The Review
of
Contemporary Fiction

Editor

JOHN O'BRIEN

Associate Editors

JACK BYRNE
DOMINIC DI BERNARDI
LOWELL DUNLAP
STEVEN MOORE

Typesetter & Designer

SHIRLEY GEEVER

Book Review Editors

THOMAS BRODERICK
KATHLEEN BURKE

T0165855

Volume 8, Number 3

Fall 1988

ISSN: 0276-0045

SUBSCRIPTIONS.   Send orders to *The Review of Contemporary Fiction*, 1817 79th Avenue, Elmwood Park, IL 60635 USA.

Single volume (three issues):

Individuals: $15.00; foreign, add $3.50;

Institutions: $22.00; foreign, add $3.50.

DISTRIBUTION.   Bookstores should send orders to:

Inland Book Company, P.O. Box 261, East Haven, CT 06512.

Bernard De Boer, 113 E. Centre St., Nutley, NJ 07110 (national distributor).

Small Press Distribution, 1814 San Pablo Ave., Berkeley, CA 94702.

Cover painting by Mary Hatch.

Indexed in *American Humanities Index, International Bibliography of Periodical Literature, International Bibliography of Book Reviews, MLA, Book Review Index.* Abstracted in *Abstracts of English Studies.*

This issue is partially supported by grants from the Illinois Arts Council, a state agency, and the National Endowment for the Arts, a federal agency, and with the assistance of Illinois Benedictine College.

The Review of Contemporary Fiction

Volume IX 1989

Spring Issue
NEW FRENCH FICTION NUMBER

Summer Issue
MILAN KUNDERA / ZULFIKAR GHOSE NUMBER

Fall Issue
KATHY ACKER / CHRISTINE BROOKE-ROSE / MARGUERITE YOUNG NUMBER

Institutions: $22.00; Individuals: $15.00.
Foreign, add $3.50; Single copy: $8.00

FUTURE ISSUES DEVOTED TO: John Barth, Joseph McElroy, Paul West, Angela Carter, Alexander Theroux.

The *Review* welcomes inquiries from qualified individuals interested in guest-editing issues on any of the following: Guillermo Cabrera Infante, José Donoso, Jacques Rouboud, Harry Mulisch, Donald Barthelme, Toby Olson, William H. Gass, Georges Perec, Philip Roth, Jerome Charyn.

John O'Brien, Editor
The Review of Contemporary Fiction
1817 North 79th Avenue
Elmwood Park, IL 60635 U.S.A.

WITTGENSTEIN'S MISTRESS. David Markson. *Wittgenstein's Mistress* is a novel unlike anything David Markson—or anyone else— has ever written before. It is the story of a woman who is convinced— and astonishingly, will ultimately convince the reader as well—that she is the only person left on earth. Presumably she is mad. And yet so appealing is her character, and so witty and seductive her narrative voice, that we will follow her hypnotically as she unloads the intellectual baggage of a lifetime in a series of irreverent meditations on everything and everybody from Brahms to sex to Heidegger to the Trojan War. *Wittgenstein's Mistress* is surely one of the few certifiably *original* novels of our time. And yet in its peculiar manner it is finally also one of the most affecting. "While Markson himself would deplore the use of a cliché, all I can say is that the book is original, beautiful, and an absolute masterpiece. Anyone who reads it can't think about the world the same way." **Ann Beattie.**
   Cloth $20.00. ISBN 0-916583-25-2

PIERROT MON AMI. Raymond Queneau. Translated from the French by Barbara Wright. In *Pierrot Mon Ami,* first published by Gallimard in 1942, we have all of the necessary elements for a coming-of-age novel: Pierrot's initiation into a world filled with manipulation, deceit, and fraud. From his short-lived job at a Paris amusement park where he helps to raise the skirts of girls to the delight of an unruly audience, to his frustrated and unsuccessful love of Yvonne, to his failed assignment of caring for the tomb of Prince Luigi, Pierrot stumbles about, nearly immune to the effects of duplicity. And if we are to take seriously the novel's closing line, we might suspect that Pierrot has understood all along what kind of world he inhabits and that he accepts it in the only way possible: with laughter. "Raymond Queneau's books are ambiguous fairylands in which the scenes of everyday life are mingled with a melancholy which is ageless. Though they are not without bitterness, their author seems always to set his face against conclusions, and to be moved by a kind of horror of seriousness. 'Foolishness,' according to Flaubert, 'consists of wanting to reach a conclusion.' One can imagine those words as the epigraph to Queneau's *Pierrot Mon Ami.*" **Albert Camus.**
   Cloth $20.00. ISBN 0-916583-24-4

Add $1.00 for postage and handling per copy. Send order and payment to:

— THE DALKEY ARCHIVE PRESS —
1817 North 79th Avenue
Elmwood Park, IL 60635 USA

Contents

"Once More unto the Breach, Dear Friends, Once More": The Publishing Scene and American Literary Art

George Garrett

> Literary mores no longer place as much
> stock in the hieratic model of the winner,
> which is just as well. Unless one is good at
> self-sacrifice, is endowed with an iron will
> and a genius-sized gift, it's likely to be a
> defeating thing to insist on producing Art
> or nothing.
>
> Theodore Solotaroff,
> *A Few Good Voices in My Head*

ONCE UPON A TIME, not so long ago, trade books published in America were conveniently divided (*segregated* might be a better word for it) by publishers into two basic categories—"popular" and "serious." It was those terms, as much as anything else, Saul Bellow was fighting against when he coined his own opposite poles—"public" and "private." We are talking about, roughly, thirty years ago: the War over with, replaced, of course, by other, smaller wars without ceasing; the last of the original millions of veterans, who had crowded the campuses as never before on the G.I. Bill and changed American education (among other things) for better and for worse forever more, gone off into their long deferred "real" lives at last; the paperback revolution which had furnished the affordable textbooks of that era and which had, for a time, revitalized the dozing, yawning American publishing business with the double whammy of fresh new money for the taking and the up-to-date sweaty greed to go out after it. About thirty years ago we had even had a little literary revolution, too, one of those once in a century or so (maybe) overturnings of the statues and monuments of the Literary Establishment and their replacement with a new set of heroes and icons. (I suppose the nearest thing to it was in seventeenth-century England when the Roundheads finally managed to kick ass on the Cavaliers and shut down all the theaters as part of what they hoped was a final solution. Of course, half a century later the theaters were back in business, but utterly different. The old Shakespearean stage as long gone and forgotten.) In our

7

own revolution, for example Faulkner, Fitzgerald, Hemingway and even Steinbeck, none of whom could be said to have prospered greatly, either in rewards or reputation in the years before the War, were now suddenly declared to be the Old Masters of the first half of this century. (You want to see how highly regarded they were during that first half-century? Go and pick up any old *New York Times Book Review* or *Herald Tribune* or *Harper's* or *Scribner's* or any other literary magazine between, say, 1920 and 1945, and you'll see who the Updikes and the Oateses of the time were, and they were sure not Faulkner, Fitzgerald, Hemingway or Steinbeck. Wolfe, maybe, but his time was brief, brief.) Needless to say, certain publishers began sifting through their backlists looking for old-timers and unknowns who maybe could be resurrected to the cheerful music of the cash register. And, do not forget, for the first time ever, courses in modern and contemporary literature were now being offered at American colleges and universities. There was going to be some good money there, too, for these lucky or clever publishers who could get their snouts up close to the edge of the trough. "Serious," or to use another synonymous term of the period, "prestige" writing just might pay off in the long run after all.

It is an important condition of modern and contemporary literary art that the most prominent and active American publishers of our times have had, at least as a secondary or "spin off" goal, the desire to be not only successful but also socially respectable. Money alone could not purchase or confer that reward. It was necessary to publish something not merely worthwhile, but *recognized* to be worthwhile, at least within the precincts of the New York City where they lived and worked and prospered. See Theodore Solotaroff's essay "What Has Happened to Publishing," in *A Few Good Voices in My Head* (1987), where he writes "of Jewish newcomers using family money to establish houses that conformed to their desire and drive to play an important cultural role in New York, much as their counterparts were doing in Vienna, Berlin, and London." We could make too much out of the special limitations, partly self-imposed, both ethnic and regional in American commercial or "mainstream" publishing. But there is a tension there and a different purpose. Insofar as Solotaroff's observation is accurate —and there is no good reason to question his authenticity—it depicts a curious cultural and social scene, at once strictly regional and of small space, and international. Looking not west of the Hudson to the huge area and population of the nation itself (which appears to figure chiefly in their calculations, *dream* if you prefer, as a source of raw materials, including writing, and of potential customers, *natives* if you would rather, caught in a classically colonial paradigm), but east, across the Atlantic to the example of European urban culture. This particular upward social mobility is not, then, an example of the *American* dream and has only a commercial need to be in touch with the larger and wider American dreams and aspirations. He said it, I didn't; but in large part it helps explain how the inordinate influence of the New York City community (as it sees itself, of course) on serious American literature came to pass.

In the meantime "popular" literature, preferably best-sellers, could keep the old cash flow flowing, pay the piper and take care of overhead—which latter included the salaries and expense accounts of people employed in the business who, if they weren't getting rich, were at least living comfortably.

It all seems so sweet and innocent and so very long ago. So long before the arrival of the "Blockbuster," and the chain bookstores and all the latest, improved means of persuasion and advertising and publicity, of the conglomerates which could afford to pay for all this. Before, also, the sudden upsurge of "creative writing" in hundreds of institutions, which soon led to hundreds of jobs for poets and fiction writers, who could be modestly supported by the patronage of the colleges and universities, provided they published and in places with enough "visibility" to bring credit on themselves and their patron institutions. And provided that they picked up enough good reviews in the right places. The "right places" being mainly and chiefly the media centered in and around New York, thus, in a serious sense, making these American educational institutions, coast to coast, curiously dependent on the good will and attention of one particular region with its own mindset and special interests. And there was also an exponential increase in the number and variety of possible grants, awards, fellowships and prizes able to be acquired if not exactly earned by writers.

Along with all of this came, hand in glove, the social twins who always arrive to accompany awakening ambition—corruption and conflict of interest. What had once, and recently enough, been a lonely and savage struggle for simple survival was radically altered, at least for some, becoming the perhaps even more ruthless and brutal battle for the fruits of personal ambition. The poets turned out to be the worst of the lot. No surprise there. They had endured the toughest times. Only the well-to-do could really afford to write poetry. Those who were not rich enough by inheritance or, by privilege, firmly set (like Williams and Stevens, for instance) in a lucrative profession, went under. Like poor old Maxwell Bodenheim. But now you could earn a half-decent salary as a teacher with a prospect of maybe tenure or even, maybe, an endowed chair someday, provided you minded your p's and q's, acted more or less the way a poet is supposed to act, and picked up enough outside support and recognition to justify your very existence. Given the prospect of comfort and a kind of junior executive security for poets, it is hardly surprising (though not in the least praiseworthy, either) that the poets in large numbers began to behave towards each other in ways which would have embarrassed Iago and to pull insider tricks and stunts which would make Ivan Boesky blink and blush. The fiction writers were only marginally better behaved, perhaps because there was/is more scrutiny devoted to them. They still had some readers and the prospect of reaching a few more. Some of them are doing rather well.

Ann Beattie, for example, who only teaches from time to time when she really has to, is quoted in *Publishers Weekly* (December 25, 1987) in a statement which less than a decade ago (and even allowing for inflation) would have aroused some hearty horse laughter among the brotherhood and sisterhood of working writers: "If I tried to support myself solely by writing short stories, I'd have an annual income of under $10,000 a year." It has been at least half a century in America since anybody came close to making that kind of money from writing short stories. The poets didn't even read each other (not even when judging or reviewing each other's work), so who cared what they did or didn't do? Those among the poets who had (somehow, as much to their own surprise as anyone else's) arrived at the top of the little heap were willing to live with things just as they are. If people started to *read* them, who knows?, they might easily be toppled from eminence and replaced by others whose names and whose works were mostly unknown. To them at least.

By now, you will have guessed, we are already located in the big middle of the here and now. And we are supposed to be talking about the publishing scene, not writers. Problem is, *truth* is, most of the writers (practically anybody you have ever heard of) are involved in a close symbiotic relationship, cosy you might say, with the publishing world. Without the acquiescence and tacit support of the writers (especially the most successful ones) the whole creaky system might collapse. They can fool you, though, the writers. Take PEN for example, forever using our dues to battle against some forms of overt censorship here and there, against racial separation and segregation in South Africa if not, say, Kenya or Ghana, firmly committed against torture everywhere in the world except in certain Eastern Bloc nations, and mostly keeping their own mouths shut tight about the inequities and injustices, trivial and profound, perpetrated on the American public by the same folks who give them their advances against royalties and publish their books. Whatever their price is, it doesn't include a vow of silence or even very much self-sacrifice.

The writers are far from blameless and they must take a good share of the blame, not only the publishers, that there is so little place for genuine experimental writing in America. By Americans. If you happen to come from another country and have to be translated out of another language and into English, you are *expected* to be a little bit off the wall.

What has happened most recently within the old system of American trade publishing is a series of slight but significant changes, chiefly during the past five years. One item is a new category, a new usage—*literary,* as in "a literary novel." A literary work has no pretensions (or hope) of somehow becoming a Blockbuster; possibly, though, it may become a best-seller. Blockbusters, the ultimate best-sellers, are the bread and butter, meat and potatoes of contemporary commercial publishing. The whole system is organized around the Blockbuster. But a great many of the type, widely advertised and expensively promoted, given every chance, have proved to be duds. Nothing is more costly or absurd than a Blockbuster which has arrived on the scene with all the excitement of a soggy firecracker. For a little while the routine was to try to line up several potential Blockbusters per season and hope that one or two caught on. This proved to be very wasteful; and whereas American commercial publishing is nothing if not widely wasteful, it was too much so for the limited resources of most publishers. Over the past few years the publishers have tended to spend more time and money and planning on fewer potential Blockbusters. For the rest of their line, many have discovered that a "literary" book will do just fine. You get a lot more attention and review space (which, at least, can be considered as a form of cheap advertising; like the publication of poetry, for instance); more so than before, because reviewers, given a choice, prefer to review literary works rather than most of the Blockbusters which don't need to be reviewed, anyway. A true Blockbuster can't be helped much by good reviews. And bad reviews? Think of Samuel Goldwyn's famous reaction to criticism: "It rolls off my back like a duck." More to the point, the literary book is, almost always, more economical. Doesn't call for an enormous advance. If good things develop, fine and dandy. If bad things accrue, why the publisher can quickly dump it, cutting losses (and they are usually *minimal* losses anyway) at a dead run. And once in a while, it is believed, a genuinely literary work can, in fact, achieve a noteworthy financial success. Can even become a bona fide best-seller. On November 30, 1987, the *Washington Post* book critic Jonathan Yardley took positive note that serious writers were beginning to show up on the best-seller lists. He cited Gail Godwin, Toni Morrison, Tom Wolfe and Scott Turow. He did not mention some others whose books had, earlier in 1987, found places on the various best-seller lists, writers like Philip Roth, Saul Bellow, Gore Vidal, John Gregory Dunne, Walker Percy, Larry McMurtry, Kurt Vonnegut, and Pat Conroy. Important thing to keep in mind is that (surprising as it may be), from the point of view of most "mainstream" publishers and the national book critics and reviewers, these writers are all equally "serious" and "literary." One should also be aware that the term "literary" has been stretched, perhaps to its extreme, to include even such things as movies, widely distributed and advertised feature films. For example, the *New York Times* (January 7, 1988) discussed *Broadcast News* as an example of the type—"The Making of a 'Literary' Film."

In some ways the fact that writers, who at least began their careers as "serious" and "literary" artists, can now produce profitable work for commercial publishers has had a negative impact on contemporary writers. The positive values, if only as a vague source of hope and of good morale, are obvious. But in many cases these people are merely the token literary artists on the publishers' lists. Which is to say there is usually not a whole lot of room left on those lists, or in the publishers' special mindset, for many new people. Or for any *rediscoveries.* The latter is, ironically, the most difficult category of all, because the publishers have by now established a deep and serious interest (it's their investment, after all) in keeping the accepted Literary Establishment intact, as firmly settled as can be. Just as, at the end of World War II, rediscovery and revisionist history were worthwhile (therefore almost inevitable) in practical, pure and simple financial terms, so from now on it would be a serious problem, in those same terms and for an entire linked chain of beings living off the literary plankton—publishers, their stables of writers, reviewers and literary journalists, critics and academics—if the Establishment were, at any point, threatened with any significant change.

Because of what happened to Faulkner, Fitzgerald, Hemingway, Steinbeck, etc., a whole generation of American writers came along believing that nothing in literary history is carved in stone, set in concrete. They learned the wrong lesson from their own immediate past; for now nothing seems so solid, secure, and untouchable as the literary pantheon as it is perceived by its supporters. The sense of revision and rediscovery has been transferred away from the contemporary scene and turned onto the redefinition of the Canon. (For a popular discussion of this, see "U.S. Literature: Canon Under Siege," *New York Times,* January 6, 1988, p. 12.) The motives here are, of course, political and social as well as personal. (The personal element is for feminist and minority critics, for example, to find things to write about and to build profitable careers upon. And it is always somewhat easier to be an instant, natural-born gender or ethnicity expert than to be the master of an extensive and approved canon.) Thus, in terms of revisionism Hawthorne and Melville and Cooper are far more vulnerable than, say, Carver or Barthelme or Beattie. These latter are, at this time, contemporary mid-list authors. That is, they do not lose a great deal of money for their sponsoring publishers; but, at the same time, they do not, not directly at least, make much for the publisher either. Their star status is partly a matter of acknowledged quality and excellence and partly a matter of publicity and promotion. The ratio of these characteristics to each other would be an interesting subject for debate if there were any place (other than this one) for even discussing such things. Never mind. I expect most readers are willing to grant those three, and others, a measure of literary excellence even if they do not necessarily take them all to be self-evidently head and shoulders above, superior to any number, a goodly number, of others among their contemporaries. The most interesting thing, here, is that unlike Roth, Bellow, Walker Percy, etc., who somehow (though not without support and supporters) earned their status in the hierarchy, the next batch of writers (here merely *represented* by Carver, Beattie, Barthelme, as if by a decent law firm) were simply awarded that status by their publishers at the outset, their installation being confirmed by continued publicity.

The inevitable next step was to see if a writer could be championed by a publisher and turned into an early best-seller. What would happen if a publisher took a book by a "serious," "literary" writer and offered the kind of massive and expensive support that is usually reserved for Blockbuster authors? There are a number of recent examples of this kind of scheme. The rise to a certain kind of notoriety of Jay McInerney (*Bright Lights, Big City*) is a result of this kind of attention. So is the career of writer Richard Ford whose two most recent books, the novel *The Sportswriter* and the collection of stories *Rock Springs,* have been given the full contemporary publicity and promotional treatment by his editor (himself much publicized) —Gary Fisketjon. Between them, Ford and Fisketjon have succeeded in giving the writer a maximum "visibility." However, Fisketjon concedes that sales have not been, except in a strictly relative sense, extraordinary. Ford is certainly well known, a "name" now and, as well, has received the kind of prominent and prompt review attention that most American writers, even among the finest and most famous, never come to know. But the full apparatus of modern "exposure" could not quite bring out book buyers and readers in the numbers (yet) which would justify the expense and effort.

More impressive, more extraordinary, and, finally and in a deadly serious sense, far more dangerous to the declining, somewhat ambiguous integrity of American literary art, has been the story of "the Brat Pack." This is a story which also involves Fisketjon, as a principal mover and shaker, among others of the so-called Baby Editors who came into the lime-light (a prominence once reserved for the likes of Maxwell Perkins and Saxe Commins) in the mid-1980s. Their latest task and challenge was at once somewhat more daunting and more cynical: to take a little group of writers —in this instance Bret Easton Ellis, Jill Eisenstadt, Tama Janowitz, and some others, all more or less in the shadow of Jay McInerney—writers of extremely limited literary talent, and somehow to sell them to the great unwashed American colonial reading public as literary celebrities and (maybe, all in due time) as at least spokespersons of their generation, if not as major literary figures and influences. What this involved was publicity, the beauty of it being that (at least in the view of the Baby Editors and their cohorts) today, as we drift into the inevitable decadence that haunts the ending of every century, it does not matter in the slightest whether the publicity be positive or negative, good or bad, the desired results will be more or less the same. The first stage proved remarkably successful. In a very short time any scholar worth his salt could have quickly put together a checklist of severely, often outrageously negative reviews in prominent places by prominent reviewers of the latest literary works of the Brat Pack. These could have then been added to an even longer list of articles about these authors as personalities, celebrities, *characters* and, as well, as social symbols of this and that, of something or other, in every kind of magazine you can think of, from the *Georgia Review* to *Vanity Fair, Gentlemen's Quarterly, People,* and the *New Yorker.* Conservative critics raged, the chic and trendy had campy good fun; but everybody mentioned the Brat Pack and usually spelled their names right. At first it was merely a whole lot of publicity, and (again) seemed to have no real effect on sales or reading habits. But, at last, by the end of 1987 the masterminds, the Baby Editors, had begun to sell some *books* on the basis of all that publicity. Whether anyone actually read or will read them remains to be seen. The important thing to note is that this late in our sad and bloody century when, it would seem, all the world would be at last more or less immune to the coarser, cruder, more vulgar and more obvious forms of hype, some cynical young people of less than (zero?) serious accomplishment could prove P. T. ("This Way to the Egress!") Barnum right as rain.

Truth is, these children of our century's old age did not invent anything. Literary journalism was already in its place and functioning, like many other forms of contemporary journalism, more as a matter of personalities and newsworthy events than matters of art and life. Mailer, of course, had seen this whole thing coming, plugged into the power of it and danced his little shocked and shocking boogaloo in *Advertisements for Myself.* But it is hard to believe that even *he* could have imagined a literary journalism which would (in 1987) devote space, energy, even some thought to such questions as the matter of Joni Evans departing from Simon and Schuster (and, simultaneously, divorcing her boss and husband there, Richard Snyder), going on to replace Howard Kaminsky (who seems to have been fired over something about a party in Frankfurt—who knows? cares?) at Random House. Then there was the hue and cry and the counterattacks of the book reviewers when, against overwhelming odds and well-laid plans (it seems), Larry Heinemann won the National Book Award for his novel *Paco's Story.* Much more space was spent on this argument than was ever (so far) allotted to reviews of the novel. And there was so much else to write about, to think about. There was the big J. D. Salinger lawsuit. There was the final departure of Shawn and the arrival of Gottlieb at the *New Yorker.* The rising and falling of certain smaller nations, some minor wars and famines attracted less press attention than that little episode. There were public accounts of odd little literary quarrels. See, for instance, "Big Fight Among the Little Magazines," the *New York Post* (June 22, 1987, p. 6), which tries to detail and make some sense out of a battle between Robert Fogarty of *Antioch Review,* Gordon Lish of the *Quarterly,* and Ben Sonnenberg of *Grand Street.* In a roundup of important events and happenings of 1987, "Updates on '87," the *Washington Post* (December 31, 1987) spent some time (as it and the *New York Times* had earlier spent a good deal of time and space) considering the sad fate of a *book proposal* (!) by Joan Braden. (If you can publicize and review book proposals, who needs to bother with books?) Equally important to the *Post* was the case of Shere Hite, "the Sean Penn of the 1987 literary circuit," whose latest opus, *Women and Love,* was one of the most prominently reviewed and publicly discussed books of the year. In fact, this may have been a moderately important story, for this was a case which ran counter to the Brat Pack Caper. In spite of everything, it failed to live up to plans and expectations. A "Knopf insider" was quoted: "The general expectation is that publicity, good or bad, generates sales. On this title, publicity generated sales but not to the magnitude it should have."

The peak of literary journalism in 1987 was probably Rust Hills's "*Esquire's* Guide to the Literary Universe" (*Esquire,* August 27, pp. 51-61), where Hills jumped aboard the bandwagon to celebrate the likes of (yes!) Gary Fisketjon, whom he declared ("The President Ordains the Bee to Be") to be "the only young editor in the business who has the power—and the inclination—to publish his contemporaries." Presumably Hills means people of Fisketjon's own age. Notice that there is no mention, not the slightest hint, of quality or excellence. Merely contemporaneity.

And that, ladies and gentlemen, is where we find ourselves as we stagger forward into the last decade of the century. What can be said of the American publishing scene in our time? That it has, in almost every way, reflected the vices and virtues of the society of which it is an odd part. That, at times and almost in spite of itself, it has allowed artists, master artists, to surface and to endure. That the great corruption, if not simply danger of the last half of the century has been the attempt on the part of the publishers to *create* (by fiat as much as fact) its own gallery of stars and master artists. That this last, while not an outright failure, for there are fine and gifted writers who have been championed by their publishers, is nevertheless not likely to improve the lot or situation of most American writers, either the discovered or undiscovered.

Nevertheless—witness this magazine, witness the incredible persistence of many small presses, the surprising success of many small regional publishers (Algonquin Books, for example)—there are other forces at work. Not the least of these is a strong new kind of regionalism in the nation, which, at the very least, goes counter to the effort to govern and control the whole country's taste from one great, dying city. And not the least force for the possible change, if not destruction of the (already) Old Order of things is technology. Even imaginable technological changes could easily constitute a revolution. But we are on the edge of almost unimaginable and surely unimagined changes which seem likely to make the whole present system of American publishing as quaintly old-fashioned as a medieval market fair. Let it come down, as the man said to Banquo.

Meantime, as if by magic alone, so many good and gifted, old and new American literary artists of all kinds carry on, often quite outside of the system. Perhaps it is appropriate to summon up magic at this point. It was no Brat or Baby Editor, but a genuine literary artist, R. V. Cassill, who has seen clearly a thing or two in a long lifetime and who said of our time: "I think we are at the end of an age, and the magicians have always appeared at the ends of ages."

Postmodernism Revisited

John Barth

1. The Tragic View of Categories

PERHAPS BECAUSE I'M a novelist by trade, I am by temperament more Aristotelian than Platonist in my attitude toward reality: more nominalist than realist, especially as regards human beings and the things they do and make. Fred and Shirley and Mike and Irma seem intuitively realer to me than does the category *human beings;* the cathedrals at Seville and Barcelona and Santiago de Compostela seem more substantial than the term *Spanish Gothic;* and the writings of Gabriel García Márquez and Italo Calvino and Salman Rushdie and Thomas Pynchon—even the writings of John Barth—have ontological primacy, to my way of thinking, over the category *Postmodern fiction.* To me it seems self-evident (though I know very well it is not) that *this* rose and *that* rose and *that* rose—Fred, Irma, and Shirley Rose—are real items in the world, whereas the term *rose* names an idea in our minds, a generality that we achieve only by ignoring enough particularity; and further, that such generalities, while they're not necessarily illusions or fictions, are of an order of reality secondary to that of individual roses. In my universe, in short, classes are not *un*real, but they're less real than their members.

On the other hand, categories and similar abstractions, such as common nouns themselves, though they are (to my way of thinking) more or less fictions, are nevertheless indispensable fictions: indispensable to thought and discourse, to cognition and comprehension, even to sanity. How blithely I have divided reality already, in just a couple of paragraphs, into Aristotelians and Platonists, classes and members, novelists and cathedrals and roses and paragraphs and human beings, like a fisherman culling his catch. How glibly I deploy even such a fishy fiction as the pronoun *I*, as if—though more than half of the cells of my physical body replace themselves in the time it takes me to write one book (and I've written ten), and I've forgotten much more than I remember about my childhood, and the fellow who did things under my name forty years ago seems as alien to me now in many ways as an extraterrestrial—as if despite those considerations there really is an antecedent to the first person singular pronoun. It is a far-fetched fiction indeed, as David Hume pointed out 250 years ago;[1] but if I did not

[1] In his *Treatise of Human Nature,* 1738.

16

presume and act upon it, not only would I go insane; I'd *be* insane.

This is the Tragic View of Categories. Terms like Romanticism, Modernism, Late-Modernism, and Postmodernism are more or less useful and necessary fictions: roughly approximate maps, more likely to lead us to something like a destination if we don't confuse them with what they're meant to be maps *of.*

Why do people bother their heads with such categories, and even write essays about them? For a number of reasons, no doubt, some implied above:

• We do it as a kind of shorthand. It's more convenient to say "post-modern architecture" than it is to recite a list of buildings here and there around the world that seem to us to share certain significant characteristics.

• We do it out of the human urge to articulate widely felt changes in perceived reality. Certain decades, for example, acquire names—the Gay Nineties, the Mauve Decade, the Roaring Twenties, the Swinging Sixties—though the fine tuning (sometimes even the gross tuning) of those terms may be problematical indeed. I may feel that "the Sixties" began on November 22, 1963, with the assassination of John F. Kennedy by Lee Harvey Oswald,[2] and ended on Yom Kippur 1973 with Egypt's attack on Israel and the consequent Arab oil embargo; you may have quite other benchmarks. One of my undergraduate professors, the Romance philologist Leo Spitzer, used to say that it's very useful for students to imagine that the Renaissance began at half past two on a Thursday afternoon in 1272, let's say, with the death of St. Thomas Aquinas, and ended with the announcement on the eleven o'clock news of October 31, 1572, that Martin Luther had nailed ninety-five theses to a church door in Wittenburg. Later on, said Spitzer, we may want to adjust those benchmarks by a decade or maybe half a century. Some revisionists may even dispute the whole concept: How many people truly swung in the Sixties, roared in the Twenties, felt a spirit of cultural rebirth in the 300 years we're calling the Renaissance? The only answer is: a small but (for users of the category) epochmaking minority.

• Finally, it must be acknowledged that in the twentieth-century art world in particular, one may "declare a kingdom in order to proclaim himself king." My Johns Hopkins colleague Hugh Kenner made this observation vis-à-vis literary Postmodernism, for which he has little use. As a general observation I would not only second it, but extend it to literary critics as well: They may declare an entire era—"the Pound era," for example—in order etc.

Confining ourselves to the more creditable of those motives just mentioned, most of us would agree, I'll bet, that our culture lives in time and that there really do seem to be significant differences of spirit between the

[2] The art critic David Hickey has declared that for him, American Postmodernism begins with this event and the subsequent assassination of the assassin: the death of a certain diehard U.S. optimism.

American 1950s and '60s, say; or between the works of the nineteenth-century painters who came to be called Impressionists and the works of the twentieth-century painters who called themselves Abstract Expressionists; or between novels that begin with sentences like "Happy families are all alike; every unhappy family is unhappy in its own way," and novels that begin with sentences like "riverrun, past Eve and Adam's, from swerve of shore to bend of bay, brings us by a commodius vicus of recirculation back to Howth Castle and Environs." We may even agree that there are significant differences of spirit between Mies van der Rohe's Seagram Building in Manhattan and Philip Johnson's AT&T Building in that same neighborhood, whatever we happen to think of the buildings themselves; and that there are aesthetic differences, perhaps even comparable ones, between the opening words of Joyce's *Finnegans Wake* and those of García Márquez's *One Hundred Years of Solitude,* as well as between the novels that follow those opening sentences.

"Many years later, as he faced the firing squad, Colonel Aureliano Buendía was to remember that distant afternoon when his father took him to discover ice." We have arrived at Postmodernism, which is where I came in a couple of decades ago.

More exactly, my first visits to that mildly vexed subject were two little essays written between novels: "The Literature of Exhaustion" (1968) and "The Literature of Replenishment" (1980). If my approach here to a revisit is particularly tentative and crabwise, that is because my experience with the term and with the various phenomena it's been used to name has been similarly so.

2. Postmodernism Arrived At

The writer of these words is a 58-year-old storyteller, mainly a novelist, who—as a student in the 1940s and '50s—cut his apprentice literary teeth on the likes of Franz Kafka, Thomas Mann, James Joyce, T. S. Eliot, and Ezra Pound: the old masters of what we now call literary High Modernism, as that last term is understood in many parts of the world.[3]

When my first novel was published in the mid-1950s, it was approved by the critic Leslie Fiedler as an example of "provincial American existentialism." The description intrigued me; like a good provincial, I set about reading Sartre and Camus to learn what Existentialism was, and I concurred

[3]But not in all: *el modernismo,* in Spain and Latin America, has a quite different reference, and when the Spanish writer Federico de Onís coined the term "postmodernism" in 1934, he was describing a Hispanic reaction within Hispanic *modernismo,* no more relevant to our subject here than Arnold Toynbee's use of the term *postmodern* a few years later in *A Study of History.* This Hispanic distinction seems still to apply: A friend from Valencia tells me that the adjective *postmoderno* is applied derisively by his students to the latest clothing styles from Madrid.

with Mr. Fiedler (who later became a colleague and friend), if not altogether with Sartre and Camus. If people had done such things in those days, I'd have had a T-shirt printed up for myself: PROVINCIAL AMERICAN EXISTENTIALIST.

My second novel, published a couple years later, was generally assigned to a new category called Black Humor. I buckled down and read such alleged fellow Black Humorists as John Hawkes, Kurt Vonnegut, Bruce Jay Friedman, and (when he arrived on the scene) Joseph Heller, and I decided that this was not a bad team to be on: the Existential Black Humorists.

But my third, fourth, and fifth books, published through the 1960s, came to be described no longer as Existentialist or Black Humorist, but as Fabulist, and the term was made retroactive to those earlier productions too, as well as to the fiction of John Hawkes again and now of Donald Barthelme, Robert Coover, Stanley Elkin, William Gass, and Thomas Pynchon, to name only some of my new (and old) teammates. As before, I dutifully did my homework: read up on those of my fellow Fabulists with whom I wasn't already familiar, and decided I liked that term—and that team—even better than I'd liked its predecessors. But of course I went right on doing what it seemed to me I'd always done: not particularly thinking in terms of Existentialism, Black Humor, or Fabulism, but putting this sentence after that one, and the next one after this one.

Sure enough, just when I'd got a pretty good idea what Fabulism was, in the 1970s the stuff began to be called Postmodernist. With increasing frequency I found myself categorized under that label, not only with my old U.S. teammates but with some new, first-rate foreign ones: Samuel Beckett, Jorge Luis Borges, Italo Calvino, Gabriel García Márquez. I had hoped some women would sign on next time the ship changed names; would *be signed on,* I should say, since the artists themselves are not normally consulted in these matters. In any case, the crew was certainly strengthened by those world-class additions. But what exactly were the critics referring to?

Not surprisingly, by this time I found that familiar question less than urgent. All the same, it interested me that those who used the term *Postmodern,* at least with respect to literature, seemed far less in agreement about its reference than had the users of labels like Fabulist and Black Humorist. If Joyce was a Modernist, was Beckett then a Postmodernist? Indeed, if the Joyce of *Ulysses* was a Modernist, had the Joyce of *Finnegans Wake* already moved on to Postmodernism? Was Laurence Sterne's *Tristram Shandy* proto-Modern or proto-Postmodern? More important, was the whole phenomenon, whatever it was, no more than a pallid ghost of the powerful cultural force that Modernism had been in the first half of this century, or was it a positive new direction in the old art of storytelling, and in other arts as well? Was it a repudiation of the great Modernists at whose figurative feet I had sat, or was it something evolved out of them, some next stage of the ongoing dialectic between artistic generations that has characterized Western Civ at least since the advent of Romanticism in (I'm going to say) the latter eighteenth century?

My opportunity to find out came at the close of the decade. The Deutsche Gesellschaft für Amerikastudien, an association of German professors of American subjects, convenes annually at Whitsuntide in one or another of their national universities, as our Modern Language Association does between Christmas and New Year's in one of our Hilton hotels. In 1979 the Gesellschaft took as the general subject of its conference "America in the 1970s," and the Literature section chose as its particular topic "Postmodern American Fiction." Three U.S. writers—William Gass, John Hawkes, and myself—were invited to Tübingen as guests of the conference, a kind of live exhibit. By that time the term really had gained wide currency in literature as well as in architecture and painting; I even had a rough idea how it might be applied to what was going on in my own shop. But when I looked over some of the standard critical texts (faithfully doing my homework again), I was surprised to find that though the century was 79% expired, there was still considerable disagreement about what *Modernism* means, or meant, not to mention Postmodernism, about which no two authorities seemed to agree.

So I leaped into the breach—rather, I sidled crabwise into it—and drafted a little talk for the Gesellschaft on what I thought the term *ought* to mean, if it was going to describe anything very good very well. Armed with my tentative definition/prescription, I went off to Tübingen with my fellow former Fabulists and found to my mild dismay that our German hosts, the object of whose meticulous curiosity we were, spoke of literary Postmodernism as if it were as indisputable a cultural-historical phenomenon as the Counter-Reformation or the Great Depression of the 1930s. Their discussion, and there was plenty, had to do with refining the boundaries and establishing the canon; there was so much confident bandying of adjectives and prefixes—High Postmodernism, Late Postmodernism, Proto-Postmodernism, Post-Postmodernism—that at the end of one session an American student remarked to me, "They forgot Post Toasties."

Moreover—perhaps on the principle that birds have no business holding forth on ornithology—our hospitable hosts weren't interested in hearing my lecture on their subject. My fellow exhibits and I read from our fiction instead, no doubt a sounder idea.

All the same, I had thought what I'd thought and I'd seen what I'd said (to myself) on the subject of postmodern fiction. When I got home I published my reflections in the *Atlantic* (the monthly magazine, not the nearby ocean), where a dozen years before I had published some reflections on what I called "the literature of exhaustion." Here is the summarized conclusion of that Tübingen essay, "The Literature of Replenishment":

If the Modernists, carrying the torch of Romanticism, taught us that linearity, rationality, consciousness, cause and effect, naive illusionism, transparent language, innocent anecdote, and middle-class moral conventions are not the whole story, then from the perspective of these closing decades of our century we may appreciate that the contraries of these things are not the whole story either. Disjunction, simultaneity, irrationalism, self-reflexiveness, medium-as-message, political olympianism[4] . . . these are not the whole story either. . . .

My ideal Postmodernist author neither merely repudiates nor merely imitates either his twentieth-century Modernist parents or his nineteenth-century pre-Modernist grandparents. He has the first half of our century under his belt, but not on his back. Without lapsing into moral or artistic simplism, shoddy craftsmanship, Madison Avenue venality, or either false or real naiveté, he nevertheless aspires to a fiction more democratic in its appeal than such late-Modernist marvels as Beckett's *Texts for Nothing*. . . . The ideal Postmodernist novel will somehow rise above the quarrel between realism and irrealism, formalism and "contentism," pure and committed literature, coterie fiction and junk fiction. . . .

What my [earlier] essay "The Literature of Exhaustion" was really about, so it seems to me now, was the effective "exhaustion" not of language or of literature but of the aesthetic of high Modernism: that admirable, not-to-be-repudiated, but essentially completed "program" of what Hugh Kenner has dubbed "the Pound era." In 1966/67 we scarcely had the term *Postmodernism* in its current literary-critical usage . . . but a number of us, in quite different ways and with varying combinations of intuitive response and conscious deliberation, were already well into the working out, not of the next-best thing after Modernism, but of the *best next* thing: what is gropingly now called Postmodernist fiction. . . .

Et cetera.

3. Postmodernism Revisited

The difference between professional intellectuals and professional artists who are perhaps amateur intellectuals is that the former publish articles and essays in order to share their learning, whereas we latter may publish the odd essay-between-novels in order to share our ignorance, so that those more learned can come to our rescue. My little essay on Postmodernism has been translated and reprinted a number of times over the past eight years, and my rescuers have been many. Though I still hold to my basic notion of what Postmodern fiction is, or ought to be if it's to deserve our attention, I have happily withdrawn from the ongoing disputes over its definition and its canon: over who should be admitted into the club or (depending on the critic's point of view) clubbed into admission. Postmodern, I tell myself serenely, is what I am; ergo, Postmodernism is whatever I do, together with my crewmates-this-time-around, until the critics rename the boat again. Moreover, *it is what I do whether I do it well or badly:* a much more

---

[4] And, I should have added, the *topos* of artist-as-hero, from Goethe through Byron down to Joyce.

important critical consideration, to which I shall return.

But as I go on doing it, I note with respect and mild interest observations on the subject made by my peers and betters. Octavio Paz, in the Mexican literary organ *La Jornada Semanal,* declared huffily that since I've got *el modernismo* all wrong (that special Hispanic distinction again), I can scarcely be trusted with *el postmodernismo,* which anyhow he was already writing about decades ago, under a different term, as I would have known were I not just one more gringo ethnocentric. *There's* a rescuer for you. The writers I call Postmodernist, Susan Sontag and William Gass call Late Modernist; for them, the American Postmoderns are the minimalist-realists of the 1970s and '80s: Raymond Carver, Ann Beattie, and company. The Australian art critic Robert Hughes dates Postmodernism, at least in its Pop Art manifestation, from that moment in Walt Disney's 1940 movie *Fantasia* when Mickey Mouse mounts the conductor's podium and shakes hands with Leopold Stokowski. I like that. But yet another art critic, Thomas McEvilley, speaks of Egyptian postmodernism from the Middle Kingdom and Roman postmodernism from the Silver Age; for McEvilley, lower-case postmodernism is the periodic swing of the pendulum of Western Civ from the spiritual-romantic (of which twentieth-century Modernism is an instance) toward the rational-skeptical.[5]

The Italian semiotician/novelist Umberto Eco, in his 1983 book *Postmodernism, Irony, the Enjoyable,* is a good deal kinder to my essay than Señor Paz was, and very illuminating on the ironic "double coding," as he calls it, characteristic of much postmodern art and life. I quote Signor Eco:

> ... the postmodern attitude [is] that of a man who loves a very sophisticated woman and knows he cannot say to her, "I love you madly," because he knows that she knows (and that she knows that he knows) that these words have already been written by Barbara Cartland. Still, there is a solution. He can say, "As Barbara Cartland would put it, I love you madly." At this point, having avoided false innocence, having said clearly that it is no longer possible to speak innocently, he will nevertheless have said what he wanted to say to the woman: that he loves her, but he loves her in an age of lost innocence. If the woman goes along with this, she will have received a declaration of love all the same. Neither of the speakers will feel innocent, both will have accepted the challenge of the past, of the already said, which cannot be eliminated, both will consciously and with pleasure play the game of irony.... But both will have succeeded, once again, in speaking of love.

I like that, too: If for "Barbara Cartland" we substitute "the history of literature up to the day before yesterday," it is the very point of my essay "The Literature of Exhaustion." It makes clear also, incidentally, the

---

[5]I too, in "The Literature of Replenishment," referred to the Middle Kingdom scribe Kakheperresenb as a postmodernist. As for twentieth-century literary Postmodernism, I date it from when many of us stopped worrying about the death of the novel (a Modernist worry) and began worrying about the death of the reader—and of the planet—instead.

difference between the premodern English novelist William Makepeace Thackeray, for example, and the Postmodern Chilean novelist José Donoso. When Thackeray, at the end of *Vanity Fair,* says of his novel and its characters, "Come, children, let us shut up the box and the puppets, for our play is played out," he is making in 1848 an author-intrusive rhetorical flourish of a sort familiar at least since the early seventeenth century (e.g., in *Don Quixote*), and he is making it in the same spirit as Cervantes; it is not really anti-illusionary at all. When such early-twentieth-century writers as the André Gide of *The Counterfeiters* and the Miguel de Unamuno of *Mist* and the Luigi Pirandello of *Six Characters in Search of an Author* begin to challenge the reality of their characters (or have their own reality challenged by their characters) and otherwise foreground the inescapable artifice of their art, we recognize that we are in the land of Modernism. But when Donoso declares to us elegantly and elaborately from time to time in *A House in the Country* (1984) that he has no wish to trick us into believing that his characters are real or that their joys and sufferings are any more than ink-marks on paper—and then immediately beguiles us back into the gorgeous, monstrous reality of his fable—he is "double coding" like Umberto Eco's lovers; he is having it both ways with illusionism and anti-illusionism. That strikes me as legitimately Postmod, and in the hands of a good storyteller it works.

I'm interested too in the observation by the British architect Charles Jencks in his 1986 treatise *What Is Post-Modernism?* that whereas for Modernist artists the subject is often the *processes* of their medium, for Postmodernist artists it is more typically the *history* of their medium. On the basis of this distinction, Jencks classifies the Pompidou Center in Paris, for example, with its abstract patterns of boldly exposed and brightly painted pipes and trusses, as Late Modernist, and Robert Graham's Olympic Arch in Los Angeles—with its truncated classical nude bronze torsos balancing on inverted metal cones on a black granite dolmen like a streamlined ruin—as Postmodernist. But I'm not sure how far this interesting distinction carries over into literature. It is true that many of the writers called Postmodern have looked to various sorts of myth for their material—whether classical myths or such pop mythologies as old Hollywood movies—as well as to pre-modern narrative forms like the tale, the fable, and the gothic or the epistolary novel; also to pre-modern narrative devices, such as Donoso's intrusive, commenting author. *I*'ve certainly made use of things like that. But so did Joyce, in *Ulysses,*[6] and if that benchmark of novelistic Modernism must be reclassified as Postmodern, I for one begin to experience vertigo. I think I'll stick with Umberto Eco's "double coding"; in fact, I think I'll stick with my own rough-and-ready definition of Postmodernism, quoted earlier.

[6]E.g., in the "Oxen of the Sun" chapter, which lovingly parodies the evolution of English literature in echo of Mrs. Purefoy's pregnancy and difficult labor.

So how is literary Postmodernism doing these days, and what Post-Post-modernism, if any, lies around the next corner? In architecture, there seems to be no question that postmodernism is where the action is, for better or worse. Almost nobody builds plain old International-Style curtain-wall boxes anymore; every new shopping mall and condo has its ironic steel-and-glass gable ends, false fronts, cupolas, quotations from the Victorian, whatever. The style has triumphed, with the usual distribution of excellent, mediocre, and horrendous specimens that one finds in any established style. But although most of the leading practitioners of what is called Postmodern fiction are by no means finished yet with their careers, and may feel them-selves to be still in the process of defining the style (just as their critics are still defining and debating the term), it cannot be doubted that in U.S. fiction, at least, the pendulum has swung from the overtly self-conscious, process-*and*-history-conscious, often fabulistic work of Barthelme, Coover, Elkin, Gass, Hawkes, Pynchon, & Co. toward that early-Hemingwayish minimalist neo-realism aforementioned, epitomized by the short stories of Carver, Beattie, Frederick Barthelme (the Houston Postmodernist's younger brother), and others. Indeed, I suppose that at present these are the two main streams of contemporary U.S. fiction of the literary sort—fiction which, in Conrad's words, "aspires to the condition of art"—though there are many who would say that the best American work in the medium is being done by writers not usually associated with either of these traditions: writers such as Saul Bellow, Norman Mailer, Joyce Oates, William Styron, Anne Tyler, John Updike. That may be.

In any case (back to my starting point), be it remembered that the question whether a particular novel or painting or building is Late Modern, Postmodern, Post-Postmodern, or none of the above, while it's not an unworthy question, is of less importance—at least it ought to be so—than the question Is it transcendently terrific?

In this connection, it's worth remarking that in literature, at least, an artist may be historically notable without being especially good. For this reader, Gertrude Stein is one of those; others will have other examples. Conversely, he may be quite good without being otherwise especially important: I think of Joyce Carey, of Henry Green, of others, living, whom I shall not name. Alas, it is the misfortune of many, many published writers, perhaps of most, to be neither especially good nor particularly important; and it is the fortune of a very few to be both artistically excellent and historically significant. Since art is long and life is short, *those* are the writers (if we can name them) to whom we ought to give our prime-time attention. Among our con-temporaries, I quite believe, a few of these few are what has come to be called Postmodern.

Writing and Writers: Disjecta Membra

Gilbert Sorrentino

WRITING IS DIFFICULT and "strange," insofar as its vision of reality is unlike our vision of reality. Some writing is so remote from us that it cannot be read at all—it repels us, or, on the contrary, seduces us. We pretend that this writing is the manifestation of a private vision, that it *sees* a world, a reality, wholly different from our own. Nothing can be further from the truth. We sequester this writing, we call it exotic, or weird, or skewed, because otherwise we would be faced with the intolerable proposition that the reality such writing offers is, indeed, our own, but that we cannot, though we live in the middle of it, recognize it. Such writing shakes our precarious sense of ourselves, so it is much safer to pretend that it is but the excrescence of a strange mind sifting through its own invented detritus.

Description: A language of cumulative detail used to describe process or thing tends naturally to "preserve itself against signification." In a paradoxical way, the more detail adduced, the further the process or thing is removed from representation.

Such detail works against the grain of narrative; such a use of language tends toward the list or catalogue, and these, by their placement of words outside the normal cohesion of the sentence, move toward a defiance of signification. We might say that a language of cumulative detail is an anti-function of narrative, which fights for the *disappearance* of the word, which in such writing is ideally transparent—we "look through it." Cumulative detail is often called unnecessary when employed in narrative—it is said to need cutting, editing, etc. And this is justifiable, perhaps, but only when the detail forms a kind of "bump" on the narrative surface. If there is no narrative apparent, the details *become* the narrative. The problem for the writer who finds himself drawn to details is to find a way of permitting these details, this description of a fine meticulousness, to *be* the narrative, and to resist the temptation to use the details as an engine to drive the narrative. In other words, the language of detail is a language that is not designed to further "the story." Such a language eerily leads the writer away from narrative and signification, and, thrusting itself into the foreground as "narrative," seems often to be clumsy, awkward, boring—a chain of *longueurs*. The difficulty for the reader may simply be put: Here is a language of non-signification (opaque), presumably functioning on the page on which he expects to find the narrative, the language of signification (transparent). But to skip the details in such works is to skip the works. (See *Watt.*)

Writers often use words up, that is, certain words or phrases become such an intimate part of a writer's vocabulary that they no longer seem to exist as "innocent" signifiers, but point only to the cosmos of the writer. "Lay" people may use such words innocently, but to the specialist they do not signify; they have dropped all pretense toward naming things, and point only to the work which has, in effect, consumed them. When we speak of a writer's vocabulary, we speak of the words that he has subverted in their primary function as signifiers. They now *belong* to him and point to his oeuvre. Who can write "gong-tormented," or "stately, plump," or "brightness falls" and insist that these formulations are innocent descriptives? These words become internally ritualized, they are "meta-clichés."

If it is a truism that a work of literature is verifiable only by itself, what of the work that is not? That is not verifiable by anything at all? Where do we locate authority? And is authority "necessary" to fiction? Where is authority when the author not only refuses to acknowledge it, but refuses, likewise, to disdain it? When it is not even a consideration?

The perfect comment on a book is the book itself. But since it cannot comment on itself, critics comment on it. This comment on the book from sources anterior to its reality purportedly leads us to its reality—which is in perfect contradiction to all that has been said about it. Problem: Comment which begins as ancillary to the book may ultimately displace the book, or pretend that the book has no reality without it. Oddly enough, this often happens to the classic, the coterie work, and the *pièce à succès;* other works stand naked.

Blanchot. Naming destroys the objects named. They "become" the language used to name them, and exist behind it, untouched. O.K. But if naming makes the object named no more than a signifier, what happens when the object is misnamed (children's play, erotic games, etc.)? It becomes, to the imagination, the wrong object (or the wrong signifier). There is a double destruction of reality here. "A" is the name given A (but is not A); then "B" is the name given "A' is the name given A (but is not A or B). There exists a kind of reincarnation of something that is not there.

Kafka is the voice of absolute authority, until we try to discover whence this authority comes, and of what nature it partakes, until, that is, we try to *find* Kafka. He is everywhere in his work, but nowhere, we know everything about him, and nothing. We are always just about to grasp him, but cannot, and when we surrender to this truth, when we realize that Kafka is nowhere to be discovered, there is Kafka. The same is true of Joyce, except that while Joyce literally pushes himself into his work, Kafka, by some impossible legerdemain, attempts to push himself out of it. We look for Joyce in his work, but discover that he is outside, looking with us; we look for Kafka outside his work, but he has never left it, he is always in the situation of one who tries to escape. Both writers are wholly subversive, Joyce pretending the authority of exterior narration, and Kafka reporting objectively from the front. But Joyce is not exterior, and Kafka is not "at the front." In terms of literary authority, neither writer gives a damn about it.

The "yes, but" of the book reviewer always means "why isn't this work more like works which I know to be literature?" That is all it ever means.

Reviewers who don't understand the work under review, or who are intimidated by this lack of understanding, are shameless in their admission of this. Most of them, in fact, can hardly wait to admit it. Their admission of ignorance, however, neither silences nor dissuades them from their tasks. On the contrary, they spend the space of their reviews pointing to the incomprehensible work before them, and this gesture is displayed as a kind of self-bestowed nobility. The work, of course, is always at fault, since the book reviewer is a bona fide literary person, perhaps an expert, else why would he be reviewing books? To admit his incapacity to review the book would never do. The book must die.

"It is at least the beginning of art." Thus Williams in *The Great American Novel* on the gaudy, the tawdry, the flamboyant in popular culture, kitsch, the extravaganza of spectacle. Williams is always worrying at this, here, in *Spring and All, The Desert Music*—throughout his entire body of work. It is a delicate proposition he comes at, and has to do with the imaginative hunger of all people for "creative energy." These people, the great mass of people who cannot "find" an art to sustain them, are the potential audience for "the new" in literature, but the paradox lies in the fact that they are never brought into contact with it. The problem may, simplistically, simplistically indeed, be stated: The real audience for "the new" is quite probably those who have been denied the very education possessed by those who despise "the new." The latter's education has prepared them for fashionable writing disguised as literature, and predisposed them against true literature. The uneducated are insulated against polite garbage. To put it even more simplistically: the potential reader of innovative literature is semiliterate; the great mass of the highly literate find their sustenance in the vague gestures of a knowing politesse. When we read, say, the *New Yorker,* we are in the presence of a lapidary literacy, a given sophistication, a mime of charm and grace, and death. Who will believe that the reader for whom the *New Yorker* is too difficult is the possible reader of John Hawkes? But he will never seek a Hawkes because the culture machine pretends that Hawkes and the *New Yorker* are equally beyond him.

Natalia Ginzburg prefaces her *Lessico Famigliare (Family Sayings)* with the comment that she has striven, in this work, to include only those things actually remembered—no assumptions, elaborations, inventions, etc., etc., are permitted. In short, the work will proffer the truth. Of course, this beautiful little book reads like a work of fiction. Why is this? Because in structuring the factual details of this period of her life, she imposes upon them the forms necessary to their elucidation, and these forms turn the facts into imaginative integers. There is nothing more fictitious than the remembered fact (divorced from the facts, unremembered, which surrounded and informed it) located in isolation within the architecture of the work. And this is not even to question the reliability of the memories, which are almost always, by definition, metamorphosed into the shapes we require in order to pretend that our lives have some transfigurative meaning.

The List: The ideal list becomes an object. It not only bypasses or thwarts the combinative processes of language, but it subverts the selective processes of language as well. In terms of the combinative, the words of such an ideal list proffer themselves as elements of a constantly surprising parataxis; and in terms of the selective, the list denies the "lateral sliding" of metaphorizing. In effect, the list reduces the machinery of signification to silence. By ignoring the sound-image/concept linkage, it paradoxically permits reality its hegemony. Reality, in the list, is allowed presence by means of the list's denial of language's "desire" to falsify it. The *real* is a list: a list is *real.*

A writer knows that he is a writer when he has lived long enough to see that his writing defines, as clearly as a graph, his life. The shock of this is not caused by anything so homely and acceptable as "the record of the passing years," or the recognition that his work is uneven or inadequate to his desire for its excellence, but by the fact that this "graph" is not a metaphor for his life, but a merciless representation of it. It is as if his work finally unmasks itself as the log wherein recorded is the vast amount of time that he has spent at a distance from the world in which everyone else lives. This log tells him that he is not quite *here.*

What a joke it is to read or hear—as I have read or heard more times than I can count—that writers "see more clearly" or "feel more deeply" than non-writers. The truth of the matter is that writers hardly "see" or "feel" at all. The disparity between a writer's works and the world per se is so great as to beggar comment. Writers who arrange their lives so as to "have experiences" in order to reduce them to contemptible linguistic recordings of these experiences are beneath contempt.

The first notion I had that writing is not the registration of one's comings and goings came with my reading, at about eighteen, of Stevens's "Sea Surface Full of Clouds" in some anthology. What I remember of that poem is the thrill of the word "chocolate" muscular and solitary on the page. This was not *chocolate*, but a manifestation of the poet's arrogant appropriation of *anything*. The word virtually sailed free of all connections.

The List: Let me propose the idea of a list of questions formulated about a given character and so proposed without complementary answers to the questions. This list forms a kind of discontinuous, scattered narrative unit. The questions allow us to know certain things about the character and also permit the reader to fill in the absent answers, the asked-for information. This occurs whether or not the reader knows the answers, that is, whether or not the character has performed in such a way as to allow the reader to come up with the answers. If there has been no information provided, so that the questions cannot be answered, the reader is, nonetheless, strangely urged to answer them with data which the questions themselves imply. This list is a kind of system of negative narrational energy.

Now, this list of questions, initially proposed as finite, that is, a list *sans* answers, creates another list (of answers) if the writer decides, later, in perhaps another work, to answer them. This list creates another scattered narrative unit. If these answers are, by means of punctuation, combined or broken up, e.g., if two answers are made into one, if one answer is made into two, etc., etc., this narrative unit becomes not only a set of answers to a set of questions but a curiously "sensible," if slightly skewed, positive addition to the text(s). The answers detach themselves from the questions which occasioned them and shift onto another narrative plane. The manipulation of the answers by the application of punctuational choices lets us see a "truth" about the character nowhere prefigured in the texts. The materials concerning the character are enriched in ways that the "imaginative" could not succeed in doing.

What is most fascinating about such an enterprise is that the list of questions, despite a lack of cohesion, commonality of themes, unity of concerns, etc., etc., will produce a list of answers that forms a coherence. It is as if the set of questions, drawn from whatever sources and with no expectation of being answered, has within itself a reliable narrative statement.

So far as I can tell, none of this will work if the answers are in hand as the questions are being drawn up, i.e., the questions must be "innocent" of expectation. In this procedure, what seems to be an aleatory exercise turns out to be exercise in prefigured form. It is another revelation of the enormous expressive power latent in the list.

Description Becomes Comedy (in 4 Steps)
1. The man fell.
2. The cow fell down.

3. The cow then fell over.
4. The armadillo collapsed.

D.H. Lawrence's Problem, or, The English Disease: Lawrence trusted his body and "the dark secret blood," etc., etc., sure. But only after he had beaten it into submission with the bludgeon of his puritanical mind. The result: a body that could not be aroused by the "obscene." So DHL's natural body is seen to be wholly unnatural. From the vantage of his purity, he presumes to call the rest of us perverse. Sade is the bitter prescription for this pettifoggery, for Sade knows that the erotic is not natural, but is controlled by the intelligence. Lawrence mistakes the erotic for the animalistic, and since he could not, of course, be an animal, he pushed the erotic into the "blood." Impossible.

Possibilities for Comic Writing
— writing is possibly comic if its signifiers are dislocated, i.e., "in the wrong places."
— or if its signifiers are treated with contempt or indifference.
— or if its signifiers are substituted for by other signifiers which mock the descriptive tasks of the first (malapropisms, neologisms, homophones, etc.).
— or if the writer is indifferent to the signifiers' accuracy of representation or communication.
Above all, comic writing disdains the easy target. It is therefore usually in conflict with the cultural locus and opinions of a socio-intellectual elite. The latter prefers comedy which is directed against those things that are at odds with currently embraced notions of sophistication and "rightness." This sort of comedy is a series of coded nudges which exist within the "closed circle of language" (Barthes) that constitutes the elite's verbal world. The catharsis of anarchism is not there operative, but the brutality of fascism is.

Toby Olson's novels propose a metaphysics of sexuality, but it has no power separate from, or outside the context of his grave rituals of action. In this sense, it is no more important to his novels than the act of, say, driving a car, or addressing a difficult lie in golf, etc. All the action in his work takes on a splendor rooted in his need to describe. But the description itself is a description not of the act, but of the ritual of which the act is celebratory. These are exhausting but exhilarating novels, since each detail of the ephemera of "everyday life" attracts the author's complete attention and is proffered with the utmost care. This is far beyond the precision of description, and cannot really be thought of as description. There is a poignant alertness to this writing, an admission, of sorts, that description falsifies reality, and that reality can only be partially allowed its presence if presented as a series of interlocking ritualizations. The language of these novels is wholly indifferent to the *facts* of "how things are" or "how things work"; it is a language that insists on the unseen processes of any and all acts. As such, the language itself becomes ritual, and permits Olson to say the most outrageous things. He blithely conjures up the baldest coincidences, he waltzes, unconcerned, through melodrama, sentimentality, scenes of laconic "machismo"—all the things that fiction is supposed to avoid. None of these things, in his novels, are handled as instances of the real toward which Olson gestures, that is, he is not at all concerned that our understanding of a given text may register "coincidence" or "sentimentality," etc., etc. Such elements escape from the aesthetic failure that should be theirs because they are set down without regard to their presence as counterparts to "coincidence" or "sentimentality" either in life or in the conventions of fiction. This incredibly blunt engagement with dangerous motifs occurs, I think, because Olson nowhere allows irony a place in these texts; a coincidence, for instance, sets up no ironic vibrations because the text in which it occurs is perfectly ingenuous, perfectly "innocent" of ironic possibilities. This is remarkable work, and oddly reminds the reader of Hemingway, although Hemingway's ritualizations are wholly concealed by the attention to surface detail (the famous eye-object linkage which *seems* to describe the real). In Olson's novels, the attention is to the processes of ritualization, the close attention to which absorbs the details. The process of the action is conflated with the outward details of the action, and the inseparable "mixture" is presented, as a profound ritual, to the reader. This is why his novels are fantastic. The mundane is subverted by its own mode of *being mundane,* its own inherent, celebratory process, the ritual proper to it. It goes without saying that these techniques are wholly free from the "symbolic," which is why they are uncomfortable, i.e., things don't represent *other* things, they reveal their own stubborn real-ness.

E.H. Gombrich: "If illusion is due to the interaction of clues and the absence of contradictory evidence, the only way to fight its transforming influence is to make the clues contradict each other and to prevent a coherent image of reality from destroying the pattern in the plane." Gombrich is writing here of Cubism, but his remarks hold true for literature if we substitute the words "syntax" or "plot" or "narrative," etc., etc., for "plane." This contradiction of clues is clearly seen occurring in lyric poetry, in which language has long since shed the burden of the referential message. But we run into trouble in fiction, no more so than in the creation and deployment of characters. Nothing in a work of fiction is more disturbing or baffling to a reader than characters who seem remote from actual people, characters who are not consistent in their actions and thoughts. A plot may be difficult or tortuously convoluted, syntax eccentric, dialogue attenuated, but if the characters present an appearance of actuality, the work is suffered because it is "true to life." It goes without saying, I hope, that I don't speak of odd or eccentric characters as inconsistent—they are consistent in their oddity.

It is precisely here, however, that the "transforming influence" of illusion is to be met head on by the writer. Readers "believe" in characters who act, so to speak, *in character.* Conventional characterization proffers us background, history, attitudes, "psychology," reactions, etc., etc., in its construction. (One might say that such characterization is the result of skills sharpened by practice.) The reader gets to know such characters, and once he does, he expects them to act in a certain way throughout the work—and so they do. I omit here, obviously, characters in works that contain elements of surprise (e.g., mysteries), the sudden light shed on what has gone before (the regressive ending), and so on. These hoary techniques are but tricks of the trade.

The reader is then to take these "in-character" characters as representative of real people. We *know* them. To allow the contradictory to appear amid the welter of consistency shakes the foundations of the reader's belief in the characters, and deprives the writer of his supposed vaunted authority.

But relentlessly intransigent characterizations let us see, as it were, only those aspects of the characters which the writer allows us to see: we *see* that which we *see,* Q.E.D. But these uniform creations, these constructions painstakingly put together to imitate reality, are but mannequins or puppets which the reader insists on thinking of as people who might *really* be alive. We are given "coherent images" of the actual. If the writer introduces contradictory elements of character, if, that is, he allows elements of characterization that are at odds with what we think the character to be to emerge (elements that the work does not demand), these elements turn the characters into bewildering and impenetrable entities. They become as perplexing as real people—a notable paradox. The more "unreal," the less consistent, the more contradictory the fictitious characters, the more are they like real people, with their shifts, changes, spurts of growth and diminution, with their hidden experiences that subvert their facades.

For the writer to do this deprives him of his authority over the mannequins who *should* be his. This loss of writerly authority prefigures a loss of the suspect wisdom about life that the writer is thought to possess. He is seen, at last, as what he is—a writer—and seen as such by readers and by himself. What has happened is that language has made his mannequins "incoherent." His authority extends only to language, at which point the "transforming influence" of the illusory may be engaged and negated within a work that speaks of human interactions by means of the adventures of invented characters; in short, within a work of fiction. A "coherent image" of reality cannot then "destroy the pattern" of language's hegemony. The characters are freed from their roles as human surrogates and become formal elements among other formal elements. They become words.

In the Pooka-Good Fairy section of *At Swim-Two-Birds,* we see the gradual emptying of significatory function of the word "kangaroo." As this function is eroded, the word asserts itself as relevant in contexts foreign to its place in the process of signification, and then (for this is not enough for O'Nolan), the hollow signifier begins to invent narrative. As the word becomes less able to perform its conventional function, it becomes a generator of comedy. This is a dazzling performance played out along the "axis of combination." Our laughter proceeds from the fact that we cannot forget the original signifying task of the word. "Kangaroo" is made comic in itself, and the comedy is heightened when it appears in new and seemingly inhospitable contexts. The writer who can bring off such effects must have a powerful distrust of language's referential precisions.

Raymond Roussel: The blinding "openness" of Roussel's language, its lack of the guile we associate with craftsmanship and style, has some of the clarity and solipsism of the play of children. In such play, the adventure to be acted out is often, if not always, carefully devised beforehand. For instance, if in children's play, a gigantic, super-strong steel door has been created and posited as an element in the narrative of the play's adventure, one child may suggest that a special device be permitted entrance into the narrative, a device made of materials stronger than the door's, etc., etc. This device is capable of smashing the door down. One child submits the idea, the others O.K. it and its right to exist within the play, and the play resumes. The device is used, the door broken down, and the narrative continues.

Roussel often works this way. In *Locus Solus,* in the story of *The Reiter,* we read that a torch made of "a certain resinous material" is "to be stuck upright in the ground *which, being loam, was easily penetrated*" (italics mine). The final phrase of this sentence corresponds to the child's invented device, and is intended to head off questions and objections as to the feasibility of a "resinous branch" being stuck "into the ground." Roussel invents the device of ground-as-loam, "easily penetrated."

Such an addendum to the given object, or, more precisely, such a declension of its properties, permits the narrative to continue in its uncanny candor. It is not enough for Roussel to call the ground loam in the first place, for Roussel's enterprise is that of making language's specific manifestations, its words and phrases, *equal to each other.* One word somehow cancels another out. Since both are equal, the quotient is equal to them. Or: the dividend (ground) is divided by the divisor (loam), giving us the quotient (ground is loam). Ground $\div$ loam = ground, loam; or $1 \div 1 = 1$.

The same process inheres in Roussel's substitutive techniques (*Comment j'ai ecrit . . .*). That all words may well be the same as all other words gives Roussel's work its astonishing clarity. Its implications—that diverse things may not ever be known through language—renders his work vertiginous.

*

The lucidity of Roussel's prose is created by his faith that there can be no understanding of anything without description of action; but this description must be joined to a description of the processes employed to effect the action.

His digressions, usually stories with the quality of fairy tales, or children's stories, have about them an air of desperation. They are generated by one specific in the action or process described, yet hovering over them is the fact that any other specific could have generated a different tale. Roussel's rigorous adherence to his generative procedures cannot obviate this ever-present possibility. He wishes his tale to be the only tale possible, but knows that this cannot be the case.

No detail is given more importance than another.

For Roussel, seeing is never enough. What is seen must be explained, but the explanation is empty without the visual accompaniment. Neither description of seen action, nor explanation of why we see what we see can stand alone. They are equal to each other in importance, and they cancel each other out. The description of the *process* of the action is another description of the *action.* We see the specific; then we see the law that rules the specific—and the latter is a translucent layer over the former.

There is no psychology in Roussel, no philosophy, no understanding of characters in terms of their pasts. They, in a sense, have no lives, they are the necessary ingredients in the actions they perform or cause to be performed, or they are the retailers of the secrets of process. They are like the corpses of *Locus Solus* who present an "illusion of life." Not of living, but of life. They *seem* alive, and are the purest characters in fiction, since they are not alive, nor does Roussel pretend that they are. All his characters are elements in a vast tableau of bewildering activity. When we discover why they act as they do, this "why" is seen to be no more than the process which governs their actions. As if one were to ask, "Why did X murder Y?" only to be answered by a description of the murderous act, followed by a detailed description of the processes involved in weaponry, body movements, etc. etc.

Canterel's corpses make all other fictional characters suspect. Or, rather, they assert the truth about fictional characterization.

*

There is no interior in Roussel's work. All is meticulous detail, exteriorized. The characters enmeshed in these outer details are discovered in predicaments that are simply scraped off the surface of "found" narratives of love, romance, melodrama.

In Roussel, we get the phenomenon in action; then the explanation of how the phenomenon has come to pass. The explanation occurs after the description, but it is an explanation of a process which occurred anterior to the phenomenon. The mechanics of the process and the process itself occur, of needs, simultaneously in the tableaux, but in the text they are split in two and take place on absolutely different levels of reality, in wholly different spaces, and at wholly different times.

For Roussel, the act, the process working itself out, is somehow suspect, somehow incomplete without the explanation and description of the "how" posited as a discrete entity. To button a jacket is an unintelligible act, since the bald action masks the mechanics it entails. It is in the separation of the act and its prior mechanics that Roussel finds his only peace. This may be why his relentlessly detailed descriptions are filled with a terrible anxiety, an almost tangible compulsion—they are the actions of a world without any meaning. His only balm is to find "meaning" in the equally relentless detailing of the necessary mechanics. But this balm is false, and the truly dreadful quality of his work becomes apparent in the detailing of the mechanics that permit the meaningless actions to occur. The explanation of the process is as void of meaning as the act. Roussel's work says that action and explanation are incapable of meaning, and that language cannot endow them with meaning; language can only register the meaningless.

When we read Roussel, we see the presence of oblivion, the emptiness of death. Without, I hope, indulging in dramatics, it seems to me that Roussel's work is like death itself. In his work, there is no hint of salvation, there is only the implied repetition of the "illusion of life," in which we are entangled. The repetitions to infinity seem to imply a freedom from chance. They do—but this is the freedom of Canterel's corpses. Weirdly, these corpses are an expression of optimism, an optimism that the emptiness of death can be cheated by a return to the emptiness of a life devoid of the aleatory, by an "illusion of life." The corpses are an expression of peace, almost of joy, since they are outside of both death and life.

Finally, there is no comedy in Roussel. Anything approaching the comic is obviated by its being caught in the machinery of performance/explanation/repetition, and instantly becomes not comic, but grotesque. What could be more eerie than watching a single instance of Charlie Chaplin's antics, listening to an explanation of that instance, then watching the action repeat itself, eternally? Ceaseless, or potentially ceaseless repetition of any act, utterance, locution, etc., is threatening, terrible, and fearsome. It is the secret face of madness.

Fictional Futures and the Conspicuously Young

David Foster Wallace

THE METRONOME OF literary fashion looks to be set on *presto.* Beginning with the high-profile appearances of David Leavitt's *Family Dancing,* Jay McInerney's *Bright Lights, Big City* and Bret Ellis's *Less Than Zero,* the last three-odd years saw a veritable explosion of good-willed critical and commercial interest in literary fiction by Conspicuously Young* writers. During this interval, certain honored traditions of starvation and apprenticeship were inverted: writers' proximity to their own puberties seemed now an asset; rumors had agents haunting prestigious writing workshops like pro scouts at Bowl games; publishers and critics jockeyed for position to proclaim their own beardless favorite "The first voice of a new generation." Too, the upscale urban young quickly established themselves as a bona fide audience (and market) for C.Y. fiction: Ellis and McInerney, Janowitz and Leavitt, Simpson and Minot enjoy a popularity with their peers unknown since the relative popular disappearance of the sixties' hip black humor squad.

As of this writing, late 1987, the backlash has been swift and severe, if not wholly unjustified. Many of the same trendy reviewers who in the mid-eighties were hailing the precocity of a New Generation now bemoan the proliferation of a literary Brat Pack. The *Village Voice,* which in 1985 formalized the apotheosis of McInerney in a gushy cover story, this autumn uses a scathing review of some McInerney disciples as occasion to headline the news that THE BRAT PACK SPITS UP, with crudely cut-out faces of Janowitz, McInerney, Ellis et al. pasted on photos of diaper models. Nineteen eighty-seven saw the staff and guests of the *New York Times Book Review* suddenly complaining of a trend toward "world-weary creative writing projects," a spate of "Y.A.W.N.S. (Young Anomic White Novelists)," an endless succession of flash-in-the-pan "short-story starlets." In its October 11 issue, no less an éminence grise than William Gass administers "A Failing Grade For the Present Tense":

You may have noticed the plague of school-styled [writers] with which our pages have been afflicted, and taken some account of the no-account magazines that exist in order to publish them. Thousands of short-story readers and writers have been

---

*Hereafter abbreviated "C.Y."

released like fingerlings into the thin mainstream of serious prose. . . . Well, young people are young people, aren't they. . . . Adolescents consume more of their psyches than soda, and more local feelings than junk food. Is no indulgence denied them? . . . I read [a recent Leavitt-edited anthology of C.Y. fiction] as a part of my researches. It is like walking through a cemetery before they've put in any graves.

What's caused this quick reversal in mood? Is it capricious and unfair, or overdue? Most interesting: what does it imply?

In my own opinion, the honeymoon's end between the literary Establishment and the C.Y. writer was an inevitable and foreseeable consequence of the same shameless hype that led to many journeyman writers' premature elevation in the first place: condescending critical indulgence and condescending critical dismissal inhabit the same coin. It's true that some cringingly bad fiction gets written by C.Y.'s. But this is hardly an explanation for anything, since the same is true of lots of older artists, many of whom have clearly shot their bolts and now hang by name and fashion alone.

More germane is the frequent charge of a certain numbing *sameness* about much contemporary young writing. To a certain extent anyone who reads widely must agree with it. The vast bulk of the vast amount of recently published C.Y. fiction reinforces the stereotype that has all young literary enterprises falling into one or more of the following three dreary camps:

(1) Neiman-Marcus Nihilism, declaimed via six-figure Uppies and their salon-tanned, morally vacant offspring, none of whom seem to be able to make it from limo door to analyst's couch without several grams of chemical encouragement;

(2) Catatonic Realism, a.k.a. Ultraminimalism, a.k.a. Bad Carver, in which suburbs are wastelands, adults automata, and narrators blank perceptual engines, intoning in run-on monosyllables the artificial ingredients of breakfast cereal and the new human non-soul;

(3) Workshop Hermeticism, fiction for which the highest praise involves the words "competent," "finished," "problem-free," fiction over which Writing-Program pre- and proscriptions loom with the enclosing force of horizons: no character without Freudian trauma in accessible past, without near-diagnostic physical description; no image undissolved into regulation Updikean metaphor; no overture without a dramatized scene to "show" what's "told"; no denouement prior to an epiphany whose approach can be charted by any Freitag on any Macintosh.

Mean, but unfortunately fair—except for the fact that, like most generalizations, these apply validly only to the inferior examples of the work at hand. Ironically for the critic who wants both to bemoan invasions and pigeonhole the invaders, the very proliferation of C.Y. fiction, with its attendant variety, raises the generation's cream above stereotype. The preternatural smarts with which a Simpson or Leavitt can render complex parental machinations through the eyes of thoroughly believable children; the gritty white-trash lyricism of Pinckney Benedict's *Town Smokes;* the wry, bitchy humor of a good Lorrie Moore or Amy Hempel or Debra Spark story; the political vision of William Vollmann's *You Bright and Risen Angels;* the conscientious exploration of *motive* behind Yuppie dissolution in McInerney's *Bright Lights*—these transcend Camp-following and, more important, merit neither head-patting nor sneers. See for yourself. Among the C.Y. writers who do, yes, seem to crowd the last half of this decade, there are some unique and worthy talents. Yes, all are raw, some more or less mature, some more or less apt at transcending the hype the hype-mills crank out daily. But more than a couple are originals.

But it's weird: all we C.Y. writers get consistently lumped together. Both lauds and pans invariably invoke a Generation that is both New and, in some odd way, One. Unfamiliar with the critical fashions of past decades, I don't know whether this perception has precedent, but I do think in certain ways it's not inappropriate. As of now, C.Y. writers, the good and the lousy, are in my opinion A Generation, conjoined less by chronology (Benedict is twenty-three, Janowitz over thirty) than by the new and singular environment in and about which we try to write fiction. This, that we are agnate, also goes a long way toward explaining the violent and conflicting critical reactions New Voices are provoking.

The argument, then, is that certain key things having to do with literary production are radically different for young American writers now; and that, fashion-flux aside, the fact that these key things affect our aesthetic values and literary choices serves at once to bind us together and to distance us from much of an Establishment—literary, intellectual, political—that reads and judges our stuff from their side of a . . . well, generation gap. There are, of course, uncountable differences between the formative experiences of consecutive generations, and to exhaust and explain all the ones relevant here would require both objective distance and a battalion of social historians. Having neither at hand, I propose to invite consideration of just three specific contemporary American phenomena, viz the impacts of television, of academic Creative Writing Programs, and of a revolution in the way educated people understand the function and possibility of literary narrative. These three because they seem at once powerfully affective and normatively complex. Great and grim, tonic and insidious, they are (I claim) undeniable and cohesive influences on this country's "New Voices."

Stats on the percentage of the average American day spent before small screens are well known. But the American generation born after, say, 1955 is the first for whom television is something to be *lived with,* not just looked at. Our parents regard the set rather as the Flapper did the automobile: a curiosity turned treat turned seduction. For us, their children, TV's as much a part of reality as Toyotas and gridlock. We quite literally cannot "imagine" life without it. As it does for so much of today's developed world, it presents and so defines our common experience; but we, unlike any elders, have no memory of a world without such electronic definition. It's built in. In my own childhood, late sixties, rural downstate Illinois, miles and mega-hertz from any center of entertainment production, familiarity with the latest developments on "Batman" or "The Wild, Wild West" was the medium of social exchange. Much of our original play was a simple reenact-ment of what we'd witnessed the night before, and verisimilitude was taken very seriously. The ability to do a passable Howard Cosell, Barney Rubble, CoCo-Puff Bird, or Gomer Pyle was a measure of status, a determination of stature.

Surely television-as-lifestyle influences the modes by which C.Y. writers understand and represent lived life. A recent issue of *Arrival* saw critic Bruce Bawer lampoon many Brat-Packers' habit of delineating characters according to the commercial slogans that appear on their T-shirts. He had a scary number of examples. It's true that there's something sad in the fact that Leavitt's sole description of some characters in, say, "Danny in Transit" consists of the fact that their shirts say "Coca Cola" in a foreign language—yet maybe more sad that, for most of his reading contemporaries, this description *does the job*. Bawer's distaste seems to me misplaced: it's more properly directed at a young culture so willingly bombarded with messages equating what one consumes with who one is that brand loyalty is now an acceptable synechdoche of identity, of character.

This schism between young writers and their older critics probably extends to the whole issue of strategic reference to "popular culture" in literary fiction. The artistic deployment of pop icons—brand names, tele-vision programs, celebrities, commercial film and music—strikes those intellectuals whose consciousness was formed before the genuine Tele-vision Age as at best frivolous tics and at worst dangerous vapidities that compromise fiction's "seriousness" by dating it out of the Platonic Always where it properly resides. A fine and conscientious writing professor once proclaimed to our class that a serious story or novel always eschews "any feature that serves to date it," to fix it in history, because "Literary fiction is always timeless." When we protested that, in his own well-known work, characters moved about in electrically lit rooms, propelled themselves in autos, spoke not Anglo-Saxon but post-WWII English, inhabited a North America already separated from Africa by continental drift, he amended his ruling's application to those explicit references that would date a story in the transient Now. Pressed by further quibbling into real precision, his interdiction turned out really to be against what he called the "mass-commercial-media" reference. At this point, I think, trans-generational discourse breaks down. For this gentleman's automobiled Timeless and our F.C.C.'d own were different. Time had changed Always.

Nor, please, is this stuff a matter of mere taste or idiosyncrasy. Most good fiction writers, even young ones, are intellectuals. So are most critics and teachers (and a surprising number of editors). And television, its advertising, and the popular culture they both reflect and define have fundamentally altered what intellectuals get to regard as the proper objects of their attention. Those cognoscenti whose values were formed before TV and advertising became psychologically pandemic are still anxious to draw a sharp distinction, à la Barbara Tuchman, between those sorts of things that have genuine "quality" and are produced and demanded by people with refined tastes, on one hand, and those sorts of things which have only "popularity" or "mass appeal," are demanded by the Great Unwashed and cheerfully supplied by those whom egalitarian capitalism has whored to the lowest of denominators, the democratic market, on the other. The enlightened older aesthete, erudite and liberal, weaned let's say between 1940 and 1960, is able to operate from a center of contradiction between genuine refinement and genuine liberalism, advertising scholars like Martin Mayer had already begun to deride by the fifties' end:

The great bulk of advertising is culturally repulsive to anyone with any developed sensitivity. So are most movies and television shows, most popular music, and a surprisingly high proportion of published books. . . . But a sensitive person can easily avoid cheap movies, cheap books, and cheap art, while there is scarcely anyone outside the jails who can avoid contact with advertising. By presenting the intellectual with a more or less accurate image of the popular culture, advertising earns his enmity and calumny. It hits him where it hurts worst: in his politically liberal and socially generous outlook—partly nourished on his avoidance of actual contact with popular taste.

I claim that intellectuals of the New Generation for whom C.Y. writers are supposed to be voices can no longer even wrap their minds around this kind of hypocrisy, much less suffer from it. Not that this "enlightenment" is earned, or even necessarily a good thing. Because it's not as though television and advertising and popular entertainments have ceased to be mostly bad art or cheap art, but just that they've imposed themselves on our generation's psyches for so long and with such power that they have entered into complicated relations with our very ideas of the world and the self. We simply cannot "relate to" the older aesthete's distanced distaste for mass entertainment and popular appeal: the distaste may well remain, but the distance has not.

And, as the pop informs our generation's ways of experiencing and reading the world, so too will it naturally affect our artistic values and expectations. Young fiction writers may spend hours each day at the writing table, performing; but we're also, each and every day, part of the great Audience. We're conditioned accordingly. We have an innate predilection for visual stimulation, colored movement, a frenetic variety, a beat you can dance to. It may be that, through hyper- and atrophy, our mental capacities themselves are different: the breadth of our attentions greater as attention spans themselves shorten. Raised on an activity at least partly passive, we experience a degree of manipulation as neutral, a fact of life. However, wooed artfully as we are for not just our loyalty but our very *attention,* we reserve for that attention the status of a commodity, a measure of power; and our choices to bestow or withhold it carry for us great weight. So does what we regard as our God-given right to be entertained—or, if not entertained, at least stimulated: the unpleasant is perfectly OK, just so long as it *rivets.*

As one can see popular icons seriously used in much C.Y. fiction as touchstones for the world we live in and try to make into art, so one might trace some of the techniques favored by many young writers to roots in our experience as consummate watchers. E.g., events often refracted through the sensibilities of more than one character; short, dense paragraphs in which coherence is often sacrificed for straight evocation; abrupt transitions in scene, setting, point of view, temporal and causal orders; a surfacy, objective, "cinematic" third-person narrative eye. Above all, though, a comparative indifference to the imperative of mimesis, combined with an absolute passion for narrative choices that conduce to what might be called "mood." For no writer can help assuming that the reader is on some level like him: already having seen, ad nauseum, what life *looks like,* he's far more interested in how it *feels* as a signpost toward what it means.

The technical coin, too, has a tails. For instance, it's not hard to see that the trendy Ultraminimalism favored by too many C.Y. writers is deeply influenced by the aesthetic norms of mass entertainment. Indeed, this fiction depends on what's little more than a crude inversion of these norms. Where television, especially its advertising, presents everything in hyperbole, Ultraminimalism is deliberately flat, understated, "undersold." Where TV seeks everywhere to render its action either dramatic or melodramatic, to move the viewer by displaying constant movement, the Minimalist describes an event as one would an object, a geometric form in stasis; and he always does so from an emotional remove of light years. Where television does and must aim always to *please,* the Catatonic writer hefts something of a finger at subject and reader alike: one has only to read a Bret Ellis sex scene (pick a page, any page) to realize that here pleasure is neither a subject nor an aim. My own aversion to Ultraminimalism, I think, stems from its naive pretension. The Catatonic Bunch seem to feel that simply by inverting the values imposed on us by television, commercial film, advertising, etc., they can automatically achieve the aesthetic depth popular entertainment so conspicuously lacks. Really, of course, the Ultraminimalists are no less infected by popular culture than other C.Y. writers: they merely choose to define their art by opposition to their own atmosphere. The attitude betrayed is similar to that of lightweight neo-classicals who felt that to be non-vulgar was not just a requirement but an *assurance* of value, or of insecure scholars who confuse obscurity with profundity. And it's just about as annoying.

Not that the Catatonic's discomfort with a culture of and by popularity isn't understandable. We're all at least a little uncomfortable with it—no?—probably because, as technicians like Mayer foresaw thirty years ago, escape from it has gone from impossible to inconceivable. That is, since today's popular TV culture is by its nature *mass, pan-,* it's of course going to impact the styles and choices and dreams not just of a few fingerling artists and their small readerships, but of the very human collectivities about which we try to write. And this impact has been overwhelming; the new Always has changed everything. I'm going to argue that it's done so in ways that are bad and have costs. "Bad" means inimical to many of the values our communities have evolved and held and cherished and taught. "Costs" means painful changes and losses for persons. Because, see, a mysterious beast like television begins, the more sophisticated it gets, to produce and live by an antinomy, a phenomenon whose strength lies in its contradiction: aimed ever and always at groups, masses, markets, collectivities, it's nevertheless true that the most powerful and lasting changes are wrought by TV on *individual persons,* each one of whom is forced every day to understand himself in relation to the Groups by virtue of which he seems to exist at all.

Think, for instance, about the way prolonged exposure to broadcast drama makes each one of us at once more self-conscious and less reflective. A culture more and more about *seeing* eventually perverts the relation of seer and seen. We watch various actors who play various characters involved in various relations and events. Seldom do we think about the fact that the single deep feature the characters share, with each other and with the actors who portray them, is that they are *watched.* The behavior of the actors, and—in a complicated way, through the drama they're inside—even the characters, is directed always at an audience for whom they behave . . . indeed, in virtue of whom they exist as actor or character in the first place, behind the screen's glass. We, the audience, receive unconscious reinforcement of the thesis that the most significant feature of persons is *watchableness,* and that contemporary human worth is not just isomorphic with but rooted in the phenomenon of watching. Precious distinctions between truly being and merely appearing get obfuscated. Imagine a Berkleyan *esse-est-percipi* universe in which God is named Nielsen.

Then consider that well-known, large, "ignorant" segment of the population that believes on a day-to-day level that what happens on televised dramas is "real." This, the enormous volume of mail addressed each day to characters and not the persons who portray them, is the iceberg's extreme tip. The berg itself is a generation (New) for whom the distinction between (real) actor artificially portraying and (pretend) character genuinely behaving gets ever more tangled. The danger of the berg is badness and cost—a shift from an understanding of self as a character in a great drama whose end is meaning to an understanding of self as an actor at a great audition whose end is *seeming,* i.e., being seen.

Actually there are uncountable ways in which efficiently conceived and disseminated popular entertainment affects the existential predicaments of both persons and groups. And if "existential" seems too weighty a term to attach to anything pop, then I think you're misunderstanding what's at stake. You're invited to consider commercial dramas that deal with violence and danger and the possibility of death. There are lots, today. Each drama has a hero. He's purposely designed so that we by our nature "identify" with him. At present this is still not hard to get us to do, for we still tend to think of our own lives this way: we're each the hero of our own drama, others around us remanded to supporting roles or (increasingly) audience status.

But now try to recall the last time you saw the "hero" die within his drama's narrative frame. It's very rarely done anymore. Entertainment professionals have apparently done research: audiences find the deaths of those with whom they identify a downer, and are less apt to watch dramas in which danger is creatively connected to the death that makes danger dangerous. The natural consequence is that today's dramatic heroes tend to be "immortal" within the frame that makes them heroes and objects of identification (for the audience, VCR- and related technology give this illusion a magnetic reality). I claim that the fact that we are strongly encouraged to identify with characters for whom death is not a significant creative possibility has real costs. We the audience, and individual you over there and me right here, lose any sense of eschatology, thus of teleology, live in a moment that is, paradoxically, both emptied of intrinsic meaning or end and quite literally *eternal.* If we're the only animals who know in advance we're going to die, we're also probably the only animals who would submit so cheerfully to the sustained denial of this undeniable and very important truth. The danger is that, as entertainment's denials of the truth get even more effective and pervasive and seductive, we will eventually forget what they're denials *of.* This is scary. Because it seems transparent to me that, if we forget how to die, we're going to forget how to live.

And if you think that contemporary literary artists, of whatever stature, are above blinking at a reality we all find unpleasant, consider the number of serious American fictional enterprises in the last decade that have dealt with what's acknowledged to be the single greatest organized threat to our persons and society. Try to name, say, two.

Maybe the real question is—how serious can people who have a *right* to be entertained permit "serious" fiction to be anymore? Because if I claimed above that the C.Y. writers' intellectual fathers held dear a contradictory blend of cutting-edge politics and old-guard aesthetics, I'm sure most of us would gladly trade it for the contradictions that are its replacement. Today's journeyman fiction writer finds himself both a lover of serious narrative and an ineluctably conditioned part of a pop-dominated culture in which the social stock of his own enterprise is falling. What we are inside of—what *comprises* us—is killing what we love.

Hyperbole? It's important to remember that most television is not just entertainment: it's also narrative. And it's so true it's trite that human beings are narrative animals: every culture countenances itself as culture via a story, whether mythopoeic or politico-economic; every whole person understands his lifetime as an organized, recountable series of events and changes with at least a beginning and middle. We need narrative like we need space-time; it's a built-in thing. In the C.Y. writers today, the narrative patterns to which literate Americans are most regularly exposed are televised. And, even on a charitable account, television is a pretty low type of narrative art. It's a narrative art that strives not to change or enlighten or broaden or reorient—not necessarily even to "entertain"—but merely and always to *engage,* to *appeal to.* Its one end—openly acknowledged—is to *ensure continued watching.* And (I claim) the metastatic efficiency with which it's done so has, as cost, inevitable and dire consequences for the level of people's tastes in narrative art. For the very *expectations* of readers in virtue of which narrative art is art.

Television's greatest appeal is that it is engaging without being at all demanding. One can rest while undergoing stimulation. Receive without giving. It's the same in all low art that has as goal continued attention and patronage: it's appealing precisely because it's at once fun and easy. And the entrenchment of a culture built on Appeal helps explain a dark and curious thing: at a time when there are more decent and good and very good serious fiction writers at work in America than ever before, an American public enjoying unprecedented literacy and disposable income spends the vast bulk of its reading time and book dollar on fiction that is, by any fair standard, trash. Trash fiction is, by design and appeal, most like televised narrative: engaging without being demanding. But trash, in terms of both quality and popularity, is a much more sinister phenomenon. For while television has from its beginnings been openly motivated by—has been *about*—considerations of mass appeal and L.C.D. and profit, our own history is chock full of evidence that readers and societies may properly expect important, lasting contributions from a narrative art that understands itself as being about considerations more important than popularity and balance sheets. Entertainers can divert and engage and maybe even console; only artists can transfigure. Today's trash writers are entertainers working artists' turf. This in itself is nothing new. But television aesthetics, and television-like economics, have clearly made their unprecedented popularity and reward possible. And there seems to me to be a real danger that not only the forms but the *norms* of televised art will begin to supplant the standards of all narrative art. This would be a disaster.

I'm worried lest I sound too much like B. Tuchman here, because my complaints about trash are different from hers, and less sophisticated. My complaint against trash fiction is not that it's plebeian, and as for its rise I don't care at all whether post-industrial liberalism squats in history as the culprit that made it inevitable. My complaint against trash isn't that it's vulgar art, or irritatingly dumb art, but that, given what makes fiction art at all, trash is simply *unreal, empty*—and that (aided by mores of and by TV) it seduces the market writers need and the culture that needs writers away from what *is* real, full, meaningful.

Even the snottiest young *artiste,* of course, probably isn't going to bear personal ill will toward writers of trash; just as, while everybody agrees that prostitution is a bad thing for everyone involved, few are apt to blame prostitutes themselves, or wish them harm. If this seems like a non sequitur, I'm going to claim the analogy is all too apt. A prostitute is someone who, in exchange for money, affords someone else the form and sensation of sexual intimacy without any of the complex emotions or responsibilities that make intimacy between two people a valuable or meaningful human enterprise. The prostitute "gives," but—demanding nothing of comparable value in return—perverts the giving, helps render what is supposed to be a revelation a transaction. The writer of trash fiction, often with admirable craft, affords his customer a narrative structure and movement that *engages* the reader—titillates, repulses, excites, transports him—without demanding of him any of the intellectual or spiritual or *artistic* responses that render verbal inter-course between writer and reader an important or even *real* activity. So when our elders tell our graduate fiction class (as they liked to do a lot) that a war for fictional art's soul is being waged in the 1980s between poetry on one side and trash on the other—to this admonishment we listen, at this we take pause. Especially when television and advertising have conditioned us to equate net worth with human worth. Sidney Sheldon, a gifted trash-master, owns jets; more people in this country write poetry than read it; the annual literary budget of the National Endowment for the Arts is less than a third of the U.S.'s yearly expenditures on military bands, less than a *tenth* of the three big networks' yearly spending on Creative Development.

Sidney Sheldon, by the way, was the Creative, Developing force behind both "I Dream of Jeannie" and "Hart to Hart." Oprah Winfrey asks him in admiration for the secret behind his success in "two such totally different media." I say to myself, "Ha," watching.

It's in terms of economics that academic Creative Writing Programs* offer their least ambiguous advantages. Published writers (assuming they them-selves have a graduate writing degree) can earn enough by workshop teaching to support themselves and their own fiction without having to resort to more numbing or time-consuming employment. On the student side, fellowships—some absurdly generous—and paid assistantships in

---

*These words are capitalized because they *understand* themselves as capitalized. Trust me on this.

teaching are usually available to almost all students. Programs tend to be a sweet deal.

And there are more such programs in this country now than anywhere anytime before. The once-lone brow of the Iowa Workshop has birthed first-rate creative departments at places like Stanford, Houston, Columbia, Johns Hopkins, Virginia, Michigan, Arizona, etc. The majority of accredited American I.H.E.s now have at least some sort of formal academic provision for students who want vocational training in fiction writing. This has all happened within the last fifteen years. It's unprecedented, and so are the effects of the trend on young U.S. fiction. Of the C.Y. writers I've mentioned above, I know of none who've not had some training in either a graduate or undergraduate writing department. Most of them hold M.F.A.'s. Some are, even as we speak, working toward a degree called a "Creative Ph.D." Never has a "literary generation" been so thoroughly and formally trained, nor has such a large percentage of aspiring fiction writers eschewed extra-mural apprenticeship for ivy and grades.

And the contributions of the academy's rise in American fiction go beyond the fiscal. The workshop phenomenon has been justly credited with a recent "renaissance of the American short story," a renaissance heralded in the late seventies with the emergence of writers like the late Raymond Carver (taught at Syracuse), Jayne Anne Phillips (M.F.A. from Iowa), and the late Breece Pancake (M.F.A. from Virginia). More small magazines devoted to short literary fiction exist today than ever before, most of them either sponsored by programs or edited and staffed by recent M.F.A.s. Short story collections, even by relative unknowns, are now halfway viable economically, and publishers have moved briskly to accommodate trend.

More important for young writers themselves, programs can afford them time, academic (and parental!) legitimacy, and an environment in which to Hone Their Craft, Grow, Find Their Voice,* etc. For the student, a community of serious, like-minded persons with whom to exchange ideas has pretty clear advantages. So, in many ways, does the fiction class itself. In a workshop, rudiments of technique and process can be taught fairly quickly to kids who might in the past have spent years in New York lofts learning basic tricks of the trade by trial and error. A classroom atmosphere of rigorous constructive criticism helps toughen young writers' hides and prepare them for the wildly disparate responses the world of real readers holds in store. Best of all, a good workshop forces students regularly to formulate consistent, reasoned criticisms of colleagues' work; and this, almost without fail, makes them far more astute about the strengths and weaknesses of their own fiction.

Still, I think it's the Program-sword's other edge that justifies the various Establishments' present disenchantment with C.Y. fiction more than

---

*On these, too: they are to Programs what *azan* are to mosques.

anything else. The dark side of the Program trend exists, grows; and it's much more than an instantiation of the standard academic lovely-in-theory-but-mangled-in-practice conundrum. So we'll leave aside nasty little issues like departmental politics, faculty power struggles that summon images of sharks fighting for control of a bathtub, the dispiriting hiss of everybody's egos in various stages of inflation or deflation, a downright unshakable publish-or-perish mentality that equates appearance in print with talent or promise. These might be particular to one student's experience. Certain problems inherent in Programs' very structure and purpose, though, are not. For one thing, the pedagogical relation between fiction professor and fiction student has unhealthiness built right in. Writing teachers are by calling writers, not teachers. The fact that most of them are teaching, not for its own sake, but to support a separate and obsessive calling, has got to be accepted, as does its consequence: every minute spent on class and department business is, for Program staff, a minute not spent working on their own art, and must to a degree be resented. The best teachers seem to acknowledge the conflict between their vocations, reach some kind of internal compromise, and go on. The rest, according to their capacities, either suppress the resentment or make sure they do the barely acceptable minimum their primary source of income requires. Almost all, though, take the resentment out in large part on the psyches of their pupils—for pupils represent artistic time wasted, an expenditure of a teacher's fiction-energy without fiction-production. It's all perfectly understandable. Clearly, though, feeling like a burden, an impediment to *real* art-production, is not going to be conducive to a student's development, to say nothing of his enthusiasm. Not to mention his basic willingness to engage his instructor in the kind of dynamic back-and-forth any real creative education requires, since it's usually the very-low-profile, docile, *undemanding* student who is favored, recruited, supported and advanced by a faculty for whom demand equals distraction.

In other words, the fact that creative writing teachers must wear two hats has unhappy implications for the quality of both M.F.A. candidates and the education they receive in Programs. And it's very unclear who if anyone's to blame. Teaching fiction writing is darn hard to do well. The conscientious teacher must not only be both highly critical and emotionally sensitive, acute in his reading and articulate about his acuity: he must be all these things with regard to precisely those issues that can be communicated to and discussed in a workshop *group*. And that inevitably yields a distorted emphasis on the sorts of simple, surface concerns that a dozen or so people can talk about coherently: straightforward mechanics of traditional fiction production like fidelity to point-of-view, consistency of tense and tone, development of character, verisimilitude of setting, etc. Faults or virtues that cannot quickly be identified or discussed between bells—little things like interestingness, depth of vision, originality, political assumptions and agendas, the question whether deviation from norm is in some cases OK—

must, for sound Program-pedagogical reasons, be ignored or discouraged.

Too, in order to remain both helpful and sane, the professional writer/ teacher has got to develop, consciously or not, an aesthetic doctrine, a static set of principles about how a "good" story works. Otherwise he'd have to start from intuitive scratch with each student piece he reads, and that way the liquor cabinet lies. But consider what this means: the Program staffer must teach the practice of art, which by its nature always exists in at least *some* state of tension with the rules of its practice, as essentially an applied system of rules. Surely this kind of *enforced* closure to further fictional possibilities isn't good for most teachers' own literary development. Nor is it at all good for their students, most of whom have been in school for at least sixteen years and know that the way the school game is played is: (1) Determine what the instructor wants; and (2) Supply it forthwith. Most Programs, then, produce two kinds of students. There are those few who, whether particularly gifted or not, have enough interest and faith in their fiction instincts to elect sometimes to deviate from professors' prescriptions. Many of these students are shown the door, or drop out, or gut out a couple years during which the door is always being pointed to, throats cleared, Fin. Aid unavailable. These turn out to be the lucky ones. The other kind are those who, the minute fanny touches chair, make the instructors' dicta their own —whether from insecurity, educational programming, or genuine agreement (rare)—who row instead of rock, play the game quietly and solidly, and begin producing solid, quiet work, most of which lands neatly in Dreary Camp #3, nice, cautious, boring Workshop Stories, stories as tough to find technical fault with as they are to remember after putting them down. *Here* are the rouged corpses for Dr. Gass's graveyard. Workshops *like* corpses. They *have* to. Because any class, even one in "creativity," is going to place supreme value on *not making mistakes.* And corpses, whatever their other faults, never ever screw up.*

I doubt whether any of this is revelatory, but I hope it's properly scary. Because Creative Writing Programs, while claiming in all good faith to train professional writers, in reality train *more teachers of Creative Writing.* The only thing a Master of Fine Arts degree actually qualifies one to do is teach ... Fine Arts. Almost all present fiction professors hold something like an M.F.A. So do most editors of literary magazines. Most M.F.A. candidates who stay in the Business will go on to teach and edit. Small wonder, then, that older critics feel in so much current C.Y. fiction the tweed breeze that

---

*Only considerations of space and legal liability restrain me from sharing with you in detail the persistent legend, at one nameless institution, of the embalmed cadaver cadged from the medical school by two deeply troubled young M.F.A. candidates, enrolled in a workshop at their proxy, smuggled pre-bell into the seminar room each week, and propped in its assigned seat, there to clutch a pencil in its white fist and stare straight ahead with an expression of somewhat rigid good cheer. The name of the legend is "The Cadaver That Got a B."

could signal a veritable storm of boredom: envision if you dare a *careful, accomplished* national literature, mistake-free, seamless as fine linoleum; fiction preoccupied with norm as value instead of value's servant; fiction by academics who were taught by academics and teach aspiring academics; novel after critique-resistant novel about tenure-angst, coed-lust, cafeteria-*schmerz.*

Railing against occluded subject matter and tradition-tested style is one thing. A larger issue is whether Writing Programs and their grinding, story-every-three-weeks workshop assembly lines could, eventually, lower all standards, precipitate a broad-level literary mediocrity, fictional equivalents of what Donald Hall calls "The McPoem." I think, if they get much more popular, and do not drop the pose of "education" in favor of a humbler and more honest self-appraisal—a form of literary patronage and an occasion for literary community—we might well end up with a McStory chain that would put Ray Kroc to shame. Because it's not just the unhealthy structure of the Program, the weird creative constraints it has to impose on instructors and students alike—it's the type of student who is attracted by such an arrangement. A sheepheaded willingness to toe any line just because it's the most comfortable way to survive is contemptible in any student. But students are just symptoms. Here's the disease: in terms of rigor, demand, intellectual and emotional requirement, a lot of Creative Writing Programs are an unfunny joke. Few require of applicants any significant preparation in history, literature, criticism, composition, foreign languages, art or philosophy; fewer still make attempts to provide it in curricula or require it as a criterion for graduation.

Part of this problem is political. Academic departments of Creative Writing and "Straight Literature" tend to hold each other in mutual contempt, a state of affairs that student, Program, and serious-fiction audience are all going to regret a lot if it continues to obtain. Way too many students are being "certified" to go out there and try to do meaningful work on the cutting edge of an artistic discipline of whose underpinnings, history, and greatest achievements they are largely ignorant. The obligatory survey of "Writers Who Are Important to *You*" at the start of each term seems to suggest that Homer and Milton, Cervantes and Shakespeare, Maupassant and Gogol—to say nothing of the Testaments—have receded into the mists of Straight Lit; that, for far too much of this generation, Salinger invented the wheel, Updike internal combustion, and Carver, Beattie and Phillips drive what's worth chasing. Forget Allan Bloom gnashing his teeth at high-school students who pretend to no aspirations past an affordable mortgage—we're supposed to want to be *writers,* here. We as a generation are in danger of justifying Eliot at his zaniest if via a blend of academic stasis and intellectual disinterest we show to the dissatisfaction of all that culture is either cumulative or it is dead, empty on either side of a social Now that admits neither passion about the future nor curiosity about the past.

The fact that we Aspiring Voices as a generation show so little intellectual curiosity is the least defensible thing of all. But it could well be that the very thing that makes our anti-intellectualism so obscene renders it also extremely temporary. Thing in question: our generation is lucky enough to have been born into an artistic climate as stormy and exciting as anything since Pound and Co. turned the world-before-last on its head. The last few generations of American writers have breathed the relatively stable air of New Criticism and an Anglo-American aesthetics untainted by Continental winds. The climate for the "next" generation of American writers—should we decide to inhale rather than die—is aswirl with what seems like long-overdue appreciation for the weird achievements of such aliens as Husserl, Heidegger, Bakhtin, Lacan, Barthes, Poulet, Gadamer, de Man. The demise of Structuralism has changed a world's outlook on language, art, and literary discourse; and the contemporary artist can simply no longer afford to regard the work of critics or theorists or philosophers—no matter how stratospheric—as divorced from his own concerns.

Crudely put, the idea that literary language is any kind of neutral medium for the transfer of _____* from artist to audience, or that it's any kind of inert tool lying there passively to be well- or ill-used by a communicator of meaning, has been cast into rich and serious question. With it, too, the stubborn Romanticist view of fiction as essentially a mirror, distinguished from the real world it reflects only by its portability and mercilessly "objective" clarity, has finally taken it on the chin. Form-content distinctions are now flat planets. Language's promotion from mirror to eye, from *organikos* to organic, is yesterday's news (except in those two lonely outposts, TV and the Creative classroom) as the tide of Post-Structuralism, Marxism, Feminism, Freudianism, Deconstruction, Semiotics, Hermeneutics, and attendant -isms and -ics moves through the ("Straight") U.S. academy and into the consciousness of the conscious American adult.

The crux being that, if mimesis isn't dead, then it's on life-support courtesy of those who soon enough will be.

And what a row C.Y. writers can see among its heirs! Only about eighty years after visual-arts movements like Dada and Cubism supplanted "referential" art (no camera inventions to threaten the sovereignty of literary mimesis, see), the *literature* of the referent, of "psychological glow," of *illusion* has finally come under constructive attack from angles as disparate as they are dazzling. The refracted world of Proust and Musil, Schulz and Stein, Borges and Faulkner has, post-War, exploded into diffraction, a weird, protracted Manhattan Project staffed by Robbe-Grillet, Grass, Nabokov, Sorrentino, Bohl, Barth, McCarthy, García Márquez, Puig, Kundera, Gass, Fuentes, Elkin, Donoso, Handke, Burroughs, Duras,

---

*Take your pick of Tolstoy, Schopenhauer or Richards and insert "feeling," "freedom from phenomena," or "relevant mental condition," respectively, in the space provided.

Elkin, Coover, Gombrowicz, LeGuin, Lessing, Acker, Gaddis, Coetzee, Ozick. To name just a few. We, the would-be heirs to a gorgeous chaos, stand witness to the rise and fall of the *nouveau roman,* Postmodernism, Metafiction, The New Lyricism, The New Realism, Minimalism, Ultra-minimalism, Performance-Theory. It's a freaking maelstrom, and the C.Y. writer who still likes to read a bit can't help feeling torn: if the Program is maddening in its stasis, the real world of serious fiction just *won't hold still.*

If one can stomach a good dose of simplification, though, there can be seen one deep feature shared by all the cutting-edge fiction that resonates with the post-Hiroshima revolution. That is its fall into time, a loss of innocence about the language that is its breath and bread. Its unblinking recognition of the fact that the relations between literary artist, literary language, and literary artifact are vastly more complex and powerful than has been realized hitherto. And the insight that is courage's reward—that it is *precisely* in those tangled relations that a forward-looking, fertile literary value may well reside.

This doesn't mean that Metafiction and Minimalism, the two most starkly self-conscious of the movements that exploit human beings' wary and excited new attention to language, compose or even indicate the directions in which the serious fiction of "whole new generations" will move. Both these forms strike me as simple engines of self-reference (Metafiction overtly so, Minimalism a bit sneakier); they are primitive, crude, and seem already to have reached the Clang-Bird-esque horizon of their own possibility—self-reference being just a tiny wrinkled subset of aboutness. I'm pretty convinced, though, that they're an early symptom of a dark new enlightenment, that quite soon no truly serious C.Y. writer will be able to pretend anymore that the use of literary expression for the construction of make-believe is a straightforward enterprise. We are the recipients of a knife unprecedentedly vulnerable to its own blade, and all the Writing Program prizes and "Mary Tyler Moore Show" reruns in the world can't hide what's in our hands forever.

Exciting is also confusing, and I'd be distrustful of any C.Y. snot who claimed to know where literary fiction will go during this generation's working lifetime. It's obviously true that the revolution I've just gushed about has yielded changes in outlook that are as yet primarily destructive: illusions exposed, assumptions overturned, dearly held prejudices debunked. We seem, now, to see our literary innocence taken from us without anything substantial to replace it. An age between. There's a marvelously apposite Heidegger quotation here, but I'll spare you.

The bold conclusion here, then, is that the concatenated New Generation with whom the critics are currently playing coy mistress is united by confusion, if nothing else. And this might be why so much of the worst C.Y. fiction fits so neatly into the Three Camps reviewers consign it to: Workshop

Hermeticism because in confusing times caution seems prudent; Catatonia because in confusing times the bare minimal seems easy; Yuppie Nihilism because the mass culture the Yuppie inhabits and instantiates is itself at best empty and at worst evil—and in confusing times the revelation of something even this obvious is, up to a point, valuable.

Well, but it's fair to ask how valuable. Of course it's true that an unprecedented number of young Americans have big disposable incomes, fine tastes, nice things, competent accountants, access to exotic intoxicants, attractive sex partners, and are still deeply unhappy. All right. Some good fiction has held up a mercilessly powder-smeared mirror to the obvious. What troubles me about the fact that the Gold-Card-fear-and-trembling fiction just keeps coming is that, if the upheavals in popular, academic and intellectual life have left people with any long-cherished conviction intact, it seems as if it should be an abiding faith that the conscientious, talented, and lucky artist of any age retains the power to effect change. And if Marx (sorry—last dropped name) derided the intellectuals of his day for merely interpreting the world when the real imperative was to change it, the derision seems even more apt today when we notice that many of our best-known C.Y. writers seem content merely to have reduced interpretation to whining. And what's frustrating for me about the whiners is that precisely the state of general affairs that *explains* a nihilistic artistic outlook makes it *imperative* that art *not* be nihilistic. I can think of no better argument for giving Mimesis-For-Mimesis'-Sake the chair than the fact that, for a young fiction writer, inclined by disposition and vocation to pay some extra attention to the way life gets lived around him, 1987's America is not a nice place to be. The last cohesive literary generation came to consciousness during the comparatively black-and-white era of Vietnam. We, though, are Watergate's children, television's audience, Reagan's draft-pool, and everyone's market. We've reached our majority in a truly bizarre period in which "Wrong is right," "Greed is good," and "It's better to look good than to feel good"—and when the poor old issue of trying to *be* good no longer even merits a straight face. It seems like one big echo of Mayer the fifties' ad-man: "In a world where private gratification seems the supreme value, all cats are grey."

Except art, is the thing. Serious, real, conscientious, aware, ambitious art is not a grey thing. It has never been a grey thing and it is not a grey thing now. This is why fiction in a grey time *may not be grey.* And why the titles of all but one or two of the best works of Neiman-Marcus Nihilism are going to induce aphasia quite soon in literate persons who read narrative art for what makes it real.

And, besides an unfair acquaintance with many young writers who are not yet Conspicuous and so not known to you, this is why I'd be willing to bet anything at least a couple and maybe a bunch of the Whole New Generation are going to make art, maybe make great art, maybe even make great art change. One thing about the Young you can trust in 1987: if we're willing to devote our lives to something, you can rest assured we get off on it. And nothing has changed about why writers who don't do it for the money write: it's art, and art is meaning, and meaning is power: power to color cats, to order chaos, to transform void into floor and debt into treasure. The best "Voices of a Generation" surely know this already; more, they let it inform them. It's quite possible that none of the best are yet among the Conspicuous. A couple might even be . . . *autodidacts*. But, especially now, none of them need worry. If fashion, flux and academy make for thin milk, at least that means the good stuff can't help but rise. I'd get ready.

Conflictual Inscriptions

Claude Ollier

THE NOTES AT HAND are an attempt to interlink a certain number of remarks touching as much upon those phenomena preexisting the decision to write as upon those intervening within the act itself—remarks drawn from a personal practice and which were developed not in the margins of an activity but within this activity itself, every graphic trace calling for an elucidation, every elucidation incorporating itself into the activity in progress and influencing its direction and meaning.

How shall we go about giving a brief account of the elements of this practice?

Let us say: Every act of writing instantaneously resolves an ensemble of socio-cultural conflicts organized in a series of schematic oppositions. Instantaneously resolves, through an immediate graphic trace of text; and at every instant, that is, in a succession of instants which comprise so many writing decisions; furthermore, resolves, but always provisionally—otherwise everything would be decided in a few words. For each graphic trace, or "proposition," introduces one or more fictional elements into circulation, which the immediately following graphic trace either confirms or denies, a contradiction that an ulterior trace will strive to reconcile. In other words, the socio-cultural conflicts inscribed in a series of oppositions are transmuted, by the act of writing, into inscribed textual conflicts, these latter as a series of fictional oppositions, either on the same fictional level or between one or the other of these levels.

Let us examine one by one these different points—not in the abstract, but by describing and analyzing the forms under which, at the different stages of the elaborative process of texts, these phenomena have manifested themselves with a relative clarity and restraint.

Considering things in the chronological order of their mobilization, we must first of all speak of those images or *syncretic figures* which are located at the origin of fiction, images that yield a global and undifferentiated apprehension of a future, or virtual, fictional object, and which long precede perception and conception in terms of clearly separate and distinct fictional elements. Here there is the blurry frame of a scene in a dream, there the configuration of a landscape, or a photograph, or a painting upon which a certain distribution of light has altered the eyes. If this figure strikes us, and is retained and privileged to the detriment of so many others that besiege us, the reason is that within itself it bears the mark of major urgent solicitations, which it collects together in a fashion, binds in a sheaf and brandishes before our eyes in order to provide their reading form. And what there is to read is more or less legibly inscribed there. At first glance there are the lines to be read, which demarcate the contrasting surfaces, perceived as fields of oppositions. Other lines of equal importance do not appear at first reading, but passing time purges this image and one must not spend too long waiting for the other force fields to grow more pronounced, revealing new series of oppositions. I mean that such a figure appears sooner or later—and rather soon, for it is very often observed, not to say that it obsesses us—as *a condensed version of the fundamental conflicts dividing us at that time.* It is like a film upon which have been fixed ongoing dramas and the imprint of all sorts of obstacles and indecisions. This figure imposes itself at the outset through an as yet dissimulated signifying power, through the richness of its signified elements which allows the few simple features inscribed there to be intuited, and gradually announces itself, with an ever-growing power, as *symbolic* of a global situation composed of fixed and unresolved tensions. This figure constitutes, if you will, not a first text but the figurative equivalent of a first text, a rebus-like pre-text—offering itself for deciphering or "development," or to be more precise, absolutely demanding deciphering and development. And it is this operation that will soon be effected by instituting the fiction.

To more clearly describe the mechanism triggered by these figures at the origin of the writing process and to show the scope of their generative role in the conception of the fiction, an example is necessary at this point. Let us choose a geographic map whose incompleteness is its chief distinguishing characteristic, marked as it is in the center by a vast, empty, roughly elliptical zone, dubbed somewhat redundantly "uncharted zone." The design of a plain is visible to the north, desert plateaus to the south, and to the east and west, a mountain range with high peaks and winding valleys. All the features of this graphic representation—lines representing waterways, roads, reliefs, names of regions and localities—which provide a relatively plentiful and precise reading at the periphery, gradually become sparser and more imprecise as they approach the central zone, at the outskirts of which they are no more than mute, stippled signs. They totally disappear shortly afterward, the geometrical locus of their disappearance tracing, by default, this ellipsis wherein there is nothing more to be read than the meager term that qualifies it.

Thus, upon this first series of customary oppositions—plain/mountain, fertility/aridity, dense population/sparse population, steppe vegetation/scrubland vegetation, Arab tribes/Berber tribes (because this takes place in a region in North Africa), Koranic law/law of custom, written language of the plain/unwritten dialect of the mountain, etc.—upon this first series a second superimposes itself, determined by the presence of this central zone, fruit of the absence of cartographical work, namely: full/empty, abundance of points of reference/elimination of all points of reference, traditional itineraries/virgin itineraries, surveyed territory/terra incognita, speech/ silence, written text/blank page, etc. And also: region conquered by the invader/rebellious region, sphere of compromise/zone of resistance, colonized people/free people. . . . All these oppositions cannot be perceived consciously and at once, only a few alone catch the eye, but if all are within a short while readable and analyzable, it is because the first momentary perception has unconsciously mobilized the ensemble of socio-cultural oppositions which have their seat in us, and the present conflicts translating them. I decipher these series of oppositions inscribed on the map, I recognize and identify them as homologous to my own, transforming them, by my "taking them on" into what will be called *conflictual inscriptions,* personal conflictual inscriptions here, distinct from those which, entirely socialized, we will soon meet. These personal inscriptions are also the product of the meeting between a figurative opposition and our own determinations (notably all those implied by a person's belonging to a determined social class, to a system of education and of reading, to a system of institutional instruction and the valorization of activities known as intellectual, to a particular culture)—inscriptions which are in the greatest measure our work and represent a whole series of acts of rebellion or adaptation, of clarification or disruption, of misrepresentation, of sidestepping or of attack, of assent or questioning, of display or dissimulation.

Here then is the deciphered and endorsed image, its series of oppositions recognized and taken into account, gradually, through renewed, meticulous observation. And this observation will give rise to a series of *secondary figures,* functioning as the analytical derivatives of the synthetic global figure of departure, which they will decompose into its simple components, linking these latter, from one figure to the other, into a sort of "progression" (as in the expression "harmonic progression") or abstract itinerary. The specific mechanisms set into motion by this phenomenon of "capture" and appropriation can already be seen, as well as the specific temptation to institute the fiction it brings into the world. To return to the preceding example, likewise it is after such a first glance that was at the origin of a rather large book, *Mise-en-Scène,* that there succeeded a long period of observation, during the course of which were gradually engendered schematic intermediate forms coming between the basic image and the first grammatical forms to be graphically traced on the blank page. Placed under observation this way, the incomplete map allowed itself to be separated from the fiction's mediating forms of approach. These *forms,* or *notions of approach,* were in the order as follows, through a transformation of sorts into filmic "dissolves": blank zone—ellipse—circle—circular itinerary— double itinerary—reverse itinerary—recurrence of actions and procedures —the positive direction of a route and the negative direction—duplication of characters—double murder—etc. Then the tripartite division: full zone—empty zone—full zone, articulated upon: in time past—today—in the future. Then: dissimulation—partial unveiling—renewed dissimulation, etc. Thus, one after the other, the derived figures come into existence, both of an arithmetical and geometrical type: graphic traces of routes and modes of behavior, relationships, progressions, keys for an encoding. These simple figures were like grids which, abstracted from the figurative inscription of departure, took form in order to act as a support for the construction of the fictional correspondences to come, or as polarizers channeling the white light emitted by the nebula of sorts which was the initial image rising within the angles of view of an attention on the alert.

If this whole process clearly and more and more precisely assumes at this point a fictional orientation, there must come a day when grammatical figures assume the roles of the derived figures that have just been described. Then, the search informs itself with graphic traces of words in lines and rhythmic games worked upon vocabulary and syntax. It might well be said that the first gesture of writing takes place at the moment when the progression of the idea by means of the proliferation of arithmetical and geometrical figures absolutely necessitates a parallel discourse, functioning as the commentary upon these figures, as well as the practical means of interlinking, combining, and turning them henceforth more effectively toward this task of staking and mapping the "blank."

Here then the second stage of the elaborative process of the fiction is attained, wherein the writing action begins and the component elements of the derived figure are refracted into *fictional elements* or *indications*. Exactly what are we saying? . . . That we seek to transmute the symbolic figures constituted by our appropriation of the basic figure and the ensemble of personal productions that our reaction to this figure has triggered in order to convert them into symbols issuing from the lexical codes and syntaxes, themselves wholly preconstituted and socialized.

These codes are, first of all, those of the language of origin, those eventually of one or several foreign languages, and those of the different languages spoken in the country of origin (standard, technical, specialized, slang, regional, academic, critical, journalistic, etc.). But they are also those of all texts, "literarily" constituted or not, which present themselves to us with their impressive catalogue of formulas: narrative, epic, dramatic, lyric, juridical, economic, scientific, pictorial, cinematographic, etc. It is upon this matter, compact, fibrous, entangled, omnipresent, which at every moment solicits and besieges us, that we are going to apply the figures arising from our personal reaction to the inscriptions of oppositions that have put us on the alert. However, this very matter which we will attempt to transform by our personal inscriptions and whose resistance and opacity we will experience at every moment, can itself be analyzed as being entirely woven, braided with conflictual inscriptions. These latter are *wholly socialized inscriptions,* preconstituted, imposed upon us well before any writing action or project, the manifestations of a prodigious perpetual constraint that is social, anonymous, ancestral, with which our own conflictual inscriptions will engage in a struggle, a marked struggle if there ever was one, of a constant and pathetic ambiguity: at once a desire to recognize and a will to mutate, a search for correspondences and an attempt at rupture, a temptation for order and a call for destruction.

It is upon this mined territory that the attempt to write will be tested out. Its closed space: the blank page. Its product: the graphic trace of the lines. And the trace of the first lines is tentative, trying, treacherous: perilously tossing a few words into the void—which ones?—in the beginning when founding the fiction. We will attempt shortly to analyze how the decisions are made, which impulses intervene at the moment of making them. Let us examine for the moment what is at stake in these decisions, toward what they tend, and what their implications are.

We have postulated that the component elements of the abstract figures of departure were going to be refracted into fictional elements or indications. Refracted how? . . . Through decomposition, or analysis—each of these elements selecting, from the ensemble of preconstituted linguistic inscriptions, a secondary ensemble of corresponding fictional elements. We pass from a catalogue of abstract symbols to a catalogue of grammatical symbols. And beginning with the first graphic traces of lines, whose forms and formulas arise from what Benveniste calls several "linguistic levels," thus immediately facing us with a highly structured matter, it appears very quickly that the fictional elements jotted down on paper organize themselves into several levels, and that between these levels a hierarchy establishes itself. In addition, immediate practice shows that the fictional components placed into circulation combine with each other according to *distributional relationships* (at each level) and *integrational relationships* (from one level to another). Furthermore, the related definition that Benveniste gives concerning form and meaning can be legitimately applied to the type of fiction being constructed. Thus, to paraphrase: "The form of a fictional unity is its ability to be decomposed to components at subsidiary levels; its meaning, its ability to integrate a unity of a higher level." It must be noted that the conflicts issuing from the distributional order between fictional elements of the same level must of necessity be resolved in the integrative order, through elevation to the higher level. It is this necessity, we believe, which makes the fictional matter progress: the obligation of finding a higher level, a territory of resolution, regardless how provisional, of the conflict between elements.

We can conclude from what has preceded that the decision to transmute the schematic symbols into grammatical symbols had for effect to transpose our conflictual inscriptions into the domain of grammar and narrative rhetoric: and until then what was happening between points, lines, surfaces, volumes, colors, numbers and simple relationships between numbers, now takes place between fictional elements and levels. The text which begins to be written is thus itself also analyzable as a conflictual inscription—a second-degree conflictual inscription, a result of applying our own inscriptions, often differed for a long while, and finally determined, upon those imposed upon us by society, its languages and its cultures.

However, just as it was revealed, from the first gesture of writing, that the fictional components were articulated according to laws and a hierarchy both quite complex, likewise it soon appears that the elements of socialized inscriptions—let us say grammatical forms and narrative formulas—that we select from the immense catalogue at our disposal, are the object of a choice involving far more than their simple initial appropriateness for the activity of mutation defined earlier. Indeed, it is very evident, from the start of this activity, that what we thought in our inexperience we were able to name very matter-of-factly a "selection" of elements from among this ensemble of languages that satisfied our intention, is inseparable from a questioning—partial, local, step by step, very swiftly generalized—of these forms and formulas among the stock we are drawing from and which we can no longer appropriate in complete innocence, for the good reason that both sets of elements, resulting from multiple conflicts in the historic space and time of their inscription, are anything but innocent. It follows that our own inscriptions can only be legitimately articulated upon those imposed upon us by society on the necessary condition that we systematically reexamine these latter in their genesis and their social functions, for fear of seeing our own blend back into the imposed ensemble and lose any specific character, thus any power to transform, thus any innovative interest.

(Here, a brief parenthesis, to specify that by "personal inscription" or "one's own" inscription, we are not by any means referring to a feature of individual originality which we alone are capable of emitting, but rather to features belonging to an ensemble of figures that we happen, through our particular social situation—family, class, nation, cultural sphere—to have distinguished. It is the ensemble of figures and their combinations on the one hand, the ensemble of the observer's social situation on the other, which has a bearing on the present case, preceding any sign of individual particularization. In the example given earlier, the features of the map that we appropriated for a fictional project might have been utilized by any other person placed in the same conditions, who then would have abstracted the same secondary figures, or others, but certainly not just any ones, because the list of these figures is necessarily limited.)

Therefore, we have tried to show what fictional writing consists of in its start-up phase, what the thrust of the text is at its very beginnings, a text whose development from now on will proceed, according to its own laws of growth, line after line, to progressively create the fiction.

Let us now suppose that the textual corpus is already substantially composed; the majority of fictional elements are in place, and have already been the object of a certain number of combinations; the integration of different levels is under way; the outcome of this activity—the fiction—is already drawn up in its broad outlines. Among the remarks that can be made at this stage, there is one which stands out, never ceasing to amaze regardless of how prepared one is: namely, that the text, through its own evolution, has taken on—a comforting sign among all—an unforeseen direction, and that this direction is opposed, to a possibly great degree, to the previous determinations fixed by the schematic figures at the start. The reason for this is that we have now entered into the third phase of fictional creation, the one where the activity is going to be nourished with interactions between the pursuit of a certain line of development that has an overtendency to expand its field, and the call to order of the schemas. We will not go into the details of this struggle, which is at the foundation of fictional development, a struggle without which this long meticulous enterprise would most likely be neither long nor meticulous anymore. In short, if the schemas regularize, as Jean Ricardou would say, the text in progress, in return, the graphic development of the text markedly distorts the schemas. And if, eventually, the fictional matter thus produced makes the meaning resonate far more than that reckoned on by the minimum interplay of foreseen combinations, then so much the worse for the schemas. Furthermore, if the writing in itself is creative, it is because the number of possible applications of a personal inscription within the socialized inscriptions is in any case very high.

This new start leads (and this is of special importance to our remarks) to the composition of a text that can be analyzed as an *ensemble signifying new conflictual inscriptions,* the outcome of the confrontation between the first set of inscriptions and the second, a product and provisional resolution of their struggle. Its hybrid character reflects, or refracts, in the grammatical and narrative order, the already hybrid character of personal inscriptions (a product, it has been seen, of the reaction of our personal determinations to the schematic inscriptions constituted beforehand). In addition, these new inscriptions—the text bearing the trace of this struggle—take place, no sooner constituted, within the body of inscriptions of the same type, that is, in the present case, within the extension of all previous fictional texts, which it enriches, at least quantitatively, by one unit. This has as a consequence that in the view of others the newly issued text speedily takes its place among the ensemble of wholly socialized inscriptions, and manifests itself to such a view with the same character of "imposition," and eventually, in the best cases, the same force, the same constraint. And the said text, no sooner completed, detaches itself from the one that constructed it, the one point in common being the memory of circumstantial connections to be assigned to the anecdote file. One further remarkable fact is that the lines of fiction, hardly traced out, are read in this way by their author, who thus finds himself always in the objective position of first reader, at an appreciable distance from what he has just marked down and which, already, impose themselves upon him.

To condense what has just been said concerning the three stages of the creative process of fiction, we propose calling:

IMPOSITIONS, the ensemble of socialized inscriptions, whether the immense preconstituted text which these latter impose upon us, or Text #1, in a general historic order (Text #2, in ours, up to this point).

OPPOSITIONS, the personal inscriptions arising from our reaction to the preceding. This will be Text #2 in the general historic order (Text #1, up to this point, in ours).

PROPOSITIONS, the newly created inscriptions, the present state of the resolution of conflicts between the first two. We will name it Text #3.

These three texts, and the meaning of their interactions, seemed to us able to be represented, as a first approximation, by the following schema:

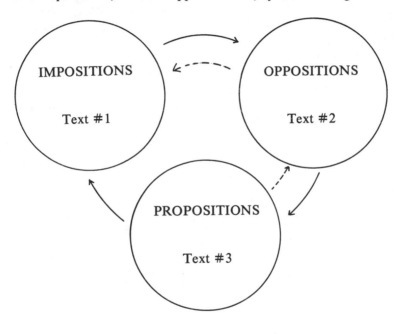

Schema #1

The dotted arrows, aiming toward dialectical effects, are meant to draw attention to the fundamental phenomenon that writing is an action, and an action in three phases, of textual modification, a *transformational action* consisting of the selective appropriation (thus of rejections) and coercive applications (thus of distortion, of diversion of meaning, of impositions of new meanings upon the matter worked upon); that writing is consequently a general action engaged in the production of social structures wherein ideology is manifested on the greatest scale, if not always with the greatest brilliance.

A total "intellectual" undertaking, therefore, in the domain of fictional, and more generally cultural, signifiers and of the re-creation of their meaning. A physical undertaking as well, and here we approach, lastly, a point that is central to the act of writing, whose coordinates are to be placed, like the personal inscriptions described earlier, in the category of reaction, in the sense of revolt, against imposed structures. Likewise, if we consider this representation of the gears of fictional mobilization, let us point out at first glance a gap, the absence of a transmission belt which will set the machinery going. However, this transmission, this current which passes (or does not pass), this energy whose output and intensity are so irregular, so precarious—it would be glaringly remiss of us not to state that our bodies are what provide it, or more precisely what could be called the *motor drives,* to be defined as the affirmation in the practical gestures of writing, of a general attitude of the body regarding the materials which it must first of all acquire a knowledge of, then possess, then transform. We will name these phenomena DISPOSITIONS (schema #2).

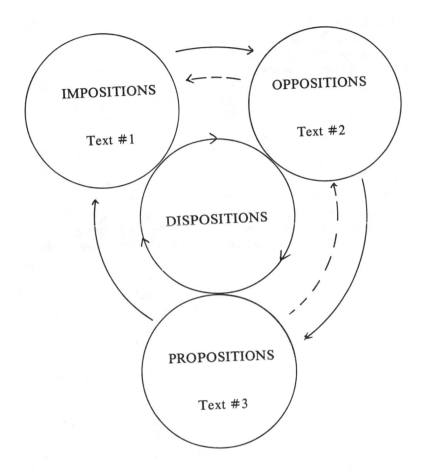

Schema #2

Namely: a knowledge acquired of the direct agent-materials in the activity: papers, inks, erasers, stylus with points; supporting material: table, chair, and clothing; neighboring materials: surfaces, colors, volumes of the dwelling circumscribing the place; the material that lights, shadows, or conceals the scene; and the ambient noises, the aural interventions produced by the surrounding material.

Next, taking possession of these materials, that is: approach, appropriation, preferential uses, accommodation, privileged localizations within the available space; position in the center, the margins, set back; postures, tilt of the body; the respective moments of immobility and movement; adaptation to temperature, lighting, sound, silence; rhythms of pauses, of rest.

Then: reactions of the body to external solicitations, such as those emanating from the matter as envisaged up until this point, as well as from the grammatical material put into play. And we believe this is where a most curious phenomenon occurs: a great many writing decisions intervene so abruptly, in such an immediate unexpected way, that it might well be said that there exists a particular attitude of our body regarding language and graphic marks, an almost autonomous versatile behavior, more or less evident according to the resistance of the material. If we were to venture a characterization, it would be in such terms: ruse, taming, suspicion, circumspection, pact, appeasement, violations, aggression, show of force, domination, coercion, exasperation, rupture, exile, return to grace, etc. It resembles a kind of elusive, dissimulated, observable symbiosis between the physiological life, particularly the nervous system's, and that of the grammatical articulations mobilized by the fictional construction. This state of veiled impulsive struggle, consisting of attraction, seduction, stimulation, repulsion, is now and then noticeable to such a degree that it seems as if the hand itself—the nerve endings in the fingers—is summoning one of these articulations in order to fix it as rapidly as possible upon the paper, in a real bid for power, without allowing time for the eye to read it and, possibly, to reject it. This is something noticeable on many occasions, particularly in that category of decision which might be grouped under the rubric of "expedient alternatives" or "shortcuts," the decisions, for example, to revise, so essential to the biology of the text, the impromptu inscriptions of lexical items excluded from the paradigm (whereas it had been thought they were going to be chosen), inscriptions of elision, of ellipses, of a condensed formula, all those inscriptions that are usually described as oversights and spelling mistakes. Then there are those which involve the relationships of fictional density and the hierarchy between levels: decisions concerning breaks, sectioning, cartographical "arrangement," short-circuit sequencing, carrying over to a new paragraph, coming to a standstill, sometimes backtracking, all by way of a strange "stuttering" of the wrist. This mechanism is particularly characteristic of the written work in every aspect that can appear, in the reading, as "notations" or "transcriptions" of sensations, impressions or images: images of sight, sound and touch of course, but especially so-called kinesthetic images— concerning the movements of parts of the body—and synesthetic—linked to the feelings of comfort or discomfort resulting from an ensemble of internal sensations. We did indeed say "can appear" as "notation" or "transcription," for these brief hasty formulations are not so much to be analyzed as efforts at translation into words of an actually received image, as to be seen as the instantaneous, nearly visceral reaction of the motor agent in the lines of the writing itself to the resistance of such and such a graphic particularity, of such and such a word inscribed on the paper, or only read in a low voice, or quietly, surreptitiously perceived, as if secretly—in brief: the motor agent's reaction to a graphic or phonetic form which the work in progress has approached, even flushed out into the open.

It is no doubt here that the pulse of a text is decided, that the distribution of plot indications finds its rhythm, that either following or preceding or during the most conscious decisions, what might be called the *palpable motor reality of a text* is determined, or at least its most obvious, palpable characteristics, those very ones which the text's composer is often very surprised to hear uttered by other readers than himself, as if there had passed through his knowledgeable elaboration, through this sieve that he believed so fine, particles of "matter" stamping his text with a scansion whose general effect has escaped him.

We are not saying that this interplay alone determines the general rhythmic characteristics of a text, or of a series of texts, considered as the personal mark of a "composer," perhaps what is classically called his "style." But that this parallel interplay, underground or barely breaking to the surface, superficial, continually participates, through the other (in principle entirely conceptual and logical) in the creation of the fiction. At any rate, it initiates the fiction, to the extent that it communicates the impulse of departure: the desire to write. It satisfies this desire the whole time that the lines are being written, and as soon as it is extinguished, as soon as it disconnects itself from the "intelligible" game, all pleasure in writing—that stupefying voluptuousness of inscription and revision—vanishes in the same stroke. The ambient space then resumes its banal turn, and time its day-to-day flux and rhythm, and the state of overactivation of the inscribed relationships in the three circles of the subject-society-language gearworks gives way again, for the space of an intermission, to a state of ordinary activation, that of expression and communication.

We have thus attempted, through the three stages of writing that we have distinguished (the formation of abstract figures, the integration of these figures with social inscriptions, the stimulation between the text in progress and the figures of departure) and through what we have given as the motor gear of the whole system, the motor drives, to enumerate and describe the different forces at work in the process of fictional creation. We have also tried to show how, by virtue of what elements and what mediating operations, a fictional object, if it is conceived and shaped with appropriate rigor and openness to the unforeseen, can appear, among other things, thanks to the multiplicity of the textual relationships brought out, as the homologue of the multiple relationships linking, in a given place and for a given personal situation, language, subject and society. The initial note of caution was, naturally, applicable at every point of this description: this work is the result of reflecting upon a personal practice, and in no way presumes to cover the whole field of fictional creation. Perhaps, here and there, such or such a remark will simply correspond with another's practice. Furthermore, certain of these developments, notably those concerning "fictional levels" or the mechanism of spontaneous inscription of scansions, may have appeared incomplete, imprecise or clumsy. Certainly, they are so: this is only the present, provisional state of a difficult clarification of the question.

Trans. DOMINIC DI BERNARDI

Editor's Note: This essay originally appeared in Claude Ollier's Nébules *(Flammarion, 1981), and is printed by permission of the author.*

Ill Locutions

Christine Brooke-Rose

THIS CENTURY SEEMS to have relived, with greater intensity and sophistication, all the ancient quarrels, and none more than the quarrel between literature and philosophy. For although this has often taken the form of a quarrel between literature and science, basically it's the same quarrel, since ancient philosophy included science, both being searches for the truth, whereas poets, as everyone knows, told lies.

Today, however, we have been brought curiously back to that age in antiquity when philosophy could embrace not only science but politics and metaphysics and literature, even if poets lied and writing was a threat to pure thought. We seem, at any rate, much closer to those times, and notably to pre-Socratic times, than we did earlier this century, when science and poetry were still deeply opposed in a two-truths theory (one for poetry and one for science), which was only a refurbished version, refurbished by the New Criticism in various guises, of the nineteenth-century two-truths theory, one for religion (a "higher" truth) and one for science.

Today we have apparently come out of our entrenchment and in various ways have stopped hiding behind the notion of a higher truth. Nevertheless, we have done this by opening out onto other disciplines which are often considered scientific, or which at least claim to use scientific methods, such as psychoanalysis, sociology, linguistics, different kinds of logic or even mathematics. And all these, like philosophy, mostly still claim to seek truth. We thus have a curious double situation.

On the one hand, the movement which led Plato to exclude poets from his Republic and writing from his notion of the truth is, according to Derrida, regularly repeated in the logocentric tradition to which we belong, recurring for example in the work of J. L. Austin and that of his disciple John Searle, whose texts, as Derrida has shown, deconstruct themselves exactly in the same way as do those of Plato or Rousseau or Saussure or Heidegger, or even, as others have shown, those of Derrida himself, in the sense that the author repeats the very gesture which he has criticized in his predecessors.

On the other hand, and largely thanks to this deconstructive activity, philosophy and literature have moved closer and closer together in the work of many scholars, who have come round to proclaim, or to admit, sometimes regretfully, that the language of all the human sciences without exception, and indeed all language, is literary through and through, rather as one might say, rotten through and through.

There is an ingenious reading of J. L. Austin for instance, by Shoshana Felman (1980, 99-210), who tries to turn Austin into Derrida, partly in order to show that Derrida has misread him. His famous act of exclusion of the "non-serious" or literary from his performative (such as promises uttered by actors in a play, or jokes, or poetry, in other words literature) is read as itself non-serious. His sentence defining the performative, which says "I must not be joking, for example, or writing a poem" is read as itself a joke, on the well-demonstrated and delightful grounds that Austin has such fun with language, takes such pleasure in it, and transforms his whole performance into a performative, which in the end, through his vocabulary of desire and excitement, itself represents promise, while the constative represents constancy and the difficulty of remaining faithful to a text.

But Jonathan Culler comments: "Still, to treat the exclusion of jokes as a joke prevents one from explaining the logical economy of Austin's project, which can admit infelicities and exploit them so profitably only by excluding the fictional and the nonserious. This logic is what is at stake, not Austin's attitude or his liking for what Felman calls 'le fun' " (1983, 118n).

I shall not enter here into the quarrel between Derrida and Speech Act Theory. What I want to do is to look at some of Austin's examples in *How to Do Things with Words,* and relate them to narrative technique, or rather, to one very particular aspect of narrative technique, namely a type of sentence which represents the two different kinds of perception—reflective and non-reflective. Most philosophers have recognized these two kinds of perception, even if they seem to have had some difficulty in representing the non-reflective, except in long-winded descriptions about someone automatically side-stepping puddles (Russell) or counting cigarettes (Sartre), and becoming conscious of this only if asked about it afterwards. The type of literary sentence which does this much better is a pure invention of narrative and cannot occur outside narrative. It is usually referred to as "free indirect discourse," but I wish to avoid the word "discourse" and follow Ann Banfield (*Unspeakable Sentences,* 1982), whom I shall be discussing in some detail and who calls it "Represented Speech and Thought," precisely because she opposes this type of "unspeakable" sentence to "discourse" in a much more specific sense, as speech act in the communications model. This opposition between "histoire" (history, not story, best translated as "narration") and "discours" (the communications model or "system of person," with deictics, etc.) is that established by Benveniste (1961), and will become clear below. It is not to be confused with the more familiar narratological opposition "histoire" (story) vs. "discours" (treatment) established by Genette (1972), which derives from the opposition "fabula/sjužet" of the Russian Formalists.

* * *

As a non-philosopher I am often surprised at the sentences that philosophers think up to make their points. With Austin in particular, it is amusing to see how many of his examples are cast in narrative form—which is odd for someone who claims to exclude fiction as non-serious. At any rate, linguistic philosophy is full of fictional suppositions such as this one:

Suppose that before Australia is discovered X says "All swans are white." If you later find a black swan in Australia, is X refuted? Is his statement false now? Not necessarily: he will take it back but he could say "I wasn't talking about swans absolutely everywhere: for example, I was not making a statement about possible swans on Mars." (143)

Under our eyes, X has become a peculiarly complex fictional character. A novelist might want to continue the dialogue to see how X could develop.

In Lecture VIII we get the odd distinction between phonetic, phatic and rhetic acts—the first not illustrated since "it is merely the act of uttering certain noises." The phatic act, however, turns out to be our old friend "direct speech" or *oratio directa* (now called "direct discourse," but I am avoiding that word):

He said "I shall be there."
He said "Get out."
He said "Is it in Oxford or Cambridge?"

while the rhetic act turns out to be our equally familiar friend *oratio obliqua* or "indirect speech":

He said he would be there.
He told me to get out.
He asked whether it was in Oxford or Cambridge. (95)

Now indirect speech is always summary: we are not given the words uttered, and this can even lead to ambiguity, as in the sentence analyzed by Quine (1976, 185-96): "Oedipus said that his mother was beautiful," which can be read in two ways (see Banfield, 17).

Austin later drops these terms, which have not survived, and calls the phatic act ("direct speech" for literary critics) *Locution,* and gives more examples:

He said to me "Shoot her!"
He said to me "You can't do that."

while the rhetic act (indirect speech) can be either *Illocution:*

He urged (advised, ordered . . .) me to shoot her.
He protested against my doing it.

or *Perlocution* (effect incorporated, two degrees):

(a) He persuaded me to shoot her.
　　He pulled me up, checked me . . .

(b) He got me to (made me) shoot her.
   He stopped me, brought me to my senses &c. (101-2)

   The philosophical reasons for these distinctions are not in question here, but formally the three types correspond to the traditional narrative distinctions that Genette (1972) classifies under *Distance* (distance between what he calls the narrator's voice and the character's actual words): direct being the least distant, indirect more so (the character's words summarized or even interpreted), and "narrativized" (a new refinement) being the most distant, the character's words transformed into an action (*stopped, brought me to my senses*) and thus even more irrecoverable than in direct speech, as in for instance "I informed him of my decision to leave."
   Clearly language has developed these different registers for specific reasons that have to do with distancing of the speaker's perception from that of the person whose words he is reporting, and hence with the indirect manipulation of his interlocutor.
   But what *don't* we find in Austin's examples? Obviously, since he excludes fiction as non-serious, what is missing is the type of sentence specific to narrative, invented by narrative and impossible in discourse, that is, in the speech situation as opposed to that of narration. What is missing is the sentence of Represented Speech and Thought (traditionally called Free Indirect Discourse, *discours indirect libre, erlebte Rede*...). This is the type of sentence which gives the vocabulary and idiom characteristic of direct speech, expressive elements such as exclamations and questions, as well as the deictics of the character in his situation (*now,* for instance, although in a narrative past); but it retains the shift of tense and the change of person from first to third which are characteristic of indirect speech. It is like indirect speech but without the impression of summary, since we get the words and expression of the character. Here is an invented example:

(1) He was walking down the street. Would he find the courage to tell his father? Yesterday there had been nothing but trust. But now, yes, oh God, he was afraid.

Note that the presence of the thinking or perceiving character is given. We get the tense-shift and change of person of indirect speech rather than those of direct speech (Shall I find the courage to tell dad . . .), but we also get the deictics and personal vocabulary and often the characteristic syntax of direct speech (question-form, exclamation, the deictics *yesterday* and *now,* although we are in the narrative past).
   Because of these dual characteristics this type of sentence—which appears spontaneously in all European narrative with the rise of the novel, but which was not formally recognized or analyzed until the end of the last century)—has been regarded as "mixed," and the traditional view has been and still is that the character's thought or speech is given in his own words but that the "narrator's voice" is also heard, in the narrational tenses and in

the distancing third person, thus creating an ironic distance and indirect comment.

This is certainly the way most people have come to read this type of sentence, which is often used for comic effects, and these are automatically attributed to an ironic over-voice. The first example below, from George Eliot, is Represented Thought, the second, from Zola, is Represented Speech:

(2) A wild idea shot through Mr Chubb's brain: could this grand visitor be Harold Transome? Excuse him: he had been given to understand by his cousin that . . .

> (Eliot, *Felix Holt*)

(3) En tout cas, Monsieur était prévenu, elle préférait flanquer son dîner au feu, si elle ratait, à cause de la révolution.

> (Zola, *Germinal*)

But we can get a represented letter or a represented conversation, as in these two examples from Forster's *A Room with a View:*

(4) Of course Miss Bartlett accepted. And equally of course, she felt that she would prove a nuisance, and begged to be given an inferior spare room—something with no view, anything. Her love to Lucy.

(5) A conversation then ensued, on not unfamiliar lines. Miss Bartlett was, after all, a wee bit tired, and thought they had better spend the morning settling in; unless Lucy would rather like to go out? Lucy would rather like to go out, as it was her first day in Florence, but, of course, she could go alone. Miss Bartlett could not allow this. Of course she would accompany Lucy everywhere. Oh, certainly not: Lucy would stop with her cousin. Oh no! that would never do! Oh yes!

By the time we get to Virginia Woolf and Joyce we have this changing viewpoint highlighted, and the supposed ironic voice seems a little louder and more intrusive; indeed in Joyce the device is already part of the parody of narrative styles displayed in *Ulysses:*

(6) "I met Clarissa in the Park this morning," said Hugh Whitbread, diving into the casserole, anxious to pay himself this little tribute, for he had only to come to London and he met everybody at once; but greedy, one of the greediest men she had known, Milly Brush thought, who observed men with unflinching rectitude.

> *(Mrs. Dalloway)*

(7) Cissy Caffrey caught the two twins and she was itching to give them a ringing good clip on the ear but she didn't because she thought he might be watching but she never made a bigger mistake in all her life because Gerty could see without looking that he never took his eyes off her.

> *(Ulysses)*

Despite the traditionally clear "said" and "thought" in (6), there is a blurring of Represented Thought and what Banfield calls narration per se, or narrative sentence, which *can* carry authorial comment (e.g., "who observed men with unflinching rectitude" could be narrator-comment or still part of Milly Brush's consciousness). And in (7), what looks here like a changing viewpoint from Cissy to Gerty is not so in context, but we do have to reread. The main ambiguity I shall be discussing, however, is that between Represented Thought and Narrative Sentence.

In practice both stylistics and linguistics treat a Narrative Sentence as Represented Thought as long as a character is clearly present as perceiver:

(8)   Emma mit un châle sur ses épaules, ouvrit la fenêtre et s'accouda. La nuit était noire. Quelques gouttes de pluie tombaient.

(Madame Bovary)

Formally there is no distinction here between a Narrative Sentence in the progressive, that tells us that the night was dark, and a sentence of Represented Thought that represents what Emma was passively perceiving (as opposed to consciously thinking). One test (apart from the presence of a perceiving character) is to see whether one can insert deictics such as *now* into that past: "the night was dark now," where a Narrative Sentence would have (unnecessarily) "the night was then dark."

This is Benveniste's famous distinction between *discours* (or speech as part of a communications model, which he calls "the system of person") and *histoire* (narration), which he clearly envisaged as both historical and fictional (history and story). For the difference between so-called truth and fiction is not linguistically marked (a "lie" uses the same syntax), any more, in fact, than is irony, since irony is saying a sentence and meaning more, or something else, even the opposite, or letting a character say a sentence that has a clear meaning for him while another interpretation is also possible for the reader. But it is made possible contextually and culturally. Parody, too, is culturally determined.

I have on purpose given examples from Banfield's book because it created quite a rumpus among literary critics, as her earlier articles had done. The debate continues. I cannot go into the detail of it here, but I do want to take up its main thesis as something that clearly interests philosophy, something that should convince literary critics more than it has so far succeeded in doing, and something that ought to make writers think.

For the spontaneous development of this device, which she calls Represented Speech and Thought because it *represents* (as opposed to imitating, as does direct speech) the words or perceptions of characters, has had two consequences: one in the way the device has been perceived by analysts of it, which is what I shall mostly deal with here; another in the way it has come to be used by writers, and this I shall touch on at the end of my paper.

* * *

Literary critics, then, have persisted in seeing a dual-voiced device, and this is because they remain in a communications model of addresser-addressee.

Certain linguists, however, make a distinction, like Benveniste, between the "discourse" of the communications model (the "system of person") and the language of narration ("histoire"), which is, literally, unspeakable: "No-one speaks here, the events seem to narrate themselves," says Benveniste (1966, 241; trans. 1971, 206). This language of narration cannot use the pronouns *I/you* (without passing into the discourse situation), or the deictics that go with these (*here, now, tomorrow, last week*, etc.), and it has its own tenses. It cannot use the present tense, for instance, or the present perfect, or the future, which belong to discourse.

The tense-system of narrative is particularly clear in French, where the *passé simple* or aorist is wholly restricted to literary narrative and unusable in speech except in mock quotes. Contrary to what some may think, it is still very much alive in narrative and necessary to it, though not, interestingly, in the second person, for the narrative sentence does not belong to the communications model and thus excludes the second person as well as its deictics. The exclusion of the *passé simple* from discourse can be dated very precisely in the sixteenth century, says Banfield, and it is not by chance that Represented Speech and Thought, which is based on the Narrative Sentence but allows certain deictics, can first be found in La Fontaine (poetic narratives) and develops with the novel, a form specifically associated with writing, as opposed to the taking down of essentially oral narratives (Banfield, chap. 6).

Benveniste's theory, as well as Käte Hamburger's work on "the epic preterite" and *erlebte Rede* (*Die Logik der Literatur*, 1973), are used by Banfield to analyze these two types of unspeakable sentences that are Narration and Represented Speech and Thought. She takes as her cue Kuroda's discovery of a literary style in Japanese that "transcends the paradigm of linguistic performance in terms of speaker and hearer" (Banfield, 11), and involves an epistemological distinction between two forms of language, one used to indicate fact, the other to express the speaker's state—thus even an emotive adjective like *sad* can indicate a fact or express a state. This distinction seems roughly equivalent to that between *énoncé* and *Enonciation*, sometimes translated as "statement" versus "utterance" (utterance not in the philosophical sense but understood here as that containing the subjective elements such as "I think," "surely," etc.). But Kuroda also distinguished between reflexive and non-reflexive consciousness. These elements enable Banfield to develop several hypotheses in a way that accounts linguistically for the types of sentence in question.

Let us go back for instance to sentence (4), Miss Bartlett's letter. Banfield stops the quotation at "Her love to Lucy." But the text goes on:

(4a)   Of course Miss Bartlett accepted. And equally of course, she felt sure that she
would prove a nuisance, and begged to be given an inferior spare room—
something with no view, anything. Her love to Lucy. And, equally of course,
George Emerson could come to tennis on the Sunday week.

Clearly the last sentence cannot represent Miss Bartlett's letter, since she is
away and quite unaware of the arrangements at the Honeychurches. We
have passed from Represented Speech (or Writing) to a narrative sentence,
but one which takes over the "and equally of course" of Miss Bartlett. The
traditional view would be that the "of course" and the "and equally of
course" come from the translator. In Banfield's theory, however, both these
would "represent" Miss Bartlett's way of writing and talking (cp. sentence
[5]), which the "narrator" *then* ironically echoes in a narrative sentence.
Another of Banfield's examples, from Jane Austen, is even more revealing,
since it can in itself be read as narration on first reading, but must be read as
Represented Thought on second reading:

(9)   He [Frank Churchill] stopped and rose again, and seemed quite embarrassed.
He was more in love with her than Emma had supposed.

(Emma)

Banfield discusses this and other examples that contain the proper name
or kinship names like *dad* or *papa* (see my sentence [1]), or even title and
surname (*Miss Bartlett*), under what she calls non-reflexive consciousness. It would be too complicated here to rehearse the details of this
essential chapter in her book, but obviously the sentence from *Emma* must
be read as character's perception second time round, since we know by then
that Emma was wrong, and a narrative sentence by convention cannot lie
(in the sense that it must be coherent with the rest of that fictional world).

Banfield's theory has been attacked not by linguists but by literary critics
who cling to various versions of the dual-voiced theory, and above all to the
notion of a narrative *voice.* Banfield on the other hand insists that the word
narrator has become a holdall substitute for the evacuated and taboo word
author, so that we now have "two competing theories about the text's unity,
one which assigns all the sentences of the text to a single narrating voice and
another which sees author and narrator as distinct constructs of literary
theory, restricting the latter to [here she cites Hamburger, 140] 'cases
where the narrating poet actually does "create" a narrator, namely the first
person narrator of the first-person narrative' " (185). And she adds that
"since the thesis of the author's silence ultimately touches the language of
the text it is fair to ask whether linguistic argumentation can enable us to
decide between these two theories." Clearly she defends the second
(narrator and author as literary constructs, narrator referring only to an
explicitly present I-narrator, not to the author behind the narration).

On the mere question of constructs and terminology we would have to ask
what useful function is fulfilled by simply substituting "narrator" where

critics used to say "author," which then forces further distinctions between explicit/implicit, reliable/unreliable and all the other terms inherited from Booth (1961). But beyond the terminology, Banfield seems to have hit somewhere below the belt of reflective consciousness, at the question of "authority"—at least judging by the acidity of the debate. Her theory essentially draws a distinction between "optionally narratorless sentences of pure narration and sentences of represented speech and thought," both "unspeakable" but representing two poles of narrative style (narration and representation of consciousness) (17, 18). And in Chapter 5 she deals with the type of "ambiguous" sentence I have just been talking about, which can be read either at one pole or at the other (but, like Wittgenstein's duck-rabbit, not both at the same time). It is this type of sentence which has become the center of the controversy, precisely because "it seems to combine features of both narration and represented speech and thought," and has been used as "counter-evidence" for a supposed "merging" of two voices, and as proof of "the constantly shifting data of literary style" (12) or the mysterious inaccessibility of literature to scientific analysis, in the kind of argument which, like religion before the onslaught of science, attacks the very attempt to define narrative style linguistically.

Banfield's thesis is presented through extremely rigorous linguistic argumentation, that shows (for example) why indirect speech cannot be derived from direct (28ff), and, more generally, that extends Chomsky's grammar to account for these "unspeakable" sentences of Narration and Represented Speech and Thought, by adding a top node E (Expression) to Chomsky's S, from which expressive elements such as Exclamations descend directly and announce subjectivity (rather in the same way as Ross [1970] posited an introductory performative to all declatory sentences); whereas deictics and evaluative words are embeddable within the S which wholly represents the announced subjectivity or character's point of view. She does not invent examples the way philosophers and linguists do, but goes through, element by element and literary example by literary example, all the formal differences between sentences that are uttered in a context of the communication model (first and second person, addressee-oriented adverbs, subject/object inversion in parentheticals, echo-questions, etc.), and shows that direct speech in a narrative naturally belongs to this system of person, since it imitates communication, whereas Narrative Sentences and sentences of Represented Speech and Thought (reflective and non-reflective) do not imitate but represent, in words, what does not occur in words (actions, gestures, expressions, objects, landscapes, etc., in the case of Narrative Sentences) or what does not necessarily occur in words (consciousness in the case of Represented Speech and Thought).

For this she posits a formula with both a SPEAKER and an ADDRESSEE/HEARER and a PRESENT for the communication model (the SPEAKER being one with the E of Expression); but a SELF for the

Unspeakable sentences, a SELF who is separated from the SPEAKER. Her formula, which has naturally received the brunt of the attacks, is 1E/ 1SELF (and of course there can be many Es, and hence SELFs, in one TEXT, however short, as we have seen from the Forster and Woolf examples). That SELF perceives in its own PRESENT which is past in the narrative (NOW = PAST is her second rule):

In discourse, the speaker's telling cannot be separated from his expression. But in narration, a sentence exists whose sole function is to tell. Alongside this sentence is another whose sole function is to represent subjectivity. When a NOW is invoked in narration, language no longer recounts: it represents. This is as true for first person narration as for third person narration. (178)

The language of narration, she goes on to show, has no "voice," no accent, no dialect (otherwise it becomes discourse, as in, say, *Huckleberry Finn* or Russian *skaz*):

If narration contains a narrator, this "I" is not speaking, quoted by an author; he is narrating. If it does not [contain a narrator], then the story "tells itself," as Benveniste has it. Rather, it is of its nature to be totally ignorant of an audience, and this fact is reflected in its very language. (179)

She goes on to say that it is the language of narrative that "realises most fully in its form and not only in its intent the essence of the literary which has for so long been taken to be the achievement of poetry," and she quotes J. S. Mills's contrast between poetry and eloquence, likening it to that between narration and discourse.

So far I have seen no convincing reply to Banfield's arguments. Literary critics tend to think that the mere producing of supposed counter-examples (assuming they are properly understood and do not prove Banfield's case) can demolish a linguistic argument, whereas, as in science, only a better linguistic argument can do so. As Banfield puts it: "For a sentence to qualify as a syntactic counter-evidence to 1E/1SELF, it must be either (i) a single E containing both a first person and a third person SELF or (ii) a single E containing more than one expressive construction, where all are not interpreted as the expression of the same SELF" (188). For instance, I myself thought I had found counter-examples from Jane Austen, but they do not fulfill these conditions and therefore can illustrate Banfield's thesis. *Emma* is imagining Jane Fairfax married to Knightley, and she wickedly imitates Jane Fairfax's companion Miss Bates:

(10)   "If it would be good to her, I am sure it would be evil to himself; a very
        shameful and degrading connection. How would he bear to have Miss Bates
        belonging to him?—To have her haunting the Abbey, and thanking him all
        day long for his great kindness in marrying Jane?—'So very kind and obliging!
        But he always had been such a very kind neighbor!' And then fly off, through
        half a sentence, to her mother's old petticoat. 'Not that it was such a very old
        petticoat either—for still it would last a great while—and, indeed, she must

thankfully say that their petticoats were all very strong.' "
"For shame, Emma! Do not mimic her!"

I quote Mrs. Weston's reproach to show that we are in dialogue (direct speech). Of course we hear another voice here, which assumes responsibility for the Represented Speech of Miss Bates exactly as an *author* does, but it is Emma's voice, and the Represented Speech, which "represents" only Miss Bates's speech, has been embedded in the direct speech, exactly as the "narrativised" speech of "thanking him all day long" or "flying to her mother's old petticoat" are embedded. For Represented Speech, although "unspeakable" (and this Banfield does not say), can be used inside direct speech, even in "real life," but only in narration, when we are telling a story and unconsciously using literary devices. And I suspect (with no "evidence") that this only occurs among fairly literate speaker-narrators, whereas non-literate ones tend to retell with direct speech ("And I sez to 'im I sez, Well, I never.... And Ow, he sez..." etc., to use an extreme example). But this is only an unresearched impression.

Or Mrs. Bennett bidding farewell to Mr. Bingley in *Pride and Prejudice:*

(11)   "Next time you call," said she, "I hope we shall be more lucky."
        He should be particularly happy at any time, &c &c; and if she would give him leave, would take an early opportunity of waiting on them.
        "Can you come tomorrow?"
        Yes, he had no engagement at all for tomorrow; and her invitation was accepted with alacrity.

Who says "&c &c"? It is very easy to hear "narrator" irony about polite formulas. But in Banfield's theory, the "&c &c" would represent the character's own awareness of them, though at a non-verbalized, semi-conscious level (formulas he could add but does not, OR formulas he is adding and still uttering, but which we are not given). We thus have a passage from Represented Speech to Represented Thought (perhaps non-reflexive). Such passages are swift in Jane Austen: even here we pass from direct speech to Represented Speech to Represented Thought, back to Represented Speech, then to Direct Speech and back again to Represented Speech, ending with a Narrative Sentence that names the acceptance without giving the words ("narrativized discourse" in Genette's system).

We have a situation, then, in which a linguist has shown the grammatical evidence for one point of view only, the character's, in Represented Speech and Thought, while non-linguists cling to a narrator's point of view as well, to which certain bits and pieces of the sentence are attributed on the ground that the character would be incapable of "thinking" those words. Thus the whole subtlety of the device, which represents the complexity of non-verbalized consciousness—and even the flashes of self-awareness a character may have about himself—this subtlety is lost, with value-judgments parcelled out to a narrator (often *also* confused with the author, despite the "taboo," e.g., "Flaubert" or "James"). "But what grammatical evidence of a narrator's point of view do we find?" Banfield asks. "This is what is problematic in the dual-voice claim. The second voice of the dual-voice position is always the narrator's, never another character's [e.g., Emma of (10)]. The logic behind the claim . . . is a case of *petitio principii.*" Certain words of narration in a sentence of Represented Speech and Thought cannot, it is said, represent the character's point of view, therefore they represent the narrator's. "But the missing premise is none other than the conclusion" (189).

The incapacity to argue in rigorous linguistic terms is understandable, if regrettable, in literary critics who attack a linguist. But what is so strange, and this will be my small contribution to that debate, is their self-deconstruction, their insistence, by way of the supposed richness and unaccountability of literature in scientific terms, on pushing narrative into discourse, on pushing the type of sentence that is unspeakable and thus absolutely specific to the novel, into the merely speakable; on pushing the type of sentence that uniquely represents two levels of perception that have long fascinated philosophers, into a banal narrator/character dichotomy that merely replaces the author/character dichotomy and harks back to the author as God, present and authoritative and omniscient in his text. And of course, the pushing of such sentences, which uniquely result from the achievement of writing, back into a communications model, repeats the very gesture that Derrida has revealed as phonocentric and logocentric, from Plato to Austin and Searle, as privileging voice and speech over what he calls *l'écriture,* that "writing in general" of which writing and speech are but particular cases. *L'écriture,* or differentiation and deferral, with its features of what Banfield, after Chomsky, calls universal grammar, realized or not in this or that feature in this or that language, is once again rejected here.

* * *

That's for the critics, and ultimately unimportant, although it has necessarily received the most space in this type of paper. What is sadder has been the misunderstanding of Represented Speech and Thought by writers. Invented spontaneously, almost unconsciously, unreflectively, then developed very reflectively indeed, Represented Speech and Thought, like most artistic devices, eventually became unconscious again, that is, it was not only used as a cliché (already parodied in Joyce), its subtlety wasted on trivia, but it was also misused because misunderstood.

Formally, as we have seen, the sentence of Represented Speech and Thought is similar to the Narrative Sentence, indeed, identical with it when deictics and other signs of E are not linguistically present, but only the presence of a perceiving character. This formal similarity led, inevitably, to these two distinct poles being fused, and the sentence of Represented Speech and Thought being used as narration, to tell, to give narrative information—whole summaries of a situation for instances, or analepses of a whole past, which are clearly there to inform the reader and not to represent a character's perceptions, save at the cost of making them rather gross. This can go on for pages. Such misuse is extremely frequent in the average modern neo-realist novel, including most classical science fiction that imitated the already worn techniques of the realist novel in an attempt to be respectable. This misuse is a direct result, not only of the post-Jamesian condemnation of "telling" in favor of "showing," but also of the concomitant attempt to eliminate the author: and since narrative information must be given, the easy solution was to "filter" it through a character's mind, however implausibly, thus thoroughly weakening the device into its opposite.

Consequently—and writers on the topic never seem to say this—the device at its best belongs wholly to the classical novel. A reaction to its weakening had to come, and it came with Camus's *L'étranger,* written in the present perfect, and especially with Beckett, who used direct speech as narrative, and with the *nouveau roman* in the fifties. Robbe-Grillet loudly dismissed the *passé simple* as *the* mark of the traditional novel, and adopted (after Dujardin and Joyce) the present tense, which he used in a brilliantly unsettling manner (since time-shifts are necessarily unmarked), though this was soon more weakly imitated. What he did not mention as a sign of the traditional novel was Represented Speech and Thought (which he would call *discours indirect libre*), but its jettisoning was implicit in his rejection of the past, as in his rejection of *le mythe de la profondeur* (psychological exploration in depth and so on). At any rate, the device disappeared, together with the traditional narrative sentence in the past tense. The novel passed for a while into discourse, a voice speaking (but not two) in Beckett, or, in Sarraute, many voices (but one at a time) speaking, thinking, perceiving, but in direct speech, or what Voloshinov (Bakhtin) has called "free direct speech." In Robbe-Grillet it was less a voice speaking than a consciousness perceiving, but in present tense deictics. And in Butor we even got the second person plural as central consciousness.

It was a necessary purge, and parallel in a way to the critics' rejection of the "unspeakable" as a concept for the "speakable," except that the critics remain in the old dispensation of the dual-voice theory which merely replaces the old author/character dichotomy, with the "narrator" as ironic God; whereas the modern novel truly dispenses with both narrator and irony and lets the character speak direct, in "free direct speech." As Sontag said long ago (1969, 34), irony, after Nietzsche, is no longer possible, has exhausted itself, and similarly Barthes (1970), for more political reasons, insists that classical irony is merely the power of one discourse over another, merely another bit of the Referential Code. None of the critics writing on

Represented Speech and Thought cite many examples after Woolf and Joyce.

It was a necessary purge, and certainly brought new ways of perceiving. Some postmodern writers have adopted this free direct mode, others play with all literary devices, but to explode or undermine them. And Represented Speech and Thought has not been renewed. Perhaps because, according to Derrida (1967, 335), representation is death. If so it would have to be renewed through some other development.

We can however, understand why Austin and other Speech Act theorists after him do not deal with this kind of sentence. First, it is fictitious and therefore non-serious—though that also applies to Austin's swan story (which, however, and I can say it now, is in direct speech and so not in a traditional narrative mode); but second, and more important, the sentences of both Narration and Represented Speech and Thought are too literary, a by-product of writing, unspeakable, ill locutions.

REFERENCES

Austin, J. L. *How To Do Things with Words* (Oxford: Oxford Univ. Press, 1962).

Banfield, Ann. *Unspeakable Sentences* (London: Routledge & Kegan Paul, 1982).

Barthes, Roland. *S/Z* (Paris: Seuil, 1970).

Benveniste, Emile. *Problèmes de linguistique générale* (Paris: Gallimard, 1966); trans. Mary Elizabeth Meek, *Problems in General Linguistics* (Coral Gables: Univ. of Miami Press, 1971).

Booth, Wayne C. *A Rhetoric of Fiction* (Chicago: Univ. of Chicago Press, 1961).

Culler, Jonathan. *On Deconstruction: Theory and Criticism after Structuralism* (London: Routledge & Kegan Paul, 1983).

Derrida, Jacques. *L'écriture et la différence* (Paris: Seuil, 1967).

Felman, Shoshana. *Le Scandale du corps parlant* (Paris: Seuil, 1980).

Genette, Gérard, "Discours du récit," in *Figures III* (Paris: Seuil, 1972).

Hamburger, Käte. *The Logic of Literature,* trans. Marilynn Rose (Bloomington: Indiana Univ. Press, 1973), 2d. rev. ed. (Originally published as *Die Logik der Dichtung,* 1957.)

Kuroda, S.-Y., "Where epistemology, style and grammar meet: a case study from the Japanese," in *A Festschrift for Morris Halle,* eds. P. Kiparsky and S. Anderson (New York: Holt, Rinehart & Winston, 1973), 377-91; cited in Banfield, 11.

——————, "Reflections on the foundations of narrative theory from a linguistic point of view," in *Pragmatics of Language and Literature,* ed. T. van Dijk (Amsterdam: North-Holland, 1976; New York: American Elsevier, 108-40); cited in Banfield, 196.

Quine, W. V., "Quantifiers and propositional attitudes," in *The Ways of Paradox and Other Essays* (Cambridge: Harvard Univ. Press, 1976).

Ross, John, "On Declarative Sentences," in *Readings in Transformational Grammar,* eds. H. Jacobs and P. Rosenbaum (Waltham, MA: Ginn, 1970), 222-72.

Sontag, Susan, "The Aesthetics of Silence," in *Styles of Radical Will* (London: Secker & Warburg, 1969).

Editor's Note: This paper was originally read at a symposium on "Narration as a Mode of Cognition" organized by the Centre for Philosophy and Literature at the University of Warwick, England, 7-8 March 1987.

Thinking of You

Robert Creeley

LISTENING TO A DISCUSSION of what the prospects were for action after postmodernism, I was moved by a colleague's getting to his feet to say it was *narrative,* the old-time river that used to be the metaphor for life itself. As it was, I'd been hearing voices for years and had thought whatever worlds a fiction could contrive would be of necessity a diversity of stances, of frames, of whatever a plurality of Harrys might say to variously common Mabels and vice versa, wherever and when. I had almost forgot that someone might be talking to me, as if I were, in fact, for real. Like, *there* you are!

In college we had had a lot of common heroes and, given the horrors of those days, we certainly needed them. We moved from the Depression to the Second World War with only a high-school diploma to qualify our outer or inner resources. On the one hand, we had Franz Kafka as genial mentor. He could make a night in jail for drunk and disorderly seem a piece of cake. Back of him was the Great Dostoyevsky, who proved an engaging twist on usual terms of Puritan guilt. I recall a story, possibly apocryphal, about his having shown up at Gorki's house late at night, pounding on the door, being let in by the housekeeper at last, waiting in the foyer for the great man to show—who does. Then Dostoyevsky falls to his knees and recounts his whole participation in the viciously sordid rape of a child he had elsewhere written of, we knew. And Gorki listens, dumbstruck, till finally Dostoyevsky finishes and Gorki can say nothing at all, so horrified is he by what he has been told. At which point Dostoyevsky looks at him with contempt, saying, "*I* am utterly to be abhorred, but you—*you* are worse!"

Another pole was Gide, with his complicated Protestant morality and sensuousness. I remember reading volume after volume of his *Journals,* looking for clues to my own location. Again we had all read *Lafcadio's Adventures* and although its terms repelled me, the *acte gratuité* was an intriguing proposition. Back of it were the bored students in Baudelaire's *Paris Spleen* who see the impoverished glazier four floors below them, call him up to their garret to which he then climbs painfully with all his wares on his back, and then they tell him they want nothing, watch him go back down all the narrow stairs to the street door, rush back to the window to lean out and drop, just as he comes out into the alley, some heavy object which hits and breaks all his precious panes of glass.

What was that story about, so to speak? Or Lawrence's "The Captain's

Doll" with those curiously powerful women? Or that women's shipboard orchestra in Conrad's *Chance*—and the way such an apparent vastness of physical place contracts to the scale of a cramped room? Then there was James, and de Maupassant, Hawthorne, Melville's *Pierre*. Céline and Stendhal both made context a disposition of energy, of literalizing attention. It was the address to a proposed "reality" that was definitive, as, in fact, it always will be. Stendhal's insistent emphasis upon style was signal that the medium was indeed the message, whatever the latter might presume itself to be otherwise.

Of course, this is all familiar ground. Parallel to the increasing emphasis upon information theory and artificial intelligence, literary forms become increasingly, almost didactically, self-conscious, so that their construct and activity per se are a significant content as in Joyce's *Finnegans Wake* (another of my generation's fetishes). It is curious to see "naturalism" at the same time turn to a flattened, popular form, most apt for classic detective stories or, better, the genre defined by the work of Hammett, Raymond Chandler (the master of its baroque period certainly), and James M. Cain (whom I felt back then a very competent and solid workman, and still do).

In any case, there seems in retrospect a drift to forms, either a playing with "systems" or else a reflective naturalism, which is also very aware of its style. So it is that John Updike finds place initially with all camps in the fifties as a striking *stylist*—in much the same way that Richard Wilbur was thought a *classically* graceful poet. It is interesting that a writer like Gilbert Sorrentino moves articulately in all these possibilities of formal determination, from *Steelwork* to *Mulligan Stew,* or the trilogy beginning with *Odd Number.* For Sorrentino it is really "how to get said what must be said" (W. C. Williams) that seems the point, and his almost anthropological ransacking of abstracting systems provides now a very droll and consistent invoice of games people play and are played by.

Games seem to be winning insofar as they permit it, that is, make a localizing ground for attention and participation. Chess must make the same invitation, to think within a system of thought. The poet Robin Blaser noted recently the intense competition that the modern framing of reality had provoked in its attempt to provide a grounding for human belief after the loss of the traditionally religious. In some respects the resulting babble of conflicting claims is deafening and disheartening—and in no respect the possible construct of a *world*. One remembers with some dismay just how literal an invention any world must be, recalling its root as "life or age of man." How curiously faded now seems that device of Lawrence Durrell's *Justine* series, just that the staticizing of such a sequence of foci is about as satisfying to the imagination of "real life" as were the function and effect of those glasses required for 3-D movies. The paraphernalia in each case was the crucial distraction. I also had one eye.

So what does a game have to be? Does it have to work, like they say?

Video games certainly have a lot of narrative, and one does or doesn't get somewhere, or survive, in a way that seems quite distinct from pinball, for instance. I don't think it's yet possible, if it ever will be, to qualify just what so-called computer technology has done to previous dispositions of epistemology. I mean, of course, what happens to knowledge when its traditional relation to ordering and retrieval (memory) is intensively modified by instrumentation exterior to its own function? Another way of putting it would be to consider how extrinsic to functions of knowledge one's own participation has curiously become (i.e., does "knowing" need us the way it used to?).

It was not so long ago that Walter Benjamin had concerns somewhat of this kind in his discussion of the storyteller and of that person's vulnerability in a world of multiplicating, anonymously generalizing report. Despite Borges's wry observation that "Walt Whitman" is one of the great literary inventions of all time, we know inherently that the presence which the words of his singular poem make real to us *is* as real as we are—simply that we so feel it—as Santa Claus, as God, as ourselves. I am too much of a New England Puritan to come to final terms with Eastern religions, as they say, but I am equally convinced that nothing is "real" beyond the experience which so defines it. I can think of no other definition for a life: it feels it is so. The storyteller is, then, either as Benjamin defines and values him, or as anyone familiar with neighborhood, family or friends might also: that one who brings the multiplicity of all that's outside us in space and time, all that *other,* into some focusing and detailing relation to the fact of ourselves, each of us, as one *and* many. Possibly you will remember in the classic account of the Kalahari that the bitter harshness of imprisonment was the effect of being separated from one's "story," from the communal recounting, the tales or telling that located each one as present. No matter the degree, finally, that circumstance is a familiar story in itself, because—at least in this society—community seems a long, long way from home.

No doubt there will be much writing now to suspend time, to vitiate its inexorable, irritating demands—"time's ravages." But that story is also an old one. I think, more likely, one will want to feel more specifically regarded, addressed—and not to be held endlessly as witness, a speechless and impotent participant. Who knows. Yet one keeps on talking.

Robert Duncan offered a lovely sense of the Ideal Reader as comfortable person in sun bonnet, attentive in interest, absorbed, apart from our bother and preoccupation with intent. It was also Duncan who told me once, apropos something we had in mind, that he couldn't remember if he wrote it or read it. Then later, speaking of the Language poets, he said, "They have no story."

The abstracting, resistant surface of much contemporary prose makes it obviously difficult to treat as transparent, just that the words are so provokingly demanding in their own isolating patterns. But we are reading something other than a usual communication—rather, this is an activity of language whose information is far more the nature of its traffic than who or what does or doesn't get home safely. In other words, all presumptions in the habitual structures of narrative are forced to the foreground and become far more the "story" than what is otherwise told. Yet the persistent public success of a writing which continues with the habitual clichés of order—the historical novel, the romance (Gothic or teenage), the private eye, etc.— does argue, paradoxically, how significant structure is to the information of narrative, independent of all else that is being said. It was Robert Penn Warren who said years ago in response to a story of mine that was to be published in the *Kenyon Review:* "Constitutionally I am in favor of plot. I believe that all stories should move from point of rest A through series of complicating actions B to point of rest C. . . ." The story in question was "The Unsuccessful Husband," and Olson called it "the most perfect Dostoyevsky imaginable." But John Crowe Ransom didn't understand it either, and it's to the point that Williams spoke of all of my prose of this time as "sketches."

So a conclusion is expectably awkward. What must have so engaged me in the persistently dislocating stories of Dostoyevsky, Gide, Lawrence, Céline, et al. was the intensive displacement of all that had been taught me as limit, as securing parameter. Whether the bleak rape of the child, or the dog fed the hook in a crust of bread, or Father Zossima's putrefying body, the world shifted and reformed in context, and I could no longer presume it simply. This specific power of story is for me its most significant one, but it has nothing to do, finally, with violence or even the unexpected. A few years ago, in Berlin and without much to read, I found some used copies of novels by Patrick White for sale—*Riders in the Chariot* and *The Vivisectionist.* We were stuck in a sparely provided apartment, limited by money and small son, and White's writing became for me an absolute refuge and resource. I was fascinated by its information of Australia, but far more by the range of sensual apprehension he was master of—odors, sounds, exquisite edges of relation. Subsequently I read a lot more, tracking back to his early work with its echoes of Virginia Woolf and Henry Green—but nothing measured to that almost raw edge of response his later work could manage. I had a like feeling about Keri Hulme's handling of the alcoholic Maori protagonist in *The Bone People;* simply I'd never been that perceptive of a classic human despair.

Build a better mousetrap, they used to say, and the world will beat a path to your door.

Notes on the Threshold of a Book

Harry Mathews

In 1983 I attended the Action Workshop created by Fernando Flores and Werner Erhard. The workshop demonstrated the proposition that "performative speech"—speech capable of guaranteeing material results —necessarily uses only four kinds of statement: requests, promises, assertions, and declarations. In order to see what consequence this notion might have in written language, I decided to try translating Ruskin's Stones of Venice *as an experiment in "performative writing." These pages constitute both a prelude to the experiment and a rehearsal of it.*

I DECLARE THAT "I" is the name I shall assign myself as I write these exploratory pages. I declare that "you" is the name I shall assign myself as I read these pages.

I declare that writing these pages means a recording of the conversation I am having with you.

I request you read these exploratory pages.

I assert that in its form a book is a request: an unopened book is asking to be opened, an open book is asking to be read. (I point out to you that right now *The Stones of Venice* is lying beside your pad, opened, not being read.)

I ask you, why does a book have particular names attached to it (title, author, publisher, at least)? I ask you to consider my answer to the question. I suggest that the names attached to a book are meant to conceal the uniformity of the experience of reading. (I point out to you that the names people have conceal their likeness in a similar way—except that in our case, I must also point out that since *our* names refer to the same object, they reveal our likeness. I suggest this may be less apparent to readers other than yourself.)

I admit to you that we are not on an equal footing: you never have a chance to speak. Only I can speak—I can declare that absolutely. I realize that I could "let you speak" by attributing words to you, which would conventionally appear in quotation marks to show that a character (a not-I) is doing the talking. But I maintain that the quotation marks and the rest of my procedure will fool nobody, that as soon as you begin speaking you will become I, I talking to you—just what is happening now.

I suggest, as a consolation, that if I alone can speak, you alone can listen: as soon as I begin to listen I become, by definition, you.

I point out again to you that *The Stones of Venice* is lying open next to your pad, asking to be read.

Now, as I begin to read or rather to look at the page that I am planning to read, I ask you another question: Do the opening sentences of a non-fictional book constitute a request or an assertion? Are the opening sentences inviting you to accept what you are going to read, or telling us that such-and-such is so?

I suggest the following answer: an essay is a request that pretends to be an assertion. I therefore accuse non-fiction by virtue of this lie to be fiction.

But wait: I make a further suggestion to you, in the form of another question: are assertions a false category altogether, being essentially requests inviting listeners to give their assent, agreement, or belief? I propose that every assertion can be rephrased as a request. Example: "Apples are often red" means "I request you to accept the proposition that apples are often red, since you can probably provide evidence to that effect or, if not, you can count on me to provide ample testimony for it."

I conjecture that this proposition, if it turns out to be true, will not affect my assertion that non-fiction is fiction. (I also point out that this assertion is consistent with my earlier one that the experience of reading is uniform.)

Now, another question: if a book is a request to you to read it, what do you ask of the book? I assume that when you begin reading, you are expecting—therefore requesting—something, which I have so far only called the experience of reading. What do you think that means?

I maintain that what you ask of a book is the possibility of learning—of knowing, in thought or feeling, something new; or something which if not new in substance will be made available in an unfamiliar way and so will be made new for you (be renewed). I suggest furthermore that since there is almost nothing that is truly new (and what there is will as soon as it is known become part of what is old) what you ask of a book is not learning as the acquisition of thoughts or feelings that you don't yet possess but learning as a process. I suggest that what you ask of a book, whether it is a book of poetry or a manual for the repair of air-conditioners, is to be given the satisfaction of experiencing the process of learning—that without this satisfaction any book you read you will reject as a waste of time. I assert that this is what is *common* to all books, common to your expectation of any book; I admit, too, that particular books must satisfy particular expectations as well—so that the air-conditioner will keep working on this stifling Saturday afternoon; so that you can know what happens when Wallace

Stevens uses the word *orange.*

I can now say that when you open *The Stones of Venice* you have the primary expectation of learning in itself, as a process, and perhaps another, particular expectation. So I ask you, is there a particular expectation?

Is there something in particular you want to learn *about?*

You want to learn about Venice
and more particularly the Stones of Venice,
        stones here standing for *building stones,* or
      architecture.

I suggest, however, that what you have already started learning about (having read no more than the title, having just opened the book) has nothing to do with Venice or architecture and everything to do with a way of using language:

      See above, "*stones* standing for . . ."

"Standing for" instead of naming. (I immediately add a more extended interpretation: *stones* stands for not only architecture but architecture considered as an important subject—stones being durable, heavy, and grave in sound; no doubt *stones* stands for much more than this.) I suggest to you that you already know that Ruskin's subject will not be architecture but its significance. Is this what you want to read about? I suggest that you already know that you will not get what you think you expect; or that by now you expect words to tell you something they are not saying—words will be standing in for other words. I insist you recognize that as soon as words stand in for other words, nominal subjects dissolve, and what is written can be "about" everything and anything.

I propose that in the matter of Ruskin's success, which led him to complain that no one listened to what he was saying and everyone praised him for the way he said it, that he was wrong and his readers were right: Ruskin spoke himself in every sentence, and what his readers loved was him, not his ideas.

A question: how can Ruskin have spoken himself in every sentence? Is this a subject open to stylistic analysis, or does the question demand bringing in matters beyond the text itself?

I advance the possibility that this alternative is a false one: stylistic analysis can discover the intentions of the writer as he wrote, and at the same time I suggest that these intentions were not necessarily confined to being expressed through writing, that they did not require writing to exist (even if they required language), that they could have been given other forms, such as the designing of a garden or an engineering project. I consider the style of Ruskin to be the way he speaks himself in that it manifests his commitment to the possibilities peculiar to written language. That is why his subject matter and his message do not matter, and his style does. I contend that the real subject of *The Stones of Venice* is not Venice or architecture but the written word. I emphasize that in saying this I do not mean to portray Ruskin as ignorant of what he was doing, because I find that the results—the effects—of his writing are close to his explicit ideas, only he demonstrated those ideas undeniably in the way he arranges words, while the points he makes about architecture are always subject to argument.

Because I'm giving up the idea of using *The Stones of Venice* as a text for translation into performative speech, and because stylistic analysis is fun and worthwhile but irrelevant to my preoccupations at this moment, I conclude my comments on Ruskin's book with the first words you read after the book's title, which form the title of the opening chapter, "The Quarry." I point out that where *stones* stood in a particular, clear way for architecture, *quarry* remains to the end of the chapter it heads definitely ambiguous. You never learn whether it means the place from which stones are extracted, or if it means the writer's (and reader's) prey. I deduce that you are then not in a world of stones at all, but one purely of words.

I confess that today (9/6/83) I cannot be sure whether there is or is not a speaker present in written language. I admit that for years I have been telling you that there isn't; now I ask you, is there any more of a one when the speaker is physically in front of you (since then, if you hear him, you are doing the speaking yourself)? If in written language there is a speaker, is he created by the reader, by you—is one of the writer's tasks to give you materials and space to create a speaker as well as all the rest? When the American Express bill thanks you for sending money, and you imagine a printing machine doing the thanking, why not?

I suggest to you that this question (still unanswered) casts light on the nature of characters in fictitious works—which means in all written works. This morning I read of Unamuno's remark that "Don Quixote is no less real than Cervantes"; to make the point even more obvious, I add that Sherlock Holmes is much more real than Conan Doyle. I can deduce at once that in these explorations I am a character who by speaking according to certain rules enables you to imagine me as *a* person, the emphasis being on the *a* as signifying unity and coherence, what I could also call personality. Then "I" am that person, and what I-Harry Mathews think about who I really am has no connection with, or at least no effect on, the me whom you are creating out of the way I express myself in these lines you are reading. Can I not now assert that in written language there is always a speaker, who is a character created by the reader out of the materials at his disposal? I can furthermore insist that this speaker does not correspond to and therefore cannot be expected to represent the individual to whom the speaking voice nominally refers—Harry Mathews here, Benjamin Franklin in his autobiography, James Reston in the articles he signs in the *New York Times*. I suggest that not only must you the reader make up the speaker for him to exist, you cannot help doing so. You use the telephone book: who is reading you that list of names and numbers? I suggest someone—or something—is.

I speculate that the genius of writing is to know how to let you imagine me as the speaker I assert myself to be, at that particular point, for my present purpose. I infer that the genius of autobiographical writing (I remind you that I find all successful writing to be autobiographical; here I mean what is overtly so) is to provide you with materials and space to create me in a way identifiable with my historical reality and with the way I assert that that historical reality should be read.

In any writing that alleges to speak in the first-person mode, I suspect that you are always what you were defined as being at the start of these explorations (the name I give myself reading) and that I am always what I was defined as being (the name I give myself writing).

Les Merveilleux Nuages

Harry Mathews

> . . . man's best-directed effort accomplishes
> a kind of dream, while God is the sole
> worker of realities.
> *The House of the Seven Gables,* XII

The Duplications is not what they seem. Kenneth Koch's book-length poem, which resembles his earlier *Ko* in size and style, is a work of many duplicities, of which the foremost is this: it is an intensely serious undertaking masquerading as preposterous entertainment. In this respect it belongs to a family of modern classics that includes *Count Orgel's Ball* and *The Baron in the Trees,* as well as stories of Kafka's such as "The Giant Mole." It also takes its place in an older tradition of inspired poetic comedy, the tradition of *The Rape of the Lock, Don Juan,* and *Orlando Furioso;* together with Ovid's *Metamorphoses,* Byron and Ariosto in fact provide its models.

The preposterousness of *The Duplications* lies more in the telling than in the tales told; but some idea of it can be given by a summary of the stories themselves; and the summary will serve, especially for those who have not read the work, as a frame of reference for discussion. The main stories are four:

1. Mickey and Minnie Mouse are driving through Greece as contestants in an automobile race. They are accompanied by Donald Duck, by Pluto, who is gay, and by Clarabelle Cow. Clarabelle manifests an attraction to Mickey that angers Minnie, who soon dispatches her to Samos. Mickey and the others drive across a bridge of spray to Crete. There Donald makes a pass at Minnie. In a jealous rage, Mickey pounds him with a rock until Minnie stops him. Donald is taken to a vet, but too late: he dies. Stricken with remorse, the mice abandon the race. They try to live a solitary life in Crete, but they are so hounded by journalists and tourists that they repair to Washington, D.C., where, thanks to a new drug, they are changed into comic-book characters. Their chief competitors in the race, Terence and Alma Rat, seem sure winners at this point; their progress is interrupted, however, by Herman Clover, a snake who anesthetizes Terence in order to make love to Alma. Meanwhile, to protest their transformation, artists display giant paintings of Mickey and Minnie in the Bosphorus. These works of art convince Mickey that he should return to the race, win it, and

confess to the murder of Donald. He and Minnie are transported to Olympus, where they soon become gods. Terence and Alma are then rescued from Herman the snake by priests from Mount Athos. Minnie, remorseful over her punishment of Clarabelle, uses her new powers to change her into a beautiful woman. Mickey likewise resurrects Donald; but because his command is imprecisely phrased, Donald is no sooner reborn than he becomes a calligram of himself. Heartbroken at his mistake, Mickey is unexpectedly visited by the turtles of Olympus, who demand self-rule. In replying to them, Mickey utters a blasphemous "Goddam!" Olympus explodes, scattering its inhabitants. Mickey and Minnie land on a Grecian highway conveniently near a Chevrolet in which they go on to win the race. The Donald calligram is taken away to a Dutch museum. On Samos, Clarabelle bumps into the Amos Frothingham statue (see 3). Amos comes to life, clasps a rapturous Clara to his bosom, and "soars straight skyward" into cloudland (where Pluto, when we last saw him, was playing golf).

2. Two characters from *Ko,* Pemmistrek and Alouette, are picnicking in Provence. Pemmistrek accidentally touches a chemical substance that turns him to glass. Alouette is so shaken by this event that she is transformed into a huge bird. She carries her lover to Rome, where he is brought back to life by Doctor McSnakes, although without his memory. The doctor advises Alouette that a certain rabbinical ritual may be able to restore her to human shape. As the couple wanders through Rome, Pemmistrek tumbles into an underground passage that leads him straight to Helsinki. Alouette is forgotten. He takes up with Ann, one of the Early Girls, winsome creatures fabricated out of Finnish soil. (When an Early Girl makes love, the replica of an existing city comes briefly into being, as Pemmistrek soon learns to his surprise.) He leaves Helsinki by train with Ann and other Early Girls. Meanwhile, Alouette goes to a Roman synagogue where a rabbi performs as an entertainment the very ritual needed to bring back her womanhood. She magically learns of her lover's whereabouts and flies to Stockholm, where Pemmistrek has arrived and narrowly escaped death. Still in the company of the Early Girls, Pemmistrek takes a train north. His memory returns. After a polar bear has knocked him off his train, he boards another that soon pulls into a station where Alouette has just arrived. The lovers are blissfully reunited. At this point Atlantis raises its watery arm to snatch the train filled with Early Girls down to its watery realm. Ann and her sisters will henceforth be companions to the all-male Atlantides.

3. Huddel, another refugee from *Ko,* survives only as a Roman statue. Brought back to life, he is immediately shattered by a passing car. But his fragments miraculously reassemble: he becomes a superman, half flesh, half concrete. He flies (not in a plane but on his own) from Rome to Samos. There an American team has gathered, determined to destroy him before the USSR enlists his powers against the West. While in Juno's temple,

Huddel recognizes one of his assailants and slays him—a sacrilege that brings about an earthquake. Samos is destroyed, although only temporarily. On the island, Huddel has met the beautiful Aqua Puncture. With her he flies to Africa. (In the meantime, Amos Frothingham deserts the American death team, devotes himself to the cause of Greece, and settles on Samos. He will later die of an insect bite, and a statue of him will be erected on the island.) Huddel and Aqua land in Tropical China, a region of Africa Italian in its customs but populated by Chinese. (During a peaceful interlude, Aqua tells Huddel her story. She is the granddaughter of an ancient Etruscan woman whose youth was preserved by a secret process through the centuries. John Ruskin had fallen in love with her; she had died bearing him a daughter, who was kidnapped by jealous archeologists and kept, drugged, in a Dutch museum. There she was discovered by Nyog Papendes, Commander Papend's father [see 4]; Aqua was their daughter.) Mugg McDrew, a member of the death team, has tracked Huddel down and tries to kill him, but he is thwarted in the attempt and himself dies. After yet another assault, this one by a pygmy, Huddel decides to leave Africa and fly with Aqua to Helsinki. On their way they discover a pleasant region in the clouds where sky vegetables are growing. They find life there exalting and go no farther. Pluto then delivers Papend's letter to Aqua (see 4). She thus learns that she has a half-brother and is filled with longing to meet him. In time a crescent-shaped car picks them up to drive them to a heavenly feast organized by Nyog Papendes.

4. High in the Peruvian Andes, Commander Papend, Nyog's son, has built a replica of Venice in which to indulge his appetite for young women. In protest against this abomination, Nature has attacked the city with swarms of giant bees. The only defense against them is the erection of large matzoh placards throughout the city. At the start of the poem, an inhabitant of Second Venice, Elizabeth Gedall, disappears into the sky while sitting by her stoop. She is later found unharmed, the momentary victim of a "gratuitous act" on the part of certain cumulus clouds. Papend knows of his half-sister Aqua's existence. Filled with a desire to know her, he persuades Pluto to deliver a letter to her. An earthquake then releases a long-buried Inca prince into Second Venice. The event leads Papend to reconsider his aims in life—a process that continues when, after a summons from his father, Papend is lifted into the sky. Visions of a better world come to him as he travels through the clouds towards Nyog Papendes' feast.

Clearly the author of *The Duplications* has no interest whatsoever in suburban realism. He entertains us with improbabilities. And these, it should be added, are riddled with further improbabilities. We are constantly being distracted from the stories here summarized by lesser incidents of varying irrelevance, as well as by a host of minor characters—fifty-nine by my count: some last only a line, like Miss Ellen Foster Tay; others, such as Norma Clune, nuclear physicist and translator of Proust into Icelandic, infiltrate several stanzas. Further interruptions, also entertaining, take the form of reflections in the manner of *Beppo* and *Don Juan,* each with its particular savor. A consideration of the transcendent moments life can offer includes these lines:

> There is the proud sensation, for example,
> Of sitting in the ocean in a car;
> Or being thrown against a Gothic temple
> By an outrageous omophagic Czar —
> No one should ever feel that he has ample
> Experiences which light him like a star:
> Stark naked hens and roosters playing cricket,
> And Juno, Mars, and Saturn in a thicket. (23/155)[1]

Those who have spent time in Venice will recognize the aptness of this observation:

> And now the Adriatic seems a pond, though
> One knows how large it is upon occasion
> When in a vaporetto to Torcello
> Going as slowly as a spoon in jello. (149/281)

Furthermore, this medley of "interruptions of interrupted interruptions" moves along *prestissimo*. Enjambment, which keeps lines and stanzas spilling forward into their sequels, is applied to the narratives as well. Ariosto told several stories at once but carefully marked off the beginnings and ends of their parts. Here there are no such pauses. We can never be sure if the next half sentence will still pertain to Mickey's and Minnie's adventures or plunge us into those of Pemmistrek and Alouette. We can only hang on as we speed along into whatever comes next.

Even as we are being so impudently entertained, we start noticing certain duplications, certain duplicities, at least the simpler ones that lie in the foreground of the text—such as that the Venice we had assumed to be the original city is a copy perched high in the Andes, or that "a tremendous goat" seen wandering through Thessaly is a disguise worn as a punishment by three monks from Mount Athos. We also notice that rhyme, that traditional duplicating procedure of verse, has a novel function: instead of emphasizing meaning or playing a counterpoint to it, it can in this poem brutally determine it:

> . . . the large Christmas turkey that No-Shu
> Sends each December to the O.N.U.,
>
> Now that Mao's China's been admitted to it.
> Norma, who loves him even though he's crazy,

---

[1] Page references are first to *The Duplications* (Random, 1977), then to Koch's omnibus volume *Seasons on Earth* (Penguin, 1987).

> Had made him go each week to Dr. Bluet,
> The psychiatric heir of Piranesi,
> Who saw man's mind as a huge, complex cruet
> In which he was imprisoned, like a daisy. (105/237)

(After this summary appearance, we hear no more of Piranesi and Dr. Bluet.)

When we read this passage, we are deep into the poem, moving fast; and since we know the lines are parenthetical ones, we do not stop to ask what kind of sense they make, or if they make any sense at all. We are willing to allow that the last four verses may have been entirely suggested by the rhyming pattern—that they may be, in other words, nonsense. Now when a writer has succeeded in creating such a state of mind in his reader, he can get away with murder. And in fact the next two lines tell us: "He'd worked with No-Shu now for eighteen months, / Who in that period had killed only once." The writer can lead a pleasantly distracted reader into the depths unsuspecting and virtually unawares. Reconsider the quotation earlier that starts "There is the proud sensation. . . ." The gods invoked in the last line of the couplet are not such auspicious ones as, say, Venus, Mercury, and Apollo, but a sinister triad standing for domestic law, war, and death. We are being entertained with murder and gods of gloom. *The Duplications* are not what it seems.

What is really going on in the poem? We can start looking for an answer in another, even less comprehensible passage. The passage cannot be said to be central to the poem, because, like *Don Juan, The Duplications* has no center; or more accurately, its center is a perpetually shifting point on its surface—the point where at any moment we are reading. Still, even at a first hurried encounter, the passage is arresting enough to make us wonder about it. It occurs just after McDrew's death in Tropical China. Meralda, a blue-eyed young woman, has just explained to a Chinese journalist named Pong that this death was brought about by an insect lodged in McDrew's heart:

> ". . . Say, have you got a match?"
> The lovely girl requested. When the TienTsin
> Reporter bent to see, she ran off dancing
>
> And screaming horrible threats into the air,
> "We'll kill you all, we bugs! Ha ha! Forget it!
> You'll never stand a chance!" No underwear!
> She rose into the sky. "What have I said? It
> Was only so I'd understand!" "Beware!"
> She rising cried. She saw a bird and met it
> With sloppy kiss. "We cure at first but then
> We do our fated work: death to all men!" (65/197)

First of all, Meralda, however mysterious, is plainly duplicity incarnate. Her change from pretty girl into prophetess of annihilation might be said to confirm the suspicions we have been starting to feel. Her threat of death furthermore thrusts into our attention a topic that we have already found—in Saturn and No-Shu—lying close to the entertaining surface of the poem. Talk of death in fact permeates *The Duplications.* Mickey's first appearance, for example, at once leads to the mention of Walt Disney's demise, and the giant Packard in which he races suggests the "bone and dust of dinosaurs." The first Mickey episode concludes with news of a murder in an Athenian restaurant. Pemmistrek's translation to Finland brings to light another murder. The "proud sensations" in the quotation earlier would seem to offer little hope of survival, and in other reflective interpolations we are told of the "meaningless violence" that plagues the world, of "decimating nations," of "the art / We waste upon ingenious ways of killing." The long reflection at the end of the first part of the poem concludes: "And so one carries on . . . with what is vital / Being a thing continually sought for — / At death it's this that we have come to nought for!" A full list of such examples would multiply them tenfold.

Death wreaks havoc as well with the cast of characters. Bit players, like Huddel's assailant on Samos or Pemmistrek's in Stockholm, are pitilessly mowed down, and at some point most of the main characters are deprived of life in one way or another. Mickey and Minnie are reduced to two dimensions, Pemmistrek is turned to glass, Aqua spends inanimate years in a museum. Amos Frothingham and Mugg McDrew both lose their lives. Huddel and Donald die twice, once literally, once figuratively. Papend leaves the world "as one dead." Nyog Papendes may be alive, or dead, or both—it hardly seems to matter.

The reason it hardly matters is that in the poem death does not always mean that life is over. For the principal characters, in fact, it is more like a new beginning. Of them only Mugg McDrew dies definitively—the peculiarity of the event is driven home by the repetition of "death" as a rhyme seven times in two stanzas (63/195). The others all recover—are reborn. (It is true that Donald Duck ends stuck in his calligram, but there is good reason for that, as we shall see.) We may ask why, aside from the animated-cartoon improbability of the work, this should be so. What kind of death can this be? The answer seems to be: it all depends. We do glean a few general hints about its nature. Death is apparently a prerequisite of freedom. Huddel declares, " 'three births remind me / That I was meant to live . . . / Above all else I prize my liberty!' " (36/168); Mugg McDrew cries, " 'A shame / That I must kill them both, but that's the game / Free life depends on!' " (58/190). Death is also close to dreaming. When Papend rises "as one dead," the poet writes, "I cannot guarantee his state was waking, / But he was wakeful in its dreamy spaces" (153/285); and Early Ann, snatched from life on earth to Atlantis, goes on loving Pemmistrek "as a dreamer / Loves someone she has never seen in daytime" (144/276). Lastly, death works a change in its victims that makes them semi-divine. Mickey and

Minnie become gods on Olympus; Huddel becomes superman; Aqua, Amos, and Papend acquire the ability to fly; Pemmistrek (in his dreamlike amnesia) leads a life of bliss miraculously shielded from the dangers that beset him.

So death in *The Duplications* is not altogether dire; it can even lead to happiness. It does, however, demolish expectations; and it remains a real, if variable, danger. Why does it happen so often? Why does it happen at all?

A short quotation will suggest the answer. By a roadside in Thessaly, the snake Herman Clover has just put Terence Rat to sleep and is turning his attention to Alma:

> He seized her in his coils, which caused a cinem-
> Athèque in Athens to explode and nine
> Persons to suffer in Constantinople
> From heart disease. (100/232)

No deaths are certified, although at least a few seem inevitable; but what emerges unambiguously from these lines is the lethal power of sexual desire. It is the desire of the male for the female that litters *The Duplications* with mortality. Desire may have consequences other than death, but it is death's certain cause.

This fact manifests itself first of all in the narratives: Donald Duck has his head bashed in for seducing Minnie; the Renaissance architect Archibald is poisoned for lusting after Leo VII's favorite; a Dallas billionaire dies after satisfying his girlfriend's whims. But it is more by poetic association that the link between desire and death is forged. Juxtaposition rather than causal sequence is what puts the point across. Some examples: Commander Papend has "sexual urges large as Lapland / And was as set for action as a gun / In madman's hands who hates the world around him" (4/136). Minnie reclaims Mickey from Clarabelle with the lusty words, "Your tough luck! / Alone with him tonight I'll squeak and fuck!" which no sooner spoken precipitate the fatal shooting in the Athenian restaurant—an event that initiates a reflection on death that brings us to Pemmistrek vitrified on a field in Provence (11-13/143-45). The passage devoted to "the art / We waste upon ingenious ways of killing" ends a list of preferable pastimes with the erotic awakening of an adolescent boy (59/191). "The beginnings of romance" are said to be "very quiet, like a sailor / Drowned in the sea" (51/183). The words already quoted—"At death it's this that we have come to nought for!"—conclude a two-page description of the attractions of different women to men, and the next stanza, which terminates the first part of the poem, contains the lines "So mourners walking down the Via Sacra / See their love's grave and feel they're buried in it / Themselves . . ." (76-77/208-9). And this is only a sampling. As its last item, a slightly different kind of fact: there is only one triple rhyme in the poem that appears four times, and it is *life, wife, knife* (15/147, 23/155, 98/230, 99/231).

Next question: why should male sexual desire cause death? We are not praying mantises; we are not even obliged to be Lacanians. Why such punishment for so "natural" an impulse? If there is a punishment, there must be a crime. What is criminal in man's desire? Two guesses.

No, one guess. Who needs to think twice about Oedipus and his mother? And this obvious answer came at once to mind. It came to my mind, and there it stayed. There was nothing in the poem to justify it. I did not, however, let the answer go. On the contrary, it could properly be said to have started bugging me. I won't say it gave me butterflies in my stomach, or ants in my pants, but it was certainly a bee in my bonnet and a flea in my ear. So I looked at the poem yet again, starting at the beginning with Papend and his duplicated city, where I read:

> Why did he want all this in Venice? Actually
> I do not know. I'm not sure he did either.
> I'd guess the city just aroused him sexually
> As Mommy's breast arouses the pre-teether. (7/139)

Why yes! And Second Venice was an "Abomination beneath the sky's blue." And what happened to it? "Nature" caused it to be attacked by "hideous monstrous bees." Then I recalled other curious details in the work: the buzz and the butterfly preceding Huddel's resurrection, the mite in McDrew's heart, the ant that revealed precious information to Alouette, the bees that helped No-Shu learn the truth about his mother, Meralda's curse on men, McStrings devoured by ants, the prohibition of females from Mount Athos so strict that "even Ann / The Ant and Fay the Firefly are excluded," and, last but not least, the poet's exclamation on Amos Frothingham's return to life: "Take that, you / Dull insect, Death!" My obvious answer lay explicit but invisible under my eyes in a metathesis at once simple and ingenious and, of course, disarming:

i n S e C t

It was no longer surprising, it even seemed perfectly fitting that *The Duplications* was so full of bugs (even if I knew that they could not be interpreted simply as allegorical or even symbolic representations of incest). The discovery, however, did nothing to answer yet another question that immediately arose: is incest really a punishable crime? Why does it lead to death?

Let's reconsider the concluding lines of the quotation above: "aroused him sexually / As Mommy's breast arouses the pre-teether." We first turn to women for nourishment, and our mothers naturally provide it. Food is a substantial, non-duplicitous gratification of our hunger: not only does our hunger disappear, we are given something tangible to make it disappear, something we can be sure of, something we can know in the act of incorporating it. But with this gratification we also get something we didn't bargain for: an awakening of sexual desire. And unlike hunger, sexual desire cannot be satisfied—by the mother or anyone else—the way hunger can. We can never possess our gratification the way we possess food; we can never be sure of it, never "know" it in so reassuring a way as incorporation. The satisfaction remains elusive and illusory.

On several occasions in the poem, hunger and sexual desire are merged in the figure of the mother: almost overtly in the remarks on Papend's preference for Venice (7/139), inferentially in the interpolation on violence and pleasure (59/191), most explicitly in a passage that follows the mention of the poet's given name and speculates how such names may be chosen:

> . . . some, romantically —
>
> If, for example, Dad once loved a lassie
> Named Billy Jo, he might call baby Billy,
> If baby is a boy, or if the chassis
> Of that small creature shows that it is silly
> To think she's the same sex as Raymond Massey
> And may one day play Lincoln, perhaps Tillie
> Might satisfy his crazed nostalgic need
> To see his old flame at his wife's breast feed. (87/219)

"Dad" is certainly a doomed man, and probably one long gone. In any case his "crazed nostalgic need" is a perfect definition of the condition that condemns the male to death. His insanity—and his crime—lies in confusing the two kinds of desire, one seemingly real, the other illusory in its gratification. By demanding a substantial gratification of sexual desire (that is, as substantial as food—something impossible) the male condemns himself to failure, hopelessness, unreality, nothingness, and so to "death." This death is then interpreted as coming from the mother herself: by luring with real satisfaction and exciting with impossible desire, she becomes unforgivably duplicitous. Incest is not lethal because of any social taboo but because the mother reveals desire as something doomed. The maternal breast is at once the source of life and death. (Cf. Meralda: "We cure at first but then / We do our fated work . . .")

It is thus that the insects of incest pester these pages with their curious itches. As we have seen, at the very outset of the poem bees attack Second Venice, where Commander Papend "made love over fifty times a day": the bees are warded off with matzoh placards "Placed on the shoreside gilding of [each] house": food—the object of innocent and necessary desire—staves off the punishment of sexuality. Interestingly enough, bees are later on specifically associated with the sexual attractiveness of the mother. No-Shu's murderously obsessive jealousy is explained in this fashion:

> His father and his mother had a dog
> Named Uncle Patsy, Ki-Wa in Chinese,
> Which bumblebees had trapped under a log.

> No-Shu, just five, ran out and chased the bees
> But then got lost, while going home, in fog
> And had a vision of his mother's knees
> With someone's hand upon them. Since that time
> He had devoted half his life to crime. (104/236)

No-Shu became a murderer of philanderers, a self-appointed punisher of sexual desire.

Now if we remember Meralda's curse (65/197)—I trust by now it has begun to make more sense—we should expect insects themselves to become the agents of retribution. After all, Meralda says they will; and occasionally they do—a bug inside a crocus, no less a one than Meralda's daughter, stings Amos Frothingham to death (72/204); McDrew dies from an insect egg planted in his heart; a praying mantis's bite turns Pong into a baby while " 'insect eyes' were decimating youth" (66/198); death is even accused of *being* an insect (147/279). But what is remarkable is how often insects fail to kill, how often, belying Meralda's words, they are harbingers of life, growth, and superior knowledge. Even in McDrew's case, it was the insect egg that enabled him to attain adult size; Pong, after his second baby-hood, grows up again; it is an insect that, plunging into Alouette's Campari as she drinks it, supplies her with the information she needs to start recovering her happiness (68/200); and at one point the insect world is praised for holding philosophical views superior to our own (28/160).

This suggests why in *The Duplications* "death" (except for the exceptional McGrew) is less than fatal and often benign. Incestuous desire may not after all be a crime, or not only that. Rather than a punishment, the death it leads to may be a kind of rite of passage. Both desire and death may reveal paths leading to the kind of knowledge that "might cure us of all grieving" (as the author says of the insects' wisdom), knowledge that will transcend the practical, provable sort and "help people love . . . their world," for all its duplicity. Certainly the desire that dooms us leads as well to developments other than death. It enables us to produce (or discover) new worlds: the ephemeral cities of the Early Girls, Second Venice itself, the new Atlantis that is its undersea counterpart (144-45/276-77), the exalting sky world in the clouds that is a dreamy version of earthly life, with fields of heavenly fruit and vegetables, sky fish, cloud golf links, and endless sky-borne thoroughfares. These various new worlds can be called metamorphoses or sublimations of ordinary reality, but in the poem's term they are most fittingly thought of as its duplications; and their existence points to duplication as the way by which we can survive desire, death, and their duplicities. For, clearly, if one can be reborn, death is *also* a duplicity. This is perhaps the wisdom of the mortal, benevolent bugs.

If that is so, we may ask what modes of duplication are available to us. Poetry is certainly one: we have not only the demonstration of the art in this particular book but the more general claims the author makes on its behalf.

(The poem itself is qualified as an attempt to speak "Of how things are on earth, and how in heaven" (84/216); earlier, the *ottava rima* stanza is praised as "a splendid churn to / Make oppositions one" (79/211). In ultimate aim as well as in immediate practice, *The Duplications* is everywhere concerned with duality and doubleness.)

But before we turn to the poet's advocacy of poetry, we should see what he has to say about the medium in which poetry operates, that is, about language. After all, we habitually think of language as a vast duplicating system: it replicates reality by assigning it names. Why can't it suffice as our means of duplication (i.e. of survival) without being subjected to the additional formalizations that poetry brings to it? Answer: by itself, language is utterly duplicitous—as duplicitous as our mothers. Language pretends one thing and does another. It pretends to give us names for things; in fact it gives us only words (which are other things). It is, in "other words," always telling lies—a fact grandly demonstrated at the opening of *The Duplications* when we are presented with a familiar Venice that dissolves a page later into something very different: "Venice, Peru, of course, is where it happened" (4/136). The strange ways personal names are given, as in the passage quoted on page 99, illuminates the naming function of language in general: the names we call things represent not those things but ambiguous histories of experience that we peremptorily associate with them.

This radical ambiguity of language is dramatized in Donald Duck's transformation into a calligram of himself. Mickey, you may remember, has killed Donald in a fit of jealousy. When he becomes God of Everything on Olympus, his first act is to resurrect his friend. But Donald has scarcely come back to life when he is turned into words—"Words everywhere feathers had been except / His beak, which stayed the same, like Uncle Sam" (135/267). The reason this happened is that Mickey's "commandment / Had some ambiguous words in it" (136/268):

> What "like to man" meant
> In resurrecting Donald — he had said
> "Bring Donald like to man to life from dead" —
>
> Was what remained unclear. Did Mickey mean
> "As man would"? Man would do it in some art,
> In picture, word, or music, and we've seen
> The natural forces carrying out this part
> Of what he said, confused, had tried to glean
> The maximum effects: first made a smart,
> Exacting, happy duck, far from acedia,
> Then turned him to a high form of mixed media.
>
> The words which make his feathers up declare,
> I think, SOMA PSYKOS SEMA ESTIN,
> "The body is the soul's prison." If you care
> For intricate deep meanings, this has been

> The best part of this story anywhere —
> Think how man's language shuts man's meanings in
> And is his prison, as his body is! (136/268)

Ambiguity creates the prison of language, which is equated with the body, itself condemned to ambiguity, as we have seen, in its confusion of palpable and imaginary longings.

So language is our second body, and it is similarly doomed: "One's words, though, once excited, mate and marry / Incessantly, incestuously, like patients / Gone mad with love . . ." (91/223). Like the body forthright in appearance, language is another instrument to delude ourselves with our desires—"to see our old flame at our wife's breast feed."

(This ambiguity of language perhaps provides one meaning of the words ". . . the fallacy / We find by being born into this galaxy" (81/213). It is worth pausing to underscore the weight of the word "born" in these lines. We find death and all the ages of man in *The Duplications,* but never birth. It is the great *non-dit* of the poem.)

If language doesn't work as a naming system, what has to be done to make it work? A possible answer may be suggested by pointing out that if language cannot properly name what is, it may be able to name what isn't. Indeed, this is what it seems to do naturally. And what might "what isn't" be? Out of the ocean of infinite possibilities rise glistening dolphins we can recognize: the creatures of our "crazed nostalgic needs," the images of our impossible desires.

Can language be compelled to perform usefully and consistently this naming of what isn't? This is where poetry comes in. Poetry transforms language into the Universal Duplicating Machine that it can never become in the world of fact. (When the author returns from an outing that filled him with inspiration for his poem, he finds that "even sometimes the very / Words I would lose en route spawned duplications / Stretching as far as sight" [91/223].) Not representation but invention—or more precisely re-invention—becomes the overt goal towards which words are directed. Here are some simple examples of what I mean.

Even in conventional poetic usage, rhyme is a procedure that is independent of the aims of representation (although it need not disrupt them): the duplication of sounds occurs for its own sake and needs no further justification. We have already noticed how in *The Duplications* rhyme can take absolute precedence over reason to determine events and even the presence of particular characters (there are many so created, beginning with E. McTizzy born from "busy," Dr. McSnakes from "shakes," Ellen Gudge from "grudge"). The usual naming function of language is reversed—now, it is realities that are assigned to names. Another kind of duplicating power can be discovered in single words by exposing second meanings. Consider the effect in these lines of "pinking" in the wake of Lisa's sunburn:

> I see the dawn
>
>> Growing more quickly than the flush of red
>> Upon the back of Lisa who has lain
>> Four hours naked in the sand instead
>> Of going to the store at Fifth and Main
>> To buy some pinking scissors as she said
>> That she was going to do, wherefore her pain. (88/220)

The passage furnishes us with another kind of example of nonrepresentational invention. The simile illustrating the dawn is carried way beyond any criterion of vividness. The visual comparison is submerged as it expands into apparent irrelevancy. And just as the comparison with the "patient etherized" obliterates the sunset at the opening of "The Love Song of J. Alfred Prufrock" but defines the speaker of that monologue, Lisa in her nakedness becomes not an image of the dawn but yet another apt if unreasonable duplication of sexual desire. Metaphor has been subverted from its explanatory prosaic function to become the recreator of a reality it does not name.

An earlier instance of simile demonstrates a comparable effect, achieved in this case through compression rather than expansion. It occurs in the description of the "giant earth- or sea-quake" that is devastating Samos after Huddel's sacrilegious act:

> [It] smote the Samian robber in his cave
> And threw the Samian shepherd from his mount
> And shot a thousand dead up from the grave
> And broke more water jars than I can count;
> And, while the island cracked, a tidal wave
> Like a huge copy of *The Sacred Fount*
> Smashed everything in sight and then retreated,
> Leaving old Damos totally depleted. (38/170)

The comparison with *The Sacred Fount* at first looks like another wacky triumph of rhyme. There is more to it than that. Waves move in succession like the turned pages of a book; a fountain or spring is very different from the sea but both are water. Why not compare a tidal wave to a book, when this tidal wave depends for its existence on the book we're reading? The undisguised imitation of Byron in the preceding lines has reminded us that we are in a world determined entirely by poetic language: water here is all words. Finally, James's novel concerns the passionate investigations of a narrator smitten with a lust for knowledge: what he relates, it turns out, may be no more than a duplication of reality created by his own desire. . . . So here, as in the case of Lisa, an extravagant simile ultimately brings us back to one of the poem's central themes.

We are now in a better position to consider the claims the author makes on behalf of poetry. Essentially, they are to be found in the long interpolation that starts the second part of the poem (78-95/210-27). Here the author speaks about the difficulty of resuming a work that has lain abandoned for two years; relates nostalgically the life he had led while he was beginning *The Duplications*—he was staying in Kinsale on the Irish coast with his friends Homer and Betty Brown; and discusses quite unsystematically the genesis of *The Duplications* and the nature of poetry.

These pages offer something of a relief after the unrelenting zaniness of the fictional narratives, and they provide a more open, more comfortable context for their resumption. Although it is the reflections on poetry that most concern us here, it is worth pointing out that the author's life in Ireland is itself presented as a kind of duplication. His friends the Browns are for the writer a "home away from home," a second family: a mother, a father, and—the only other occupant besides himself—their daughter Katherine. At the same time, we learn that *The Duplications* was born at least in part of desire. The poet says that now, years later, his mind will be "less leaping / Than when I saw you last when I was sleeping / And saw you blossom for me every night" (79/211). This unidentified "you" was present to the poet as a dream of desire ("But I've stopped dreaming of you / In that particular way, which made me wild" [80/212]); and, elsewhere in the house, Betty Brown was dispensing motherly care. While the writer worked on his poem in a room upstairs, she "diced, sliced, and carved and sieved in / The kitchen which was under it." In the neighboring upstairs room was Katherine, "whom her mother / Would sing to sleep two times a day or once, / Depending if she was in a napping period" (86/218). And it is precisely after evoking this double image of woman as the inaccessible object of desire and the tender, providing mother that the author writes (remembering the non-napping baby's cries):

> I've always thought I should be more forgiving
> And not be seized by the desire to kill
> When someone interrupts me at my knitting
> Of words together, but I'm that way still.
> I've not, however, murdered anyone,
> I swear, as I am Stuart and Lillian's son. (87/219)

Thus in the midst of comfortable domesticity are evoked, and clinched with a propitiatory oath, the interwoven strands of desire, death, and the mother that so entwine the fictional narratives.[2]

[2]No sooner have the narratives resumed than these three themes are again sounded together with, as here, the vengeful child appearing as the possible agent of death (cf. No-Shu's story, 104-105/236-37). After Herman Clover, the lecherous snake, attacks Alma Rat, Pemmistrek and Early Ann are almost run over:

> My God! it must be smart
> To find a way to be as the first man was,
> Adam, I mean, exempt from, in the soft spring,

It could hardly be otherwise. To this poet, poetry is never imagined as an escape from desire and its consequences: poetry *is* desire. He describes himself as "burning / To carry on this discourse with my head / The world calls poetry and I call yearning . . ." (85/217). The equation is made explicit. He can have no hope of avoiding death. (Is the interruption of the poem its death, its resumption a rebirth?) Writing poetry, however, leads beyond "death" to the satisfactions of understanding and even of mastering the fate to which we are condemned. Poetry, we are told, is "a fabric to deceive and undeceive" (79/211). Through it we can discover "the sole true story of man's secret mind" (91/223). It can "change / What seems disparate into what alone / Can make us happy: re-possession" (94/226). The three statements can be taken together as one: man's true story is hidden by the incapacity of ordinary language to tell it, and only the deliberately "false" duplications of poetry can reveal it and so make it available to repossession.

How this actually happens is something of a mystery, and the author of *The Duplications* leaves the mystery unexplained. Doing otherwise would mean subverting the poem. He must, after all, remain the absent creator, even in the Irish interpolation, which for all we know may be as fictitious as the rest of the poem. Even if it isn't, neither the more personal "I" he assumes in it nor the confession of certain events in his life should be read as signifying more than the author pointing to the mask he has chosen to wear. The mask has its own necessary mystery, and this may be part of the mystery of how poetry accomplishes the transformations the author claims for it.

The mystery is not explained, but it is not concealed, either; and here we discover a more interesting reason for the lack of explanation. Towards the end of the Irish section, the author asks himself how the life he had then lived might be related to his poem: "There were, doubtless, certain real connections / Of other kinds between my life and work . . . / Some ways in which cool Kinsale did concur / With Aqua, but I don't know what they were" (92/224). And later, at the very end of the poem, he admits "I've / No knowledge of transfinite life-death distance, / So I shall leave them, without more insistence . . ." (153/285). Since *The Duplications* has been largely about travels in "life-death distance," this admission of ignorance is striking.

Attack from others, either strange or offspring!

But not since then, I think, has any managed
To have complete protection. Even Adam
Was by his earthly consort disadvantaged
When she brought him an apple. Thank you, Madam.
Oh well, all right! Then boom! Boom, doom, and damaged,
We have not yet recovered from that datum
(If it is true, which cannot be gone into) . . . (102/234)

The mystery is not explained because the poet does not know its solution, or perhaps because he knows that a true mystery has no solution. The "them" he leaves in the last quotation are the several characters en route to the feast of reunion and reconciliation organized by Nyog Papendes. By this time they, and we, are high in the clouds—deep, that is, inside the world of duplications. The poet is saying in effect that he does not know how we got there. But perhaps there is no way he could, if knowledge is only possible *within* that world beyond reason, beyond "death."

No matter how one does reach the world of poetic duplications, it is certainly worth getting to. When Huddel and Aqua discover their first sky-vegetable patch in the clouds, they are pervaded with a "sweet, pure grandeur" for which anyone on earth would gladly abandon wealth and success (76/208). When he rises into the sky, Papend finds himself "confused, inspired":

> He goes on thinking, which, on such occasions
> i.e. when one is in convulsive flight
> Away from what one knows and with sensations
> That mix the energies of day and night
> May bring about the birth of those creations
> All kinds of artists treasure, and they're right . . . (152/284)

He is filled with "the confidence and lack of fear of death . . . / That power gives, like that of innocence . . . ." "Strange new energies became unfastened" in him, and he sees his life as he had never been able to see it on earth, conceiving of a new Venice greater than the one he built.

Curiously, when these grand revelations come to Papend, he may actually be asleep: "I cannot guarantee his state was waking / But he was wakeful in its dreamy spaces." We may then deduce that the world of poetic duplications is one of dream, as well as of desire and death. . . . Papend's experience confirms the notion that this second world of dream is the best and perhaps only place in which to apprehend and recreate our earthly reality.

But Papend may not necessarily be sleeping, or only sleeping, because he is dead or very close to death (149/281); and so presumably are the others who like him are making their way at the poem's end to Nyog Papendes' feast: Clarabelle, Amos Frothingham, Huddel, Aqua, Pluto, and even Elizabeth Gedall. How could they not have died when the yearning that is poetry has brought them here? They are furthermore entering the realm of their own desires, going to "where what they know of things will be increased" (147/279), "to where they feel it is they're wanted" (154/286). They are doomed; and what of it? In this dream duplication of earth, the veil of duplicity will be cast aside and things be shown as they are—something that is revealed to Papend as a perception of desire innocently repossessed:

> Then into fading, then more faded, blue,

> Until all colors are completely gone
> And everything a quite light light-white hue
> Like petticoats stretched out upon a lawn
> To dry on Easter morning, when the Shoe,
> Which children think the Rabbit has put on,
> Has left its tracks and also precious eggs
> To which the children run on trembling legs
>
> And cry, "Why are there petticoats out here?"
> In fact, there aren't. It was the mere appearance
> Of petticoats, was frost, which, in the clear-
> Er later morning sky is gone, as Terence
> Was gone from consciousness, as from the beer
> The foam is gone, as from the throne room Clarence.
> And Papend goes on sailing through this ether
> Where clouds, air, everything he sees, is see-through. (151/283)

Desire repossessed: is anything else more desirable? In any case, it seems improbable that the heavenly travelers will find anything else to enjoy, since there is no certainty that they will reach their destination: "I wonder if they ever will arrive?" (153/285). In fact, they have already arrived, although not at the feast of Nyog, "the Lord of Sad and Happy Endings." What they have reached *is* their desire: the perfect consummation of desire is its own duplication. We leave them journeying through the sky in everlasting flight. This is a last duplicity on the author's part.

Or next-to-last. Much earlier in the poem, during the Irish interpolation, there is a long passage about the dawn and early morning—it begins with the simile of Lisa pinking. The passage associates daybreak with poetic creation and introduces the reflections on poetry that we discussed. Now, in the very last lines of *The Duplications,* we read that Nyog Papendes' guests

> . . . all, soaring in their flight,
> Are fading fast, or covered by the awning,
> Which everyone can see, of early morning. (154/286)

They are, in other words, hidden by what inspired their existence: they disappear from our view beyond an oxymoron that tells us that our sight is darkened not merely by light, but by the light of revelation itself.

Poundian Romance:
Investigating Thomas McEvilley's Novel,
North of Yesterday

Robert Kelly

> "a hungry book, reading the readers"
> Thomas McEvilley, *North of Yesterday,*
> *or, Flowers of Waz* (1987)

THE COINCIDENCE OF MEANS with goal is, in this world and beyond it, the special quality both of the illuminative path and of the highest energies of literature—one of the many reasons writers constantly confuse their practice with religion. It was the particular triumph of Modernism to create —in Pound, Joyce, Stein, Proust, Mann, Broch, Beckett, Céline, even Rilke —a determinedly secular epos to enshrine, instruct or transform our secular world. (The fact that poets are religious about Pound and novelists about Proust shows merely that religion can embed itself in the secular, snug as an abbé in a Neuilly salon.)

In *North of Yesterday,* modern dreams open out onto a late Egyptian mystery, and from its perfervid sensual nightmares some characters discovered lurking in the mind of the teller (like Lovecraft's Old Ones, ever watchful for their chance to speak and move), proffer to the Narrator (the voice we get to know) three fateful flowers. Their petals, eaten, produce effects which are coincident with history arrowing its way to the novelist's now, coincident with the drugs he and his beloved are forever high on or low from, coincident with the very book itself, sent from Back Then and always being lost Here and Now, a book that turns ineluctably into the novel we are reading. Classical modernism and classical mystery story at once. I found pleasure in the fact, though, that the self-reflexiveness of this novel is relaxed, even genial; it is not at all portentous, clever, or French. McEvilley takes for granted a novel's (and our own) capacity for being fascinated by its own coming into being. We are souls making souls in a vale of soul-making, we are part of theogony. We like the smell of our own armpits better than that of others—this fatal penchant is the root of self-awareness in modern texts. We are fascinated by our own dreams. The narrator in *North of Yesterday* spends a lot of the time dreaming, with and without the help of sleep.

PAUSE NOW FOR: LYRIC MYTHEME FROM THE TURN OF THE CENTURY

On a warm night a long trolley ride from Market Street, when the wicker porch furniture groaned and cracked under the quiet passion of a young couple sitting close not quite furtively in the dark, in June, with mosquitoes sibilant and the dog asleep, with parents not far and society in love with lovers as it always is, summer warmth around the turn of the century, Ezra Loomis Pound and Hilda Doolittle were, a little bit, making love. Damp clothes and quick breaths, a hand here, a hand there, all of it unsatisfactory, enthralling, fulfilling, incomplete. By midnight the mustachioed swain had risen for his long walk home, the girl (exhausted by sheer feeling, pre-orgasmic excitement swollen and released to post-orgasmic irritable lassitude without ever the Everest of orgasm proper in between) watched his athlete's body move with a fencer's short neat steps to the sidewalk and disappear beyond the meager porch light.

In the gorgeous simplistic bargain basement called Literary History, it is a commonplace to believe that Ezra Pound spent the rest of his life fleeing such feelings and such tendresses, and that H.D. spent the rest of hers trying to sustain that evening forever, projecting it into past and future, Egypt and Greece, Rome and Bethlehem, always, the throb of that not-quite-unspeakable, deeply articulate, yearning. Boys will be boys, girls will be girls.

It is true that the *idle* reader of the *Cantos* looks in vain for the author's amours, or any love stories more recent than rainy Toulouse in the thirteenth century, or some Renaissance affair too complicated by family history and real-estate manipulations to have much gyzm. The subtle reader is, as usual, better rewarded. Busy writing the *Cantos* for himself in the acoustic reverberation of the master (for one must chant the *Cantos* that one hears, that is the secret, we must write the book we read), the reader soon learns that many of the *Cantos,* especially the later ones, are concerned with the articulation of the heart's poise in a world of passion. Poise, the pivot. Pound chose as one of his most important glyphs the ideogram (found in the very name of China) which can mean the middle, the heart of the target. He writes of the Unwobbling Pivot. We recall him, Pound, in his power, as the one who stood by his words, unwobbling, and we remember also the man between two women, a man between two works, a man between two worlds. Olga and Dorothy, Poetics and Economics, Antiquity and Cathay—a man trying to be just the one he is, no other. Pound is patron saint of our modern polytheism, even as, in the mighty agon of the Pisan nightmare, he began to cast away this idiocy of a self. No wonder the impassivity of the Confucian acrobat so pleased Pound, who tried to hold his own at the pulsing heart of the, of any, dialectic.

Surely H.D. in her own work sought and found such balances, such chambers and alcoves of desire between the determination of her heart to find comfort and love's mating, and the determination, Isis-like in her tenacity, not to give up one iota of all the world that has been.

Her mode became the *palimpsest,* as Ezra's the *ideogram.* These two modes are the Eve and Adam of modernism—by which *ism* I mean to indicate not an historic period but a watershed of spirit from which we still are plentifully supplied.

Palimpsest: the inscription of a new text on an old parchment from which the former words had been scraped away. With time (or with infra-red photography after the turn of the century), both messages come through. Layer upon layer of meanings, narrations, build up. This touch touches every touch before, skin upon skin. The palimpsestical method studies the overlay of all that has been spoken. It is the method of *superimposition.* On the other hand, the ideogrammatic method works by *juxtaposition,* assembling entities, objects, words into a speaking structure, a structure whose unity-of-saying is a function of the very diversity from which the complex image is welded by ear.

The ideogrammatic method. This was Pound's great formal declaration, and the awe-filled, god-crazed spaces of the *Cantos* (especially those canto-beginnings, those fair embarkations at the start of many of the individual cantos, ideograms that commence the journey outward, each time, from the silence of his life or the deeper silence of his logic, his terrifying "So that" which ends the first canto), those spaces ripple with light and dazzle with the congestion of thought in all its *substances,* packed tight; these passages are in fact the ideograms themselves of a great new language Pound only began.

END OF RETROSPECTION. BACK TO MCEVILLEY.

This is not the place to remark yet again Pound's immense influence on twentieth-century poetry and poetics. We all know that. Here I just want to sketch, draw the bow almost at random, in hailing this lovely, intricate new book of McEvilley as a rare thing, a new thing, an instance of Pound's not hitherto much noticed pressure on the novel.

Pound's snows of Lydia and golden lyres transcend their local times and occasions. In McEvilley's urgent rhythms, Pound's poetic of image / ideogram / cluster turns to a *narrative syntax,* an alternative excellence at last to those of Paul Metcalf and Guy Davenport as our most notable Poundian novelists (and they more so by the coalescence of concerns than by templating of method). In McEvilley's work, variation and repetition, the rich bottom-work of the round dance, make the ground on which his dancers move, never stable, never pausing. Every recurrence is a jolt, not a serenity. His images dance round and slap our faces, our meek modern faces. Pound's measures are set to new burdens, and Pound's haughty spondees and clangorous troches (read out loud page 58!) tell H.D.'s stories, classic entablatures made to writhe with the serpentine delusions of the heart. McEvilley is running away from the classic world Pound still (per aspera ad astra) hungers for as *norm of spirit.*

The deeds and transforms of this novel are not serene. A hero lost at sea (over and over: Egypt, Turkey, Yucatan) is born or reborn a sea monster— he is, or someone is. In a passage of great beauty, a woman is missing from her bed while her lover searches, haunts, through all the houses of the town looking at the sleepers still or restless in their silent beds. A criminous old procurer lives forever, an ancient poet refuses to desist in his discourse. Things happen, or seem to. What else is new? Peopled with fascinating language, this book tells plenty. But what does it tell?

All events are myth. Insofar as we can recognize them as *events* at all, not just as shadowy smears, blurs, pixels of discrete light, to that extent it means they participate in myth, rehearse myth, renew myth, or simply present myth. Myth means that which we have no other way of apprehending than as a whole. Any event is myth, and any person is myth. As Barthes pointed out in the same brilliant year that Olson wrote *Projective Verse,* the capacity of language to use the *passé défini,* the simple past tense (he came; it fell), implies a dependence, both naive and functional, on some imputed creator/observer who can measure the boundaries of process itself, and determine when an event is, and when it is finished. (I write this on Good Friday, and recall with a shiver that the God we call Our Lord said, "It is finished" as he stood against the wood of the cross.)

So the tendency of the modern novelist to erode the edges of the event, deny its close-endedness, abrogate the privilege of its ego and the ego of the character—this tendency is not a fashion (though it may be fashionable at times) but a breakthrough in the Tacit Communal Theology that runs the mind of the West. In *North of Yesterday,* each act knows itself as several, not as single. This novel, excitingly obedient to its hypermodern[1] agenda, calls into question the very nature of "event," "person," "character." And in doing so, it does not appear to pay even lip service to some inherited wistfulness towards unity. (We are states united, but states apart, in gods we trust, but take no refuge in them.)

This deliquescence of character and event enrolls McEvilley's book in the glamorous army of books found hard to read. (One newspaper reviewer found the sentences detestable and their purport obscure, if I remember aright.) What an interesting thing it is, to be hard to read! Or be, really, as

---

[1] Whatever Postmodern may finally come to mean, I want there to be a term to mean, and I am using *hypermodern* to do so, strategies or enterprises which carry forward the basic modernist devotion to technique ("technic"), as well as modernism's characteristic methods: fragmentation, ideogram, palimpsest, alienation, analysis (as in Cubism), etymology. Modernism's deep, almost mystical belief in the *means* at hand—"a man at the mercy of his means"—seems still to go on generating work of great power—Brakhage's films come to mind, and Zukofsky's late poetry as it helps to shape current poetics, or the work of Jackson Mac Low, or the polytheistic psychology of James Hillman.

this book truly is, very easy to read, a lollop every moment, easy to read but hard to understand. By understand, I mean a nervous and insecure questing for connections faster than the author cares to supply them.

Egypt is fanciful, and Greece a poetic land of the lost. Not much special knowledge is needed to read this book, just delight in language, a pagan lust for imagery, along with patience for the figures of the dance as they wind and unwind themselves. (One of the dumbest things in the world is to look at a dance and want it to be architecture.) The novel sprouts a few local thorn bushes of arcane reference, which are also things we might be happy to learn about. And it is alas only too likely that many a reader won't recognize Quintus Smyrnaeus, though it would help to—an often deprecated later Greek writer whose accurate homeric metrics and plausible homeric language, used in an epic that tells (as Homer's did not) about the Fall of Troy, combine with a fine bloody imagination and great imagistic powers to make much more than a pastiche of Homer. Quintus is an important character in this novel, partly used (I suspect) as an affectionate teasing of the Ezra Pound whose oeuvre seems so basic a donation, or permission, to McEvilley, partly as a link in a tradition of writers reading writers—a poignant avowal of demure humility, if McEvilley is to Quintus Smyrnaeus as Quintus Smyrnaeus is to Homer. It is from Quintus that the little book is sent that the narrator learns to read, and in reading writes the book we read, and in that book learns the solution to the mystery Quintus had stumbled on in Egypt. But for all its authors, there is only one book, ever.

At a rare moment of solemnity, the narrator confesses:

It is difficult to explain what has happened to me since I began this book. How many have I looked for on the river? When I found them, what was it? A flutter at the heart, a mouth pulsing at the hand. A tenderness that stuns the brain, casts a mist around the head, and we fall.

This book. The converse of the singleness of the Book is *all* the books that any book is, all the ways of reading, revealing, and hiding itself away that a text has. "My" book is missing, and Quintus's book is not "his."

This multifariousness conditions delight. The pleasure in *North of Yesterday* is the pleasure of *reading,* not that species of remembering we call "plot" or "understanding." The pleasure goes on in the text the way swimming goes on in the water; not without dullness can it be extracted therefrom. The pleasure is in the text as we pass, almost bewildered by the diversity of resources and presentments McEvilley, a very generous writer indeed, provides. We are lifelike readers in a lifelike manifold of provocations. As readers, we are tired of paying writers to simplify our experiences and abort our destinies. So though there are some things in *North of Yesterday* I don't like (just as there are some bad restaurants in Paris and some dull poems by Yeats), I like well the amplitude of registrations and remembrances he has brought to tell a story that is, when you get down to it, painfully simple.

I like this book. I like its blend, a wonderfully fatal mixture in the author, I guess, of prank and pomp, each outwitting the other:

. . . she crawls from the water on all fours and looks about strangely, remembering nothing. And I take her, sleek and soft, to my chest, and kiss her in the dream, not caring.

"*Venus decumbent: sunstroke, puking fevers, pulsatilla.*"

I discover a critical opposition coming, Uranus in Cancer and Neptune in Capricorn, and dash off a note to the papers: "There will be famine in India, civil strife in North Africa . . ." . . .

She crawls onto me, slopping her breasts on my face like slopping waves, wheels slowly, like a cow in a stall, and sucks at my cock, her head rising and falling wetly, ruminatively, tongue etching language of serpents on my spine.

I look it up.

"*Venus at midheaven: dancing; gold and silver; skill at chess.*"

I like the blend of what is happening here, the dance of registers, and so on, but I don't like the way he lets his narrator see, and his characters use, women. Perhaps it is our way, our pre-modernist way, here analyzed in one of its typical acts of humiliation. No part of this book pleases me less than such incessant blowing of the flesh-flute (fond as we all are of the flesh); the women "gobble" or "suck." That they seem to do so in a parodistic way is no excuse, and no surprise. It may be parody, but I hate it anyhow. Parody only makes things worse; what malady has parody ever cured, what tyrant has it ever toppled? Parody only adds to the obnoxiousness of the thing it has chosen to target the additional offensiveness of flippancy—a double assault on the reader's sensibility. And here the very thing parodied should not be woman's behavior but the habits of male obsession. Men are, in *North of Yesterday,* maybe not much better—but *they have language,* while women are mumblers and gobblers, literally (in the instance of the far beloved Della) faceless, or veiled. The book has its revenges on male lust: The bloated Roman governor Lucius Porcius, thinking he is rogering a choice young harlot (the same whose fortunes dominate the secret history of the novel) finds he has been buggering a man, an old man at that, a dead old man. But one suspects that Lucius is punished more for being old and fat than for being (as his name suggests) an early instance of Male C. Pig.

Long ago every boy noticed that Grail is an anagram for A Girl. In *North of Yesterday,* a girl is duly sought, Della, and found, Waz, who is or is like unto Isis; she is the veiled woman who is both goal of quest and core of nightmare. Her name sounds to me like one name for the papyrus itself, as if she is the paper (our word is from the plant's name) and the book, the virgin ground it is the male's High Destiny to inscribe. Things that are sought for are, after all, *things,* and I have already mentioned my dislike for the humiliated status of the feminine in *North of Yesterday.* There are ancient Gnostic undertakings that hint at the necessity of humiliation if a certain transformation of one's destiny is to be achieved—but this is not the place to talk about them, and this is not a decade in which they can be heard. Instead, pass with me to the lilt of the Nilotic barcarolle and enjoy an

INTERMEZZO: THE EGYPT OF NORMANDI ELLIS

Midway through my reading of *North of Yesterday,* I received a manuscript of a book I had read passages from a few years before: Normandi Ellis's "translations" of Ancient Egyptian texts, *Awakening Osiris.* These translations had haunted me—and again I felt something close to me as I read them. I delighted in her grasp of some surer image or tone, religion, gently mocking her own lovely unreformed American language still thick with things to feel and things to see. Egypt is so many things, or there are so many Egypts. Hers seemed to be an Egypt that the body could reach its way to if only the ear listened carefully. It is a country of substance stronger than image, of aspiration more than theology. Things yearn, and Normandi Ellis is adept at catching the voice of their clamor. Like McEvilley, she was *hearing* the world. What a fine writer she is, I thought, as I read. What a sucker I am for fine writing, I thought, delighting in it here in Ellis's Egypt, and in McEvilley's Egypt, not at all alike, land or writing, but each immensely participating in the act of inscription, the act (to give it a gypsy name), The Act of Making the World Be There By Opening Your Mouth.

Everything I remember, everything that we can remember, is far as Egypt from us now, since every past we remember becomes our own past, part and parcel, silent and fervent, and from it we can speak. Ellis speaks from her strength of language and living, evidently, muscular from the stresses of a life of reading, living, listening and clearly responding in what is remarkably one voice to a host of early and middle Egyptian texts. It is a beautiful book, *Awakening Osiris,* now announced for publication by the Phanes Press in Grand Rapids.

END OF INTERMEZZO. BACK TO MCEVILLEY AGAIN.

There are so many Egypts. The Egypt of Breasted and Wallis Budge, those old scholars, of Champollion and Gardiner, of Aleister Crowley on that red-letter day in the Cairo Museum, of J.A. West, the thoughtful, measured Egypt of R.A. Schwaller de Lubicz (my own favored guide), the Egypt of Herodotus, of Solon, of Aristocles (whom we with unintentional boon-camaraderie call Plato)—none of these Egypts help here.

Menacing us all in America is the Egypt that the nineteenth century thought it knew about, of towns grandly named Memphis (TN) or Cairo (NY), of Shriners' temples and lotus columns, Grauman's Egyptian Theater and Goudy's Egyptian Extra Bold. This is the Egypt that seems to summon forth a kind of Low Church pomposity: we find it in séance transcripts and mimeographed wisdom lessons from Southern California;

we meet the same tone of hushed solemn stiltedness in Norman Mailer's *Ancient Evenings.* We don't find it in Ellis or in McEvilley.

Different as those books are, they renew Egypt in the same way, a way that strikes me as very fresh: reinterpreting the past through our own bodies (i.e., through our own capacity to experience pain, pleasure, bewilderment, dismay). Their Egypt is watered by *doubt,* and serves us.

Other modern versions of Egypt do not prepare us for what goes on here. Not even Cavafy's wonderful learned afternoons, lewd as an old coin still warm from its passage through so many hands. Certainly not Durrell's conspiratorial Egypt or Forster's clear-eyed sideshow. One begins to get a flavor of McEvilley's Egypt maybe in Strauss's later opera *The Egyptian Helen,* given its own curious temporal and narrative resonances, almost interferences with, H.D.'s *Helen in Egypt,* our greatest narrative love poem. But McEvilley's Egypt is mostly the fringe land of the later Greeks, a hotbed of sex and mysteriousness, violent and swollen and orgiastic, but finally human—in a way that technocratic Rome was not. This is the Egypt to which Christ was carried by his family to escape from the quisling running-dog vassal of Roman hegemony, King Herod. Perhaps that is the best time to find Egypt, between the coming of Christ and the coming of Christianity, a long century or two of dwindling Hellenism and gathering Gnosis.

We do not hear Isis's side of the story in McEvilley's book; a little bit we do in Ellis's—not because Ellis is a young woman but because she will not leave any item unconsidered, untouched, untasted. That is the task of Isis, is it not, to reassemble the world by noticing it, part by part, to achieve that all-satisfying multiplicity of and in which she is the only unity? Strangely, as I finished *North of Yesterday,* I found myself thinking back on H.D.'s great poem, its girlish solemnity, its utter accuracy of feeling-in-remembrance.

I think in fact that McEvilley is trying for that, and what is really most consequential about this book of his, a book I will not forget, is his urgent attempt to combine the methods I have ascribed respectively to Pound and H.D. In the start of *North of Yesterday* the ideogrammatic method is used elaborately, while the last chapters yield the shimmering texts of palimpsest, voice over voice recorded and recalled, a stately antiphon of loss and presentness. Is our author leading Pound back to H.D., this curiously learnèd novelist/critic/scholar, holding aloft the hymeneal torch to light them, and us, to the thalamus, the bridal chamber from which a new mode of writing is expected soon to be born? I only ask, and ask again, in case you were wondering why I bothered earlier on with Ezra and Hilda canoodling on the porch.

So this is the sort of scope or ambition I sense in McEvilley. Like the young ingénues on the French stage in the old days, all our young geniuses are around fifty. The soon-to-be quinquagenarian McEvilley has come forward with this powerful novel. It is not his first, yet it clearly feels to me in many senses a First Novel. It is the first novel you write (for we are somehow writing it, of course, modernist text that it is) after first reading *Steppenwolf,* you are suddenly seventeen again, whatever your age, and beginning to realize that your disordered quest for your mistress is not too different from the universe's quest for meaning—the girl as God. It's the first novel you write, too, after reading Homer or Edward Dahlberg or Savage Landor, or someone else for whom the old gods and the old neighborhoods (Lydia, Attica, Egypt) are still playfully alive. It's the first novel you write after reading Pascal Quignard (of whom we should hear much more in these U.S.) or Guy Davenport, and realizing that Rome's senescence is a topological fold of our own bumptious salad days, that kind of rehabilitation of Late Antiquity into the recent past, viz., one's grandmother's gauzy summer evenings, turn of the, always the same, century. Egypt is born again with the nineteenth century in its teeth, the Musée d'Orsay and Greyhound buses faltering through antique American landscapes of the future. That is what Pound and H.D. left us with: the past is our only future. And who knows that better than the young person telling the story, the Actual Story, of his or her first love? Where nothing is so important as what really happened?

This mature and conscious writer has written a young man's book, desperate, taking every risk, believing immensely in his own feelings and his abilities to record them. The ambition is endearing too in all that it confesses: the first novel that you write when you want at last to admit to yourself and the rest of the world that the simplest things please you best: sex and slivovitz, palm trees and evening stars.

Shadows and Marble: Richard Brautigan

Keith Abbott

> "What I desired to do in marble, I can poke my shadow through."
> —Richard Brautigan, from an unpublished short story "The F. Scott Fitzgerald Ahhhhhhhhhhh, Pt. 2"

SINCE RICHARD BRAUTIGAN'S DEATH, his reputation has hardly been cast in marble. His writing has been relegated to the shadowland of popular flashes, that peculiar American graveyard of overnight sensations. When a writer dies, appreciation of his work seldom reverses field, but continues in the direction that it was headed at the moment of death, and this has been true for Brautigan. Even during Brautigan's best-seller years in the United States, critical studies of his work were few in number. What there were never exerted a strong influence on the big chiefs of the American critical establishment.

Since he was both a popular and a West-Coast writer, his work has been easy to ignore. There are no critical journals on the West Coast which can sustain a writer's career, as there are on the East Coast. His popularity among the young dumped his work with literary lightweights, such as Richard Bach or Eric Segal, and counterculture fads as Abbie Hoffman, Jerry Rubin, or Charles Reich.

Curiously, a critical climate of open hostility to Brautigan's work prevailed on the eastern seaboard and his work was perceived as a threat. From the first, it was an object of ridicule, receiving much the same treatment as Jack Kerouac's novels did in the 1950s. Brautigan's literary position for his generation also was similar to the one Kerouac provided for the Beats: Brautigan became the most famous novelist for a social movement whose literary constituency was almost solely poets. Speaking politically, most poets have little recourse to effective literary power, lacking steady income, steady publication and/or reviewing positions. Brautigan did not have the safety of a group of novelists or a regular circle of reviewers friendly to his aesthetics; consequently, he had few defenders. Brautigan did not write reviews himself, or even issue manifestos. He was perceived as the stray, and so to attack his work risked no reply. In the *Vanity Fair* article published after Brautigan's death, the playwright and

117

poet Michael McClure acknowledged this hostility and offered this re-evaluation: "His wasn't a dangerous voice so much as a voice of diversity, potentially liberating in that it showed the possibilities of dreaming, of beauty and the playfulness of the imagination."

With the burden of a ridiculed sociological movement attached to his work, positive literary criticism was sparse. Often what commentary there was tried to talk about both the hippie community and Brautigan's fiction, and failed at both. Ironically, his first four novels were written before the hippie phenomenon, and the relationship between the two was an accident of chronology at first, and then a media cliché.

While his prolific output generated plentiful newspaper reviews, these usually functioned as simple indicators of his perceived fame. Most echoed previous prejudice that he was a whimsical writer for cultural dropouts, and neither his writing nor his supposed subjects were to be considered important. What has to be remembered about criticism is that even serious critics seldom create much lasting literature themselves, and most newspaper reviewers are inevitably trafficking in fishwrap.

The true test of a creative writer is whether the literature is remembered by good writers and begets more excellent work. Other authors have acknowledged Brautigan's influence. Ishmael Reed applauded Brautigan's courage in experimenting with genres in his later novels and claimed this had an effect on his own experimental and highly acclaimed novels of the 1970s. In 1985, the popular and respected novelist W. P. Kinsella published *The Alligator Report,* containing short stories which he dubbed "Brautigans." In his foreword he spoke of how this work arose directly from Brautigan's fictional strategies, stating, "I can't think of another writer who has influenced my life and career as much."

The spare early stories of Raymond Carver have always seemed to me to show a strong connection, stylistically and culturally, to Brautigan's first two novels and short stories. Both writers create a similar West-Coast landscape of unemployed men, dreaming women, or failed artists trapped in domestic and economic limbos while attempting to maintain their distinctly Western myths of self-sufficient individuality.

Implicit in most negative criticism of Brautigan is the charge that he wrote fantasies about cultural aberrations, such as the hippies, with little connection to important levels of American life. I think this is mistaken. A strong cultural reality can be found in his work, that of people on the bottom rungs of American society, living out their unnoticed and idiosyncratic existences. Traditionally this class has been one of the resources for American literature. While discussing *Huckleberry Finn,* V. S. Pritchett writes that one of America's cultural heroes is "a natural anarchist and bum" and called the book "the first of those typical American portraits of the underdog, which have culminated in the poor white literature. . . ." Many of Brautigan's works are rooted in this underclass and his people are, in

Pritchett's words, the "underdog who gets along on horse sense."

It is often the fate for writers of American popular culture that their work is not taken seriously here, and they find an audience in foreign countries. During his lifetime, Brautigan's writing was translated into seventeen languages. Internationally, Brautigan's work commands respect and continues to generate comment. In Japan, where twelve of his books have been translated, he is considered an important American writer. (And it is of interest that Carver's fiction now enjoys an equally high level of popularity in Japan.) In Europe, West Germany continues to publish his work and a television documentary on him is under way. In France, Marc Chénetier's excellent book-length study was published with accompanying translations of three Brautigan novels. This critical work was later translated into English as part of Methuen's excellent Contemporary Writers series.

In the America of the 1980s, Brautigan's work is treated only as an object for nostalgia, and confined to rehashes of the love generation. When roll calls of fictional innovators are published in critical articles, his name has been dropped off the list of Ishmael Reed, John Barth, Donald Barthelme, Robert Coover, and others.

Brautigan's work remains the best way we have to regard him, other than as an historical figure. As a writer, I have to think the work is what really matters. Whatever follies, sins or beauties a writer might be said to possess, they are secondary considerations to the complete body of writing.

In a useful observation on Brautigan's poetry, Robert Creeley commented, "I don't think Richard is interested in so-called melopoeia, he said he wants to say things using the simplest possible unit of statement as the module." Simple sentences and minimal rhythms occur in Brautigan's fiction, too, but they work with his metaphors to obtain a more complex effect than in his poetry. By controlling the colloquial sound of his prose, Brautigan developed a strategy for releasing emotion while utilizing the anarchic and comical responses of his imagination.

"The Kool-Aid Wino" chapter in *Trout Fishing in America* provides an example of this strategy:

When I was a child I had a friend who became a Kool-Aid wino as the result of a rupture. He was a member of a very large and poor German family. All the older children in the family had to work in the fields during the summer, picking beans for two-and-one-half cents a pound to keep the family going. Everyone worked except my friend who couldn't because he was ruptured. There was no money for an operation. There wasn't even enough money to buy him a truss. So he stayed home and became a Kool-Aid wino.

What can be said about this? First, except for the fanciful notion of a Kool-Aid wino, this paragraph has the sound of the English plain style.

Brautigan wrote in a colloquial voice, but sometimes it had a curiously unmelodic and muted quality. The voice sounded as if the speaker were talking, but not always consciously aware of being heard. This might account for what other people have dubbed the naive quality of Brautigan's fiction: the tone of a child talking to himself. And for all his colloquial rhythms, slang or common nursery-rhyme devices, such as alliteration and internal rhyme, are carefully rationed, because both require that the reader *hear* them. In the paragraph, two incongruous states, being ruptured and being a wino, are joined, but the last has a rider attached, modifying it with a fairy-tale quality of special powers derived from common objects:

One morning in August I went over to his house. He was still in bed. He looked up at me from underneath a tattered revolution of old blankets. He had never slept under a sheet in his life.
   "Did you bring the nickel you promised?" he asked.
   "Yeah," I said. "It's here in my pocket."
   "Good."

While the scene is being set, Brautigan slips in the metaphor of the blankets, but in a sentence that has the same declarative rhythm as the sentences just before and after it. This blanket metaphor sounds rhythmically no more important or remarkable than the lack of an operation or the absence of a truss, but the metaphor is, in this context, spectacularly surreal.

He also used very little rhythmic speech in his dialogue. Often his dialogue is even more uninflected than his narrative passages. As Tom McGuane writes, "His dialogue is supernaturally exact." Muting rhythm in dialogue and in narrative passages dampens down the emotional content. This has an interesting effect because hearing a voice calls for a much more emotional reaction than silent narrative passages. This is why "dialect" novels are so exhausting to read. They require much more concentration and emotional response. First-person narrative calls for more effort from the reader than third-person because we are listening and responding to one person. Brautigan often got a third-person objectivity while writing in first person.

Brautigan's strategy was to control and minimize the reader's responses until he was ready to tap into them. For both his dialogue and narrative, Brautigan habitually tried for emotionally neutral sentences. While still maintaining a colloquial tone, the narrative sentences *sound* normal, the dialogue sounds minimally conversational, so they may slide by unchallenged by a reader's emotional response. What is crucial to Brautigan's style is that both dialogue and narrative strike a similar *sound* and that a neutral equality be created between them.

Once Brautigan establishes this pattern in a work, then simple statements of fact could be followed by a simple sentence bearing a fantastic and imaginative statement. The strategy is, accept A, accept B, therefore accept off-the-wall C. The poet Philip Whalen explains the effect of Brautigan's style this way, finding "in Brautigan for example complete clarity and complete exact use of words and at the same time this lunatic imagination and excitement all going 100 miles an hour."

To change to a biological metaphor, what happens in Brautigan's prose is that the parasitical imagination invades and occupies the host of precise, orderly prose, subverting, disrupting and eventually usurping the factual prose's function.

He was careful to see that the jar did not overflow and the precious Kool-Aid spill out onto the ground. When the jar was full he turned the water off with a sudden but delicate motion like a famous brain surgeon removing a disordered portion of the imagination. Then he screwed the lid tightly onto the top of the jar and gave it a good shake.

To give a realistic base for his fiction, Brautigan often started with mundane social situations and built from there, carefully placing one rhythmically neutral sentence on top of another. This lulls the reader into a false sense of security, and a false sense of security is a good first step for comic writing. By doing this, Brautigan sensed the emotional vibrations that are inevitable in the simplest sentences, so he could then upset these and introduce that lovely sense of comic panic.

Of course, there is a problem with this strategy. No matter how short, factual, or laconic sentences may be, writing always carries some shade of voice. The human voice resonates feeling and Brautigan knew this. By creating a kind of equal neutrality between the factual sound and fanciful content through the use of similar sentence structures, Brautigan tried to solve the problem of how to return to a realistic narrative once he had disrupted it with his metaphors. At times he simply alternated between the two, giving the fantastic equal time with the mundane.

"Hello," said the grocer. He was bald with a red birthmark on his head. The birthmark looked just like an old car parked on his head. He automatically reached for a package of grape Kool-Aid and put it on the counter.
    "Five cents."
    "He's got it," my friend said.
    I reached into my pocket and gave the nickel to the grocer. He nodded and the old red car wobbled back and forth on the road as if the driver were having an epileptic seizure.

Or, at times, he would let the metaphor grow from a single sentence about a commonplace until it took over the paragraph. In this example from *Confederate General,* the rhythm speeds up as the metaphor expands.

Night was coming on in, borrowing the light. It had started out borrowing just a few cents worth of the light, but now it was borrowing thousands of dollars worth of the light every second. The light would soon be gone, the bank closed, the tellers unemployed, the bank president a suicide.

Fiction must have drama, however minimal, but given this strategy in Brautigan's prose, often the drama is on the surface of the writing itself. The tension between the two poles of Brautigan's style, the plain and the meta-phorical, creates the conflict in his fiction. In the passage quoted above, the first-person character/narrator is so hyped up about visiting his eccentric Kool-Aid wino friend and witnessing his rituals that his imagination runs wild. But no one in the story notices this, so this potential conflict is confined to the prose itself. Just as the "I" character remains undercover in the mundane tale of buying Kool-Aid, the fantasy remains undercover in a plain prose.

Brautigan's writing has been called undramatic, because in a conven-tional sense it is. His style provides what drama there is more often than his characters. His metaphors function as dramatic resolutions, if subversion of common reality with imaginative thought can be called a resolution. (One of Brautigan's themes is that ultimately this strategy subverts and disrupts the very act of writing fiction.) The fanciful notion of a Kool-Aid wino provides the impetus to continue reading, not any drama between the characters. The Kool-Aid wino will nowhere insist on the strangeness of his behavior while the narrator will provide the tension with his perceptions of that behavior as *being very special in a magical world.* Often the rhythms do not insist that this is a special occasion any more than does the Kool-Aid wino. The sentences chart a rather unremarkable exchange between the two char-acters but this exchange is seen by a quite metaphorical intelligence, and so the prose itself enacts the eventual theme of the piece, that illumination comes from within: "He created his own Kool-Aid reality and was able to illuminate himself by it."

Besides a plain, slightly colloquial style, Brautigan also favored the structure of facts to give a neutral tone to his sentences. Facts are meant to be understood, not heard and savored on their own. Brautigan loved to infiltrate and sabotage them. Here's an example from the opening chapter of *A Confederate General From Big Sur.*

I've heard that the population of Big Sur in those Civil War days was mostly just some Digger Indians. I've heard that the Digger Indians down there didn't wear any clothes. They didn't have any fire or shelter or culture. They didn't grow anything. They didn't hunt and they didn't fish. They didn't bury their dead or give birth to their children. They lived on roots and limpets and sat pleasantly out in the rain.

During this masquerade of historical prose, the manipulation of a catalog style develops a strange emotional equivalency between the sentences which their content quietly disrupts. One source of this technique comes from the Western tall-tale, where a narrator, disguised as an expert, mixes the fantastic with the normal in equal portions. This passage somewhat reminds me of Twain in his role as the seasoned traveler in *A Tramp Abroad:*

The table d'hote was served by waitresses dressed in the quaint and comely costume of the Swiss peasant. This consists of a simple gros de laine trimmed with ashes of roses with overskirt of sacre blue ventre saint gris, cut bias on the off-side, with facings of petit polanaise and narrow insertions of pate de foie gras backstitched to the mise en scene in the form of a jeu d'espirit. It gives the wearer a singularly piquant and alluring aspect.

In both Twain and Brautigan's paragraphs, an anarchy is hatched inside the standardized English. Twain's prose has the trotting rhythm of standard fill-in-the-blanks travel or fashion writing. Brautigan's prose creates his bland rhythms through the careful alternation of "and"s and "or"s in factual sentences designed to be read and forgotten. Twain's intent is burlesque, while Brautigan's opts for a quieter anarchy. But the strategies for both seem similar.

A more complicated example of Brautigan's technique with this factual sound can be found in his short story "Pacific Radio Fire." The opening paragraph begins: "The largest ocean in the world starts or ends at Monterey, California." There's no sense of who is saying this. Since the story title has a radio in it, the voice could be someone on the radio, but it doesn't have to be, it could be anybody. Then Brautigan adds the next fact: "It depends on what language you are speaking." These two statements are acceptable, reasonable, and dispassionate. Nothing in their rhythm seems emotional or unusual. Put them together and they enact only a slightly different way of viewing the universe: "The largest ocean in the world starts or ends at Monterey, California. It depends on what language you are speaking." However, one thing has changed. With the use of *you,* the reader is now addressed, and his presence is acknowledged, giving a slightly more colloquial edge to the second sentence than the first, an intimacy. Then the third sentence plunges us into an emotional, very intimate situation—but *without* any corresponding passionate rhythm: "The largest ocean in the world starts or ends at Monterey, California. It depends on what language you are speaking. My friend's wife had just left him." Now, these three sentences present a fact followed by another fact followed by a third fact, but the last one is wildly removed from the reality of the first two. More importantly, the third sentence is *colloquially* factual. The first two have the tone of the mundane media facts that wash over us daily, while the third sentence belongs to the everyday world of emotional distress. The third sentence is something that any private person could say, just as any public commentator could say the first two.

This sequence establishes what I call an equal neutrality between the three sentences. The shift cracks the emotionless facade that the paragraph starts with and abruptly releases humor. While the language remains low-key, its arrangement yields the drama.

This linguistic shift is also curiously realistic, and I mean realistic in the manner that these verbal traumas occur. To my ear, this shift mimes the kind of dislocations that result when someone is trying to tell you how something bad happened, but doesn't know how to start. Instead they talk about the weather, the scenery, and then suddenly blurt out their distress without any rhythmic or emotional buildup. A familiar "out-of-the-blue" quality to the rapid shift from impersonal to personal occurs. Here, it works as comic timing:

The largest ocean in the world starts or ends at Monterey, California. It depends on what language you are speaking. My friend's wife had just left him. She walked right out the door and didn't even say goodbye. We went and got two fifths of port and headed for the Pacific.

What makes this more than a mere joke is that there is a vibration set off by the word "language" in the second sentence and the fact that the wife left without using any language. Brautigan at his best discovers a taut, underground humor in his prose by suppressing connections that other writers might make obvious. Someone else might have written, "and didn't even use language to say goodbye." One of the strengths of Brautigan's style is that he leaves the right things unsaid and trusts the placement of his language to supply the emotions.

When Brautigan tries to reverse this progression, going from the colloquial emotional truth to the dry facts, from the fantastic to the mundane, the humor sometimes is less natural, a tad more bizarre. Here are the opening paragraphs from a chapter in *A Confederate General From Big Sur,* "The Tide Teeth of Lee Mellon":

It is important before I go any further in this military narrative to talk about the teeth of Lee Mellon. They need talking about. During these five years that I have known Lee Mellon, he has probably had 175 teeth in his mouth.

This is due to a truly gifted faculty for getting his teeth knocked out. It almost approaches genius. They say that John Stuart Mill could read Greek when he was three years old and had written a history of Rome at the age of six and a half.

The reverse doesn't work as humor quite as well as the previous example because the neutral sentences are not part of the set-up, but are used to finish the joke. There's a deadpan humor to this strategy, of the bizarre masquerading as the everyday, but the implied connection between the historical fact of John Stuart Mill's genius and the asserted "genius" of Lee Mellon's losing his teeth either seems funny or it doesn't. At his best, Brautigan doesn't allow that much leeway for the reader's responses.

Timing was an essential ingredient in Brautigan's finest writing, and he understood the virtues of the simple buildup. According to his first wife, and Brautigan's own account of his early apprenticeship as a writer, he worked for years on writing the simple sentences of his prose. In a notebook located in Brautigan's archive at UC Berkeley, an early draft of the chapter "Sea-Sea Rider" in *Trout Fishing* showed how he divided the prose into lines of verse, carefully trying to isolate each of the phrases by rhythm, by their cadence, revising for the simplest sound possible. Accompanying this draft is an aborted journal, written in 1960 and titled "August." In a rare moment of self-analysis, Brautigan wrote: "The idea of this journal is I want to make something other than a poem. . . . One of the frustrations of my work is my own failure to establish adequate movement. . . . I want the reality in my work to move less obviously, and it [is] very difficult for me." What Brautigan means by movement is, I would guess, the switch from his metaphorical intelligence in and out of his mundane situations. In order to be less obvious, the transition between the fantastic and quotidian had to be eased by giving both the same rhythms.

His poetry sometimes forced the connection between the mundane and his imaginative fancies by combining them in one sentence. The effect was artificial and clever, and so it lacked the careful, timed setups of his prose. What made his prose remarkable was his ability to sense those moments when his imagination could occupy the larger factual rhythms of his paragraphs. This might be what he meant by "adequate movement." When he strayed too far from the mundane and/or factual setups, the cleverness had only itself to sustain, and his fiction suffered from the same defects as his poetry.

His fiction has its own peculiar vision and a sometimes satori-like sharpness. There's a humanity to Brautigan's discoveries that sets them apart from mere humorous writing. The opening paragraphs of the chapter "Room 208, Hotel Trout Fishing in America" serve as a final example of Brautigan's skills as a writer, how in a few words he could blend a prosaic vision of the world and at the same time infiltrate it with his own imagination and turn the mundane into something quicksilver, moving and alive:

Half a block from Broadway and Columbus is Hotel Trout Fishing in America, a cheap hotel. It is very old and run by some Chinese. They are young and ambitious Chinese and the lobby is filled with the smell of Lysol.

The Lysol sits like another guest on the stuffed furniture, reading a copy of the *Chronicle,* the Sports Section. It is the only furniture I have ever seen in my life that looks like baby food.

And the Lysol sits asleep next to an old Italian pensioner who listens to the heavy ticking of the clock and dreams of eternity's golden pasta, sweet basil and Jesus Christ.

Inspector Javert's Moment of Pure Aeschylus

Paul West

BECAUSE IT HAD BEEN repainted with a free hand, in what my boy's imagination called mustard-gas brown, the door of the book cupboard creaked, a dead giveaway if you were perched on a chair, trying to get at the "grown-up" books on the top shelf. This was my mother's music room, where the echoes never ceased, with always, for me, a faint twang of piano wire, a rumble from among bass keys.

It wasn't my mother, though, whom I sensed behind me as I fumbled for forbidden fruit, but Victor Hugo's blue-lipped implacable detective, Javert, a monstrous apparition somewhere between Frankenstein's creature and the masked mastermind who, every Saturday afternoon on the silver screen, worked his vicious will and groped edgily with his deformed arm in the serial called *The Clutching Hand.*

The paradox, of course, is that, in order to think Javert was behind me, I must have already dipped a couple of times into the book I was climbing to. Until I had in part read *Les Misérables* I had no one to rebuke me for reading it. My mother must have seen me straining toward the top shelf, but she never said, and all she did was tidy the way I had put the book back and dust the shelf a bit. So I was alone with that demon of rectitude, that biped monolith of pursuit and stark vengeance, and one day he would pounce. He was after me as well as after Jean Valjean. Was *I* somehow Jean Valjean? Had *I* committed some hidden theft for which I was bound to pay? Would Javert's black apparition hunt me down for reading the book he was in, with at his command a veritable arsenal of Hugo's horrors: toads, hangmen, monsters and waterspouts, witches and fork-tailed demons, and of course hunchbacks too? I knew from the book's Book One that Javert "had suffered some great interior commotion" and showed in his demeanor "the natural, cold rudeness of a man who was never kind, but has always been patient." He was all gloom, granite, and abasement. One wrong step, I knew, and *he* would turn into a hunchback. Some unspeakable malediction kept him back from human delight. He was not a hero or a jock. He was a force of the night, an ogre of the underworld, intent upon exposing the demons in everyone else because he knew the demon within himself was the worst one of all, yearning, I thought (I was a bookish kid), to be Milton's Satan, but reconciled to being what I now recognize as a bureaucratic bogeyman, whose dark raiment gathered up all the midnight black in the tunics of the British police, and whose corrupt pallor echoed the face of Hugo's Sister Simplice: "Her smile was white, her look was white. There was not a spider's web, not a speck of dust upon the glass of that conscience." She was loftily pure and he was basely so. I did not know then that the word *black* is the other etymological face of the word *white,* but my imagination assumed as much, and the more I read *Les Misérables* the more I came to think of Javert as someone poignantly gruesome, anglicizing him as I did into the mispronounced personification "Les Miserables," to be said aloud as if Les was short for Leslie and Miserables was his surname. He was the Les of the Miserables family, a man so awful in mind and feature that his very surname seemed fierce: an under-the-breath expletive, even a curse.

Fortunately the chair on which I balanced even as, through the years, my legs grew longer, never toppled over, and Javert never got me, not even to accompany him as a little drowner when he flung himself into the Seine, that chasm, that gulf, that gliding sewer. It was years before I reached the place at which, as a tall black form a passerby might have taken for a phantom, he fell straight into the darkness with "a dull splash; and the shadow alone was in the secret of the convulsions of that obscure form which had disappeared under the water." Exit a legal tiger, as Hugo says, blinded by a moral sun. Javert's going at once took him into the realm of the cat people, who growled around the edges of deserted indoor pools in rancid-smelling basements and sometimes, if you ventured downstairs, dragged you in and down.

It was a natural step from Javert to such other police figures of my childhood as the SS, in their white-collared way almost as prim-looking as Javert himself in his black, which was theirs too. It was beside the point that they were psychopathic dandies from hell, hoodlums made over into spic and span predators. After all, wasn't Jean Valjean a retread criminal, Javert a punishable extreme of virtue? Valjean too had a number, 24601, which now gives him an up-to-date echo in the aftermath of the camps, whether one has learned about them from the nine-hour film *Shoah,* by being mentally disemboweled in the most restrained way, or from Solzhenitsyn's full-length *Gulag Archipelago,* by being told that the Russian camps this century have wiped out some sixty million undesirables, roughly the population of Great Britain. This is an odd context for Victor Hugo, yet not altogether; he did after all write a whole book called *God;* and one of the main themes of *Les Misérables* is rehabilitation and redemption. Valjean's offenses—stealing bread and silver (as if all along he meant to compile a holy ritual)—are just as minor as the "offenses" for which millions were deported, tortured, and killed; and Valjean hidden away in Paris, through whose sewers he will carry Marius, is very much a figure on the run, a man proscribed. And Solzhenitsyn's vision is no more Dante-like than Hugo's, whose night-and-fog (*Nacht und Nebel* as the Nazis resonantly put it) includes human destiny seen in subterranean terms, with society become a vast mine. My little boy's brain had tapped the Zeitgeist, it seems, looking for grown-up things and discovering more than it had bargained for: ghouls amid their robot paroxysms, whether for crooked cross or hammer and sickle. The horrors *meant* for boys—outrageous mutants with horns growing out of their eyes and tongues hammered flat to serve as bibs—were there on the lower shelves, easily reached, just as easily put back. In Javert, the presumably forbidden image, I had found someone virginal, cold, idea-mad, a zealot who was a scourge, a totalitarian tool whose excuse, until the very end, was that he was only obeying the orders he gave himself. Not exactly a Klaus Barbie (Barbie seems to have had more fun in his loathsome way), but a sibling demon.

And now we have him back among us, impersonated on-stage by the jut-jawed Terrence Mann, the very image of the glacial, poised, finically rehearsed fanatic as whom we little boys in the darkest days of World War II had dressed up, pretending to be SS, in our whitest shirts, our darkest blue blazers, our shiniest leather belts, and cracking the toy whips with which we otherwise thrashed tops. I think we wanted to be on what seemed the winning side, but we were also flirting, obscenely, with the trappings of a power which "our side" seemed to have no access to, whether in their sloppy battledress of that same mustard-gas brown, or in quiet tunics of blue serge. Like Mr. Mann the other evening, power and the obsession that oils its exercise wore black with beleaguered-looking white trim. Looking at this latest Javert, I had my childhood all over again. I once more in a guilty fusion of the nineteenth and twentieth centuries saw the visage of those who were going to come and *get* us, and remembered that, in aping the Javert-SS mentality, we were planning to become our own executioners, as if the tracking down of victims had no more moral repercussion than playing with a toy train on its tiny track across the living-room floor.

I got other things too, most of all from John Napier's extraordinary set, in the main made up of two huge stacks of jetsam, one on either side of the stage, which at times come together like two mangled jetties mating, as if to portray the heedless profusion and wastefulness of the universe. Bedsteads, shutters, wheels, fences, barrels all end up on or in this field-gray heap lit by an acrid light. This is the stuff that millions have used and will outlive them, surely not that far a cry from the signal boxes and railroad switches photographed with such relentless attentiveness in *Shoa*—the station nameplate still reads "Treblinka," as if the few who cared in that accursed place were torn between the obscenity of the name's remaining and the obscenity of daring to profane it by removing it. There are no nameplates in the stacks of remnants in the musical made from *Les Misérables,* but the wasteland feeling is there all right, as if to remind us of Saul Bellow's dictum that without a wasteland there is no age of gold. I at once linked the matching dumps of debris with the wreckage left behind him by Javert, and I think I was meant to: at one point we see Javert perched on the conjoint stack of it, as if *riding* it, a warlock on the most disheveled broomstick ever seen. Is that why he got an extra burst of applause when he took his bow at the end? Were the spectators applauding their own bad dreams? I think so. He had provided the frisson, the scare, the little flicker of semi-pornographic aversion that accompanies the hand reaching for an atrocity book emblazoned with swastikas or the crooked-lightning insignia of the SS. He is purgative, emetic, but also a cousin, a double. This "monk and corporal" is the dynamo of the novel, and his resonance goes far beyond his ultimate self-disgust, not least because Jean Valjean is a bit of a bore, almost less exciting than Camus's hero Clamence, the Parisian attorney who in *La Chute (The Fall)* ceaselessly interrogates himself because he heard a woman drowning in the Seine and did not try to save her.

An "odd mixture of the Roman, the Spartan" (which accurately sums up the Javert of Charles Laughton, who was corseted and somehow tautened for the movie version), Javert is the Quasimodo—the merely sort-of-human creature—in *Les Misérables.* And, like Anthony Hopkins in the recent remake of *Notre-Dame de Paris,* Mr. Mann finds the indelible Laughton in his way, but survives by doing it à la Laughton. However he be acted, hunchfront Javert has a looming, residual awfulness, whose explanation may be found in Antonin Artaud's idea in *The Theater and Its Double* of "a fabricated Being, made of wood and cloth, entirely invented, corresponding to nothing, yet disquieting by nature, capable of reintroducing on the stage a little breath of . . . metaphysical fear." Javert is not a part to be played, but a gargoyle to be installed; an evil engine to be wound up; an insane sentry to be marched up to the human condition and never relieved. The worse you act him, the more commandingly hideous he becomes—the man whose addiction to the law takes him beyond the range of familiar obsessives, such as Ahab and King Lear even, into the twilight zone of the Eichmanns, the Barbies, the Mengeles, who all thought they were doing right. Mr. Mann, whose Kenneth Tynanish looks we last saw when he played Larry in the film *A Chorus Line,* acts out the part with antiseptic nature, as indeed of the role of debris in forming the barricade that dominates the musical's second half.

At one point Valjean smashes a chair down to its component staves, and we all of a sudden learn to build that set, that barricade, on which so many die to detonations of blanks. Only Valjean, carrying the unconscious Marius, survives: a bit too neat, a bit creaky, of course, but we are dealing here not with plausibility but with absolutes. Little Gavroche gets killed by a shot that seems to come from *beneath* the barricade. What unhinges Javert in the end is that he lets go the Valjean who has let him go: the perfect form of his ego, that *machine infernale* predicated on the letter of the law, cracks, and "normality" returns, as when the thousand-year Reich ends after a decade or so.

Yet ponder this also. Javert, for all his warts, has the unswerving zeal of the Nazi-hunter too, and that thought in its turn took me back to the old revenge dramas, in which the avenger stopped at nothing. We are supposed to learn, from those plays and *Les Misérables* and human history, that human beings fare better when they stop at something. Wind-up toys we are not, but frail subjective pawns with wanton will. When Javert at last goes down, he does so by virtue of a meshy backdrop's suddenly going up behind him, as if this were a variant of the old Einstein chestnut: "Does Princeton stop at this train?" The universe is withdrawn from him in one scenic instant both ravaging and utterly in accord with his own mechanistic instinct. I remembered the glass pane dividing humans from God in *Notre-Dame de Paris.* In this case the deity performed a prodigy of subtraction. It was not so much that Javert was no longer in the world as that it was no longer in him. Baudelaire and Flaubert despised this rather hamfisted novel; but, amid the prettily sung rather vapid lyrics tacked on to Hugo's plot, the fall and going of Javert, in which he neither fell nor budged, was a moment of pure Aeschylus.

Strange Attraction: Exaltation and Calculation in the Poetry of James Schuyler

James McCourt

A few almond trees
had a few flowers, like a few snowflakes
out of the blue looking pink in the light.
A gray hush
in which the boxy trucks roll up Second Avenue
into the sky. They're just
going over the hill.
The green leaves of the tulips on my desk
like grass light on flesh,
and a green-copper steeple
and streaks of cloud beginning to glow.
I can't get over
how it all works in together

      —from "February"

"Here, just for you, is a rose made out of a real rose . . ."
      —from "Fabergé"

Along with a theory he was building a methodology.
Ordinarily a computer user would construct a problem,
feed it in, and wait for the machine to calculate its solution—one problem, one solution. Feigenbaum . . .
needed more . . . needed . . . to create miniature uni-
verses and observe their evolution . . . change this
feature or that and observe the changed paths that would
result . . . armed with a new conviction, after all, that
tiny changes in certain features could lead to remarkable changes in overall character.
—James Gleick, *Chaos: Making a New Science* (1987)

". . . it's quite a story. Addison could make quite a thing
of it . . . and still write nothing but the truth."
   —Eve Harrington, in Joseph L. Mankiewicz's
      All about Eve (1950)

I RECENTLY CONFIDED to a young poet and doctor of literature, who has just secured an appointment on the faculty at Yale, that I was tied in a knot over how to begin writing about James Schuyler's *Selected Poems* (Farrar Straus Giroux). "He is the best," the young man said. "Do you really think so?" "Oh, yes. Every time I read 'Hymn to Life,' I burst out crying." "Well, will you tell them that—your students—when you get up to The Vatican?" "Of course—why not?"

Why not? Why not admit that when I read through this volume, read poems I've been reading for years, my desire is not to *say* or *write* anything at all: it is to go running screaming into the street. That says it all? I wish it could. Samuel Beckett said "all poetry, as discriminated from the various paradigms of prosody, is prayer." Virginia Woolf, writing about Henry James *(The Golden Bowl),* said he was "one of the few who attempt to picture people as they are. But again, though he is almost overscrupulous not to exaggerate, to see people as they are and the lives that they really lead, it is naturally through his own eyes that he sees them—eyes [that] we are led to think, must be provided with some extra fine lens, the number of things he sees is so extraordinary." (Readers who remember that this cunning tickle of VW's formed the lead-in to what was essentially a "significant form" pan of the gorgeous book, will perhaps also realize—if they are aware of how James Schuyler operates at all—that this same kind of seemingly respectful nod toward the great labors of evidentiary culling behind the poems is often used to form a point-coordinate parabola with which to whip-snap a summary "Who cares?" "So what?" back at them— the poems "about" Jane and Joe and Kenward and Doug and Frank and Fairfield and Darragh, and the other (long dead) Frank, and the very much alive and prized "dear John," etc., etc. Even the feinters with damned praise—poets mainly, of his generation, who liken this evolved master to some lark out on a tree limb somewhere in literary Nether Yaphank—go in for it: Schuyler, of course, is *lovely;* he could "read" the telephone book. But that's just *it:* he *does* "read" the telephone book; he "reads" the white *and* the yellow pages. So what? Who cares? I once dutifully, and gratefully, audited a pair of lectures on contemporary poetry given by Harold Bloom at the New School. In the corridor, during a chatty recessional, I asked one or two of his most obviously keen and brilliant students did they value the poetry of James Schuyler. "Who?")

The greatest poetry is not merely delightful; it is categorically utilitarian; it throws us its readers lifelines when we need them. My strong feeling is that at a certain point in life, you could die from not knowing the poetry of James Schuyler. Close reading of the dextrously tesselated verbal events of "The Crystal Lithium," "Hymn to Life," "The Morning of the Poem," and "A Few Days" (not this is like that is like those is like them—not "the noise"; rather they *are* this, that, those which, them; what, I you, us—the true Such: What's What) can, literally, save a reading life.

If I were teaching this poetry—analyzing its prosodic corpuscularity, instead of merely prescribing it, and using it myself for transfusions in a distressed, bi-polar mood-life (and, not so incidentally, as a source of practical historical and literary privity for my own work), I would probably begin by asking students to copy out two poems: the sestina after Dante, "I have reached, alas, the long shadow," and the next poem—a fractive sestina-collage called "An Almanac." Then I'd have them make a chart . . . you know the drill: you would most certainly find what I found. Plot the push-pull coordinates in the sestina's thirty-nine lines against the equivalents—mostly in the assonantal and interior echoes of the seventeen-line "Almanac." Do you hear in the pulse the presence of the strange attractor? Of course you do; it's a heartbeat, ready for combat.

An analogy from science, after a fragment from Wallace Stevens:

> And yet relation appears,
> A small relation expanding like the shade
> Of a cloud on sand, a shape on the side of a hill.
> —from "Connoisseur of Chaos"

He was studying attractors. The steady equilibrium reached by his mappings is a fixed point that attracts all others—no matter what the starting "population" it will bounce steadily in toward the attractor. Then with the first period doubling, the attractor splits in two, like a dividing cell. At first these two points are practically together; then as the parameter rises, they float apart. Then another period-doubling: each point on the attractor divides again at the same moment. Feigenbaum's number (4.6692016090) let him predict when the period doublings would occur. Now he discovered that he could also predict the precise values of each point on this ever-more complicated attractor—two points, four points, eight points. . . . (Gleick)

Compare the openings of, first, "The Crystal Lithium" and "Hymn to Life," then of "The Morning of the Poem" and "A Few Days":

The smell of snow, stinging in nostrils as the wind lifts it from a beach
Eye-shuttering, mixed with sand, or when snow lies under the street lamps and on all
And the air is emptied to an uplifting gassiness
That turns lungs to winter waterwings, buoying, and the bright white night
Freezes in sight a lapse of waves, balsamic, salty, unexpected:
Hours after swimming, sitting thinking biting at a hangnail
And the taste of the—to your eyes—invisible crystals irradiates the world
"The sea is salt"
"And so am I"

> The wind rests its cheek upon the ground and feels the cool damp
> And lifts its head with twigs and small dead blades of grass
> Pressed into it as you might at the beach rise up and brush away
> The sand. The day is cool and says, "I'm just staying overnight."
> The world is filled with music, and in between the music, silence
> And varying the silence all sorts of sounds, natural and man-made:

There goes a plane, some cars, geese that honk and, not here, but
Not so far away, a scream so rending that to hear it is to be
Never again the same. "What, this is hell." Out of the death breeding
Soil, here, rise emblems of innocence, snowdrops that struggle
Easily into life and hang their white enamel heads toward the dirt
And in the yellow grass are small wild crocuses from hills goats
Have cropped to barrenness.

    July 8 or July 9, the eighth surely, certainly
      1976 that I know
    Awakening in western New York blurred barely
      morning sopping dawn
    Globules face to my face, a beautiful face, not
      mine: Baudelaire's skull:
    Force, fate, will, and, you being you: a
      painter, you drink
    Your Ovaltine, and climb to the city roof, "to
      find a view," and
    I being whoever I am get out of bed holding
      my cock and go to piss
    Then to the kitchen to make coffee and toast
      with jam and see out
    The window two blue jays ripping something white
      while from my mother's
    Room the radio purls: it plays all night she leaves
      it on to hear
    The midnight news then sleeps and dozes
      until the day which now it is,
    Wakening today in green more gray, why did
      your lithe blondness
    In Remsen handsomness mix in my mind with
      Baudelaire's skull? which
    Stands for strength and fierceness, the dedication
      of the artist?

[A Few Days]
are all we have. So count them as they pass. They pass
  too quickly
out of breath: don't dwell on the grave, which yawns for
  one and all.
Will you be buried in the yard? Sorry, it's against
  the law. You can only
lie in an authorized plot but you won't be there to
  know it so why worry
about it? Here I am at my brother's house in western
  New York: I came
here yesterday on the Empire State Express, eight hours
  of boredom on the train
A pretty blond child sat next to me for a while. She

had a winning smile,
but I couldn't talk to her, beyond "What happened to
  your shoes?" "I put them under the seat." And
so she had. She pressed the button that released the
  seat and sank
back like an old woman. Outside, purple loosestrife
  bloomed in swathes
that turned the railway ditch and fields into a
  sunset-reflecting lake
And there was goldenrod and tattered Queen Anne's Lace
  and the noble Hudson
on which just one sailboat sailed, billowing, on a weekday
  afternoon.

The design of the line, or phrase of a line, or of one stanza, is the design of the poem, is the design of the collection—self-similarity throughout. ("Turns-in-on-itself" the nervous comment goes, from those whom prayer enrages.) Using the four elements earth, air, fire, water for the imagery, and the two forces gravity and levity to negotiate among them, gives the first two of the four dimensions, linearity and stature (extent and height). The "weak" force and the "strong" force, in argument (stress count/vocalic value = prosody) render the third and fourth dimensions, depth (inscape) and time. The formation will be that of the coordinates flung out from a spinal (idea) stem, forming the pattern of a leaf. As in each leaf the branch and so the tree is figured (probably the origin of the practice of awarding laurels to accomplished composer-singers), the leaf is the stanza, the branch the poem, the tree the Work.

The smell of snow, stinging in nostrils as the wind lifts it from a beach
The smell of snow (water)
stinging (fire)
beach (earth)
snow/beach = gravity
wind/sting = levity (inhalation:dream)
from gravity to levity = the lift-off of the poem.

The wind rests its cheek upon the ground and feels the cool damp
damp
wind
rests its cheek (abrasion:fire)
ground
cool damp
Proceed as above . . .

Awakening in western New York = (geography: earth) (gravity)
sopping dawn (water/fire) (toward levity:evaporation)

Globules (water) (gravity)
beautiful face = dream (air) (toward levity:idea)

A Few Days (concept: idea: levity)
are all we have. So count them as they pass They pass too quickly
too quickly (burned up: fire) (levity in process) (flowing fast: water:
    levity pulled back by gravity)
out of breath, don't dwell on the grave, which yawns for one and all
= desperate (despite the order "don't," the reader does) reach toward
    levity
grave (earth) (gravity)
yawns (gasping: air: attempted levity . . .)
Proceed, doubling, doubling back.

I merely wish to indicate by means of this analogical grid-play what I take
to be the obvious. It has been said, kindly, by poets, that James Schuyler
has succeeded in making the lyric dramatic. What I would insist is that he
has subsumed the lyric and the dramatic in the epic: Euterpe, Melpomene
and Thalia are the backup trio in the pageant that only Calliope, in all her
majesty, can lead. What sort of epic? Not of arms and the man; rather of the
man in his arms—although, as in "Dream lover put your arms around you,"
as in Samuel Beckett (writing about Marcel Proust), "Writing is the
apotheosis of solitude," that means merely and always the epic of the Self
accounting for itself—"Here!"

Along the way, Self, everyone you ever knew, or read about or thought of,
or willed killed, or thought up out of the entropic, chaotic, pleonastic,
capably-negative, southpaw pis-aller of ideation and recourse. All that
heaven allows; all it thinks is just not nice. Make a wish upon a strange
attractor; hitch-hike; take the consequences; write when you find work.

Of course I find the actual life this poet has led greatly heroic; of course I
do. Of course, that isn't the point—not even a little? No? Yes, and no. The
point is the work—the rose made out of the rose? Yes. Yes, and yes.

The time, the place, the matter, the investigation. From World War II
("we won the war!") to the present ("Oh?") in New York and its satellite
Edens (those little places just two, three, four hours . . .). The one life we
have to live. Meticulous, seeming-offhand: a kind of dowsing; uncanny
receipts for recall and reiteration carried about in a memorized breviary of
"influences," from—but *no, not that!* It is an epic of a life that came into its
maturity at the exact moment when the city assumed its capital-of-the-
planet status—the period of Abstract Expressionism, of Balanchine and the
first generation of NYCB divinities, of Martha Graham (culminating in
Agon), of first-run film noir, of Great Evenings in The Theater, of the
postwar explosion of Free Love (especially this last, in a headlong-hellbent
era when to do for it was not, necessarily, to die for it). It is a great pilgrim's
progress: the out-of-town apple-knocker postulant ("You look interesting.

Here's a copy of my new little magazine, *Upstate*"), the navy veteran, the big bad boy, erratic and brilliant from the first—stretched on the spokes of the wheel of life, like in the lyric from Billy Strayhorn's "Lush Life"; wondering half out loud whether James Joyce was any good (and why not?). Looking, looking, listening, listening. Attending the New York first night of *The Cocktail Party* with Auden ("The World and its mother were there"). Sprung for a season, off to Italy: Naples, Ischia, big-time (Visconti) theater. Shakespeare in Italian ("*Tutto il mondo e un palco scenico...*"). Then back; working at MOMA. Found out, labeled as founding coconspirator of "The New York School." Embraced, ensnared (he might have agreed with Dorothy Parker: "I've always said, that's the way I am; take me or leave me, or as in the usual order, both"). (And as he himself says of Cole Porter, as sung by Ethel Waters, "and I / May be misquoting.") Published, noticed; considered disturbing, disturbed. Netted, sequestered, enduring, and, though it's something you won't find trumpeted in the work, beloved. The great friendship with a great American painter, with poets, with . . .

I want to close what I've opened only the least crack with a glance at "Buried at Springs," the poem in memory of Frank O'Hara, dead twenty-two years last summer—the period in which Schuyler has published the four poems that have brought him to greatness. O'Hara will be remembered as a poet of stunning and stinging brilliance, I believe, and Schuyler, as I have said, is, to my mind, immortal. Reading "Buried at Springs" is not a lesson, nor is it not not:

> There is a hornet in the room
> and one of us will have to go
> out the window into the late
> August mid-afternoon sun. I
> won.
>
> . . . .
>
> The rapid running of the
> lapping water a hollow knock
> of someone shipping oars:
> it's eleven years since
> Frank sat at this desk and
> saw and heard it all.

Ezra Pound said, didn't he, that it was necessary that masterpieces be written; it was of no great importance by whom. The hornet is gone out into the empyrean; the desk—"this," not "his"—belongs to whoever hears the water, who still withstands the shock of the hollow knock—which is the heartbeat, saying again and again "not yet," and after and after, "I won." The poet contemplates his dead poet friend's absent shape, something quite like mind-caressing the archaic torso of an (American) Apollo, and says, day-in, day-out, as was suggested by that even earlier prayer-poet, "Why not change your life?"

Reactionary

Thomas McGonigle

THIS IS AN AUTOBIOGRAPHICAL essay written a year after the publication of my first hardcover novel, an essay composed of my own words, overheard remarks and clippings saved up, a partial description of the world through which I move as a writer.

*

The traditional rebuke to the writer: no one asked you to be a writer.

*

"Ten years is too long to spend on a book that will live less than one." Wilfrid Sheed.

*

Albert Jay Nock has argued that before the age of so-called literacy there were higher standards of literature . . . simply because publishers did not have to pander . . . that the best bookstore he encountered in Europe in the 1930s was in Lisbon and at that time Portugal had probably the lowest level of literacy in all of Europe. (Go in to the Dalton's in Indianapolis, for instance, as I have done, and I would swear that you would not find midst the thousands of books fifteen of literary merit, and all of *them* would be reprints.) Those who read knew how to read. They were not processors of books, as is the case with the masses today who forget the book before they have probably finished processing it. They know they have read a book when they have hit the last page; they are ready for the next bit of name-brand product. And it is an iron law: the mediocre drives out the good.

*

"In terms of the entertainment media, publishing is nothing more than a wart on the eyeball of a fly." Ron Busch, a now-dead executive in publishing.

*

Or so they say and have said for as long as . . .

*

If you counted up on your fingers the number of real literary bookstores in the United States, you would have fingers to spare.

*

"It is a bit much to expect an editor to read." William Cole, former editor and anthologist, 18 August 1987.

*

In two recent issues of the *Michigan Quarterly Review,* forty-nine writers were asked to comment on the state of literature in the United States. In passing, they mentioned as significant 255 writers, and in my rough survey the most frequently mentioned authors were, in descending order: Raymond Carver, Russell Banks, Louise Erdrich, Don DeLillo, Philip Roth, Richard Ford, John Gardner. I really can't go on listing. These forty-nine writers failed to mention: Paul Bowles, William Burroughs, Jack Kerouac, Hubert Selby, Charles Bukowski. . . .

Of course one can talk about the abundance of talent, the richness of the literature, the diversity, how lucky we all are, and still there is the nagging feeling—this is not a very good time and it seems at least to me that George Saintsbury hit the proverbial nail on the head when writing at the end of the nineteenth century about the literature that he was surrounded with at that moment:

Cacophony jostles preciousness in novel and newspaper; attempts at contorted epigram appear side by side with slips showing that the writer has not the slightest knowledge of the classics in the old sense, and knows exceedingly little of anything that can be called classic in the widest possible acceptation of the term. Tyrannies cease when the cobblers begin to fear them; fashions, especially literary fashions, when the cobblers take them up.

Yet the production of what must or may be called literature is now so large, and in consequence of the spread of what is called education the appetite so largely exceeds the taste for it, that it is not so easy as it would once have been to forecast the extent and validity of any reaction that may take place.

If, without undue praising of times past, without pleading guilty to the prejudices sometimes attributed to an academic education, and also without trespassing beyond the proper limits of this book, it may be permitted to express an opinion on the present state of English literature, that opinion, while it need not be very gloomy, can hardly be very sanguine. And one ground for discouragement, which very especially concerns us, lies in the fact that on the whole we are now *too* "literary." Not, as has been said, that the general taste is too refined, but that there is a too indiscriminate appetite in the general; not that the actual original force of our writers is, with rare exceptions, at all alarming, but that a certain amount of literary crafts-manship, a certain knowledge of the past and present of literature, is with us in a rather inconvenient degree. The public demands quantity, not quality; and it is ready, for a time at any rate, to pay for its quantity with almost unheard of returns, both, as the homely old phrase goes, in praise and in pudding. And the writer, though seldom hampered by too exact an education in form, has had books, as a rule, too much with him. Sometimes he simply copies, and knows that he copies; oftener, without knowing it, he follows and imitates, while he thinks that he is doing original work.

*

Recently, Beloit College announced that a million-dollar endowed chair in creative writing was being established. The race was on to find the writer, and it was still on a year later. It couldn't be just any writer: the writer had to be a crowd pleaser for the students; the writer had to get along with the president of the college whose major field of interest is political science; the writer had to be able to sit down and have a successful dinner with the man who was putting up the million dollars in honor of his wife's memory; the writer had to be willing to be used for publicity purposes by the college; the writer had to be willing to come to give a sort of audition lecture to the assembled college "community"; the writer had to be "world class."

*

I have problems with the phrase "trash novel," not because I admire what's between the covers of such a book but because I think the term is demeaning to the person who reads it. The line between reading for entertainment—whether it's the latest John Updike, the latest Jackie Collins, or this month's Harlequin Romance—and watching a movie on videotape can be difficult to draw. They are both forms of entertainment. And those so-called trash novels pay the rent and provide the capital that allows us to carry other titles. I hate to belittle the customer who chooses to buy these books. Each bookseller must try to analyze what his or her customers want.

William P. Edwards, Vice President of B. Dalton

*

One day in Sofia I was telling Ivialo, a younger Bulgarian writer with two collections of stories published, that there are a number of American writers who envy writers in Eastern Europe because even though there is the problem of severe censorship, at least your writing gets read for the form and content whereas in the United States a writer's work is read in terms of the bottom line and that final approval in all too many cases lies with the sales force or the editor's idea of what it is possible to sell to the sales force. Ivialo smiled and said when his first book of stories was coming out, the publishing house asked him to write a description of the book that would be put in the catalog to circulate to the managers of the bookstores across Bulgaria and that he was to make sure he mentioned that there was a lot of sexuality in the book. Ivialo said he told the editor there was very little sex in the book and his editor replied that he had to write that there was a lot of sexuality in the book when describing it because if he didn't the managers wouldn't stock the book and anyway that is the only thing they care about, the description in the catalog and . . .

*

It has been suggested that almost 80 percent of America's *literate,* educated teen-agers can no longer read without an attendant noise (music) in the background or a television screen flickering at the corner of their field of perception. We know very little about the cortex and how it deals with simultaneous conflicting input, but every common-sense hunch suggests we should be profoundly alarmed.

George Steiner

*

Of course those difficult, demanding long books still get written and sometimes even get published.

*

People tell the writer to get an agent, while the agent replies, I got to eat. A book like yours, the agent will say, just ain't worth my time. I got to eat. It's a matter of eating. You can't eat the ten percent of nothing I could get for a book like yours.

*

High art is meant for rare festivals, where anticipation is followed by exhilaration and the aftermath is meditation and recollection in tranquillity. The glut has made us into gluttons, who gorge and do not digest.

Such a condition disables one for judging new art. The eager or dutiful persons who subject themselves to these tidal waves of the classics and the moderns find everything wonderful in an absent-minded way. The wonder washes over them rather than into them, and one of its effects is to make anything shocking or odd suddenly "interesting." *Interesting* is the word you will most often hear from devotees of the arts when faced with new tricks cleverly contrived. And so another byproduct of our come one, come all policy is the tendency to reward cleverness, not art, and to put one more hurdle in the path of the truly original artist.

Jacques Barzun

*

We are eager for something to happen. No one likes to think they live in an uninteresting time. The same goes for editors and reviewers. Newspapers and magazines have to come out every day, every week, every month. You've got to deal with what's at hand. And how many times have you heard: why are you so negative, why can't you be positive? We know what you're saying. We don't publish masterpieces every week, every month, every year. No one is going to pay us for publishing blank pages where those masterpieces are supposed to be.

*

"I am thoroughly convinced that our literature would become quite respectable if half our people, at the very least, were illiterate; I should put it, in fact, at three-quarters." Albert Jay Nock.

*

And there is now a great incentive to be positive. Someday the author of a book you told the truth about might be on a panel giving out money, might be at a college where it might be nice to work, might even be at a publishing house. The world of writing is so small. Nothing is forgotten, nothing is learned. Maybe things were better when there were personally wealthy and powerful individual patrons. A writer had to write a fawning page or two at the front of the book and then get on with what he had to do. Now you keep your mouth shut, the pen on hold because you never know . . .

*

You might say: People are in distress the world over, writing will not relieve them (or make them worse off). Why not take the money there is for a magazine like this and give it away—as food—to the bums, for instance, living in packing cases over near the East River these winter nights?

But what makes you think money has any value? there's food enough rotting now in the world, even within sight of the place where these men are hanging out, to feed them every day in the year. Money has nothing to do with it. Bad writing has though: it's the same sort of stupidity.

William Carlos Williams

*

And would I be writing this if my recent novel had sold thousands of copies, if it had been picked up by the book clubs, sold into foreign editions, made into a movie? Glad you asked.

*

"They had obviously forgotten that every first-rate novelist writes a 'new' kind of novel." Leon S. Roudiez.

*

A year or so ago my novel, *The Corpse Dream of N. Petkov,* was published by the Dalkey Archive Press. There were five reviews including a favorable half-page in the *New York Times;* also two further factual mentions of it, and two talks were devoted to the book on the Bulgarian service of Radio Free Europe.

I have had a person whom I had not seen since 1965 get in touch with me after she saw the book at a fair in Miami. There have been no further surprises. The Bulgarian authorities, if they know of the book since it dealt with a still-sensitive moment in recent Bulgarian history, have not responded. A Bulgarian émigré doctor in New York bought three copies of the book to give to friends.

The book is in a certain number of libraries in this country and as far as I know in no foreign libraries. I was invited to read from the book by four colleges and art centers in the middle part of the country as a result of the publication of the book or, as is more likely, as a result of the publication of the review in the *New York Times.* I was invited to join PEN.

I plan, in my head, to send a packet of these reviews to paperback editors but a feeling of futility overwhelms me and nothing comes of it. A friend who is also an agent, but doesn't really represent books like mine, says he will see what he can do, but realistically—everyone in New York publishing is happy for the appearance of the book and they are all glad they didn't have to publish it.

And while I knew this was pretty much what would come to pass and am not disappointed, I am enough of a creature of this city, New York, to day-dream: what if . . . and the dream provides the run of the mill tawdry ache of the hunger for recognition unfulfilled but then there was the shadow: if I didn't want this to come to pass, why choose to write a novel about the last twelve or so minutes in the life of a Bulgarian political figure who was hanged in 1947?

I had talked about rescuing Petkov from forgetfulness but now he and a novel about him are . . .

I go on, resisting imperfectly my cup of bitterness . . .

Some days I am consumed with disgust at the acclaim certain trash writers are given for their celebrations of fashionable killers.

Some days, in Edward Dahlberg's phrase, all the well-known bad writers are out there, metaphorically, on the street peddling their books, and it is as if they alone constituted the world . . .

I take consolation in the ability of my Guardian Angel to shrug my shoulders.

*

It is idle to talk about preventing the wreck of Western civilization. It is already a wreck from within. That is why we can hope to do little more now than snatch a fingernail of a saint from the rack or a handful of ashes from the faggots, and bury them secretly in a flowerpot against the day, ages hence, when a few men begin again to dare to believe that there was once something else, that something else is thinkable, and need some evidence of what it was and the fortifying knowledge that there were those who, at the great nightfall, took loving thought to preserve the tokens of hope and truth.

Whittaker Chambers

*

I finished writing this essay on 4 February 1988.

Felipe Alfau's Locos

Mary McCarthy

FIFTY-TWO YEARS AGO, on June 27, 1936, I reviewed a book in the *Nation.* Very favorably. The author, Felipe Alfau, was said to be a young Spaniard writing in English. Spain was Republican then; the Franco revolt that turned into the Spanish Civil War began on July 19, three weeks and a day later. The charm exercised on me by *Locos,* therefore, cannot have been a matter of politics. And I was ignorant of Spain and Spanish. It was more like love. I was enamored of that book and never forgot it, though my memory of it, I now perceive on rereading, is somewhat distorted, as of an excited young love affair. Alfau, or his book, was evidently my fatal type, which I would meet again in Vladimir Nabokov's *Pale Fire* and more than once in Italo Calvino. But *Locos* was the first. And it appears to have been the author's unique book, fittingly, as it were. I never heard of Alfau again, though for a time I used to ask about him whenever I met a Spaniard; not one knew his name. Maybe that was because he lived in the United States, if indeed he did. But in this country I never found anyone besides me who had read *Locos.* Now the book is being reissued. Launched more than fifty years ago by a Farrar and Rinehart club of so-called "Discoverers," it has been rediscovered, by what means I don't know.

To come back to it has been a bit eerie, at least on first sight—a cross between recognition and non-recognition. For example, what has stuck in my memory is a lengthy account of a police convention in Madrid that coincided merrily with a crime wave, the one giving rise to the other: crooks converged on the city, free to practice their trade while the police attended panel discussions and lectures on criminality. Well, it would be too much to say that none of that is in *Locos;* it *is* there but in the space of a few sentences and as a mere suggestion.

The fifth chapter, "The Wallet," begins: "During the 19— police convention at Madrid, a very unfortunate occurrence took place. Something went wrong with the lighting system of the city and the whole metropolis was left in complete darkness." It is the power failure that offers the assembled criminals their opportunity. "It was a most deplorable thing, for it coincided with the undesirable immigration of a regular herd of international crooks who since the beginning of the World War had migrated into Spain and now cooperated with resident crooks in a most energetic manner. . . . As if all these people had been waiting for that rare opportunity,

145

the moment the lights went out in Madrid, thieves, gunmen, holdup men, pickpockets, in short all the members of the outlaw family, sprang up in every corner as though by enchantment." Then: ". . . it came to pass that during the Police Convention of 19—, Madrid had a criminal convention as well. Of course, the police were bestowing all their efforts and time upon discussing matters of regulation, discipline and now and then how to improve the method of hunting criminals . . . and naturally, after each session . . . had neither time nor energy to put a check to the outrages. . . . Therefore all crooks felt safer and freer to perform their duty in Madrid, where the cream of the police were gathered, than anywhere else."

That is all, a preamble. The body of the chapter has to do with the stolen wallet of the Prefect of Police. The power failure, which provides a realistic explanation, had slipped my memory, and I was left with the delightful illogic—or logic—of parallel conventions of police and criminals. The purest Alfau, a distillate.

"The Wallet," actually, may be the center of the book, whose subject is Spain regarded as an absurdity, a compound of beggars, pimps, policemen, nuns, thieves, priests, murderers, confidence artists. The title, meaning "The Crazies," refers to a Café de los Locos in Toledo, where in the first chapter virtually all the principal characters are introduced as habitués suited to be "characters" for the bad fiction writers who, like the author, drop in to observe them. There are Dr. de los Rios, the medical attendant of most of the human wreckage washed up at those tables; Gaston Bejarano, a pimp known as El Cogote; Don Laureano Baez, a well-to-do professional beggar; his maid/daughter Lunarito, Sister Carmela, who is the same as Carmen, a runaway nun; Garcia, a poet who becomes a fingerprint expert; Padre Inocencio, a Salesian monk; Don Benito, the Prefect of Police; Felipe Alfau; Don Gil Bejarano, a junk dealer, uncle of El Cogote; Pepe Bejarano, a good-looking young man, brother of El Cogote; Doña Micaela Valverde, a triple widow and necrophile.

Only missing is the highly significant Señor Olózaga, at one time known as the Black Mandarin, a giant, former galley slave, baptized and brought up by Spanish monks in China, former butterfly charmer in a circus, former potentate in the Spanish Philippines, now running a bizarre agency for the collection of delinquent debts and another for buying and selling dead people's clothes. But he is connected with the other "characters" of the Café de los Locos both in his own right and by marriage to Tía Mariquita, his fifth wife, who lives in a house that coughs—their secretary, mistaken for her husband, is murdered by Don Laureano Baez and his daughter/maid Lunarito—one of many cases of mistaken identity. As the Black Mandarin in the Philippines, he has sought the hand of the blue-eyed daughter of Don Esteban Bejarano y Ulloa, a Spanish official, and been rejected because of his color. This, precisely, was the father of Don Gil Bejarano (see above), the brother-in-law of the Prefect of Police and inventor of a theory of fingerprints, which pops up in Chapter 4, where, incidentally, we find Padre Inocencio playing cards with the Bejarano family while the young daughter, Carmen, is having sex with her brother Gaston.

Such underground—or underworld—links are characteristic and combine with the rather giddy mutability displayed by the characters. Lunarito is Carmen, who is going to be Sister Carmela; at one point we find her married to El Cogote, none other than her brother Gaston, who cannot, of course, *be* her brother if she is the daughter of the beggar, Don Laureano Baez. And yet Don Laureano's wife, when we are introduced to him as the bartender of the Café de los Locos, is Felisa, which is the name of Carmen's mother, the sister of Don Benito, the Prefect of Police. . . . In the Prologue, and occasionally thereafter, the author makes a great point of the uncontrollability of his characters, but this familiar notion (as in "Falstaff got away from Shakespeare") is the least interesting feature. The changing and interchanging of the people, resembling "shot" silk, has no need of the whimsy of a loss of auctorial control. If any aspect of the book has aged, it is this whimsicality.

It is not only the characters of *Locos* that have that queer shimmer or iridescence. Place and time are subject to it as well. A fact I think I missed back in 1936 is the discrepancy between the location of the Café de los Locos—Toledo—where the "characters" are gathered for inspection, and their actual residence—Madrid. What are these Madrileños doing in Toledo? I suppose it must be because of the reputation of Toledo as a mad, fantastic city, a myth, a city, as Alfau says, that "died in the Renaissance"; he speaks of "Toledo on its hill . . . like a petrified forest of centuries." The city that died in the Renaissance and lives on, petrified, can of course figure as an image of Spain. One more quotation may be relevant to the underlying theme of impersonation as a national trait: "the action of this book develops mainly in Spain, a land in which not the thought nor the word, but the action with a meaning—the gesture—has grown into a national specialty. . . ."

Spain and its former possessions—Cuba and the Philippines—constitute the scene; their obverse is China, for a Spaniard the other end of the world, and here the provenance of Señor Olózaga, baptized "Juan Chinelato" by the bearded, tobacco-smoking monks who raised him.

One thing that certainly escaped me as a young reviewer is the hidden presence of this "Juan Chinelato" in the first chapter, the one called "Identity" and laid in the Café of the Crazies. He is there in the form of a little Chinese figure made of porcelain being hawked by Don Gil Bejarano in his character of junk dealer. "Don Gil approached us," writes Alfau. " 'Here is a real bargain,' he said, tossing the porcelain figure on the palm of his hand. 'It is a real old work of art made in China. What do you say?' I looked at the figure which was delicately made. It represented a herculean warrior with drooping mustache and a ferocious expression. He had a butterfly on his shoulder. The color of the face was not yellow but a darker color, more like bronze. . . . 'Perhaps it is not Chinese but Indian.' Don Gil . . . looked slightly annoyed. 'No, it is Chinese,' he said." And he continues to praise it: " 'Yes, this is a real Chinese mandarin or warrior, I don't know which, and it is a real bargain.' " A minute later, thanks to an inadvertent movement, the figure is smashed to pieces on the marble-topped café table.

This is a beautifully constructed book and full of surprises. Another example: one does not notice in this opening chapter the unusually small hand of Don Gil, seen only as a mark on a whitewashed wall. The lightly dropped hint is picked up unobtrusively like a palmed coin several chapters later when Don Gil is being arrested at the reluctant order of his brother-in-law because his fingerprints have been found all over the scene of a crime: "Don Gil had very small hands . . . and the handcuffs did not fit securely enough. . . . 'Officer, those handcuffs are too big for me. You had better get a rope or something.' " In his conversations with the Prefect, he has kept working "the man from China," that is, the man who has the perfect alibi but is tracked down by science through the prints his hands have left. His last article, published in a Madrid newspaper on the day of his apprehension, is entitled "Fingerprints, a sure antidote against all alibis," and his last words, which he keeps reiterating as he is carried off in the police wagon, are "I am the man from China. . . . Fingerprints never fail."

Perhaps police work and criminality, just as much as mad, fantastic Spain, are the subject of *Locos*. And considerable detection is required on the reader's part, to be repaid, as in the hunt for "Wanted" lawbreakers, with a handsome reward. For instance, among the clues planted to the mute presence of Señor Olózaga in the Café of the Crazies there is simply the word "butterfly"; I failed to catch the signal until the third reading. And I still have a lot of sleuthing to do on Carmen-Carmela-Lunarito and the beauty spot on Lunarito's body that she charges a fee to show. A knowledge of Spanish might help. In the Spanish light, each figure is dogged by a shadow, like a spy or tailing detective, though sometimes the long shadow is ahead: "She stood at the end of her own shadow against the far diffused light of the corner lamp post and there was something ominous in that." It may be that this is the link between the theme of Spain and the theme of the criminal with his attendant policeman. In some moods *Locos* could be classed as "luminist" fiction. But I must leave some work (which translates into pleasure) for the reader.

If *Locos* is, or was, my fatal type, what I fell in love with, all unknowing, was the modernist novel as detective story. There is detective work, surely, supplied by Nabokov for the reader of *Pale Fire*. I mentioned Calvino, too, but there is another, quite recent example, which I nearly overlooked. *The Name of the Rose*, of course. It is not only a detective story in itself but it also contains an allusion to Sherlock Holmes and *The Hound of the Baskervilles*. But in *Locos* Sherlock Holmes is already present: while in England Pepe Bejarano pretends to have studied under him, which explains his uncanny ability to recover his uncle, the Prefect's, wallet. The grateful police officer, who does not know whether Conan Doyle's creation is a real person or not, wants to express his thanks. " 'Yes, Pepe, yes. I should like to write an official letter to that gentleman, to that great man—Cherlomsky, is that the name?' "

Yes, there is a family resemblance to Nabokov, to Calvino, to Eco. And perhaps, though I cannot vouch for it, to Borges, too.

Editor's Note: This essay will appear as the Afterword to Locos, *to be published by the Dalkey Archive Press in the fall of 1988.*

Book Reviews

Harry Mathews. *Cigarettes.* Weidenfeld & Nicolson, 1988. $17.95.

It is easy to dismiss this book as a wonderfully funny picture of the contemporary art world, but we must be carefully alert to Mathews's philosophical structures. *Cigarettes* is—to put it bluntly—a major exploration of our deepest longings. It is a complex work—one which will remain in our minds for decades.

Mathews uses as an epigraph the following conversation from Wilde's "The Devoted Friend":

"Let me tell you a story on the subject," said the Linnet.
"Is this story about me?" asked the Water-rat. "If so, I will listen to it, for I am extremely fond of fiction."

The epigraph is odd. It stresses the meaning of "me," "fiction," "subject."

Mathews recognizes that perception is at the heart of the matter; he offers us a work which is deeply devoted to the significance of words. Can we understand love, friendship, theological designs? Can we "live" in a world which is a "fiction," a structure we assume is real life?

Mathews offers us an elaborate, tangled structure. His characters move in and out of one time—the novel is, among other things, about the nature of time —and appear at perversely strange moments. The characters "know" their friends—Wilde's "devoted friend" is in question—but at the same time they realize that their knowledge is limited, obscure, incomplete. There is, indeed, no full knowledge; there is *speculation.* Thus the elaborate design of the novel is playful; the structure hides holes. We must read between the lines to begin an explanation of the structure, a structure which is an "anti-structure" or, better yet, a series of disturbing obscurities.

The "center" of the novel is a portrait of Elizabeth. The portrait is in everyone's mind; it is desperately desired. But the portrait—an art-structure—is not the real Elizabeth. The "real" Elizabeth is, of course, different from the painted Elizabeth; she is, however, a mysterious character who cannot stand still. She is always moving; she tempts us to say that she doesn't *exist.*

The characters, including Elizabeth, want possession. Do they want the person and/or the portrait? They don't know because their perceptions change. They are, indeed, at times unsure about possession. The novel is thus also a meditation on "presence" and "exile," on the "whole" and the "hole." It is a "holy" scripture.

Every page offers the imagery of secrecy, misunderstanding, mutability, although we don't *see* it at first. I quote representative sentences: "In imagined time his course approached infinity, and during it he met other figures less palpable and more real. . . . He recognized truth as both absolute and incommunable, time itself as irreversible and irrelevant." One character "took an eyeliner pencil and with a grunt of satisfaction drew blue whiskers across

Elizabeth's [the portrait] ivory-gold cheeks." Elsewhere: "He shyly glanced at others near him: veterans of one summer afternoon, each encased in his mind, each accumulating incongruities, pains, shames, even signs of happiness, to conceal that uncanny light—their masks, their lives." Elsewhere: "If we admit that Nature works upon the mind, war is a question of mind."

We want a "full explanation"—to use Mathews's phrase—and we search for clues. We look at imagery, characters, time frames. We, in fact, act like the characters in the novel. We, however, know that we are "real," not "fictional." But are we? Perhaps we are in some disturbing work—the world?—and do not see it. We "float" mysteriously.

In the last chapter there is a "surprise." I will not give it away, but I think it undermines the underground of the novel and compels us to reread it, to change our previous reading. We have looked at the "words" in one way; we now have to look at them in another way.

Cigarettes is, therefore, a changing novel; it cannot be possessed. (It resembles the portrait.) It is about explanation, interpretation, design. It playfully (seriously) "explains itself," but it questions its own existence. It somehow appears and disappears, forcing us to say that it *is*. But, of course, even that explanation is open. [Irving Malin]

*

Natalia Ginzburg. *All Our Yesterdays.* Trans. Angus Davidson. Seaver Books, 1986. Paper: $8.95; *Valentino and Sagittarius.* Trans. Avril Bardoni. Seaver Books, 1988. $17.95.

At long last, America has discovered the fiction of Natalia Ginzburg, a deft, enigmatic writer whose work has been savored by Italian and British readers for years. If you like Chekhov, you'll love Ginzburg, for, like the Russian story-teller whose work she deeply admired, she has the same downshifted narrative poise, the same gift for understated but piquant irony. Critics have sometimes mistaken her unaffected style for fake naiveté, but it is a willed, purposeful naiveté that rises from the survivor's bloodless struggle against bitterness.

In her third novel, *All Our Yesterdays,* first published in Italy in 1952, Ginzburg assumes her favorite role as family archivist to narrate the parallel lives of two Italian families during the years 1939-44. Graying down the backdrop of intensifying Fascist oppression, she sharpens her focus on the quirky, vibrant central characters. There is never any danger of confusing characters in Ginzburg's fiction, for she attaches a clear characterizing emblem to each one. Thus, the presence of the shy but tenacious narrator Anna is repeatedly suggested by the image of a tiny insect stubbornly clinging to the leaf, while the gentle laughter of her friend Emanuele always evokes the muffled sobbing of doves. For before Ginzburg was a novelist, she was a poet, and her ease with the figurative image assures our engagement and belief.

In the disarmingly candid preface to Ginzburg's latest novel, *The City and the House,* she reflects on the fragmentation of modern life. She is convinced that the suicide of her friend Cesare Pavese was a result of his impatience with the quotidian, his failure to outwait and decode its secrets. This triumph over the imperious tedium of daily reality also eludes the main characters in her two early novellas, *Valentino* (1951) and *Sagittarius* (1957).

Both stories recount the decline of family lives, embodied in their slowly dissolving dreams. In *Valentino,* the patient hopes of self-sacrificing parents and sisters are fixed on a handsome but childlike son, whom the father believed "would become a great man." More compelled by mirror-gazing than the discipline of medical study, Valentino makes a disastrous marriage and ends up shuffling aimlessly about the apartment of his sister, whose suppressed rage has anesthetized her into baffled submission: "So there is no one to whom I can speak the words that most need to be spoken . . . and there are times when they threaten to choke me." Valentino's narcissism finds a counterpart in the vain widow of *Sagittarius* who dreams of opening up an art gallery to which the city's smart set will flock. But when her prospective partner drugs her and leaves with her life savings, she too is left with a bewildered sense of loss.

Because both translators have used their powers of restraint in preserving Ginzburg's plain vocabulary and hauntingly spare sentences, their texts are reliable equivalents of the Italian original. Ginzburg's style is modest and detached—like forlorn shadows from Dante's *Purgatory,* her characters pause and pass. But they leave indelible prints on our sensibilities. [Rita Signorelli-Pappas]

*

G. Cabrera Infante. *Holy Smoke.* Harper and Row, 1985. $16.95; Faber and Faber, 1988. Paper: $8.95.

It is not quite accurate for the jacket of Infante's delightful tome about tobacco, *Holy Smoke,* to say that it "is the outrageous and informative story of the cigar and of those who have smoked it—in all walks of life, in literature, and in film. Cabrera Infante tells the story of cigars and cigar smoking from Columbus to Castro." All of this is true, in the sense that John Aubrey's *Brief Lives* is autobiographical, Robert Burton's *The Anatomy of Melancholy* is about melancholia, or Sir Thomas Browne's *Hydriotaphia, or Urn-Burial* is about the "Sepulchrial Urns Lately Found in Norfolk." Like Aubrey, Burton, Browne, and other truly original stylists who make a subject their own—Freud and dreams, Conan Doyle and crime, Joyce and Dublin—Infante uses tobacco (cigars, cigarettes, pipes, snuff, chewing tobacco), but especially the cigar, as his subject for a history, but what a history! Macaronic, full of puns, literary, autobiographical, erudite, philosophical, Infante has made the subject of smoking his own, like Johnson and his dictionary or Mencken and his *The American Language.*

Perhaps the most striking feature of this collection of notes and reflections on the wonderful weed is the overwhelming number of references to films and film stars. One need only refer to the cover showing a supine Groucho Marx with a cigar in his mouth or the opening passage which refers to the scene in *The Bride of Frankenstein* where Dr. Pretorius, seeing the monster, says, "Have a cigar. . . . It's my only vice" to know that *Holy Smoke* is not going to be another boring disquisition on one of the South's favorite cash crops. Rather it is a veritable introduction to the movies by a buff who loves films almost as much as he loves cigars. Hundreds of films and stars are referred to throughout, from Bogey, "the greatest cigarette smoker in moviedom," to Edward G. Robinson, "the greatest cigar smoker ever," from Marlene Dietrich, with her "languid cigarette at the end of a limp wrist," to Percy Kilbride, "the best tobacco chewer in the movies."

Holy Smoke has little to do with whether the reader is a smoker or not. Rather it is a tour de force that succeeds brilliantly. In keeping with Cabrera's personal style and structure, there are no chapters or sections except for an eighty-seven-page collection of literary excerpts under the title "La Vague Litterature." These are usually one-page excerpts from the works of writers with titles by Cabrera: Defoe, "The Plague Meets Robinson Crusoe," Poe, "Edgarpo," Tolstoy, "Tolstoys in the Attic," Conan Doyle, "Holmes Sweet Holmes, Said Watson," Fitzgerald, "The Prisoner of Zelda," Dashiell Hammett, "If I Had a Hammett," P.G. Wodehouse, "Set Wodehouse on Fire," Budd Schulberg, "What Makes Schulberg Write?" are a few examples of his punning.

Unfortunately for those of us who wish to refer to the wealth of material and references in such a valuable compilation, there is no index, no glossary, no bibliography, only a few pages of "Acknowledgments," a sad commentary on contemporary publishing as practiced by the denizens of Publishers Row in Gotham City. As Big Daddy in *Cat on a Hot Tin Roof* puts it, "What's that smell in this room? . . . There ain't nothin' more powerful than the odor of mendacity." [Jack Byrne]

*

Kathy Acker. *Literal Madness: Kathy Goes to Haiti; My Death My Life by Pier Paolo Pasolino; Florida.* Grove Press, 1988. $20.00.

Once we read a "novel" by Kathy Acker, we are trapped in her consciousness. She uses "mad" imagery and philosophy to control our rational inclinations. The novels (which often deal with "blood and guts") assault traditional, ordinary expectations, so that we cannot find comfort in old-fashioned criticism. We scream because she violates the rules of the game (of writer and reader). We suffer our madness.

It is, therefore, interesting that Acker calls these three novels "literal madness." Certainly there are crazy inversions (perversions) of literary traditions, loony and unbelievable characters, absurd happenings. Acker understands that words are mad because they purport to describe reality. Words and reality are on different planes; language lies because it distorts events.

Acker's early novel *Kathy Goes to Haiti* seems at first to be a banal travelogue. We learn about poverty, lust, drugs in Haiti, but we are soon deceived. The travelogue is, after all, an imagined country, "a country of the mind." It is Kathy's mind that we enter. And this mind is filled with contradictions, duplicities, false clues. The imagery points to these. When the voodoo doctor treats her, he "sticks the mirror in front of her face so she has to look at herself. Kathy's almost unconscious. He passes the mirror around her head three times." The mirror is the clue to the "madness." Kathy recognizes that she can never cross boundaries (of race, sex, nationality) because *she* creates them unconsciously. And her inability to cross boundaries suggests that she is assaulted by freakish narcissism. I particularly like the last sentence: "She's more dazed than before." The entire novel (or dream or life) is a curious daze which defies coherent explanation.

In the second novel, *My Death My Life by Pier Paolo Pasolini* (her most recent work), Acker fuses the mystery of the Italian's death (and life), *Romeo and Juliet, Hamlet,* and philosophical analysis to create an even more "dazed" (dazzling) work than *Haiti.*

The doom has become more pronounced; the unexpected becomes the ordinary. Boundaries are fluid. We are told that "the water our mirror reflects the relinquishment of the language. . . ." Acker is sad because she understands that she is lost in *her* country, that she cannot get a passport from us. Her words will never be interpreted correctly; indeed, they will always be private, obsessive, self-contained.

But there is also an air of accomplishment. Acker *accepts* her *mirror-language,* recognizing that she is writer *and* reader; that, indeed, she is a curiously fused, monstrous, freakish creature—an artist.

Florida is the third novel. It is Acker's version of *Key Largo;* her critical interpretation is, of course, highly personal, but it catches the doom she has courted previously. *Florida* is another philosophical travelogue. Acker tends here to use a montage of quotations (from the film) and speculation about the quotations. The montage reminds us of fusions of the other novels, but it is basic for her reading and writing. Acker wants to connect things (people, words); at the same time she accepts estrangement. *Florida* ends with an Acker song: "So listen girls, do what you can / find a horny loving man. / Give him all you've got to give, / Give him more so you can live." Does the stanza suggest the power of relinquishment? Is the stanza religious?

We cannot immediately answer these questions, but we can say that Acker always gives us more. Her vibrant prose and intellect challenge us. They make us look in the mirror. [Irving Malin]

*

Ingeborg Bachmann. *The Thirtieth Year.* Trans. Michael Bullock. Holmes & Meier, 1987. $19.95.

Anyone with more than a passing interest in modern German literature is no doubt familiar with the Austrian writer Ingeborg Bachmann, whose literary reputation was enviable even before her first book of poetry appeared in 1953.

As her career progressed, that reputation grew, surpassed only by the myth of her life, a fascination with her as, in the words of Karen Achberger (who supplies the present edition with a helpful introduction), "the timid, existential outsider as intellectual, suffering woman." This image was enhanced by Bachmann's freakish death in 1973, and today she is a canonized figure held to be one of Austria's most important and influential postwar writers. Given Bachmann's significance and the centrality of her work to feminist and new historicist concerns, it is good to see her first story collection (released in Germany in 1961) back in print in the fine Michael Bullock translation first published by Knopf in 1964. (Holmes & Meier has also published *Simultaneous,* her second collection.)

The Thirtieth Year contains seven stories. Two short pieces—"Life in an Austrian Town," a child's-eye prose poem about growing up under fascism, and "Undine Goes," a reworking of the myth of a water nymph who rejects the world of humanity—frame five more conventional narratives. In "The Thirtieth Year" a nameless narrator painfully examines his ordinary, unsatisfactory life in a voice reminiscent of Dostoevsky's Underground Man, while in "Everything" a father explains his rejection of his child, whose ordinariness defeats his father's hope that his son might "redeem the world." Turning from the tyranny of family and conventional life, "Among Murderers and Madmen" presents a Viennese Jew's account of evenings spent among former fascists and his effortless accommodation to what Hannah Arendt has taught us to see as the banality of evil. Accommodation is likewise central to "A Step Towards Gomorrah," which tells of a young woman's flirtation with and rejection of a lesbian relationship and the freedom it might have provided from the male-dominated world she inhabits. Finally, "A Wildermuth" concerns a truth-obsessed magistrate's breakdown following his realization that truth is unattainable.

These stories may not be every reader's glass of schnapps. Indeed, they are, as Achberger explains, "not narratives in the conventional sense" but "rather moments of reflection, lyrical impressions, monologues, tightly composed images to suggest a radical rebellion. . ."; they are also heavy on Sturm und Drang breast-beating and given to flights of Germanic philosophizing:

The mind which my flesh houses is an even greater deceiver than its sanctimonious host. To meet it is something I must fear above all. For nothing I think has anything to do with me. Every thought is nothing but the germination of alien seeds. I am not capable of thinking any of the things that have touched me, and I think things that have not touched me.

Still, for all their mannered excess, these are serious stories of men and women walking psychic borderlines and attempting to cross over into future possibilities by making troubled sense of their past and present lives. Often ambivalent and cryptic, these are, in short, modern stories speaking not only to postwar Europeans but to all of us who live powerlessly in a world we might wish were otherwise. Bullock's translations, I should add in closing, do Bachmann justice, capturing as they do the evocation of mood and tone so important to her work's emotional impact. [Brooke K. Horvath]

*

Paul West. *The Place in Flowers Where Pollen Rests.* Doubleday, 1988. $19.95.

The Hopi word *koyaanisqatsi,* meaning "life out of balance," came into some prominence five years ago in the Philip Glass-scored film of the same name, which eschewed narrative and dialogue in favor of a rapidly shifting montage of scenes from contemporary life. The Hopi word is used early in Paul West's extraordinary new novel, which likewise forgoes a traditional linear narrative and instead features a series of reveries, arranged not so much in chronological order as in an associative manner, one memory leading to another, with all memories existing in a kind of eternal present tense that mirrors the grammatical structure of the Hopi language.

Life is hideously out of balance for Oswald Beautiful Badger Going Over the Hill. As a teenager in the early sixties, he leaves the Hopi reservation in northeastern Arizona for Hollywood; but failing to find legitimate acting work, he descends into the trashy world of pornographic movies. During one of his cinematic orgies, a porn actress suffocates—a breathtakingly beautiful description of her repose in death opens the novel—and while Oswald is not directly responsible, his horror sends him back to the reservation to attend to his uncle, a carver of kachina dolls named George The Place in Flowers Where Pollen Rests. After his uncle's death (actually his father, though they both kept up the pretense), Oswald leaves again, this time for the war in Vietnam, an official obscenity linked to the underground obscenity of the porn world Oswald had left behind. Surviving a massacre and experiencing a kind of rebirth, he returns once more to the reservation and tries to restore some balance to his life. By way of what might be called stellar mysticism, he is able to find the balance between the individual and the cosmos, the past and the present, and reintegrates himself into Hopi society, first by recounting a traditional (and grisly) tale, and second by impersonating a kachina, Mastop the death fly.

Extracting this narrative from the novel is a challenge, for the reveries that make up *The Place in Flowers* are densely printed monologues without paragraphing or much regard for chronology. Uncle George possesses "the waterfall of a worn-out voice," and West's verbal waterfall fills a vast narrative pool five hundred pages deep, where chronology dissolves and narrative events purl in a simultaneous present that can be dipped into by characters at any time. "We are tenseless and timeless," Uncle George boasts, and it is amazing how West has managed to convey not only the Hopi culture but its linguistic structure as well. One is forced to read this novel differently than one reads an "Anglo" novel; Oswald had "learned from his tribe, his uncle especially, the sovereign slowness of things, the way in which ongoingness was better than any outcome," and it is the "ongoingness" of this novel rather than its outcome that commands the reader's attention—an attention that must be slowed down in this case, not racing forward to see what happens next. Reading slowly, the reader can better appreciate the detailed, visceral texture of the places West describes: the smells, the weather, the taste of food, the feel of clothes—which is all the more remarkable since West is describing experiences (the war in Vietnam, life on a Hopi reservation, the porn industry) that are quite alien to this transplanted Englishman who teaches at Penn State. (And how ironic that it took a Britisher to write what may very well be the Great Amer-Indian Novel.)

The traditional tale Oswald finally learns to tell also places emphasis on the telling rather than the outcome, with the more details the better. We too have heard this tale before, in a sense. The hero wears a thousand faces, Joseph Campbell tells us, and Paul West has given us an exotic new version of the oldest tale there is, one of urgent relevance in this new age of *koyaanisqatsi*. [Steven Moore]

*

Gordon Lish. *Mourner at the Door.* Viking, 1988. $16.95.

I must quote the following long epigraph because it is the key to Lish's amazing collection:

It is reported that Wittgenstein's last words were these: "Tell them that I had a wonderful life." Perhaps he did and perhaps he did not—have a wonderful life. But how could Wittgenstein have known one way or the other? As to a further matter, suppose that these were not the words—suppose the words were German words. What I want to know is this—is it the same thing to have a wonderful life in another language? Or put it this way—if another language was the language that Wittgenstein had it in, then how could it have been a wonderful life?

If we look at the twisted, tortured paths of these sentences we see that Lish is trying to understand the relationship of "life" to "language," of the "world" to the "word." Do "words" have any significance in our lives? How do we gain knowledge? Can we ever bridge the gap between experience and description—an experience itself!—of experience? The epigraph contains sardonic, "metaphysical" circles.

I have spent so much time on the epigraph that I cannot do justice to the brilliant stories. The stories are, first of all, deliberately short. They inform us that basic questions of "life" are abrupt, shocking, and minimal. The stories are "amazing"—to use one of Lish's favorite words—because they recognize that we (or the characters or, rather, the words) cannot offer full explanation.

"The Death of Me" repeats compulsively that "I wanted to be amazing. I wanted to be so amazing. I had already been amazing up to a certain point. But I was tired of being at that point. I wanted to go past that point." Consider the repetitions, the ritualistic compulsions. What is the "point"? Isn't the "point" Wittgenstein's? How do we move past the past? How do we go beyond? And how do we ever know, if we do? The story doesn't inform us, doesn't give answers. It ends in a kind of silence as the adults merely pat the child-narrator on the head.

I quote lines from other stories. Here are some from "Last Descent to Earth":

"One had words galore. One had words to burn. One had to beat them off with a stick. I myself had words to kill, and did away with as many as one could." The narrator wants to destroy "words"—to *kill* them, to *burn* them—because he recognizes that we live in a fallen world in which we cannot understand our "descent."

In another story, we have the ending: "Adjectives—oh *Christ!*" There is the linkage between "description" and religion. Can we ever get answers? Can we get to the point of life and death?

I merely list titles: "Don't Die," "Spell Bereavement" (a pun?), "Agony," "Knowledge," "The Death of Me." I see that Lish cannot control his anguish of non-knowledge, his inability to capture meanings. Now I understand that his previous works—full of murder, torture, sadism—fit into the pattern I have been tracing. They also deal with frustrated narrators who try desperately to find final solutions.

Why does Lish give us *Mourner at the Door* as the title of this book? We recognize that *we* are before the doors of Heaven; we can't get *in* because we don't know the right words, the passwords. We mourn our inabilities, our "death-in-life" (whatever these words *mean*). We remain silent, hoping, perhaps, that silence is the answer.

Lish's collection is an important literary event, a book which uses words to battle words. It is a murder-suicide because it gets to the "point" in an amazing manner. It wins as it loses. [Irving Malin]

*

Guy Davenport. *The Jules Verne Steam Balloon.* North Point Press, 1987. $21.95; paper: $11.95; Robert Kelly. *Doctor of Silence.* McPherson & Co., 1988. $20.00; paper: $10.00; Pamela Zoline. *The Heat Death of the Universe and Other Stories.* McPherson & Co., 1988. $20.00; paper: $10.00.

There is a difference between fads in short fiction and genuine developments, and while the larger commercial presses can be counted on to supply plenty of the former, the smaller independent presses are more reliable for the latter. In his latest collection of short fiction, Guy Davenport continues to build on the aesthetics of the early modernists to create the most intellectually engaging fiction of our time. As "seriously silly" as the youngsters he writes of with such affection, Davenport creates a world of sex and scholarship, where eroticism and education go hand in hand. The Dutch and Danish settings of the longer stories in this collection are presented in collages of erotic vignettes, entries from botany handbooks, mini-lectures, and quotations from a variety of texts (including the famous Quinet quotation in *Finnegans Wake*), written in a Danish Modern style of clarity and elegance. Other stories concern historical characters antithetical to the Fourierism Davenport champions: Pyrrhon of Elis, who "denied that anything exists"; a petty and vindictive Jonah; and a sympathetic profile of Hitler as it might have been written by a totalitarian toady. But in the other stories Davenport writes of an idyllic world in the same generous spirit as one of his protagonists, the schoolteacher Hugo Tvemunding, "superb lover in both flesh and spirit," who tries "to paint because I want to show others what I think is beautiful."

Robert Kelly's fictions also take place in a different world than most pop fiction does—a world less idyllic and more supernatural than Davenport's, but like his a world of intelligence, scholarship, and grace. Ranging in length from half a page to thirty-five pages, these fictions defamiliarize both the world and the short story genre; where Davenport is indebted to the generation of 1914, Kelly builds on Borges and European fabulists. In a short piece entitled "Hypnogeography," Kelly states: "I have a feeling that the Dream Representation of place can tell us a lot about what we think of as the 'real' place. . . . I want to learn, and want us to learn, how our countries and cities represent in dream." While his stories are not dreams, strictly speaking, they do read like dream representations of places, reminiscent at times of H. P. Lovecraft's oneiric alternate worlds (though without his gothic gush), more compact than the fictions in his previous collection *A Transparent Tree,* but tantalizing and unsettling, wondrous strange.

The Heat Death of the Universe is Pamela Zoline's first collection of stories, some dating from the 1960s, most of which appeared in new wave sci-fi magazines. Many science fiction writers begin with an ingenious premise but wrap it in plodding prose; Zoline however matches her ingenious premises with postmodern strategies, a playful sense of humor, and colorful writing to produce a dazzling collection of stories. The longest and most inventive story, "Sheep," is made up of an insomniac's encyclopedic ramblings in quest of sleep. Another story features a boy whose geneology consists of the most accident-prone family in literary history, while another offers a different view of Davenport's Holland, though in a college style similar to his. Zoline joins Davenport and Kelly in the small circle of writers who are making genuine contributions to the short-fiction form. [Steven Moore]

*

Ludovic Janvier. *Monstre, Va.* Gallimard, 1988. 79 Fr.

In this his fourth novel, Ludovic Janvier aims to depict the horrific aftermath of an unspeakable crime: matricide. Narrated by the murderer himself, the colloquial confession draws us in by its very weirdness and black humor. We hear of the difficulties of the clean-up and body disposal, the infernal bickering between the abandoned, impoverished woman and her semi-retarded son. Indeed, the narrator reminds us that if he is sent to prison for life, he will have fulfilled one of his mother's dearest held dreams for him: state employment. Yet what begins in horror ends in mere literary posturing. The ghost of Norman Bates looms over these pages, but what in Hitchcock's film was a rather complex, comically perverse presence, becomes in this novel still another pretext for textual production. Perhaps in an age when sociopaths can make their own literary fortunes (note Arthur Bremer's *An Assassin's Diary,* that postmodern addition to the sociopathic canon that perhaps begins with De Sade, and of course Jack Abbott's *In the Belly of the Beast*), such a fictional enterprise cannot match the unselfconscious crackpot energy and unpredictability of the real-life versions. Arthur Bremer, for example, displayed an intuitive grasp of the revolutionary impact of flat description and anomic character portrayal, an aesthetic program that inspired a whole generation of fiction minimalists. In Janvier's novel, the overwriterly concerns of the narrator—his annoyingly convenient "interest" in words, his unconvincing knowledge of some English, the very fact he shares the same first name with the author—contribute to ultimately dissipate the horror, humor and poignancy of the tale of this lost soul. [Dominic Di Bernardi]

*

Milan Kundera. *The Unbearable Lightness of Being.* Trans. Michael Henry Heim. Harper and Row, 1984. $15.95; Harper and Row, 1987. Paper: $8.95.

Milan Kundera's *The Unbearable Lightness of Being* bears a striking resemblance in its theme to his first novel *The Joke.* Both plots turn on unfortunate political gaffes by their protagonists: Ludvik, in *The Joke,* sends a postcard to his girlfriend as a prank—"Optimism is the opium of the people! A healthy atmosphere stinks of stupidity! Long Live Trotsky!" He is expelled from the university and the Party and sent to an army penal battalion for years. Tomas, in *The Unbearable Lightness of Being,* writes an article for a newspaper published by the Union of Czech Writers, in which he makes a classic comparison between Oedipus and the Czech communists, who, prior to the Prague Spring of 1968, were guilty of judicial murders. Tomas, speaking analagously, questions the guilty—"How can you stand the sight of what you've done? How is it you're not horrified? Have you no eyes to see? If you had eyes, you would have to put them out and wander away from Thebes!" His fate is to go from brain surgeon to window washer to worker on a collective farm. Humor and irony are not the stuff of totalitarian regimes! They are, rather, at the heart of Kundera's work.

But there is also the other element in these novels, the importance of sex played against the background of postwar politics, Czech nationalism turned totalitarian, and Russian intervention with its image out of *1984* ("If you want a picture of the future, imagine a boot stamping on a human face—forever"). Sex, to Kundera, is not casual in its connection to the politics of Central Europe. It is equal to the reality of politics, like the second eagle in the well-known double eagle. For him Eros and *politika* go together. They are the love that dares to speak its name! A most successful updating of Trollope and Conrad, *Unbearable Lightness* draws for us the kinds of triangles reminiscent of Ibsen—Tomas, his favorite mistress Sabina, and his wife Tereza; Sabina, Franz, and his wife Marie-Claude; Franz, Marie-Claud, and his student mistress; even Tomas, Tereza, and their beloved dog Kerenin. Lightness for Tomas is sex without love; marriage is the unbearable weight of love and faithfulness. Tomas, the womanizer who counts his sexual affairs in the hundreds, is torn between

Sabina (lightness) and Tereza (weight). Sabina skips lightly from Prague to Switzerland to Paris to California. Tomas and Tereza return to Prague from Switzerland where they end their lives together in the countryside. As Tomas says, *"Einmalist keinmal"* (What happens but once might as well not have happened at all). As Kundera says, referring, I believe, to both Eros and *politika,* "History is as light as individual life, unbearably light, light as a feather, as dust swirling into the air, as whatever will no longer exist tomorrow." [Jack Byrne]

*

Frederic Tuten. *Tallien: A Brief Romance.* Farrar Straus Giroux, 1988. $16.95.

"It was really good, looked like a little nothing, then it went sailing off and sped deep into the heart." This response by the character Tallien to a brief letter from his former benefactor is likely to be the reader's to Frederic Tuten's splendid new novel, his first since the innovative *Adventures of Mao on the Long March* in 1971. *Tallien* is a novella in size and seems simple in structure: a middle-aged man visits the deathbed of his father who abandoned him thirty years earlier, a radical activist named Rex. Inspired for years by an idealized version of his father, the disillusioned son now wishes he could tell him the story of the French revolutionary Jean Lambert Tallien (1772-1820), a historical figure whose biography takes up most of Tuten's novella. An idealist whose erotic obsession with a noblewoman named Thérèse destroys his ideals, Tallien exemplifies a truth the son wishes he could impress upon his father: that a revolution may begin with the best of intentions, but quickly brings out the worst in people.

The stories of Rex and Tallien are linked both in broad outlines and by numerous subtle details (the son wishes for a blanket to keep off the freezing December nights in the Bronx, while Thérèse leaves Tallien for a banker who makes his fortune selling thin blankets to soldiers trying to keep from freezing). The stories also share a colorful vernacular style, maximalist prose within minimalist perimeters. Tuten brilliantly captures the gut-level anxieties of revolutionary activity and the inevitable betrayals—of friends and family, ideals and principles—that attend most attempts to pound the square peg of an ideal into the round hole of reality. The son never tells this cautionary tale to his father but he tells it to us, and for that we should be grateful. [Steven Moore]

*

Janet Pérez. *Contemporary Women Writers of Spain.* Twayne, 1988. $24.95.

This work serves as an excellent introduction to Spain's women writers that provides both biographical and critical information, while also placing these writers in a feminist tradition. Although a few of these writers have been translated sporadically into English, most have not: Rosa Chacel, Carmen Conde Abellán, Ana María Moix, Esther Tusquets, Rosa Montero, Lourdes Ortiz, Olga Xirinacs, Nùria Serrahima, Antonia Vicens, Maria Antònia Oliver, Carme Riera, Carmen Martín Gaite, Ana María Matute, Mercè Rodoreda, and many, many others. Pérez is completely successful at uncovering and lucidly describing writers who otherwise would be ignored in America. [Kathleen Burke]

*

Alberto Savinio. *Childhood of Nivasio Dolcemare.* Trans. Richard Pevear. Eridanos Press (Hygiene, CO), 1987. $21.00; paper: $12.00.

If Laurence Sterne had read Raymond Roussel and then sat down to parody Henry James (a task that may remind many of Dick Cavett's expressed desire to write a comic version of *Gilligan's Island*), he might have written *Childhood of Nivasio Dolcemare;* Alberto Savinio's 1941 novel (only now seeing publication in America in a translation by Richard Pavear) must be judged successful if capturing the humor and wordplay of the original is any mark of success (and it is).

Set in turn-of-the-century Athens, the autobiographical *Nivasio Dolcemare* is Savinio's comic look at a cosmopolitan society composed, as he writes in his preface, "of the local aristocracy, the court, select members of the various European 'colonies,' and the entire diplomatic corps." He continues:

There could have been no more favorable place for learning the feel of that limp, drawing-room Europe, that Europe of "good Europeans," which threw up its already weak and debilitated hands with the first cannon shots of 1914, and in September 1939 saw even the bones in those hands turn to dust.

Through this world moves the young Nivasio, a naive yet precocious observer and sometime participant, a "collector of experiences" whose world is presented in a loosely tied bundle of mildly surreal vignettes composed of black humor, Mediterranean nostalgia, mock-serious explanatory footnotes, slapstick narration, subtle to shameful wordplay, and deadpan description:

Mothers of marriageable daughters were most incensed against "those strumpets" [living across from Casa Dolcemare], and among the fiercest was the Generaless Papatrapatakos, whose daughter Pipizza, breastless and chlorotic, was at that time, and in the most perfect conditions of nubility, just rounding the cape of forty.

Yet interesting as Savinio's novel is for its burlesque of the Balkan Belle Epoque, it is equally noteworthy as a singular manifestation of surrealist poetics and as a fine introduction to the work of a central if long-neglected member of the European avant-garde. Savinio, the pen name of Andrea de Chirico (1891-1952), brother of the painter, was a close friend of Picasso, Apollinaire, Breton, and others and was himself active as a painter, composer, violinist, playwright, stage designer, and critic as well as being influential as a novelist. Enjoying a posthumous rediscovery today, Savinio has been called by Leonardo Sciascia "the most interesting Italian writer between the two wars." Yet as Dore Ashton observes in her introduction, one should not forget that *Nivasio Dolcemare* is "downright funny" and "ought not to be freighted with theoretical literary discussions." True enough: from its account of Nivasio's mistaking the proprietor of the Saranti Employment Agency for the Greek demiurge to the revelation that the new maid has been entertaining in her bed an entire Greek army regiment, the novel (and the two short stories the volume also contains and in which Nivasio figures tangentially) should please even readers with no interest in class satire or surrealist folderol. [Brooke K. Horvath]

*

Annie Ernaux. *La Place.* Gallimard, 1983. 16.50 Fr.; *Une Femme.* Gallimard, 1987. 52 Fr.

Annie Ernaux, a novelist concentrating on autobiographical themes, offers in *La Place* and *Une Femme* an account of the lives of her father and mother, respectively. The story of her father centers on his social ambition—"the place" he wished to make for himself and that he was fiercely conscious of keeping when faced with his social superiors, among whom is his university-educated daughter. On the other hand, her mother is examined as the affective link with the world the writer left, whose very physical presence, "words, hands, gestures, her way of walking and laughing are what united the woman I am to the child I was." Small shopkeepers who had risen from the peasantry in the social upheavals following World War I, they retained a sense of their own inferiority even as they allowed their daughter to pursue her upward path into the teaching establishment. Yet this success is tormented for the daughter; what works upon her is a sense of betrayal, perhaps one that marks most intellectuals who have progressed beyond their parents' level of education. Annie Ernaux unflinch-ingly examines the peculiar network of guilt that marks her even as a successful writer, seeing this success as a function of the very ambitions of members of a class whose narrowness she learned—quite literally—to despise. This heavy self-consciousness pervades language itself: she remembers her father's obses-sion with not using the wrong words, or her own fear about using words that were above her parents. Perhaps the most poignant episode on this theme is the single visit she and her father paid to the city library, which ended in embarrass-ment for both since they had no titles in mind to request from the librarian (French stacks being closed). These concerns also explain her style: bare, unadorned, a series of short passages, almost as if she continued to perceive her own parents as the ultimate readers, who, she tells us, would have seen any stylistic efforts in the letters she sent home to them from university as "an attempt to keep them at a distance."

The author notes that she was reading *Les Mandarins* while watching over her father in his final hours, and that her mother died "eight days after Simone de Beauvoir." Indeed, her two works inevitably recall Simone de Beauvoir's

Une Mort Tres Douce (the merciless depiction of her mother's death agony), not only in apparent subject but also in that we are given a "real life" document to counteract, amend, expand, a pre-existing oeuvre, especially Ernaux's first novel, the ferocious, bilious *Les Armoires Vides*.

Ernaux, however, is not interested in a phenomenological description of the last hours but rather in the shape of the lives that have shaped hers: "This way of writing . . . strikes me as moving in the direction of truth, helps me out of the loneliness and obscurity of individual memory, through the discovery of a more general meaning." Yet she finds herself constantly struggling against this goal since there is "something" within her that seeks to preserve "purely emotional images" of the woman she is depicting. Her "desire to remain, in a certain way, on the underside of literature" is a rather peculiar goal: after all, it is the emotional intensity she brings to her task, as well as her sharply observed portraits of her parents from youth to old age, and in death, that distinguish these texts. Perhaps we should see her undertaking not so much as anti-autobiography as anti-Proust. In *La Place,* she tells us that she could not count on "reminiscence"—"the tinkling of the bell of an old store, the smell of an over-ripe melon"—for such would merely lead her to herself. Rather "it is in the way people sit and are bored in waiting rooms, call out to their children, say good-bye on train platforms that I sought the figure of my father." Indeed, within the space of these two texts we observe a rapidly changing France: in 1967 her father is shown dying in his own bed to which a priest had been summoned, and his body is left there the three days until his burial; in 1986 her mother dies in an old-age home, from Alzheimer's disease, and her funeral mass is held in a church across from a supermarket, with organ music provided by a cassette the priest pops into a player.

On the last page of *Une Femme* Annie Ernaux states: "This is not a biography, nor a novel naturally, perhaps a cross between literature, sociology and history. It was necessary that my mother become history, born as she was in a dominated milieu, one she wanted to leave, so that I would feel less alone and factitious in the dominant world of words and ideas to which, according to her desire, I acceded." As provocative as the texts themselves is their implicit challenge—namely, that we all recount the "history" made up by our parents' lives, in the same way that the next generation will only be able to grasp our own lives as stories they tell themselves about us. [Dominic Di Bernardi]

*

John Hawkes. *Whistlejacket.* Weidenfeld & Nicolson, 1988. $17.95.

Ostensibly a murder mystery involving a horse, John Hawkes's new novel bears similarity with his earlier one, *The Lime Twig.* This novel, however, examines how the written narrative compares with the artistic creations of the photographer and the painter. A meditation on being a novelist, *Whistlejacket* explores the technical, aesthetic questions of how writing fiction differs from painting and photography. For Michael, the twenty-eight-year-old fashion photographer and narrator of the story, "the photograph for which the artist strives has no story. Story is the anathema of the true photographer. Narrative, dull narrative, [is] of interest only to those who sit or stand at the frame's center or lurk at its edges trying to squeeze themselves into the picture."

The word *buttocks,* a plural without a singular form, helps demonstrate the relationship between writing, painting and photography. Language can at best "designate but never evoke their anatomical referent." The photographer or the painter can capture the derriere in a much fuller representation. Boucher's *Mademoiselle O'Murphy* exemplifies this kind of painting: "thanks to her bare buttocks [Miss O'Murphy] was assured her place in art and history." At the same time, however, "the noun for all this is missing." Thus, a photographer who prefers the concrete while avoiding the metaphor articulates a subtle critique of the power of prose to convey reality.

The role of pornography in framing the examination of the relationship between the artist and erotic truth informs much of the novel. With a photographer most enamored with "mouth shots" and "rearviews," Michael elicits recurrent male heterosexual fantasies. As in other Hawkes novels, though, *Whistlejacket* demands a critical look at what those fantasies are and why they are so dominant.

Even with these formalistic concerns notwithstanding, Hawkes's new novel is perhaps essentially an examination of justifiable homicide by a woman who has experienced intense humiliation from her husband. From Papa in *Travesty* to, most notably for this novel, Eva Laubenstein in *The Passion Artist,* Hawkes's fiction explores the criminal potential in us all. [Peter F. Murphy]

*

James McConkey. *To a Distant Island.* Dutton, 1987. Paper: $8.95.

James McConkey is one of our best writers. He refuses to be confined within one easy genre; his estrangement from the usual genres helps our literary establishment to disregard his works. McConkey writes in a clear, beautiful way about spiritual *moments*. He relates the present vision to the past; it is little wonder that he entitles one of his books *Court of Memory*. Another title is *Crossroads*.

This haunting book makes me see that I don't have to look at typographical tricks, to listen to endless "tapes," so that I can shiver with delight. McConkey's narrator is, for many of the novels, an aging, intelligent, spiritual man who wants to "confess"—one of his titles is *The Tree House Confessions* —his sins and virtues. He wants his full manhood.

He decides here to write about "a distant island." The island is Sakhalin— the island is, of course, the one Chekhov saw at thirty. We have Chekhov's account of the island; we have commentary on this action. McConkey tries to understand several things: Why did Chekhov go *there?* Why does *he* become obsessed with Chekhov's past voyage? Can he *fuse* biography, autobiography, and fiction so that he can get at the heart of the matter? Is he writing in an impure, hybrid genre which ignores important details?

Let me quote McConkey: "To reconstruct his journey is to acknowledge its influence on me, its continuing hold on my imagination, feelings, and personal experiences; in such subjective matters, there always exists the possibility of misreading from a personal need." McConkey fears that he cannot get the facts into a decent shape; so did Chekhov. What explains the hold—as obsessive as it seems—of Chekhov's island-account on this book?

And McConkey reaches another important point: "Misreading" may recur. Of course, Bloom has made the word famous, but he had not seen that any critic (McConkey) misreads so that he can construct a new "house of fiction." (Bloom seems to misread more for destruction than for construction. He fuses the two.)

McConkey may not be Chekhov—he adores the writer—but I am not McConkey. You, my dear reader, are not Chekhov, McConkey, or this sly reviewer. You must remember, however, that in order to evaluate these various sentences, *you* have to start on the journey; you have to travel to "that distant island." But where is the island? On this page? On a map? In Chekhov's book? In McConkey's book?

I wish you well. Bon voyage. [Irving Malin]

*

Susan Daitch. *L.C.* Harcourt Brace Jovanovich, 1987. $17.95.

This intriguing and very accomplished first novel is concerned with the efforts of three women to redress personal and political inequality through the manipulation of texts. The novel begins with an editor's introduction to her own translation of a journal kept by one Lucienne Crozier, a proto-feminist witness to the February 1848 Revolution in Paris. All seems well at first, but irregularities begin appearing: the language is not that of a twenty-four-year-old Frenchwoman of the last century but of an older one of this century; the editor's signature to the annotations shrinks from Willa Rehnfield to W.R., then expands back to the full name, then is joined by annotations by a Jane Amme (a nom de guerre), writing fourteen years after Rehnfield's 1968 translation. When Lucienne's diary comes to an end halfway through the novel, Amme steps in and explains Rehnfield's reasons for doctoring her translation. The fact that Rehnfield wrote in 1968, a year of revolutionary activity as futile as that in France 120 years earlier, points to the identification the reclusive Rehnfield feels for Lucienne. Amme, on the other hand, was a participant in the Berkeley riots of 1968 and consequently has her own reasons for identifying with L.C. She offers her own translation of the last section of L.C.'s diary—radically different from the Rehnfield version—and as text competes with text, questions arise concerning the recording of history, the nature of translation, and the ultimate subjectivity of all texts.

Dozens of cross-references link L.C. with her twentieth-century annotators, and Daitch brilliantly underscores the similarities between the socio-political injustices that led to the revolts of 1848 and 1968. She's clearly done her homework in both eras (she was only fourteen in 1968 herself) and demonstrates a vivid historical imagination. The role of woman vis-à-vis history—from spectator and victim to participant—runs through this tale of two cities, a stunning debut by a young writer clearly worth watching. [Steven Moore]

*

Joseph McElroy. *The Letter Left to Me.* Knopf, 1988. $16.95.

"What do you do once you've written a 1200-plus-page novel?" The straight answer, which Joseph McElroy gave to Bradford Morrow in last year's *Conjunctions* interview, is that one writes "a short book so that it has a chance of getting finished and coming out." But that, McElroy goes on to suggest, may not be so easy as it sounds, for he had already discovered that "the book you dreamed, with hope in your heart, of writing, getting to, when you finished the big monster of a book, turns out to be as impossible as anything else you ever wrote." After *Women and Men,* a book that is little short of planetary in what it attempts to include, probably the greatest challenge left to McElroy was to simplify, to write a novel as "transparent and plain" as he could make it. And if that meant putting aside for the moment his largest, most complex ambitions, it in no way lessens the interest of this remarkable novel, *The Letter Left to Me.*

Less daunting at 152 pages than *Women and Men,* the new novel nonetheless presents its own technical challenge, which is to see how far one can go with "literal memory" without losing the mythic and invented qualities of fiction. Set in Brooklyn Heights in the mid-forties, and later in Williams College, the novel is a meditation on a letter given to McElroy just after his father died, when McElroy was fifteen. From the opening scene, in which events from McElroy's boyhood are presented in a style that is uniquely his, we are aware of having had opened up to us an intensely private world. The fluid, abstract, slightly obsessed observations of the "city apartment" where the author grew up, in particular the attention paid to "a drop-leaf desk made by an early nineteenth-century cousin of my mother's," evoke a world of familiar objects made strange by death. McElroy is attempting in these opening pages not only to remember his father and the events surrounding his death, but to recreate the events as they appeared to him *then,* in all his adolescent confusion. This makes the book not a literal memoir so much as an arrangement of the narrator's perceptions and emotions "amid my father's death, which schedules everything to perfection and puts yesterday on top of tomorrow if I try to think when things happened."

"Building backwards naturally" is the recurring phrase McElroy uses for the book's composition, which is a way of imagining himself into an earlier life. A few days after his father's death, a boy is handed a letter the father had written and held for him (in a safe-deposit box in Manhattan) more than two years before. "Poised, dumbfounded," coming to grips with death for the first time, the boy is suddenly faced with a new entity, as strange and potentially disruptive as the death itself. The book is about what happens to the letter, how the family decides—with the boy's unspoken (and unasked-for) consent—to print it up in a hundred copies, and how later, in college, he allows a new printing of the letter to be sent to his classmates. The first three chapters depict the boy's unspoken confusions of pride, irritation, resentment, and eventual cool disinterest at having the letter spread around this way. He lets it happen, though through it all he is aware, without consciously thinking about it, of a certain lack of authenticity in the letter's reception, and of the related possibility that "reactions to the letter in the family hollowed the true volume my father could no longer occupy."

This feeling of displacement, of the letter's interference with his own recollection of a living father, becomes even more pronounced after the letter is read on campus. With the shift into college scenes, the pace of the narrative quickens, and the novel begins to read more like autobiography. Here we have the first-year student, not explicitly identified as a writer-to-be, who reads around in the history of ideas and is excited by the notion that there are "ideas waiting to be used"; the artist as a young man appears a likable, mildly eccentric freshman who writes home conscientiously, forgets about lectures, clandestinely occupies other students' rooms, and develops the mannerism—at once intimidating and disarming—of letting a moment pass before nodding to an acquaintance. Most importantly for McElroy as a writer, he learns in college "that one had to *decide* to think":

I make such a decision—like enlisting—and feel ignorantly obliged. Like I'll probably get my head handed to me. Push it further: that my father's death left too many things unsaid. Too many for him? I speak for others, I can't not. Would they be interested? I was shot through with things unsaid.

While living at home, secure within his family, the narrator held on to a strange passivity, and the letter was railroaded through without anyone asking his opinion. At college he sees the letter's dissemination clearly as "a deed I could have vetoed," though—again—he lets it happen. But in seeing the letter through other eyes—of college classmates, teachers, and the community at large—he begins consciously to understand how much it fails to say. "The letter left out things—more than things." And it is the novelist's concern (and presumption) to deal freely with "things unsaid."

At issue is the question of who defines one's private reality, and it is an indication of McElroy's achievement in this novel that he presents the issue in all its original, personal immediacy. In the end, the reactions to the letter in the family and at college take second place to the narrator's own mature reflections. The novel closes, appropriately, with two people—the narrator and a woman from a nearby college—discussing the letter unreservedly. Sex is near, and the emotional confusion of half-formed thoughts has given way in the narrator to a new clarity. He has grown beyond the "secure," passive world of his boyhood, to the point where he might truly share the letter with another person. And it is with something of the same intimacy that McElroy shares the letter with his readers. [Joseph Tabbi]

*

John Fante. *Full of Life*. Black Sparrow Press, 1988. $17.50; paper: $9.00.

In 1980 Black Sparrow Press began what Michael Mullen in *The Dictionary of Literary Biography* has dubbed "the Fante revival" by reissuing *Ask the Dust* (1939), considered the author's finest effort by those few Fante enthusiasts in a position to make such a pronouncement. Since then Black Sparrow has continued to publish Fante's happy-sad fiction, including his final novel, *Dreams from Bunker Hill* (released a year before the author's death in 1983), several previously unpublished works, and, most recently, *Full of Life*.

Published originally in 1952, *Full of Life* was John Fante's most commercially successful novel, condensed in *Reader's Digest,* translated into Italian and German, and filmed in 1957 with a screenplay by Fante, who worked for years as a screenwriter. Having much in common with his other work—particularly the novels chronicling the adventures of Arturo Bandino, an aspiring Italian-American writer—*Full of Life* reveals the autobiographical sources of Fante's inspiration by presenting Fante, his wife, and father stripped of fictional camouflage: "I walked out into my front yard and stood among roses and gloated over my house. The rewards of authorship. Me, author, John Fante." Indeed, as Mullen notes, the novel was so manifestly autobiographical, it was marketed initially as nonfiction.

The story, a small masterpiece of quiet comedy, follows Fante through the months of his wife's first pregnancy, during which time she suffers a conversion to Catholicism and begins to dote on her father-in-law, a stereotypical yet warmly drawn Italian immigrant fetched from his Sacramento Valley home to repair his son's new but termite-infested house beautiful. Papa Fante, who likewise dotes on his daughter-in-law (always referring to her as Miss Joyce), finds little to applaud in the city-slick ways of his son, who makes his living, good Lord, writing stories! Papa's presence in the house off Wilshire at this tense and trying time makes for much comedy—and for much touching sentiment, as in this scene after Joyce has given birth to the grandson papa has been awaiting for so long:

Papa was standing at the window in the waiting room. I put my hand on his shoulder and he turned. I didn't have to say anything. He began to cry. He laid his head on my shoulder and his weeping was very painful. I felt the bones of his shoulders, the old softening muscles, and I smelled the smell of my father, the sweat of my father, the origin of my life. I felt his hot tears and the loneliness of man and the sweetness of all men and the aching haunting beauty of the living.

It is this warm humanness, this sorrow-laced love—pushing on but never breaking through the boundary between sentiment and sentimentality—that makes Fante more than an American P.G. Wodehouse. Given the qualities of the fiction we often value today, *Full of Life* will seem to many a terribly unfashionable novel, which is too bad for us. It is a novel, in short, full of life, and we must thank Black Sparrow for giving it new life. [Brooke K. Horvath]

*

Arthur and Kit Knight, eds. *Kerouac and the Beats: A Second Sourcebook.* Paragon House, 1988. $22.95; paper: $9.95; Jay Landesman. *Rebel Without Applause.* Permanent Press, 1987. $18.95; *Neurotica: The Authentic Voice of the Beat Generation.* Jay Landesman (London), 1981. £15.00; Chandler Brossard. *Postcards: Don't You Just Wish You Were Here.* Redbeck Press (Heslington), 1987. Paper: £4.95; Alan Ansen. *The Vigilantes: A Fragment.* Water Row Press, 1987. Paper: $5.00.

The Knights have followed last year's *The Beat Vision* (*RCF* 7:3) with another collection of pieces from their Beat journal *the unspeakable visions of the individual:* interviews with Burroughs, Whalen, Jan Kerouac, Holmes, McClure, and Ginsberg; essays by Carolyn Cassady, Hubert Huncke, and Frankie Edith Kerouac Parker; and letters by Jack Kerouac and Clellon Holmes (along with excerpts from Holmes's journal). The result is another invaluable sourcebook, all primary material exciting to read and essential to anyone working in this field. Especially good are the four letters by Kerouac, each as long as a short story, and all establishing Kerouac as one of the great letter writers of our age. In his foreword, John Tytell speaks of the resistance the academic community still puts up against Beat writers, but well-edited, well-presented collections like *Kerouac and the Beats* demonstrate that a counter-cultural academic community is not only possible but vital.

Rebel Without Applause looks and often reads like one of those shallow show-biz memoirs, but don't be deceived: there is invaluable material on the early days of the Beat movement here that has appeared nowhere else. Landesman was the founder and editor of *Neurotica,* that seminal St. Louis magazine that set the agenda for much of the writing that followed in the fifties and sixties. During his recruiting trips to New York City (and his later residence there), Landesman met and worked with such people as Kerouac, Holmes, Brossard, Ginsberg, and Carl Solomon, all of whom are featured here in revealing vignettes. Kerouac especially brings a boozy vitality to these other-wise genteel memoirs: enlivening Landesman's parties with the best scat singing he'd ever heard, impressing him with a gentleness and vulnerability belied by his drunken antics, and even modeling as the "original beatnik" in Landesman's novel, *The Nervous Set.* Although the novel was never published, it was converted into a musical that premiered on Broadway on 11 May 1959, in which the Kerouac role was played by none other than *Dallas*'s Larry Hagman! Kerouac attended the premiere, but slept through most of it, awaking only when his name was used in such songs as "Fun Life": "Let's just have fun / Let's not be serious / Shakespeare was a hack / So we read Kerouac."

Among others portrayed in *The Nervous Set* were Holmes, essayist Anatole Broyard, and the legendary sexologist Gershon Legman, who co-edited *Neurotica* for a few issues. Legman looms over these memoirs like an avenging angel, burning with an iconoclastic moral energy that kept Landesman "honest" for a while (as he admits) before he gave it all up to return to St. Louis to open a cabaret. But the material on the Beats is terrific and consequently *Rebel Without Applause* belongs on every Beat scholar's shelf, as does the recent one-volume edition of *Neurotica,* which contains an informative introduction by the late Holmes.

Chandler Brossard and Alan Ansen are often associated with the Beats, more on social grounds than on literary ones. Brossard is closer to European surrealists, and Ansen to his mentor W. H. Auden, than to anyone in the Beat movement. For example, *Postcards* is unlike anything you've ever read: it consists of eighteen descriptions of such towns as Down But Not Out, Idaho, and The Cat's Meow, Michigan. Imagine Rimbaud as a Welcome Wagon hostess, Kafka as a Chamber of Commerce PR man, Céline as a walking-tour guide. Folksy geniality walks arm in arm with off-the-wall sociological analysis, rendered in a hilarious melange of puns, non-sequiturs, and inventive wordplay. This is the funniest, most original Michelin guide to that non-sequitur called America as you're likely to read. (The book lacks a U.S. distributor, but is available for $10 postpaid from the author at 132 W. 73rd St., NYC 10023.)

Ansen's *The Vigilantes* began as what Ginsberg described as "a strange literary but very sad novel about a spectre of a party at Cannastra's." After Ansen completed four chapters, Ginsberg tried to interest Carl Solomon's uncle A. A. Wyn of Ace Books in the novel—as he had with Burroughs's *Junkie* —but Wyn showed insufficient interest and Ansen abandoned the work. "A study of the milieu," as Wyn called it, *The Vigilantes* captures even in its fragmentary state the civilized frivolity of Ansen's world in the late forties, a world of liquor and opera, nostalgia and nightmare. The fragment holds additional interest as an attempt to adapt operatic form to fiction, and it is regrettable that Ansen never completed this tantalizing look at the other, more "civilized" side of the Bohemian coin. [Steven Moore]

*

Richard F. Patteson. *A World Outside: The Fiction of Paul Bowles.* Univ. of Texas Press, 1987. Paper: $7.95.

Patteson has written a valuable, necessary book on Bowles. He refuses to be content with the usual words—"exotic," "perverse," "exile"—which appear in most discussions of this neglected writer.

Patteson uses images—window, shelter, "interiors and exteriors"—which he convinces us are recurring ones in Bowles's fiction. They are, indeed, *obsessive* ones because they in fact stem from lucidly remembered details (recounted in *Without Stopping*). Although Patteson alertly notices the recurrence of these —and many other—images, he never really questions that *Without Stopping* is an odd "autobiography." In a recent issue of *Twentieth Century Literature* (coedited with Edward Butscher), we include a fascinating essay on the "autobiography" as "fiction" by Marilyn Moss. I am not completely sure about Bowles's "autobiography," but I believe, with Moss, that it is consciously deceptive. Deception itself is, of course, another obsession of Bowles.

Patteson recognizes that art is a "shelter" for Bowles; the novels and stories are safe houses—to use a spy phrase—because they are constructed in great detail by Bowles. They serve to rescue him from victimization and authoritarianism. I assume that all art is an escape; in these works my assumption is correct.

I could argue with Patteson—are Bowles's translations his? Do they belong in his canon?—but I do not want to ask the questions Patteson omits or does not ask fully. I am pleased that Patteson explicates many patterns disregarded by other critics. This book is essential reading for the admirers of Bowles's lasting work. [Irving Malin]

*

Guy Vanderhaeghe. *My Present Age.* Ticknor and Fields, 1985. $15.95.

Two quotes set the tone and character of this very funny study of the "New Man gone hopelessly awry": (1) "But the present generation, wearied by its chimerical efforts, relapses into complete indolence. Its condition is that of a man who has only fallen asleep towards morning: first of all come great dreams, then a feeling of laziness, and finally a witty or clever excuse for remaining in bed" (Soren Kierkegaard, *The Present Age*); (2) "Black-comedy gold. A protagonist comical, flaky, and unreliable enough to rival Duddy Kravitz" (*Ottawa Citizen*).

Kierkegaardian, Kravitzian, Canadian, our hero, Ed, is "rude, witty, and exorbitantly funny." He's also given to excesses both of the flesh and the imagination—he drinks and eats too much and he reverts regularly to the fantasies within his strange imagination, fantasies based on the rereading of his childhood favorites, now that he's unemployed and estranged from his beloved wife, Victoria—*The Last of the Mohicans, The Heart of Midlothian, Shane, Kidnapped, The Adventures of Huckleberry Finn,* with emphasis on Huck and Jim on the raft. Before his nervous breakdown (followed by the then customary shock treatment), a Dr. Brandt, psychiatrist, labeled his "attitude towards Victoria as unhealthy and described it as 'infantile separation anxiety.' " Most of this witty study of life on Canada's boring border deals with Ed's awkward attempts to alleviate his anxiety by restoring a marital relationship that never had a chance. As Marsha, a mutual friend of both Ed and Victoria, puts it when suggesting that Bill, her ex, had a thing for Victoria, Bill sees Victoria " 'as a victim, rather like the wife of that disgusting bureaucrat in *Crime and Punishment.* I can't recall his name at the moment. Can you believe it? I just read the book a month ago and now I can't remember the goddamn name. Isn't that crazy?' 'Marmaledov,' I say, 'his name is Marmaledov.' Marsha looks sceptical, considers, and then replies: 'Why, you're right. It *is* Marmaledov.' 'Of course I'm right.' 'Poor Ed. Right about everything that doesn't really matter and wrong about everything that does.' "

Poor Ed and Victoria fight over what Pierre Renoir called "The Rules of the Game," or what Hollywood called the Mating Game or the Tender Trap.

Whatever you call it, the game is still under litigation and the outcome will probably be decided five to four (God bless the Supreme Court). As a philosophical race track tout once put it, never dreaming that his natural wisdom superceded our highest court, "everything is life is 6 to 5 against." [Jack Byrne]

*

R. H. W. Dillard. *Understanding George Garrett.* Univ. of South Carolina Press, 1988.

The University of South Carolina Press's "Understanding Contemporary American Literature" series is geared for high-school students and undergraduates and thus would not normally warrant attention here if not for the fact that it is beginning to include a few authors not often written about. George Garrett is just such an author, and R. H. W. Dillard here offers an overview of Garrett's large body of work. The emphasis is on the novels: separate chapters are devoted to each of his half dozen novels—with the two Elizabethan novels *Death of the Fox* and *The Succession* combined for a longer chapter—but short stories and poems are frequently cited for the light they shed on the novel's thematic concerns. Charting Garrett's progression from traditional realism to "metafictional complexities," Dillard finds the "two-dimensionality of modern public life" to be the thematic common denominator of much of the work, linking the politicians of his first novel *The Finished Man* to the pin-up girls of his most recent novel, *Poison Pen.* This is a partisan account by an old friend who shares the author's Christian orientation, and since Garrett lent his support to the book, *Understanding George Garrett* might even be considered an "authorized" reading. [Steven Moore]

*

Augusto Roa Bastos. *I The Supreme.* Trans. Helen Lane. Aventura, 1987. Paper: $10.95.

This remarkable novel is about many things—the nature of revolution, reason and madness, properties of language. It is, if you will, a fictional encyclopedia.

Perhaps the most significant object of our attention is the obsessive quest for the correct, pure Word. On almost every page the narrator—or the compiler or the "supreme" artist—discusses the powers of language. At times he suggests that words control him; often he suggests that he controls them. Thus he frequently interrupts his narration to break down words and/or to worship them.

I offer some examples: "Forms disappear, words remain, to signify the impossible. No story can be told. No story worth the telling. But true language hasn't yet been born." The narrator suggests "free space" for words. "A memory of their own. Words that subsisted alone." Obviously, he is confused —or brilliantly mad. How can we ever reach a magical realm, an open space, uncluttered by false words? How can words stand alone? How can they be understood by the happy few? The narrator comments once more: he wants to "attune words to the sound of thought." Why is thought "a sound"? Is it noisy or quiet?

I can continue quoting from the novel, but I cannot discover the right words for it. The novel is not only a plea for perfect, holy language but for truthful silence. The matter is, of course, more complex because we are dealing with books *within* this one. We have a "perpetual," "circular" narration; a private notebook (written by the narrator?); a compiler's text. The text as a whole becomes, as it were, a series of *differing times, interpretations, contexts.* The novel ends with the final compiler's note: the note informs us that the "story that should have been told in them has not been told. As a consequence, the characters and facts that figure in them have earned, through the fatality of the written language, the right to a fictitious and autonomous existence in the service of the no less fictitious and autonomous reader."

What are we to make of these sentences? It appears that words create new beings, virginal words; but the new creations cannot exist peacefully because we misread sentences. There is a maze; so many speculations—or commentaries—exist that they defy rationalist, linear comprehension.

And yet, ironically, the novel is a grand design—a huge mosaic of marks. The narrator is scarred; the reader is scarred. Through the various "visions and revisions" we see the paradoxes which confront us daily. Should we remain mute? Should we use words obsessively? Can we understand the huge *and* little details? This novel is an extreme attempt to capture—and to question—the unbelievable, subtle mines of words. [Irving Malin]

*

David Seed. *The Fictional Labyrinths of Thomas Pynchon.* Univ. of Iowa Press, 1988. $25.00; Steven Weisenburger. *A "Gravity's Rainbow" Companion.* Univ. of Georgia Press, 1988. $30.00; paper: $12.95.

During the last six or seven years, Seed and Weisenburger have been among the most frequent contributors to *Pynchon Notes,* an erratically published but invaluable forum for primary research. Both have now published their findings in book form, riding the crest of a new wave of Pynchon criticism (a half-dozen books in the last two years). Both are interested in facts: what's the source for this particular datum; what's the significance of this particular allusion; what was Pynchon reading at certain stages of composition? Such documentary criticism is not in fashion in many academic quarters these days, yet when the fashions change (as they will), these books will remain valuable precisely because of their density of detail and specificity of source material.

Seed surveys all of Pynchon's work in chronological order, both isolating unique features and sources for each book and searching for recurrent obsessions and concerns and constructing Pynchon's voice from these continuities. Seed even analyzes Pynchon's dozen or so blurbs to refine further the reclusive novelist's aesthetics and somehow gained permission to reprint an invaluable letter from Pynchon to a graduate student on his research methods. Seed anchors each book in the intellectual currents of its time, stressing how each book is a response to specific socio-political tensions in the air at the time Pynchon was writing—a fact lost on less historically-minded critics and one that underscores Pynchon's sincere engagement with such issues. This is the best overview of Pynchon's oeuvre to date.

Weisenburger's *Companion* is a line-by-line annotation of *Gravity's Rainbow* and is indeed, as he points out, "eight resources in one: a source study, encyclopedia, handbook, motif index, dictionary, explicator, gazetteer, and list of textual errors." Two previous attempts have been made at such a book—Kihm Winship's unpublished index-guide, and a book by Douglas Fowler that many Pynchon critics wish had never been published—but Weisenburger's is easily the most comprehensive, authoritative, and reliable study yet on Pynchon's masterwork. He shows how "marginal, footnoted material is transmuted into fictional reference and event" and even how "many of the novel's episodes draw their backgrounds, references, even details of plotting, from a central source text." There are concise plot summaries for each section, precise chronologies (derived from Pynchon's own historically precise and symbolically provocative chronology), and an index that doubles as an index to the novel itself. Of the dozen or so books now available on *Gravity's Rainbow,* this is the only one that is truly indispensable, a stunning piece of scholarship on one of the greatest novels of our time. [Steven Moore]

*

Benito Perez Galdos. *Our Friend Manso.* Trans. Robert Russell. Columbia Univ. Press, 1987. $20.00.

Although I admire the criticism of "post-modern" literature, I am afraid that many of our critics have not truly *confronted* those historical works which have paved the way for contemporary literature. Our critics will mention the "metafictions" of Cervantes or Sterne, but they don't realize that other, more obscure writers have also grappled with problems of "character," "reality," and "realism." I am pleased that Columbia University Press has started a series of new translations of relatively unknown novels which deal with the very problems troubling us.

In *Our Friend Manso,* published originally in 1882, Galdos begins the novel with these "odd" sentences: "I do not exist. And just in case some untrusting, stubborn, ill-meaning person should refuse to believe what I say so plainly, or should demand some sworn testimony before believing it—I swear, I solemnly swear that I do not exist. . . ."

The narrator is, indeed, angry; "he" proclaims that "he" doesn't exist. In many ways "he" is surely correct. "He" is merely a group of words. But the non-existence bothers us. "He" is contradictory, foolish—and "he" possesses many qualities of human beings. Galdoz is questioning the nature of existence, the value of language, the origins of identity. But he is not solemn. He regards the philosophical, literary problems as a kind of never-ending joke.

Thus he continues to play with us: "I enjoy my nonexistence, I watch the senseless passing of infinite time which is so boring that it holds my attention, and I begin to wonder whether being nobody isn't the same as being every-body. . . ." "I" is a serious man; "he" is *so* serious that "he" makes us laugh *and* cry. Although "he" doesn't exist—"he" is not made of flesh—"he" disturbs us because "he" makes *us* wonder about *our* identity. Are *we* in some grand design? Are *we* dreams?

The narrator is especially troubled because "his" "friends"—who also don't exist—start disturbing "his" rational, angry statements. "They" force "him" to do things—to scowl, scream, plot "his" rise—and "they" begin to control "him." The comedy is truly ironic because at times we are so convinced of the reality of these beings that we feel base or sublime sensations. We *forget* that "they" are simply words.

The narrator is shocked. At times he declares that he will disappear—as if "he" *could*—and he regrets his part in the stupid plotting of others.

Galdos deserves to be read. He is not only a comic (serious) genius; he is part of the ongoing tradition we are facing today. [Irving Malin]

*

Francine Prose. *Bigfoot Dreams.* Viking, 1987. Paper: $6.95.

Although Francine Prose has written many novels (which contain meditations on fiction), she has, as far as I can tell, never received serious attention. She is usually dismissed as a "fine stylist."

I'm tempted to call attention to her most recent book. Her heroine writes loony articles for a trash-filled newspaper. She is fascinated by impossible, occult rites and practices; she is, however, ironic about these "passions." She laughs at Bigfoot headlines—she writes stories which are "lies." They can't possibly happen!

Vera writes one story, however, about kids selling lemonade (special) in Brooklyn. She gives names, addresses—these, she believes, are completely *made up.* But it seems that the Muse has somehow gone *beyond* the probable. The improbable—let's call it the miraculous—occurs and the funny tale is "true." Vera almost breaks down; she suddenly recognizes that writing—even trash—is risky. We, of course, do not know what to make of the event. Do higher powers write *us?* What is the source of the creative process? What, in heaven's name, is going on?

Vera begins to think of Blake, dark voices, mysterious fields of cosmic energy. We are amused by the "craziness" of life; at the same time we begin, like Vera, to see omens in letters. The words seem to dominate the world—they have unlimited power.

And the words are linked in *kabbalistic* ways. Vera remembers her Jewish roots—the "magical" interconnection of codes and letters in the Hebrew alphabet. At one point she thinks: "We Jews often make tragic mistakes. Vera knows hers is not realizing: when you are looking for signs, you see them. But how to stop? Just trying reminds her of a story she heard about some alchemist who believed that the secret of making gold was going through the process without once thinking of the word *hippopotamus.*"

Thus the novel is more than another clever fiction. By dealing with coincidences, dreams, words, Prose suggests that something is happening; that words are prophetic—at least—and that we must connect happenings. [Irving Malin]

*

Heidi Ziegler, ed. *Facing Texts: Encounters between Contemporary Writers and Critics.* Duke Univ. Press, 1988. $40.00; paper: $16.95.

The concept behind this anthology is simple but ingenious: ask ten of the more interesting writers to submit a new piece, then match ten critics to comment on the pieces, working without the usual safety nets of received opinions, reviews, or any of the other apparatus usually at hand when a critic goes to work on an author. Editor Heidi Ziegler's purpose was to "defy the chronological secondariness of critical interpretation," to "make the relationship between author and critic an unmediated encounter, with authors and critics becoming one another's ideal readers." The result is a book whose appeal is two-fold: an engaging collection of new writings (essays by Elkin and Barth; fiction by Barthelme, Coover, Davenport, Sontag, Abish, Gass, Hawkes, and McElroy) as well as an anthology of critical strategies, ranging from close readings to more speculative essays.

For the reader, it's a kind of luxury to have a piece analyzed immediately upon turning the last page. Usually months or years elapse between reading a piece of fiction and reading a competent criticism of it. Here, it is like having the answers to a quiz printed upside-down on the same page, or a slo-mo with commentary after a dazzling athletic feat. The author/critic duet welcomes the reader into a literary ménage à trois.

None of these intriguing concepts would work, of course, without first-rate pieces to begin with, and Ziegler's selection is indeed first-rate. All of her authors are at their best here, and they seem to bring out the best in their critics (many of whom were chosen by the authors). Especially good are Marc Chénetier on Coover and Tony Tanner on Gass, but everyone turns in a fine performance. Brilliant concept, splendid results; this book deserves the widest readership. [Steven Moore]

*

Books Received

Adams, Alice. *Second Chances.* Knopf, 1988. $18.95. (F)

Ascher, Carol. *The Flood.* The Crossing Press, 1987. Paper: $8.95. (F)

Ascher/Straus. *The Other Planet.* McPherson & Co., 1988. $15.95. (F)

Assouline, Pierre. *Gaston Gallimard.* Trans. Harold J. Salemson. Harcourt Brace Jovanovich, 1988. $35.00.

Astley, Thea. *Two by Astley: "A Kindness Cup" and "The Acolyte."* Putnam, 1988. $18.95. (F)

Auerbach, Jessica. *Painting on Glass.* Norton, 1988. $16.95. (F)

Bail, Murray, ed. *The Faber Book of Contemporary Australian Short Stories.* Faber & Faber, 1988. Paper: £5.95.

Baker, Nicholson. *The Mezzanine.* Weidenfeld & Nicolson, 1988. $14.95. (F)

Ballard, J. G. *The Day of Creation.* Farrar Straus Giroux, 1988. $17.95. (F)

_____. *The Crystal World.* Farrar Straus Giroux, 1988. Paper: $7.95. (F)

Barnes, Julian. *Staring at the Sun.* Harper & Row, 1988. Paper: $7.95. (F)

Barthelme, Frederick. *Two against One.* Weidenfeld & Nicolson, 1988. $17.95. (F)

Barthes, Roland. *The Semiotic Challenge.* Trans. Richard Howard. Farrar Straus Giroux, 1988. $30.00.

Bates, H. E. *A Party for the Girls.* New Directions, 1988. $21.95. (F)

Bates, Natalie. *Friend of the Family.* Atheneum, 1988. $16.95. (F)

Birstein, Ann. *The Last of the True Believers.* Norton, 1988. $17.95. (F)

Boyle, Kay. *Life Being the Best and Other Stories.* New Directions, 1988. $18.95. (F)

Bradbury, Malcolm, ed. *The Penguin Book of Modern British Short Stories.* Viking, 1987. $18.95. (F)

_____. *No, Not Bloomsbury.* Columbia Univ., 1988. $27.50.

Briskin, Mae. *A Boy Like Astrid's Mother.* Norton, 1988. $16.95. (F)

Brombert, Victor. *The Hidden Reader: Stendhal, Balzac, Hugo, Baudelaire, Flaubert.* Harvard, 1988. $27.50.

Burroughs, William. *Three Novels.* Grove, 1988. Paper: $8.95.

Butts, Mary. *The Crystal Cabinet.* Beacon, 1988. $19.95.

Campobello, Nellie. *"Cartucho" and "Mother's Hands."* Trans. Doris Meyer and Irene Matthews. Univ. of Texas, 1988. Paper: $7.95. (F)

Carpelan, Bo. *Voices at the Late Hour.* Trans. Irma Margareta Martin. Univ. of Georgia, 1988. Paper: $8.95. (F)

Carroll, David. *Paraesthetics: Foucault, Lyotard, Derrida.* Methuen, 1987. Paper.

Carver, Raymond. *Where I'm Calling From.* Atlantic Monthly, 1988. $19.95. (F)

Cohen, Arthur. *An Admirable Woman.* Godine, 1988. Paper: $8.95. (F)

Cohen, Richard. *Say You Want Me.* Soho, 1988. $17.95. (F)

Coleman, Wanda. *A War of Eyes and Other Stories.* Black Sparrow, 1988. Paper: $10.00. (F)

Collins, Michael. *Towards Post-Modernism: Decorative Arts and Design since 1951.* Little, Brown, 1987. $19.95.

Crawford, Stanley. *Mayordomo: Chronicle of an Accquia in Northern New Mexico.* Univ. of New Mexico, 1988. $16.95.

Dawson, Fielding. *Will She Understand?* Black Sparrow, 1988. Paper: $10.00. (F)

Del Giudice, Daniele. *Lines of Light.* Trans. Norman MacAfee. Harcourt Brace Jovanovich, 1988. $19.95. (F)

Deleuze, Gilles. *Foucault.* Trans. Seán Hand. Univ. of Minnesota, 1988. $29.50; paper: $12.95.

Deleuze, Gilles, and Claire Parnet. *Dialogues.* Trans. Hugh Tomlinson and Barbara Habberjam. Columbia Univ., 1988.

Delibes, Miguel. *Five Hours without Mario.* Trans. Frances M. López-Morillas. Columbia Univ., 1988. $25.00. (F)

Dickinson, Charles. *With or Without.* Collier/Macmillan, 1988. Paper: $7.95. (F)

Diehl, Margaret. *Men.* Soho, 1988. $17.95. (F)

Disch, Thomas M. *The Brave Little Toaster Goes to Mars.* Doubleday, 1988. $11.95. (F)

Djian, Philippe. *Betty Blue.* Trans. Howard Buten. Weidenfeld & Nicolson, 1988. $17.95. (F)

Duras, Marguerite. *The Malady of Death.* Trans. Barbara Bray. Grove, 1986. Paper: $5.95. (F)

Eisenbach, Helen. *Loonglow.* Farrar Straus Giroux, 1988. $16.95. (F)

Elliott, Emory, ed. *Columbia Literary History of the United States.* Columbia, 1987. $59.95.

Fante, John. *The Brotherhood of the Grape.* Black Sparrow, 1988. Paper: $10.00. (F)

Fizer, John. *Alexander A. Potebnja's Psycholinguistic Theory of Literature.* Harvard, 1988.

Ford, Hugh. *Published in Paris: A Literary Chronicle of Paris in the 1920s and 1930s.* Collier/Macmillan, 1988. Paper: $14.95.

Forest, Leon. *Two Wings to Veil My Face.* Another Chicago Press, 1988. Paper: $8.95. (F)

Fuentes, Carlos. *Myself with Others.* Farrar Straus Giroux, 1988. $19.95.

Garfield, Evelyn Picon, ed. and trans. *Women's Fiction from Latin America.* Wayne State, 1988. Paper: $13.95. (F)

Gébler, Carlo. *Work and Play.* St. Martin's, 1987. $12.95. (F)

Gerber, Alain. *The Short Happy Life of Mister Ghichka.* Trans. Jeremy

Leggatt. Mercury House, 1988. $14.95. (F)

Gingher, Marianne. *Teen Angel.* Atheneum, 1988. $17.95. (F)

Godbout, Jacques. *An American Story.* Trans. Yves Saint-Pierre. Univ. of Minnesota, 1988. Paper: $8.95. (F)

Green, Geoffrey. *Freud and Nabakov.* Univ. of Nebraska, 1988. $15.95.

Handke, Peter. *Slow Homecoming.* Trans. Ralph Manheim. Collier/ Macmillan, 1988. Paper: $8.95. (F)

—————. *Repetition.* Trans. Ralph Manheim. Farrar Straus Giroux, 1988. $18.95. (F)

Havazalet, Ehud. *What Is It Then Between Us?* Scribners, 1988. $15.95. (F)

Hite, Molly. *Class Porn.* The Crossing Press, 1987. Paper: $8.95. (F)

Hoffman, Michael, and Patrick Murphy, eds. *Essentials of the Theory of Fiction.* Duke, 1988. Paper.

Jabès, Edmund. *Selected Poems.* Trans. Keith Waldrop. Station Hill, 1988. $16.95.

Jameson, Fredric. *The Ideologies of Theory: Essays 1971-1986.* Vol. I. Univ. of Minnesota, 1988. $35.00; paper: $12.95.

—————. *The Ideologies of Theory.* Vol. 2. Univ. of Minnesota, 1988. $35.00; paper: $12.95.

Johnson, Denis. *The Stars at Noon.* Vintage, 1988. Paper: $5.95. (F)

Kaminski, André. *Kith and Kin.* Trans. Harry Zohn. Fromm International, 1988. $19.95. (F)

Kane, Richard C. *Iris Murdoch, Muriel Spark, and John Fowles.* Fairleigh Dickinson, 1988. $28.50.

Karl, Frederick. *Modern and Modernism.* Atheneum, 1988. Paper: $14.95.

Kasack, Wolfgang. *Dictionary of Roman Literature since 1917.* Columbia, 1988. $55.00.

Kaufman, Joan. *Dogs, Dreams, and Men.* Atheneum, 1988. $16.95. (F)

Kelly, Robert. *Doctor of Silence.* McPherson & Co., 1988. Paper: $10.00. (F)

Kennedy, Raymond. *Lulu Incognito.* Vintage, 1988. Paper: $7.95. (F)

Kiely, Benedict. *A Letter to Peachtree.* Godine, 1988. $17.95. (F)

King, Francis. *The Woman Who Was God.* Weidenfeld & Nicolson, 1988. $17.95. (F)

Klíma, Juan. *My First Loves.* Trans. Ewald Osers. Harper & Row, 1988. $14.95. (F)

Korczak, Janusz. *King Matt the First.* Trans. Richard Laurie. Farrar Straux Giroux, 1988. Paper: $8.95. (F)

Kosinski, Jerzy. *The Hermit of 69th Street.* Seaver/Holt, 1988. $19.95. (F)

Lafayette, Madame de. *The Princess of Cleves.* Trans. Nancy Mitford. New Directions, 1988. Paper: $8.95. (F)

Lazarre, Jane. *The Powers of Charlotte.* The Crossing Press, 1988. $18.95. (F)

Leiris, Michel. *Nights as Day; Days as Nights.* Trans. Richard Sieburth. Eridanos, 1987. Paper: $13.00.

Lesser, Ellen. *The Other Woman.* Simon & Schuster, 1988. $17.95. (F)

Lind, Jakov. *The Inventor.* Braziller, 1988. $15.95. (F)

Lispector, Clarice. *The Passion According to G. H.* Trans. Ronald W. Sousa. Univ. of Minnesota, 1988. Paper: $8.95. (F)

Lustig, Arnošt. *Indecent Dreams.* Northwestern, 1988. $17.95. (F)

Lyotard, Jean-François. *Peregrinations: Law, Form, Event.* Columbia, 1988. $20.00.

Machaverty, Bernard. *The Great Profundo and Other Stories.* Grove, 1988. $15.95. (F)

Mariani, Dacia. *Letters to Marina.* Trans. Dick Kitto and Elspeth Spottiswood. The Crossing Press, 1987. Paper: $8.95. (F)

Maron, Monika. *The Defector.* Trans. David Newton Marinelli. Readers International, 1988. $16.95; paper: $8.95. (F)

Marquez, Gabriel García. *Love in the Time of Cholera.* Trans. Edith Grossman. Knopf, 1988. $18.95. (F)

Mason, Bobbie Ann. *Spence & Lila.* Harper & Row, 1988. $12.95. (F)

Masters, Olga. *Amy's Children.* Norton, 1988. $16.95. (F)

McDermot, Alice. *That Night.* Harper & Row, 1988. Paper: $6.95. (F)

McLaurin, Tim. *The Acorn Plan.* Norton, 1988. $16.95. (F)

Morrow, Bradford. *Come Sunday.* Weidenfeld & Nicolson, 1988. $19.95. (F)

Morselli, Guido. *Divertimento 1889.* Trans. Hugh Shankland. Dutton, 1988. Paper: $7.95. (F)

Moskowitz, Faye. *Whoever Finds This: I Love You.* Godine, 1988. $15.95. (F)

Moyer, Kermit. *Tumbling.* Univ. of Illinois, 1988. $11.95. (F)

Murayama, Milton. *All I Ask for Is My Body.* Univ. of Hawaii, 1988. Paper: $4.95. (F)

Murray, Melissa. *Changlings.* Attic Press (Dublin), 1988. Paper: £4.95. (F)

Norris, Helen. *Water into Wine.* Univ. of Illinois, 1988. $11.95. (F)

Otto, Lon. *Cover Me.* Coffee House, 1988. Paper: $9.95. (F)

Parotti, Phillip. *The Trojan Generals Talk.* Univ. of Illinois, 1988. $11.95. (F)

Perrin, Noel. *A Reader's Delight.* Dartmouth, 1988. Paper: $9.95.

Phillips, Caryl. *A State of Independence.* Collier/Macmillan, 1988. Paper: $6.95. (F)

Pirandello, Luigi. *Tales of Suicide.* Trans. Giovanni Bussino. Dante Univ. Press, 1988. Paper: $11.95. (F)

_____. *The Late Mattia Pascal.* Trans. William Weaver. Eridanos, 1988. Paper: $14.00. (F)

Plante, David. *The Native.* Atheneum, 1988. $13.95. (F)

Radcliff-Umstead, Douglas. *The Exile into Eternity: A Study of the Narrative of Giorgio Bassani.* Fairleigh Dickinson, 1987. $26.50.

Raynor, Richard. *Los Angeles Without a Map.* Weidenfeld & Nicolson, 1989. $16.95. (F)

Rechy, John. *Marilyn's Daughter.* Carroll & Graf, 1988. $18.95. (F)

Reed, Ishmael. *Writin' Is Fightin'.* Atheneum, 1988. $18.95.

——————. *Reckless Eyeballing.* Atheneum, 1988. Paper: $7.95. (F)

——————. *The Terrible Twos.* Atheneum, 1988. Paper: $8.95. (F)

Ricoeur, Paul. *Time and Narrative.* Trans. Kathleen Blamey and David Pellauer. Vol. 3. Univ. of Chicago, 1988.

Roberts, Thom. *A Born Carpenter.* Weidenfeld & Nicolson. $17.95. (F)

Rosca, Ninotchka. *State of War.* Norton, 1988. $17.95. (F)

Rybakov, Anatoli. *Children of the Arbat.* Trans. Harold Shukman. Little, Brown, 1988. $19.95. (F)

Salusinszky, Imre. *Criticism in Society.* Methuen, 1987.

Savic, Sally. *Elysian Fields.* Scribners, 1988. $14.95. (F)

Schwaiger, Brigitte. *Why Is There Salt in the Sea?* Trans. Sieglinde Lug. Univ. of Nebraska, 1988. $15.95. (F)

Singer, Alan. *The Charnel Imp.* Fiction Collective, 1988. Paper: $8.95. (F)

Skvorecky, Josef. *Dvorak in Love.* Trans. Paul Wilson. Norton, 1988. Paper: $7.95. (F)

Sorokin, Vladimir. *The Queue.* Trans. Sally Laird. Readers International, 1988. Paper: $8.95. (F)

Spanbauer, Tom. *Faraway Places.* Putnam, 1988. $16.95. (F)

Spark, Muriel. *A Far Cry from Kensington.* Houghton Mifflin, 1988. $17.95. (F)

Spender, Stephen. *The Temple.* Grove, 1988. $15.95. (F)

Stonehill, Brian. *The Self-Conscious Novel.* Univ. of Pennsylvania, 1988. $26.95.

Tardat, Claude. *Sweet Death.* Trans. Linda Coverdale. Overlook Press, 1987.

Taylor, Richard, and Ian Christie, eds. *The Film Factory: Russian and Soviet Cinema in Documents 1896-1939.* Harvard, 1988.

Thomas, Brian. *An Underground Fate: The Idiom of Romance in the Later Novels of Graham Greene.* Univ. of Georgia, 1988. $28.00.

Timms, Edward, and Peter Collier, eds. *Visions and Blueprints: Avant-Garde Culture and Radical Politics in Early Twentieth-Century Europe.* St. Martin's, 1988. $39.95.

Tucholsky, Kurt. *Castle Gripsholm.* Trans. Michael Hoffman. Overlook Press, 1988. $16.95. (F)

Twiggs, James. *Transferences.* Univ. of Arkansas, 1988. (F)

Updike, David. *Out on the Marsh.* Godine, 1988. $16.95.

Valenzuela, Luisa. *Open Door.* Trans. Helen Lane et al. North Point, 1988.

Paper: $12.95. (F)

Vendler, Helen. *The Music of What Happens: Poems, Poets, Critics.* Harvard, 1988. $29.50.

Vizenor, Gerald. *The Trickster of Liberty.* Univ. of Minnesota, 1988. Paper: $8.95. (F)

Von Doderer, Heimito. *The Waterfalls of Slunj.* Trans. Eithne Wilkins and Ernest Kaiser. Eridanos, 1988. Paper: $15.00. (F)

Whelan, Gloria. *Playing with Shadows.* Univ. of Illinois, 1988. $11.95. (F)

Wiebe, Dallas. *Going to the Mountain.* Burning Deck, 1988. Paper: $10.00. (F)

Winton, Tim. *Minimum of Two.* Atheneum, 1988. $14.95. (F)

Woiwode, Larry. *Born Brothers.* Farrar Straus Giroux, 1988. $19.95. (F)

Zahava, Irene, ed. *Love, Struggle and Change: Stories by Women.* The Crossing Press, 1988. $8.95. (F)

Contributors

KEITH ABBOTT is the author of three novels and is currently at work on a six-book fiction series. The present essay is from his forthcoming *Downriver from Trout Fishing in America: A Memoir of Richard Brautigan.*

JOHN BARTH has published nine books of fiction, many of them reissued in paper earlier this year by Doubleday/Anchor. His latest novel, *The Tidewater Tales,* was recently published in paper by Fawcett/Columbine.

CHRISTINE BROOKE-ROSE'S most recent novels are *Xorander* and *Amalgamemnon.* Four of her earlier novels were recently published in an omnibus edition by Carcanet.

ROBERT CREELEY is best known as a poet, but he has also published fiction and criticism. His *Collected Prose* was recently reissued in paper by the University of California Press, which will publish his *Collected Essays* next year.

GEORGE GARRETT is the author of several books of fiction, most recently *Poison Pen.* His critical study *Understanding Mary Lee Settle* was published earlier this year by the University of South Carolina Press.

ROBERT KELLY'S 1967 novel *The Scorpions* was recently reissued in paper by Station Hill Press. His latest books are *Doctor of Silence* (short fiction) and *The Flowers of Unceasing Coincidence* (poetry).

MARY MCCARTHY has published several well-known novels. Her latest book is *How I Grew* (Harcourt Brace Jovanovich).

JAMES MCCOURT has written two novels, *Mawrdew Czgowchwz* and *Kaye Wayfaring in "Avenged."* He is completing a sequel to the first, *Time Out of Mind,* to be published by Knopf.

THOMAS MCGONIGLE is the author of *The Corpse Dream of N. Petkov,* published by Dalkey Archive Press, which will also be publishing his next novel, *Going to Patchogue.*

HARRY MATHEWS is the author of *Cigarettes* and three earlier novels (being reissued by Carcanet). His *20 Lines a Day* was published last summer by Dalkey Archive Press.

CLAUDE OLLIER is the author of more than fifteen books, including novels, plays, and criticism. The English translation of his first novel *The Mise-en-Scène* was published last spring by Dalkey Archive.

GILBERT SORRENTINO is the author of numerous books of fiction and poetry. His most recent novels, *Odd Number* and *Rose Theatre,* are part of a trilogy that will be completed next year.

DAVID FOSTER WALLACE is a 1985 graduate of Amherst College. His well-received first novel *The Broom of the System* was published in 1987 by Viking/Penguin, which will bring out his *Girl with Curious Hair: Stories and Novellas* this winter.

PAUL WEST has published some twenty books, half of them novels. His latest is *The Place in Flowers Where Pollen Rests* from Doubleday, which will publish next year a historical novel tentatively titled *Polidori: Byron's Doctor.*

Annual Index

Number references indicate issue and page respectively.

Contributors

Books Reviewed

STORYQUARTERLY 25

Single Issue $4/4 Issues $12
P.O. Box 1416, Northbrook, IL 60065

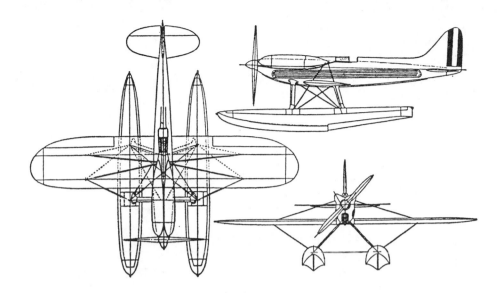

"Reading *Gargoyle Magazine* is like visiting a cafe in space." —*Choice*

Marie-Claire Blais * Paul Bowles * T. Coraghessan Boyle * Michael Brondoli

Chandler Brossard * Charles Bukowski * Rita Dove * Elaine Equi

Roy Fisher * John Gardner * Helen Garner * Ken Gangemi

Allen Ginsberg * Ivy Goodman * Jaimy Gordon * Todd Grimson

Cathryn Hankla * Ted Joans * Mary Mackey * Michael Martone

George Myers Jr. * Linda Pastan * Constance Pierce * Edouard Roditi

Jonathan Strong * Elizabeth Tallent * Henry Taylor * Rosmarie Waldrop

G A R G O Y L E * M A G A Z I N E

Fiction/Poetry/Interviews/Graphics/Reviews

P.O. Box 30906, Bethesda, Maryland 20814

$7.95/issue $15/year

The Journal of
Aesthetics and Art Criticism

VOLUME XLVI   Special Issue

Editor: John Fisher, Temple University, Philadelphia, Pa. 19122
Annual Subscription: $20.00 to individuals

MEMPHIS STATE REVIEW

POETRY • FICTION • INTERVIEWS

AMONG OUR CONTRIBUTORS:

JAMES DICKEY,

ROBERT PENN WARREN,

PHILIP LEVINE,

W.D. SNODGRASS,

JOHN ASHBERY,

MAXINE KUMIN,

DONALD JUSTICE,

MARY OLIVER,

ROBERT BLY,

DAVID IGNATOW,

WILLIAM STAFFORD,

MARVIN BELL,

FREDERICK BUSCH

BIANNUAL
SUBSCRIPTIONS
$3 PER ISSUE
$5/Year Individual
$6/Year Organization

MEMPHIS STATE REVIEW
Editor, Sharon Bryan
Department of English
Memphis State University
Memphis, TN 38152

An Equal Opportunity/Affirmative Action University

Studies in 20th Century Literature

A JOURNAL DEVOTED TO LITERARY THEORY AND PRACTICAL CRITICISM OF FRENCH, GERMAN, RUSSIAN AND SPANISH LITERATURE OF THE TWENTIETH CENTURY

Volume XII, Number 2 (Spring, 1988)

Essays by : John Daniel Stahl, Sydney Lévy, Arkady Plotnitsky, Leonard M. Olschner, Lawrence R. Schehr, Leona Toker

A Special Issue on CONTEMPORARY FRENCH POETRY
Volume XIII, Number 1
(To appear Fall, 1988)

Guest Editor: Richard Stamelman; Contributors include Roger Little, Suzanne Nash, John Naughton, Richard Stamelman, Yves Bonnefoy, Adelaide Russo, Rosmarie Waldrop, Michael Bishop, Laurie Edson

Also in preparation: A Special Latin-American Issue
Guest Editor: Jean Franco

Subscriptions: $20 for one year ($35 for two years)--institutions
$15 for one year ($28 for two years)--individuals
add $5 for air mail

Address:

Michael Ossar, Editor
Modern Languages
Eisenhower 13
Kansas State University
Manhattan, KS 66506
Submissions in:
  German and Russian

Bruce Erlich & Marshall Olds, Editors
Modern Languages & Literatures
Oldfather Hall
University of Nebraska
Lincoln, NE 68588-0315
Submissions in:
  French and Spanish

THE LOST SALT GIFT OF BLOOD
OF BLOOD
New & Selected Stories
Alistair MacLeod

One of Canada's most acclaimed short story writers, Alistair MacLeod makes his American debut in these eleven unforgettable tales, in which powerfully depicted men and women—farmers, fishermen, miners, lighthouse keepers—realize their individual destinies in scenes of intense drama. Set amid the stark beauty of Cape Breton, the stories are both hauntingly elegiac and vigorous, confirming Hugh MacLennan's judgment that MacLeod is "one of the finest short story writers now living."

"This is a 'regional' world that, like those of Eudora Welty, D.H. Lawrence, and Edna O'Brien, transcends its setting in stories of consummate artistry." —Joyce Carol Oates

"I salute here Alistair MacLeod."* —Andre Dubus

June / $10.95 paperback

TOWN SMOKES
Stories by Pinckney Benedict

"We have been introduced to an original." —Eudora Welty

"An often heart-stopping literary performance."
—The New York Times Book Review

"A stunning debut." *—The Atlanta Journal-Constitution*

Recently published / $9.95 paperback

 *Ontario Review Press*

*From his Introduction to The Times Are Never So Bad, Penguin Books (Canada), 1986.

MISE-EN-SCÈNE. Claude Ollier. Translated from the French by Dominic Di Bernardi. First published in France in 1958 and winner of the prestigious Prix Medecis, *Mise-en-Scène* takes place in the mountains of Morocco when the French still controlled North Africa. The novel is a detailed inquiry into the meaning of actions and the impossibility of determining what happens. The reader is kept guessing and wondering at what he thinks he knows but cannot be sure of. In part a detective novel and in part an investigation into the nature of knowledge, *Mise-en-Scène* is controlled by a tone and style that are spellbinding. "Superbly constructed . . . a strong and original book. . . . Rarely have I read such a spell-binding novel." **l'Aurora.** "Everything in this book is fresh and surprising. . . . A beautiful and mysterious story . . . which enriches the reader with a whole new experience of adventure and anguish. " **Le Journal de Genève.** "This anti-story ultimately becomes a fantasy tale, a nightmare of lines and light, obsessive, invasive, omnipresent. . . . *Mise-en-Scène* is close to being the masterpiece expressing that most subjective of human passions: anguish." **Les Lettres Françaises.**
   Cloth $20.00, ISBN 0-916583-26-0

---

20 LINES A DAY. Harry Mathews. For a period of just over a year, Harry Mathews set about following Stendhal's dictum for writers of "twenty lines a day, genius or not." What resulted is a book that is part journal, part biography, part writer's manual, and part genius. First undertaken as a kind of discipline, the work molds itself into a penetrating reflection on daily events in Mathews's life, his friends, himself, and the act of writing. Insisting on maintaining the integrity of the process, Mathews has altered little of his manuscript while preparing it for publication; the procedure was begun to determine what would result from such "forced" writing, and Mathews has not compromised what happened. In the process, he has given us a work that shows close-up the life of the writer, deromanticizing most of what we might think it to be while also producing a work whose style and thought are original and engaging, an absolutely remarkable demonstration of the writer's craft.
   Cloth $20.00, ISBN 0-916583-27-9

Add $1.00 for postage and handling per copy. Send order and payment to:

THE DALKEY ARCHIVE PRESS

1817 North 79th Avenue
Elmwood Park, IL 60635 USA

ODILE
RAYMOND QUENEAU
Translation and Introduction by Carol Sanders

"Even though I can't remember my childhood, my memory being as if ravaged by some disaster, there nevertheless remains a series of images from the time before my birth . . . of my first twenty years, only ruins are left in a memory devastated by unhappiness."

These opening lines from Queneau's novel, first published in France in 1937, are a brilliant, moving introduction to a story about the devastating psychological effects of war, about falling in love and being transformed by love, about politics subverting human relationships, about life in Paris during the early 1930s amid intellectuals and artists whose activities range from writing for radical magazines to conjuring the ghost of Lenin in seances. Most of all, it's about Roland Travy's agonizing search for happiness after having been conditioned to live unhappily but safely for so long, about his growing self-awareness and need for another human being, about his willingness to shed his fears and accept his humanity.

Using the down-and-outs of Parisian intelligentsia as his backdrop, Queneau has written a profoundly moving yet wryly comic story of a man's attempt to discover meaning, as well as his attempts to protect himself against the pain of understanding himself.

"I must underline here the importance of the novels of Raymond Queneau, whose texture often and whose movement always are strictly those of the imagination." **Alain Robbe-Grillet.** "We always feel good reading a Queneau novel; he is the least depressing of the moderns, the least heavy, with something Mozartian about the easy, self-pleasing flow of his absurd plots." **John Updike, New Yorker**

$19.95 hard bound $1.00 postage & handling per copy
ISBN: 0-916583-34-1

Send order and payment to:

THE DALKEY ARCHIVE PRESS
1817 79th Avenue
Elmwood Park, IL 60635 USA

STREET GIRL
MURIEL CERF
Translated by Dominic Di Bernardi

Street Girl is no ordinary coming-of-age novel, but rather an apprenticeship of the imagination. Lydie Tristan, a renegade born into a postwar European world that craves stability, is nourished in childhood by exotic fantasies while menaced by real-life teachers and parents who lash out with the fury of primitive demons. In the soon-to-end innocence of the early 1960s, her world is shaped by: Polline, her friend in arms, with whom she discovers Rin Tin Tin, boys in black leather, and the famous Drugstore; the prostitute Hughette, who talks of philosophy as easily as of the hair-raising episodes of her own youth and the tricks she turned; Abel, her stand-in pimp, a homosexual who exposes Lydie and friend to the world of art and culture and Wilhelm Reich; her Aunt Ro, sweet and spacey, a fairy godmother who facilitates her revolt, herself rumored to have murdered her husband soon after their wedding; and her grandfather, who bequeaths to her deluxe editions of the *Iliad* and the *Odyssey,* which she cherishes as talismans of her future calling.

With the rigor and tenderness that characterize François Truffaut's film *The 400 Blows,* Cerf follows her innocent *enfant terrible* along her path of rebellion through the early '60s, which ultimately leads her, in joy and sorrow, across the borders of her homeland, the whole world now her home. *Street Girl* is a vision of youth to come in the '70s and '80s, expressing a raw anger at the world of adults, school, authority, and society.

"We are mirrored in this '60s generation, which went into ecstasies at the first strains of rock and became flustered by kisses exchanged at dance parties. . . . And for once a teenager discovers her sexuality (in particular her period) not with dread, but with curiosity and satisfaction." **Le Magazine du Maisis.** "The author drinks in life through all her pores: everything that can be breathed in, seen, touched, tasted finds an echo within her. . . . It is Proust revised by a cultured school kid." **Bibliothèques pour Tous.** "Memories of childhood, of adolescence . . . transmuted by Muriel Cerf's writing, her style, her vocabulary. . . . A cascade of words, a torrent of images, accurate and funny, a cataract of expressions, a deluge of evocations." **Le Magazine Littéraire**

$19.95 hard bound $1.00 postage & handling per copy
ISBN: 0-916583-33-3

Send order and payment to:

THE DALKEY ARCHIVE PRESS
1817 79th Avenue
Elmwood Park, IL 60635 USA

LOCOS: A COMEDY OF GESTURES
FELIPE ALFAU
Afterword by Mary McCarthy

The interconnected stories that form this novel take place in a Madrid as exotic as the Baghdad of the *1001 Arabian Nights* and feature unforgettable characters in revolt against their young "author." "For them," he complains, "reality is what fiction is to real people; they simply love it and make for it against my almost heroic opposition. . . . By the end of this book my characters are no longer a tool for my expression, but I am a helpless instrument of their whims and absurd contretemps. . . . In short, my characters have taken seriously the saying that 'truth is stranger than fiction' and I have failed in my attempts to convince them of the contrary."

These fables of identity are enchanting despite Alfau's frequent reminders that these are mere puppets, figures of the imagination; nor can the reader fail to find, despite Alfau's mock warning, "beneath a more or less entertaining comedy of meaningless gestures, the vulgar aspects of a common tragedy."

First published in 1936 and undeservedly neglected for the last fifty years, *Locos* anticipated the "magic realism" of the Latin Americans as well as the inventions of such later writers as Jorge Luis Borges, Flann O'Brien, John Barth, and Donald Barthelme. Modern readers are now in a better position to appreciate Alfau's ingenuity and art, and to wonder how such a book, whose place in modern fiction is now so clear, could have gone unrecognized for so many years.

"A witty, fantastic novel of modern Spain, a novel of forms and surfaces, commanding comparison not with literature but with art." **Mary McCarthy, Nation.** "I am quite confident that some of the implications of Alfau's intricate, complex story escaped me but I am also certain that I enjoyed every moment of his dark and lively tale. Its surface shines with wit and character and even a reader who allows Mr. Alfau to get away with all his mad pretenses will be gainer not loser for being fooled." **Saturday Review**

$19.95 hard bound
ISBN: 0-916583-30-9

$1.00 postage & handling per copy

Send order and payment to:

THE DALKEY ARCHIVE PRESS
1817 79th Avenue
Elmwood Park, IL 60635 USA

MORDECHAI SCHAMZ
MARC CHOLODENKO
Translated by Dominic Di Bernardi

Mordechai Schamz is a quite ordinary man who has an extraordinary curiosity about his world, a curiosity matched only by his compulsion to find words for his observations and endless questions. Dumbfounded at every turn by his inability to make sense of himself and the world around him, he creates nonsense that is sustained by his determination to carry every argument to outrageous conclusion ("I believe only what I do not see"). Undiscouraged by—perhaps even unaware of—his failures, he confidently gets lost in the labyrinth of his investigations. A descendent of Flaubert's Bouvard and Pécuchet, and a contemporary of Calvino's Mr. Palomar and Beckett's Watt, Mordechai Schamz ponders the mysteries of life through clichés and solipcisms, making himself the master of the illogical and the clown of the absurd.

In a series of comic monologues, interrupted by quirky letters to G. and the girl he loves, Marc Cholodenko creates a character who is witty, crazed, passionate, and wily. Inventing a style that is as stilted and convoluted as the mind of his character, Cholodenko allows us to know everything about what Mordechai thinks and feels, while keeping us strangely ignorant about almost all of the externals of his character's life, except that he wears an oversized overcoat. We are given an imagination that is as twisted as it is funny, and as brilliantly ironic as it may be insane.

"A strange, quietly desperate novel, this elusive book is assuredly by a great writer." **Le Matin.** "If ridiculing philosophy is still to philosophize, then Marc Cholodenko offers us—wearing the cap of old man Godot—the maddest guided tour that has ever been organized." **Nouvelles Littéraires**

$19.95 hard bound $1.00 postage & handling per copy
ISBN: 0-916583-31-7

Send order and payment to:

THE DALKEY ARCHIVE PRESS
1817 79th Avenue
Elmwood Park, IL 60635 USA

INTERVIEWS WITH LATIN AND SOUTH AMERICAN WRITERS
MARIE-LISE GAZARIAN GAUTIER
Introduction by the Author

No other group of writers in the last twenty years has created so much interest throughout the world than have Latin and South American writers. Here in one volume are extensive interviews with fifteen of the most influential of them, including Carlos Fuentes, Mario Vargas Llosa, Manuel Puig, José Donoso, Juan Carlos Onetti, Guillermo Cabrera Infante, Luisa Valenzuela, Rosario Ferre, Isaac Goldemberg, Nicanor Parra, Ernesto Sabato, Severo Sarduy, Luis Rafael Sánchez, and Isabel Allende.

With an introduction to the interviews by the editor, along with a list of the authors' books, this is a ground-breaking work that will have an immediate appeal to anyone interested in this literature and will exercise a permanent influence on readers and critics for years to come. Marie-Lise Gazarian Gautier has a remarkable ability to bring out the best of these writers in an interview format, serving to introduce both the writer and the work.

"Her questions explore many angles: they come from all directions and one has to fight the impulse to duck under a table or behind a chair. At the end, however, what was vague in one's mind becomes better organized, more forceful, more creative. The good interviews, such as those contained in this book, are a catharsis or, if you prefer, a housecleaning. At the end of it everything is in its place, dust and cobwebs are gone, opinions and ideas shine once more like freshly minted coins." **Manuel Durán, Yale University**

$19.95 hard bound $1.00 postage & handling per copy
ISBN: 0-916583-32-5

Send order and payment to:

THE DALKEY ARCHIVE PRESS
1817 79th Avenue
Elmwood Park, IL 60635 USA

A *Gravity's Rainbow* Companion

Sources and Contexts for Pynchon's Novel

Steven C. Weisenburger

Disarming Pynchon's complex masterpiece, Steven Weisenburger provides a page-by-page, often line-by-line, guide to the welter of historical references, scientific data, cultural fragments, anthropological research, jokes, and puns woven throughout the novel. $30.00 cloth; $12.95 paper

Reading Race

White American Poets and the Racial Discourse in the Twentieth Century

Aldon Lynn Nielsen

Winner of the 1986 South Atlantic Modern Language Association Award

Examining the work of twentieth-century white American poets—including Carl Sandburg, Adrienne Rich, Allen Tate, Ezra Pound, and Allen Ginsburg—*Reading Race* traces the persistence of a language that treats blacks as an abstract, romanticized "other." $24.00

The Art of John Fowles

Katherine Tarbox

Katherine Tarbox explores the teeming substance of Fowles's novels, revealing his texts as journeys toward comprehending and unifying all the seemingly disparate elements of the self and the world. $26.00

An Underground Fate

The Idiom of Romance in the Later Novels of Graham Greene

Brian Thomas

Recognizing the changing tone of Graham Greene's fictional voice, Brian Thomas traces through novels from *The Third Man* to *Travels with My Aunt* an idiom of romance—an exploration of death and rebirth that emerged from the dark irony and tragedy of Greene's earlier novels. $28.00

The University of Georgia Press • Athens 30602